IF THE STAIRWELL WAS A GOOD PLACE TO GET MUGGED, THE ELEVATOR WAS EVEN BETTER. . . .

I leaned on the button continuously. "Come on," I pleaded.

A woman's scream pierced the ambient sound of TVs and ghetto blasters. "He's an old man, leave him alone!" Smack! Then a baby was bawling.

Tito and I swapped looks. We bolted down the corridor. A spindly black girl, a bawling child on her hip, sobbed into her hand. Four goons were working someone over.

Tito leveled the Nikon to his eye and fired. They froze like statues. The flash etched them on my retina. One was Angel. The bandaged one was James. The other two were strangers. An old man was lying on the floor.

"Yo, James, lookee 'ere." Angel grinned, his vision clearing.

One of them flicked open a switchblade. The four of them advanced.

Tito and I began backpedaling. I sighted my camera and let them have a blast of strobe. The flashes took forty seconds to recharge, an eternity. We'd shot our load. . . .

"Get 'em," Angel barked. . . .

Books by George Adams

Swindle
Insider's Price

Published by POCKET BOOKS

INSIDER'S PRICE

PRICE

GEORGE ADAMS

POCKET BOOKS

New York   London   Toronto   Sydney   Tokyo   Singapore

An *Original* Publication of POCKET BOOKS

POCKET BOOKS, a division of Simon & Schuster Inc.
1230 Avenue of the Americas, New York, NY 10020

ISBN: 0-671-70171-1

First Pocket Books printing September 1993

10 9 8 7 6 5 4 3 2 1

POCKET and colophon are registered trademarks of Simon & Schuster Inc.

Cover art by Dan Cosgrove

Printed in the U.S.A.

For Jennifer Alice Adams

Many thanks to Carol Abramovitz, Rebecca Mullen, Tom Tracy, and Lester Harris, the gang at Legal Aid, for their expert advice and help. Ditto Mark Loiseaux of Controlled Demolition, Inc. I would like to also thank Roy Kuhlman and Dave Stahlberg for their support and encouragement. I owe a special note of gratitude to Jane Chelius, Michael Sanders, Bridget Mellon, and Rena Howland Adams for their assistance in helping me unravel this mystery.

1

It's a toss-up whether it started the evening Sharon Raynes's body was dumped in the courtyard in back of her ritzy upper East Side co-op or that sweltering August night I first laid eyes on them—or the dog, anyway.

I was coming home from doing a few laps on the bike in Central Park, and they'd checked into the doorway next to mine. The cardboard carton bed was screened off by a couple of Duane Reade plastic tote bags and a shopping cart full of junk. Pretty funky accommodations. No "Magic Fingers," no "Fun Flicks" cable TV, no nothing. It was a whole lot less dangerous a flop than the city shelter, though. And besides, it wasn't a bad night for sleeping outdoors.

It was the dog that stopped me. I like dogs. I've got a real soft spot for them. They make me smile. And when I pet them, I get a glow on. They make me feel good.

This one was a German shepherd. Not a remarkable dog, I'll grant you, but big, and nearly as difficult to keep in Manhattan as an elephant, or a woman for that matter.

Which is probably why you don't see too many homeless people with German shepherds.

The dog was curled up against a pile of rags, under which his owner hunkered down for the night. The shepherd's head rested on his paws, his expression was hangdog.

Dogs aren't stupid, they know, I thought, moving in for a closer look.

His head shot up and he warned me off with a low growl.

"Easy, fella," I murmured, backing off.

The dog sighed and dropped his head back down on his paws.

"Good dog," I said softly.

He blinked dolefully.

There was no telling about the owner, buried under the rags, but the dog looked well fed. A friend of mine once observed, no matter how poor people were, and lacking in life's essentials—food, clothing, and shelter—in this country, at least, you never saw anyone so poor they were naked, and only rarely did anyone look like they were starving. Whoever was hiding under that heap of rags seemed to be able to swing two out of three of life's essentials, and man's best friend. Two out of three is good if you are playing tennis, and it's great if it's hits for times at bat, but two out of three stinks when it comes to the essentials. And the essential that always seems to go first is shelter.

I hiked the Lejeune up on its rear wheel and rolled it through the plate-glass doors of my building, wishing I could afford a dog. I had to settle for cats.

My cats' names are Morbid and Curiosity. I'd just finished feeding them their Tender Vittles and poured myself a third cup of coffee the next morning, when the phone rang. It was the first call of the day. "Hello, studio," I said, trying to sound businesslike.

"Is this Charlie Byrne?" asked a tentative voice.

"Yes, it is," I said. "Is this JoJo Cyzeski?" I recognized the voice immediately.

She emitted a throaty sound of pleasure. "Charlie, you remembered me."

"How could I forget you, JoJo?" I replied. Lightly

pitched, assertive, and with a note of mockery running through it, her voice could be as irritating as a scratch in the paint job of a new car. You weren't likely to forget once you'd heard it.

"Easily," she laughed, "but I'm glad you didn't . . . and, Charlie, it's Josephine now."

"Josephine, huh? Sounds so formal."

"Just more dignified," she explained. "Charlie, the reason I called is I need a photographer, and I spotted your name in the yellow pages."

"Ah, I don't do passport photos, Jo . . . er, Josephine," I said. That's what the odd call from the yellow pages was usually about. "But I'd make an exception in your case."

"You're very kind. I'll keep that in mind if I should need one," she said. "What I need is a photograph of a tapestry, an Aubusson. Do you do that sort of thing?"

"Like a copy photograph?"

"Yes, for insurance purpose, and an auction catalog."

"I can do that."

"It's large, nine-by-twelve, and, well, I haven't got much money to spend. Think you'd be interested?"

"How much is not much?"

"Five hundred . . . plus expenses."

"I'm interested, Jo . . . Josephine," I said, nearly tripping on her dignity. A copy job like that wouldn't take more than a couple of hours of my time. Five hundred dollars had a nice solid ring to it, and she had said plus expenses.

"Good, it's settled, then," she said. "How long has it been, Charlie?"

"It's been a few years, hasn't it?" I said, wondering how she was holding up.

"I suppose you've got a mortgage and a couple of kids."

"Not yet."

"Really, well, I hope you haven't gone gay."

"I don't think so."

"In that case, I'll expect a dinner."

Josephine Cyzeski, I remembered, was not the kind of woman who was waiting for the Equal Rights Amendment to pass to get what she wanted. "Okay, but is dinner the 'plus expenses'?"

"It's fee, dude," she said flatly.

I remembered also that her body language was more eloquent than her speech. "Have anyplace special in mind?"

"I'll leave that up to you. I'm free tonight, though, if you'd like to call me back." She gave me the number and hung up.

I'd just come back from camping out in a farmer's sunflower patch in Dawson, Georgia, swatting mosquitoes the size of parakeets while keeping one eye peeled for diamondback rattlesnakes as fat as your arm. I hate snakes. So, of course, I was thrilled to learn, before taking to the field, that the rattlers lurked in the nearby swamps, appearing in the evening to hunt field mice and cottontails. Like a Patriot missile, they homed in on Mickey Mouse and Bugs Bunny with the help of heat-seeking sensors in their tongues, or snouts. When I wasn't swatting mosquitoes or keeping an eye out for snakes, I was taking time-lapse photographs of sunflowers blooming.

To eliminate weather problems, and control lighting, we were shooting under rubberized construction tarps. Two MX Arriflex motion picture cameras, each in its own tent, were taking a single-frame exposure of a promising sunflower once every fifteen minutes. There was a generator and four 750-watt tungsten lights in each tent. Because the hot lights forced the plants to bloom, we had to shoot around the clock.

The art director insisted in the preproduction meeting that this was the way to shoot the job. My protests were in vain. Sunflowers, however, unlike photographers, don't take orders from little dictators. If you've never been in Georgia in August, believe me when I tell you it gets hot there, and humid, too. The temperatures under those tarps soared above a hundred degrees, and the humidity hovered near a hundred percent. Bud after bud peeked open, checked out the scene, said, this bud's not for you, and nosedived.

Each time this happened, the whole setup, tent, lights, generator, tripod and camera, had to be moved to a new location for fresh fodder. It didn't take many of these moves before the crew began to wilt and shrivel like the sunflowers. It was ugly.

The way I'd wanted to do the job was to cut the flowers and air-freight them to the studio, stick them in sugar and water, and let them bloom like roses. But no, we had to waste an acre of the farmer's sunflower crop before the stubborn little prick art director got the message: this was not going to work.

Mr. Smarty Pants soon became desperate. He had nothing to lose except his pride by trying it my way. So, while he and the producer tromped out into the field in the cool of the evening, along with the mice and the rabbits, to gather their buds while they may, I improvised a studio in a motel room. When they returned unmolested from the field with the sunflowers, I was ready to go. Four Nikon cameras, each with its own cool strobe lighting, and regulated by intervalometers, snapped a single frame once every fifteen minutes. In two days we captured the bloom of more than a dozen plants on Kodachrome.

All this effort was expended on behalf of five seconds of film; the opening of a television commercial hawking a brand of margarine that promised to never clog your pipes, and to keep you looking thirty-nine forever.

Sunflowers and Georgia are another song, though.

The point is, it took me until I got back to New York to discover I'd been snake-bitten. While I was laboring in the sunflower patch, my agent dropped me for another photographer.

Seems she called on a punk art director to show my portfolio. Instead of selling him on me, he sold her on his own guy, a photographer with a more upscale operation than mine. And a hardcore following of similar runny-nosed punks. Image is everything in the ad game. And mine needed work.

Nothing personal, she said, explaining the switch, but this was a career move. She hoped I'd understand. I said, sure, I understood. We'd only been together for a short time, but she'd kept me busy from the beginning. Losing her was a real blow—the lady knew how to sell, and the phone had been mighty quiet ever since. JoJo's call seemed like a good omen. Entropy sets in quick when there's no work in the shop. You start wondering whether you'll ever work again.

When the phone finally does ring, it always seems that the jobs come in twos or threes, so maybe I was due for a change of luck. Anyway, five hundred bucks wasn't too shabby for photographing a tapestry.

When I called JoJo back at noon and said, let's have dinner and renew old acquaintances, she said, sorry, but she couldn't make it tonight after all. How about next week? I said okay, and she said she needed the picture sooner than expected. Could I possibly do it tomorrow? Otherwise, she'd have to find another photographer. No problem, I said, tomorrow it is. She gave me instructions on where to go, and who to see, and where to deliver the transparencies. She wished me luck, told me to call her next week, and hung up.

The last time I'd seen JoJo Cyzeski she was a stringer for UPI in Pakistan, and I was trotting around the global village wearing a necklace of Nikons, doing my impression of a photojournalist. Although there was a lot of talk about her in the press corps, we hadn't done any more than flirt.

I wondered where I should take her for dinner, and how she was looking, and whether we'd do more than flirt.

2

They were there again the next morning when I went to pick up the paper. This time I got a good look at the master, or more correctly, the mistress. Her chair was a plastic milk crate, and the dog lay at her feet on the cardboard carpet. Framed in the doorway, they reminded me of a diorama at the Museum of Natural History. "Homelessness in America, circa 1990," might be the title. I was tempted to go back and get a camera.

They were dining al fresco. The dog was wolfing down his kibble from a plastic bowl. His owner sat with a clear plastic container—the kind you get at a Korean salad bar—perched on her knees buffet style. She was absorbed in a paperback novel, *Fools Die* by Mario Puzo. With plastic flatware, she picked at a dinner combination of tortellini, broccoli spears, chick-peas, and beets, which she washed down with a can of Diet Pepsi. The breakfast of champions, I thought.

"Nice dog," I said. "What's it's name?"

The woman looked up from the book. "Socrates," she

said, beaming, stroking the pooch's head fondly. Socrates responded by thumping his tail vigorously against the cardboard.

She wasn't young, she wasn't old, and she wasn't a half-bad-looking woman, either. Her face was pleasant and matronly, its most notable feature a pair of evenly spaced, clear blue eyes the color of a gas jet flame. Her hair was an unremarkable shade of brown, graying at the temples and widow's peak, and she wore it up. The skin on her face and the backs of her hands was like fine leather from constant exposure to weather, but otherwise she appeared no worse for wear, looking clean and healthy. Her costume was as colorful as it was unusual. She was cinched at the waist by a broad, scarlet satin sash over a moss-green turtleneck sweater topped by an orange velour vest, below which she wore a voluminous blue skirt to the ankles, and canvas, camouflage Timberland boots. For good measure, or wretched excess, she completed the outfit with a navy-blue down parka. It was plain there were several more bizarre costumes beneath this one. I wondered how many. My friend was right—even in the warmest weather you don't see homeless people running around naked. Was it because they had no closet space that they went in for the layered look? Was it because layers of clothing offered a lot of hiding places? Or was it a fashion statement on their part, the urban survivalist look? Whatever it was, even with all those layers of clothing on, you could tell she still had a shape. And that she was in no danger of hypothermia.

"Interesting name," I said.

"He's a thinker, aren't you, Socrates?" she said, scratching the blissful canine's ear.

Uncertain how to respond, I said, "Well, they're smarter than most people think."

"No doubt about it. My name's Dolly Varden," she said.

"Dolly Parton?" That was the way I heard it.

"*V*, like Victor, Varden . . . Dolly Varden," she said.

"Ah-ha, Dolly Varden," I repeated as though I were dense. "Like the trout."

"Like in Dickens," she corrected me.

"Oh, I see," I said, trying to edge away. "Nice meeting you, Dolly."

"What's your name?"

"Charlie Byrne."

"Common enough," she said.

"Yes . . . but I'm used to it. Gotta run, Dolly."

"You got a dollar, Charlie?"

"A dollar? Ah, sure." I fumbled in my wallet. "Here," I said, handing it over. Our mayor frowned on this form of charity.

"Thanks." She stashed it somewhere deep in the folds of her wardrobe.

I let the back of my hand linger momentarily in front of Socrates's snout, and he gave it a lick. "Good dog," I said, patting his head. "See you, Dolly."

"Sure," she said, and returned to her novel.

It was about four o'clock in the afternoon when Tito and I arrived at the address Josephine had given me. The temperature was a sizzling ninety-seven, the humidity a greasy ninety percent. The sky was black and blue with the threat of a cloudburst. The weather was brutal.

A tall, gaunt figure dressed in a blue blazer, gray flannel trousers, white shirt, and rep tie stood ready to receive us at the service entrance. "I am William," he announced with a diffident smile. "Mr. Ransom's man."

"I'm Charles Byrne," I said mildly. "This is my assistant, Tito Lopez. Josephine Cyzeski asked us to photograph a tapestry."

"Yes, of course, Mr. Byrne. Miss Cyzeski mentioned we could expect you. She has instructed us to show you to the tapestry, and give you any assistance you should require."

"That's very kind of you."

"Perhaps I can help you with your equipment?" He hardly looked strong enough to tote a tray of drinks.

"Why don't you show us the tapestry, and we'll come back for our gear. It'll be safe here, won't it?"

"Definitely."

"Lead on, then."

"As you wish." This guy was stiffer than a starched collar, but I guess that's what you look for in a butler.

Tito and I followed him through the pantry into the kitchen.

"The photographers are here, Brigit," he announced.

Brigit would be the cook. We swapped grins. Hers was as broad and as open as the rest of her ruddy face. There was nothing shy about her. She would be in her forties, and stood, sturdy and robust, hands on her hips, studying me with lively eyes. Her steel-gray hair was up in a bun, and her clothes, a pair of brown polyester slacks and a yellow blouse, were neat, if dowdy. She was a dead ringer for my aunt, who raised me, and coincidentally, she had made her living cooking for the rich, too.

"Charles Byrne," I said, extending my hand to her.

"Hello, pleased to meet you, Mr. Byrne," she said, beaming. She was from the same aspic mold as my aunt, no doubt about it.

"This is Tito Lopez, my assistant."

They shook hands and agreed they were pleased to meet.

"This way, Mr. Byrne," said William. He sailed off into a second pantry, the butler's pantry, and Tito and I followed. From there, he led us into the main hall.

"Charlie," Tito murmured, his eyes bugging out with amazement, "you could put the whole studio inside this room."

"It's big," I agreed.

William paused, letting us take it all in.

I had a feeling of déjà vu. It had begun with Brigit, the cook, or maybe even with the Park Avenue address, and now this strangely familiar room . . . it was like falling backward in time, like watching a tape of my life on rapid rewind. I had been here before, or in other rooms like this one. I gazed around me in awe.

Those had not been the best of times. When I was a kid, home for the holidays from whatever crummy boarding school I happened to be attending at that time, I remember being dragged by my aunt from apartment to apartment, each like this one, where she went to cook dinner parties for the rich. To kill time while I waited for her to finish work, I'd taught myself to play the harmonica. One night, as I was doing what I was supposed to do—stay out of the way in the servants' quarters at the back of the apartment—my aunt, eager to show me off, pressed me and my harmonica into service. She wanted me to play "Happy Birthday" for the lady of the house.

I was no Stevie Wonder, but I thought I sounded pretty good. Then I caught the frozen smiles on the faces of the birthday girl and her guests. My well-meaning aunt, certain she was as good as anyone and better than most, was oblivious of their condescension. Their empty applause was a stinging humiliation for a ten-year-old kid.

William cleared his throat, snapping me out of it. I'd forgotten there were places like this in New York, floor-through elegance, twelve-foot ceilings, marble floor underfoot. This was first class.

I nodded. "Very nice," I said. Tito was stunned by the splendor. Whole limbs of flowering trees and shrubs climbed from Oriental vases nearly to the ceiling in artful display. Someone had to come in daily and perform that trick. The monthly tab for the flowers alone was probably equal to a mortgage in Westport.

I inspected a pair of prints. The signature said Klee. A still life of a brace of grouse, a charming oil sketch, was signed by Degas. Even my untutored eye could see that every stick of furniture was either a Louis-the-this or a Queen Anne-the-that, and of museum quality. The carpets, too, Oriental and venerable, had pedigrees.

William cleared his throat a second time. "This way, please," he murmured.

We moved on to an adjoining room, furnished in similar fashion. A Bosendorfer piano, replete with a vase of fresh-cut flowers, suggested this was the music room. "Here we are," declared William, with an airy wave of the hand and indicating a tapestry hanging on the wall beyond the piano, "the new tapestry."

It was a pastoral scene of nymphs, knights, blackamoors, unicorns, a whole menagerie of fanciful beasts and exotic fruits and vegetables. Whatever its meaning, it was safe to say that it was no longer accessible to the casual viewer. "Handsome," I felt compelled to say.

"It is an Aubusson," William said reverentially.

"We'll have to move the piano," I said.

"Oh dear, I feared as much. You will be careful?"

"We will be extremely careful," I assured him, eschewing the contraction. I felt that if I could hang out with William for a week, it would do wonders for my English.

"We are insured, of course."

"Of course."

"But as you can see, these objects are priceless."

"We will be extremely careful," I repeated.

He smiled. "Well then, if you need any further assistance, you will find me in the pantry." He bowed slightly, excusing himself, and backed out of the room.

"The first thing I'd do if I lived here," Tito began, "is I'd hang a nice moonlight-on-the-water scene right there, over the piano. You know, the kind painted on black velvet. Then I'd have the sofas and chairs all reupholstered in leopard and zebra skin, I think. And the—"

"Don't tell me. Let me guess. You'd hang photos of Martin Luther King, Jr., and JFK. On the piano you'd have a two-foot-high plastic Madonna. Right?"

"How'd you know?" He grinned.

"Come on, gimme a hand moving this stuff."

After shifting the furniture, we moved the equipment into the room and began setting up the lights and camera. My eight-by-ten Deardorff camera, with it's brass fittings and cherrywood body, is frequently mistaken for an antique by clients. When the camera was set on the tripod, it looked right at home among Ransom's antiques.

William materialized with a plate of cookies as we were busy framing up, focusing, and preparing to make a Polaroid. "Brigit's chocolate chip cookies," he said, eyeing the alterations skeptically.

Tito helped himself to a cookie and his eyes glazed with pleasure. I popped one in my mouth. It was buttery and sublime, the best chocolate chip cookie I'd ever tasted. "Delicious. My compliments to Brigit," I said.

"Yes, they are," said William, plainly distracted. "You will be careful moving things?" he pleaded.

"Of course."

"Would you like something to drink?"

"A couple of beers would be nice," I said hopefully, glancing at Tito. He bobbed his head, his mouth full.

"Very well," said William, disappearing again.

"Has that bird got his eye on us, or what?" said Tito.

"Can't blame him. We pocket an ashtray and it's a couple of grand."

"Don't give me any ideas."

William returned with two bottles of Heineken and a pair of tall glasses on a silver serving tray. He placed them on one of the end tables next to the cookie plate. "Whenever you are ready," he said, the tray under his arm. He stood watching us work. "It must be fascinating," he said.

"What's that?"

"Photography, of course."

"It beats heavy lifting," I said.

"Do you mind if I watch?"

"Not at all."

"Surely that cannot be the photograph," he said, watching me like a hawk as I inserted the Polaroid back into the film holder and pulled out the slip sheet.

"It is not," I replied, eschewing the contraction again. Then I blew it. "We're making a Polaroid to find our exposure."

"I see."

Tito stood by the lens and cocked the shutter. I pressed the release cable. The strobes flashed. And the place was plunged into darkness.

"What happened? Did we blow a fuse?" I said.

"Oh, dear," murmured William.

"I don't think it's a fuse, Charlie," said Tito. "Look out the window. I don't see any lights."

He was right; the street was dark. A harsh, blue-white light illuminated the buildings across the street fleetingly, then it was dark again. Wind and rain rattled the windowpanes. Thunder boomed.

"I think we have us a brownout," said Tito.

13

"Shit!" I muttered, forgetting William. "Couldn't it wait until we got the shot?"

"Oh dear, oh dear," went William.

"Whatta we do now?" said Tito.

"What can we do? Are we in your way, William?"

"Not at all, Mr. Byrne. Mr. Ransom is at his summer residence on the Vineyard."

"We're here, and we're ready to shoot. We might as well wait. Con Ed's not gonna leave the ruling class without their juice for very long. Is that okay with you, William?"

"As you wish, Mr. Byrne."

"Fine, we'll wait then."

"We do have a small lounge in the rear of the apartment," said William. "May I, er, suggest that you would be more comfortable waiting there."

"Whatever you say, William." Our eyes were growing accustomed to the dark. I grabbed a bottle of beer and a handful of cookies. Tito did the same. "After you, my man," I said. Tito chuckled softly.

"Do be careful," William cautioned us as we felt our way through the dark apartment. Lightning crackled. Our passage down a long, narrow hallway was momentarily illuminated, and then we were left blind again. Rolling thunder reverberated down Park Avenue a couple of seconds later. William pulled us into a room on our right. "Oh my," he said. "This will never do. Just give me a moment while I get a candle."

"Oh my, oh my," mimicked Tito. We clowned around in the dark, feeling for something to sit on, and finally collapsed on a couch.

William appeared like an apparition, his gaunt features raked from below by the beam of a flashlight. He was carrying a pair of candles.

"Oh dear, oh dear." Tito giggled. "This is like a spook movie."

Unamused, William lit the candles. "If you need anything, there is the bell. Feel free to ring," he said, and vaporized like a ghost.

My eyes grew accustomed to the light, and I saw that we were back in the servants' quarters once more. There was nothing of value in the room. The furnishings were vaguely contemporary and shabby. There was an upright piano against one wall, and a television set. The carpeting was wall-to-wall. Tito and I stretched out on separate couches. We were in the rear of the building, and I could see across a small courtyard to an adjacent building. I watched candles flicker in the neighbors' windows.

"Wake me up when the lights come on," said Tito.

"All right," I said, and closed my eyes. The apartment was stifling without air-conditioning, and the beer had made us drowsy.

Still, I didn't find it easy to sleep. I wondered if all of Manhattan was out, or only the upper East Side. Maybe the whole city was out. I wondered where Josephine was. I wondered if microwaves, CBs, PCs, CDs, TVs, and VCRs were being liberated in the Bronx, Harlem, and Brooklyn. I wondered if these seasonal power outages weren't harbingers of greater catastrophes to come. Weren't there too many of us? Who said the lights had to come back on anyway?

3

I bolted upright. Had I been dreaming? I thought I'd heard a scream, and the sound of breaking glass. I ran to the window. The lights were back on.

"Did you hear that?" said Tito, right behind me.

"I heard something."

"It was a scream."

I peered outside into the rain, and lowered my gaze to the courtyard below. It looked like a woman's body lying on the wet concrete.

"Jesus," Tito muttered.

"Wait here," I said.

I raced from room to room, looking for a phone. I finally found one and dialed 911. It was busy. They were probably jammed because of the power outage. I dashed back to the window. The body was still there. The scream, the sound of breaking glass had been real. I hadn't dreamed it.

"I gotta get down there," I said. "She might still be alive."

"We couldn't be the only ones who heard it, Charlie."

"There's a phone in a bedroom down the hall. Keep trying 911."

"There's no one at the windows. Someone else had to hear it happen. What's the matter with these people?"

"They don't want to know. Remember Kitty Genovese?"

"Who?"

"Never mind. Call 911."

I ran into William in the main hall. "Mr. Byrne?" he said, startled. "I was about to look in on you."

"Someone fell out a window."

"Out a window, you say? Oh dear, how awful."

"Didn't you hear it?"

"I am afraid not. Not your colleague, I hope?"

"No, not Tito. We're wasting time, William. I've got to get down there."

"Of course. How can I help?"

"Call 911. Tell them it's around the corner, on Seventy-seventh."

"Two eleven?"

"If you say so. Hurry."

"Of course," he murmured, and flew to the pantry.

As I remembered from my childhood, there was a small holding foyer in the middle of the hall that led to the front elevator. I leaned on the button until the car came. It took forever. Before the door closed, I snatched an umbrella from the stand in the foyer. Two doormen were on duty as I burst out of the elevator. They blocked my path, the front door firmly shut. "I'm the photographer. From Ransom's apartment," I said, in the face of a pair of hard stares. "Check it out with William, the butler."

One of them went to the intercom.

"Listen, I'd love to chat, but someone just fell out a window."

"Fell out a window?"

"There's an echo in here. That's what I said. Around the corner." I pointed in the direction.

"Two eleven?"

"Two eleven," I echoed.

"William says he's okay, Joe," said his pal from the intercom. Joe stepped aside and held the door for me.

"If the cops come here, send 'em around the corner, okay?"

"Two eleven?" he repeated.

"You got it."

I dashed around the corner, only to find the doorman at 211 barring my way. "Help you, mister?"

"Someone in this building just fell out the window. They're in the courtyard. They may still be alive." My guess was he was a cop moonlighting as a doorman.

He held his ground impassively. "Yeah, yeah," he said, humoring me, "we know all about it. We got it under control."

"You do, huh?" Oh, man, the rich and their fucking security.

"You heard me. Now be a good fella, and take off."

"Oh . . . okay." I wasn't about to stand there arguing with this donkey. I turned, as if to leave. He relaxed, his chest caving in and sliding back down to his belt. I teed off and smacked him in the head with the handle of the umbrella. That stunned him. I sprinted through the lobby for the stairwell door and bounded down the steps three at a time. He lumbered after me. Too many doors momentarily confused me, and I lost a few seconds figuring out which one led to the courtyard. Outside, I skidded to a halt beside the body. The doorman, trucking after me, pulled up short beside me and muttered, "Oh, shit."

We gazed mutely at a well-kept, thirty-something blonde. She was on her back, staring at the sky, her face wet. A child could see this was the face of death.

"Know who she is?" I asked.

"Her name's Sharon Raynes. She was new in the building."

I indicated the window with the angry teeth of glass protruding from the casement frame. "That her apartment?"

"Yeah," he said, staring up slack-jawed, breathing through his mouth.

"Someone's trying to get through to 911," I said.

"I better call the management."

"Be sure their asses are covered, huh?"

He gave me a dirty look. "Don't touch anything."

"Not a chance," I said. "Call upstairs and see if anyone's in the lady's apartment, while you're at it. The lights are on."

"I'll be right back," he said, and waddled off.

Tito was faintly visible through the roil of mist and fog that shrouded the building. He signaled that the cops were on the way. I was getting soaked, my teeth beginning to chatter. It was a futile gesture, but I opened the umbrella and tried to shield the indifferent woman from the rain. I wished the cops would hurry. . . .

She looked as though she'd dressed in a hurry. Her clothes were in disarray, the skirt on backward, the buttons of her blouse not lined up right. She wasn't wearing a bra, or stockings. A shoe, dislodged by the impact, lay near the body. Her makeup was a mess, and she wore no jewelry. It seemed strange there were no cuts on her face or hands from the broken glass. There were no marks anywhere that I could see, but then the light was bad. She looked crumpled up and discarded, broken up inside. I looked away, and felt her sightless stare on the back of my neck.

". . . a jumper . . . yeah, female, Caucasian, thirty to forty years of age . . ." a pint-sized woman cop was saying into a walkie-talkie.

The courtyard was crowded with bodies in slickers and blaze-orange vests. Police radios crackled, and flashlight beams raked the yard and climbed the walls of the surrounding buildings. The deaf, dumb, and blind neighbors seemed to have recovered their senses, and were hanging out their windows, getting a buzz off of a stranger's misfortune.

Then a tall woman in a trench coat made an entrance. She was escorted by a burly, red-faced man in a suit too rich for a policeman's salary. I recognized him from TV as Matty Fallon, a political flack, and spokesman for the mayor. The cops, plainclothes and brass, who moments earlier had been laughing and joking among themselves, stood aside, faces solemn, and let Fallon and the woman pass. An EMS team had already gone through the motions of checking for vital signs, and was now waiting to take away the body.

The woman viewed the body somberly, hands jammed deep in the pockets of the trench coat. Eventually, she turned and said something to Fallon. Fallon, in turn, conferred with a plainclothes cop, and a gold badge. The plainclothes cop took notes. The cop flipped his notebook closed, and Fallon turned his attention to the doorman, who nodded briefly in my direction. He rejoined the woman in the trench coat as the EMS crew were slipping the corpse in a body bag. He leaned toward her, said something, and she looked my way. Then he took her by the elbow and they approached.

"Matty Fallon," he announced bluntly.

"I know who you are," I said. "I'm Charlie Byrne."

"This is Mrs. Ferrante," he said.

"Susan Ferrante," she said with a fleeting, polite smile.

"Charlie Byrne," I repeated.

She was tall. I'm nearly six feet, and in her flats she looked me in the eye. Her hair, which looked dark and shoulder-length, was matted to her skull from the rain, which made her bold features seem all the more pronounced. She had a long, intelligent face, which looked pale as ivory in the dim light. Her mouth was broad and expressive, with lips that were generous. Her eyes were large and well spaced. I couldn't see the color, but they seemed to shine in the dark. Her nose was large, too, but a match for the rest of her face.

"They tell me you were the one who found her, Mr. Byrne," she said.

"Yes."

"She was my sister," she said simply, her gaze fixed on the EMS crew. They were lifting the gurney through the basement door now.

"Oh . . . I'm sorry," I mumbled. "I wish I could have gotten to her sooner."

"I'm grateful you got to her when you did," she replied.

I was searching for something further to say when a gray-haired cop with lieutenant's bars intruded. "We're finished here, Matty," he said. "No reason to hang around."

"Susan, why don't you go along with Frank," said Fallon. "I'll be right with you. I'd like a word with Mr. Byrne."

"Good-bye, Mr. Byrne," she said. "And thank you for your concern."

I said good-bye and watched her leave.

"So tell me, Mr. Byrne," said Fallon, "how is it you happened to be the one who found her?"

It wasn't exactly a hostile question, but it wasn't friendly, either. Let's just say he wasn't wasting any of his famous Irish charm on me. He was probably saving it for the television camera. "Just lucky, I guess," I said. I can cop an attitude as quick as the next person.

"Take it easy, I'm just asking," he said.

"I was working in an apartment around the block when the lights went out. That's how I happened to be in the area."

"Uh-huh, the lights went out . . . then what happened?"

I nodded at Ransom's apartment. Tito was standing in the window. "My assistant and I—"

Fallon looked up. "That him?"

"Yes."

"That isn't Marc Ransom's apartment, is it?"

"That's right, you know him?"

"I know Marc," he admitted. "Go on."

"As I was saying, we were waiting for the lights to come back on when we heard a scream, a crash, the sound of broken glass. We ran to the window and saw the body lying in the courtyard."

"Was that it?"

"What do you mean?"

"Was that all you saw?" he asked with a hard look.

"That was all. My assistant called 911, and I got down here as fast as I could, but it was too late. Then the cops came, you came—"

"And that was it?"

"That was it."

He seemed to relax a bit. "Live in the city?" he asked amiably.

"Manhattan. I'm in the phone book."

"Thanks again, Mr. Byrne," he said, regarding me speculatively. "We'll be in touch if we have any further questions."

I watched him hustle out of the courtyard, thinking that was a line the lieutenant should have said. In fact, it was an interview the lieutenant should have conducted. I looked up at the shattered window. The cop on the walkie-talkie had called Raynes a jumper. Wouldn't a suicide have opened the window first if he was going to jump? I wondered. I looked over again at Ransom's apartment. William and Brigit were standing in one window, Tito in another. Tito waved impatiently for me to come back upstairs.

I made my way through the basement and out to the street, one of the last to leave the courtyard. Patrolmen were telling the curious to move along, the excitement was over. The EMS ambulance was pulling away from the curb. There was no sign of Fallon or Susan Ferrante anywhere. One by one, patrol cars were leaving the scene, gumdrops flashing. I slipped through the police lines like a shadow and hurried back to Ransom's.

William greeted me with a towel, but what I needed was a change of clothes. "Was that Mr. Fallon I saw with you?" William wanted to know. "And who was the woman with him?"

"That was Matty Fallon, and the woman was Susan Ferrante, the sister of the dead woman," I said.

"Oh dear, how dreadful," he murmured. "Brigit, we have had Mrs. Ferrante to dinner, remember?"

"Go on, William," said the cook, giving him a playful poke. "Do you think I pay any mind who comes to dinner here?"

"Yes, Mrs. Ferrante has been to dinner here on more than one occasion," William said gravely.

"With Fallon?" I asked.

"With Mr. Fallon, and others," he replied.

"Come on, Charlie, let's wrap this job and get out of here," Tito said. "If we hang around much longer, they'll be charging us rent."

"Let's do it," I agreed. I was as anxious as he was to get out of there.

Everything was standing just as we'd left it. Our lights were set. We pulled a Polaroid immediately. It took four of them before we got one we liked. The rest was automatic. Three film holders, six sheets of eight-by-ten Ektachrome, and bing, bang, boom, we were packing up the equipment and saying our good-byes—praising Brigit's cookies and thanking William for the beers. We flew out of Ransom's luxe co-op faster than a landlord can slap a tenant with a dispossess.

Dinner's on me when the crew works past eight P.M., and it was ten o'clock before we dropped the equipment off at the studio. I'd given up any hope of turning a profit on this job. "Hey, look, a dog," said Tito, spotting Socrates and Dolly Varden as the cab pulled up to our door.

"The new tenants," I said. "They moved in a couple of days ago."

"Man, can you believe that, a dog. I can't afford a dog."

"I know what you mean. His name's Socrates. The owner's name is Dolly Varden."

"Yeah. How do you know that?"

"I welcomed them on behalf of the Block Association."

"What kinda names are those?"

"Greek, I guess."

Tito put away the gear, and I changed into dry clothes. We went around to Lexington Avenue and Thirty-seventh to B.B.'s Ribs, a chicken and rib joint. It's got sawdust on the floor, free peanuts in the shell, which you throw on the floor, live C&W, and the Mets on the TV at the bar. The food's decent, and reasonable, and they serve late. The clientele are mostly bosses and their secretaries. It's a regular low-rent rendezvous.

I ordered baby back ribs, a baked potato, and a draft of Samuel Adams. Tito ordered a draft of the same and the rib roast. Starting with a brick of fried onions—we were in the mood for some grease—we wolfed down supper with one eye on the television set. The Mets were at Chicago, getting creamed by the Cubs. They were fifteen games off the pace, playing less than .500 ball. Tito, whom I deferred to on these matters, blamed the disastrous season on management.

"They're always fixing what isn't broken. Watch and see," he predicted sourly, "they'll trade a .300 hitter for a .250 in the off-season."

We burped and pushed aside our plates. The waitress asked if we'd like doggy bags. B.B.'s was that kind of place, it prided itself on sending the patrons home with doggy bags. The Mets would have trouble putting all the food away. Tito had had enough and waved her off. I asked for his as well as mine, plus an extra baked potato. I paid the tab, and we strolled over to Fifth Avenue. I waited with him while he hailed a cab, and gave him the fare—another late-night emolument. It was past eleven when I started back to the studio alone.

Before I turned the corner, I could hear her. It was like walking into a wall of sound. Dolly Varden's figure materialized out of the dark. Drawing nearer, I could see her eyes bulging, her face flushed, the veins in her neck throbbing as she fowled the night with demented obscenities. She was as original as she was inventive, suggesting any number of droll sexual possibilities. Her faithful pooch stood by her side looking sheepish and embarrassed. Occasionally he'd join in a chorus, emitting a howl that wavered between a call of the wild and a whimper, between a cry of defiance and a moan of pain and of humiliation. Tell me dogs don't know.

Should I interrupt her, I wondered, and risk drawing her fire? The wisest, and best, policy is to give the street loonies wide berth. Why get involved, right? Right. "Er, Dolly," I began. She went right on ranting. "Dolly," I tried again. She was oblivious to me. "Dolly!" I yelled finally at the top of my lungs.

That seemed to get her attention because she clammed right up. Her eyes receded back into their sockets. She glared at me, like, this better be good, buster. "Are you speaking to me?" she asked reasonably.

"Dolly, I've brought some food for you and Socrates— ribs, and roast beef . . . a baked potato."

She computed this information and said, "Whatta ya think you are, some kinda fuckin' good Samaritan?"

What did I expect? "Here," I said, undaunted. I offered the doggy bag.

She snatched the bag from me with contempt and fumbled to open it. She stuck her nose in it and sniffed. "Don't eat meat," she announced, lifting her eyes to meet mine.

"Okay, lemme have it, I'll eat it tomorrow, for lunch."

"Socrates eats meat," she said, clinging to the doggy bag. Socrates concurred, beating his tail on the sidewalk.

"All right, give it to Socrates." I turned to go, anxious to get upstairs and put this day behind me.

"Charlie! Gotta dollar?" She grinned.

"Yeah, sure," I sighed. I whipped out my wallet and forked over a bill. It disappeared into the layers of her wardrobe with the speed of light.

I reached down and scratched Socrates behind the ears. He reciprocated with an amiable lick of the back of my hand.

"Good night," she said.

I was crouching, working the key in the bottom lock of the plate-glass doors, when she went off like a rocket on another blue streak. "Cocksucker . . . motherfucker . . ." she screamed. Reluctant and mournful, Socrates joined in the chorus.

I realized she wasn't shouting at me, but rather at some black hole in the universe. Even so, the scalding hot tirade blistered the back of my neck and sent me scurrying for cover behind the silent sanity of the thick plate glass. This had been one of those days.

4

The restaurant JoJo and I had settled on was around the corner from City Center. The gimmick was wine tasting, and an awesome array of the grape was on display, sold by the glass at prices higher than the whole bottle cost retail.

I paused at the reservations desk, and a wispy, bearded blond in the last dregs of his youth greeted me with a false smile. He was wearing chinos, a blue oxford cloth shirt, a black knit tie, and a denim apron. We were going to be two for dinner, I told him, and we didn't have reservations. No problem, he assured me, ushering me to a table in the dining room and slipping me the wine list as soon as I was seated. He hovered over me while I studied the list, at the ready and expecting to be quizzed.

"Is it too late for last year's Beaujolais nouveau?" I asked, hoping my enological ignorance wasn't showing.

"We haven't had the Beaujolais nouveau since November," he informed me.

"Too bad," I mumbled, feeling about as in touch as a coma victim.

"Is it a red wine you're interested in?"

"Yes, I think so."

"Well, in that case, may I recommend the Cabernet Sauvignon '82, or the Châteauneuf-du-Pape '85. Both excellent vintages."

"The Pape," I said, and handed the list to him.

"Will that be a taste, or the six-ounce glass?"

What did it take to shake this guy? "How many ounces to the taste?" I asked, playing along.

"A taste is two and a half ounces."

"The economy size, the six," I said.

"Certainly," he murmured, and glided across the floor to a cruvenet machine with more taps than a centipede has legs.

I eyeballed the premises. The dark, raw wood; exposed brick; blue and white checkered tablecloths; the lighting, which cunningly caught a glint off the flatware and put the sparkle on the stemware, conspiring to lend an ambience of the intimate boîte; and Julian Bream's guitar filtering through the stereo in muted tones. A cozy atmosphere where a wino with an educated palate could get ripped.

The wine steward, or whatever he was, returned beaming, and bearing my glass of Châteauneuf-du-Pape '85 on a round bar tray. He placed the glass before me gently, and hesitated.

I passed the glass under my nose and sniffed. He watched anxiously. "Mm . . . fruity," I said, "yet with a hearty, full-bodied bouquet." His head bobbed affirmatively. I sipped, and smiled. "Insouciant . . . and yet . . . ineffably piquant." I was pushing my luck. I had never used those three words before in my life, let alone all in one sentence. But, hey, it was that kind of place. Blondie kvelled with bliss.

"Exactly, a spectacular vintage," he exclaimed. "Enjoy!" he commanded, before turning on heel, leaving me, finally, to myself.

I was still nursing the six ounces of Châteauneuf-du-Pape '85 when Josephine made her entrance twenty minutes later. I stood to greet her, and she beamed as she spotted me. She was lithe and chic in a dark gray linen business suit, a pale green silk blouse, and a twist of gold chain. The hem of her skirt brushed her knees, showing off limbs unusually long for a Chinese woman, and as nicely turned as the legs of a Queen Anne chair. More than one pair of envious eyes tracked her as she pranced over to the table.

"JoJo." I grinned in a foolish pleasure.

"Josephine," she was quick to correct me, as she extended a lacquered hand, which I cupped in both of mine.

"You look wonderful," I gushed. I'd guess she was thirty-five, or forty, no kid, but she could easily pass for twenty-five. Whatever her age, she was a spectacular vintage herself.

"Thank you." She smiled. "And you're as handsome as ever, Charlie." She folded her skirt beneath her and took her seat.

Blondie was Johnny-on-the-spot with the wine list. Josephine gave it a glance and said, "Kristal champagne."

"A bottle?" Blondie breathed.

Kristal? A bottle? What was this guy, high on the grape? A bottle must go for a hundred and fifty bucks or more in this place. "A glass," I said, "and another Pape." I was determined to break even on this deal.

"Yessir," Blondie murmured, slinking away.

"So, Josephine, what's been happening to you since I saw you last?" That should get the ball rolling, I figured. Her favorite topic of conversation had always been herself. I gazed at her, not remembering her eyes so perfectly almond-shaped or so darkly luminous. Nor did I remember her cheekbones so pronounced, her neck so long and slim. I didn't remember her so drop-dead beautiful.

"Well . . . I was divorced," she replied.

"From Cyzeski?"

"Who else?"

"I dunno. Sorry to hear that," I said, feeling an expression of sympathy was in order.

"Don't be," she giggled, "he was a turd."

English definitely wasn't her second language. "Well, in that case," I said, "I'm happy for you." I'd have to take her word for it that Cyzeski was a turd. Aside from the scuttlebutt in the press corps, and the odd fact that she was a farm girl—her folks grew vegetables underwater for Chinese restaurants, things like watercress, water chestnuts, sprouts, and rice—I didn't know much about her. "Anyway, you look like a million bucks," I said.

"Thanks." She grinned.

"You must be doing well."

"I've got no complaints." Blondie materialized, and we leaned back to let him serve the drinks.

"Do you work for this Ransom guy?"

"Uh-huh," she said, and sipped the Kristal.

"Looks like he's rolling in dough. What's his racket?"

"He's a real estate developer."

"Real estate? Jesus, Josephine."

"You sound like a renter, Charlie." She laughed.

"And proud of it," I said. I've been renting in Manhattan since Elizabeth Taylor was a virgin, and I remember when real estate was just another dumb, boring business, like selling insurance or bond trading. Who wanted to waste their lives money-grubbing in those businesses? But now money was everything, and a goon with an MBA was as glamorous as a rock star. There was a time when you could get by with a savings account and a lease. Now the financial wiseguys had it rigged so you needed a CD, an IRA, a money market account, a Visa card, and a co-op. The same roach ranch that used to rent for two or three hundred dollars a month now costs $2500 a month in mortgage and maintenance and is called a co-op instead of an apartment. That's progress for you.

The studio rent had soared from six hundred dollars a month a decade ago to more than three thousand dollars a month today. And all that bought me was a short count on 2100 square feet in a building that, in spring and fall, when the boiler was down, you could age prime beef. The roof leaked so badly you could take a shower under it when it rained. And the elevators were thrill rides. You could smoke crack, shoot dope, get laid or mugged in the stairwells, but you'd better come up with the rent on the first of the month. Raymond Chandler described a building like mine as "the kind of building a business crawls into to die."

"What exactly is it that you do for Ransom, broker, sell co-ops?"

"No."

"Hustle tax shelters?"

"Not allowed anymore."

"You gonna keep me guessing?"

"It's my job to see that his life goes as smoothly as possible, that there are no glitches."

"What's that mean? You lick his stamps, pick the shirts up from the laundry, tell the tradespeople the check's in the mail, and mix the martinis?"

"Hardly, the help does those things," she said loftily. "I supervise them and keep his calendar. I shop for him when he needs to give a gift. I deal with the decorators, represent him at auctions . . . that sort of thing. I do whatever needs doing."

"Like a private or social secretary, huh?"

"You might say that."

"Is he married?"

"Widowed."

"How delightful, and you run the household."

"Yes."

"The majordomo," I said, still fishing, "the lady of the house, as it were . . . in all but name, that is."

"You might say that." She smiled coyly.

"Park and Seventy-sixth is the high-rent district, and his apartment was like a museum. How rich is he?"

"Do you know what a unit is, Charlie?"

"Like a rental unit, you mean?"

"A unit," she explained, "is one hundred million dollars."

"You don't say. That's a lot of money. I'm still slumming in the four zero neighborhood myself."

"Marc has five units," she informed me, giving the high-five sign with a well-manicured hand.

"Well, I'll be darned, he's on his way to being a billionaire. How come I've never heard of the guy before? Most of the real estate barons have egos the size of Giants Stadium, and they aren't shy about flaunting it."

"Marc would rather die than see his name in the newspaper."

"Marc?" I smiled.

"Marc." She smiled right back. "Everyone thinks I sleep with him, but I can't help what people think."

I didn't remember asking whether she slept with Marc, but I think I was meant to think what everyone thought. "Well, he's so low-profile I haven't a clue what's his."

"You've heard of the Thackeray, I presume?"

"Do I look like a hick?"

She answered with an enigmatic smile.

Everyone in New York had heard of the Thackeray. It was an old SRO hotel in Murray Hill they refurbished a couple of years ago. Now it's infested with trendy boutiques instead of crackheads. It comes complete with the de rigueur piano player doing show tunes out of key in the café. The well-heeled who wouldn't have been caught dead below Fifty-seventh Street shack up there now while their apartments are being redecorated, or they're getting a divorce, or having a thing with a hairdresser. Chic to die.

"Marc owns it." She smiled.

Like I was supposed to be impressed. "That's nice," I said. "Probably writes off most of his personal living against the hotel."

"They all do it."

"Anyway, I'll bet Ransom has no secrets from you."

"None." She grinned.

"Shall we order?" I said, reaching for the menu.

"I'm famished."

Blondie appeared. Josephine ordered something called Carpaccio gold, which turned out to be a tricked-up steak Tartar—even the restaurant business had gone bananas overnight. New dishes were being invented by the minute. Chefs were nearly as glamorous as MBAs. The Pepsi Generation had to eat. I stuck to the trite but true, sole meunière. Both dishes were served with julienne potatoes, and broccoli al dente. She had another glass of champagne, while I stayed with the Châteauneuf-du-Pape. Blondie sniffed his disapproval. Apparently, iconoclasm was frowned on in enological circles.

I learned more than I needed or wanted to know about Ransom. He was all she wanted to talk about. I learned the man was in his middle fifties and had a daughter, a burden to her father. I also learned that Ransom's sex life was busier than a standing stud at a breeding farm, and Josephine devoted considerable time to juggling the mounting schedule. Furthermore, the fillies and mares weren't necessarily all thoroughbreds—they ranged from the maids to society women. I didn't ask, but I couldn't help wondering how Josephine got along with the rest of the stable; after all, here was a stud with five big units up for grabs. I didn't sense any jealousy on her part.

I let her babble on, only to learn that Ransom also had his dark side. He could be demanding, and demeaning, a tyrant, in fact, and was not above reducing faithful retainers to tears, Josephine included, when it suited his mood.

"Bad manners," I murmured, although I couldn't image him bullying Brigit, the cook, and it's a cinch he'd never have bullied my aunt. She wouldn't care how many units the guy had, she'd tell him to take the job and shove it. And she'd be working somewhere else the next day. Good cooks are always at a premium.

"Yes," she conceded, but she was working on him. "I consider it part of my job to make a gentleman out of him," she declared primly.

Good luck, I thought.

By now we were sipping coffee and brandy, and I was feeling pretty mellow. I signaled Blondie for the check. It came to ninety-two and change. I put five twenties and a ten in the leatherette folder and got to my feet. It occurred to me that this was no way to go about putting together a unit. Whatever hope I'd had of breaking even on the tapestry job, I'd just blown on dinner.

"How about a nightcap at my place?" Josephine said, uncoiling her legs and standing.

5

The theater hadn't broken yet, and we had no trouble flagging a cab. She gave the driver an address on West End Avenue in the eighties. The cab dropped us in front of a pre–World War II building, brick, and trimmed with faux Greek architectural details in white limestone.

"Good evening, Luis," she said, as we breezed past the fat, middle-aged Puerto Rican holding the door.

"Good evening, Mrs. Cyzeski," he answered politely.

We rode up to the twelfth floor in a clean, freshly lemon-oiled, wood-paneled elevator that still bore the scars of the vandals who had occupied the building in the days before gentrification. Epithets like "cheech," "pussy," and "blood" were among the more legible, along with a "Yo, Loretta."

"Yo, Josephine," I said, as she turned the key in the lock of apartment 12B, "you own?"

"Naturally, dude," she said, ushering me into a large foyer, and then an even more spacious, high-ceilinged living room with a southern exposure.

"Very nice, must have cost an arm and a leg," I said, doing a quick three sixty.

"This is one of Marc's buildings," she said, watching as my eyes roamed the room. "I was able to get a really marvelous deal."

"The insider's price?"

"Below the insider's price," she bragged. "Excuse the appearance, I'm still working on the place. Would you like a tour?"

"Why not?"

"Follow me."

"These old West Side apartments are something. They don't build them on this scale anymore."

"I love it," she said, leading the way down the hall off the foyer. "My bedroom." She gestured to our left. We looked in on a large, comfortable room done in pale yellow and cornflower-blue. A frilly, inviting four-poster bed dominated the room; that, and an almost floor-to-ceiling plate-glass mirror. There were also a Sony TV and VCR, a traditional chest of drawers, a hope chest at the foot of the bed, and a pair of linen-covered night tables.

"Very nice," I said.

"Thank you. I've done more with the bedroom. I like my comforts. The kitchen," she said, indicating the room across the hall. With raw wood, old tile, and generous proportions, it had lots of charm. The gas stove and deep, double-basin sink were genuine antiques.

"You've kept the old fixtures—clever."

"I like the old stuff," she said. We continued down the hall, where there was a smaller bedroom, bare but for a single, unmade bed. "The guest room," she said, and I nodded. "As you can see, I haven't gotten around to it yet." I nodded again.

Finally, at the end of the hall, we came to a large, old-fashioned West Side bathroom featuring a claw-footed bathtub big enough for three, and, like the kitchen, another acre of tile. The toilet was a pull-chain affair with the reservoir overhead. Dried herbs and flowers and a display of apothecary jars and cosmetics accented the anachronistic facilities.

I smiled approvingly. "Real nice crib, Josephine. People have been known to kill for apartments like these."

"I like it." She smiled. "About that nightcap, I have some cognac."

"Fine."

We trooped back to the kitchen. She rustled up a pair of glasses and a bottle, moving swiftly and with an economy of motion. "Sorry, but no snifters," she said, pouring the cognac in rocks glasses.

"That's all right," I said. "I'll have a glass of ice water, too, please."

We took our drinks and moved back to the living room. She gestured with her glass to an overstuffed sofa. "Have a seat," she said. "I'll put on some music."

I settled down in a corner of the sofa. My eyes automatically tracked her as she moved to the credenza. She dropped a CD in the player. It sounded like Fleetwood Mac. Then she folded herself into a wing chair, her bangled wrist decorating the armrest. "To whatever," she said, hoisting her glass.

"To Pakistan, and the good old days," I suggested.

"The good old days," she agreed, and drank. She sank back in the chair and swung one leg over the other. "I understand, from William, there was some excitement the other day at Marc's," she said, studying me.

"You heard about it?" I'd meant to mention it, but she had me so distracted, it had slipped my mind. "Does the name Sharon Raynes mean anything to you?"

"A friend of Marc's," she said laconically. "How did you know her name?"

"From the doorman. And her sister, Susan Ferrante, and Matty Fallon identified the body. It was strange there was nothing in the paper or on television about it."

"Matty probably had it hushed up as a favor to Susan. Besides, the blackout was the big story. Did you see her jump?" she asked. She began drawing circles in the air with the toe of her pump.

"I heard the sound of breaking glass, rushed to the window and looked down, and there she was."

"That was all?"

"That was it, pretty much. I lost a few minutes getting down to her. That might have made a difference. And when I did get there, all the doorman did was call the management company. . . ."

"Marc owns the building. That's how she got the apartment."

"How's he taking it?"

She shrugged, and half smiled. "He is upset, naturally. . . ."

"Naturally."

She was grinning. "He used to call her Acid Raynes," she said.

"I thought you said they were friends."

"They were."

"You think she was pushed?"

"What makes you say that?" She recrossed her legs and began jiggling her foot.

"If you were going to commit suicide by jumping out a window, wouldn't you open the window first?"

"You didn't know Sharon. There was no telling what she might do."

It was getting late, and this line of patter was too gloomy to lead anywhere. "Maybe. I guess I'd open the window first," I said, and polished off the cognac. I got to my feet. "Thanks for the drink. Like your place, Josephine."

"What's your hurry?" she said with an inscrutable face.

"No hurry, it's late."

"I thought you'd be glad to see me." She pried off one pump with the other. "Have another one," she said, letting the other shoe drop.

"A short one, maybe."

"Help yourself, you know where it is." She smiled. "I'll be right with you."

I watched her pad off in stocking feet, my throat dry. I heard the bathroom door shut. I took a swallow of ice water. I don't know what I expected, but this wasn't exactly it. One minute she was all business, and the next she was ready to fool around. You never know.

I found the cognac bottle and poured myself three fingers. I could hear the water running in the bathroom and wondered whether I needed a shower. I wandered into the bedroom, sat down on the bed and unbuttoned my shirt and kicked off my shoes. I heard the toilet flush and the door open.

She came into the room wearing only her bangles and perfume. Her breasts were small and high, her belly flat. Her skin was flawless, and the color of butterscotch. The trace of black in the confluence of her thighs made me think of licorice. She lit a candle. "It's a Riger," she said. "Smell it."

"Smells like cedar." I remembered the smell from Ransom's.

"Isn't it nice? They're the Rolls-Royce of candles. I order them by the case for Marc. How about a tape?" She grinned.

"Sure."

She inserted a videocassette into the VCR.

"Oh, that kind of tape," I said. "Thought you meant music."

"Would you prefer music?"

"Whatever you like." It was her show. The picture tube blinked on.

She flicked off the lights. Her skin turned opalescent in the cold light of the television.

"I like them almost as much as music," she said, and wiggled her hips. "You still have your pants on."

I fumbled with my belt buckle.

"Come 'ere!" She crouched. I stared at her reflection in the big, plate-glass mirror. She unbuckled my pants and dropped them to my ankles. A couple of babes were going down on a guy on the television screen.

She glanced at the action, then turned to me with eyes glazed. "Ever have two girls?" she asked. She took me in her mouth without waiting for the answer.

My gaze fell on her backside with its compression of curves. Wide shoulders narrowed quickly, like an arrowhead, to the waist, and then flared out again into the fullness of her hips. I ran my fingers through her hair. We hadn't even kissed. I wondered how I measured up to the guy with the five big units.

* * *

I left Josephine's early next morning as the sun was rising up out of Astoria. It was going to be a real dog day. The big units would be chilling out in the Hamptons or the Vineyard.

The cab dropped me at the corner of Fifth and Thirty-eighth, where Dolly Varden had tapped a hydrant and was in the midst of her morning toilet. Stripped to a T-shirt and jogging shorts, she was bent over, head in the rush of water, singing, on key, "Splish, Splash, I Was Takin' a Bath." Socrates, dragging his leash, was doing a Hoover maneuver on the gutter, sniffing out intriguing aromas.

I walked over to Sixth Avenue to pick up a copy of the *Times,* and went to the Greek's for breakfast. Over scrambled eggs and coffee, I scanned the front page. The paper said that it had been a summer of record high temperatures. This was news? Crops were burning up in the Midwest, forests were burning up in the West. There was a problem with the ozone layer. Bad news for emphysema and skin cancer sufferers. And to top it all off, because of the greenhouse effect, the polar ice caps were melting and Central Park would soon be lousy with bougainvillea and coconuts. Other than that, there was no earthshaking news.

I paid my check and picked up two containers of coffee and a couple of bagels at the takeout counter. Dolly Varden, now dressed for business—panhandling—was brushing out her hair when I crossed the street.

"Good morning, Dolly," I said.

She eyed me suspiciously.

"Charlie Byrne, remember?" I took a container of coffee and one of the bagels out of the paper bag. "How about coffee and a bagel?" I said, and offered her the bag. She hesitated before accepting it, peering cautiously into the open bag. I showed her the bagel I was holding. "For Socrates," I said. "May I?"

"I'll feed him," she said, dunking her bagel in the coffee.

"Here you go," I said, passing her the other bagel. Socrates's eyes were glued to it. Dolly handed the bagel to him and went back to dunking. Socrates gulped down the treat with a couple of quick snaps and looked up at me hopefully. I reached to pet him.

"Don't touch the dog," said Dolly.

I pulled my hand back. "Whatever you say. Well, you two have a nice day."

"Got a dollar, Charlie?"

"Er, sure." I gave her a buck.

She snatched it from me and stuffed it in her clothing.

"Thanks for the coffee."

"Anytime," I said.

6

The week before Labor Day, the drought broke. The phone seemed to be ringing off the hook. It was enough to make me believe in divine providence, thank God. A client had come through with a package of six newspaper ads for a local bank, which we were busy getting into production, and another art director had referred a new agent to me, a smooth young guy with a forty-dollar haircut and a seven-hundred-dollar suit. The courting had begun. We were sniffing each other out, trying to figure out who was the bitch and who was the dog.

Josephine called, too. Ransom was happy with the tapestry pictures, and she'd have the accountant cut the check right away. Atta girl, Josephine. Oh, and by the way, was I free to attend a dinner dance September twelfth, at the Thackeray? Marc Ransom's mother, Florine, the dowager queen of Manhattan real estate, was having a birthday party.

The twelfth was a Sunday, a little more than a week away.

Too short a notice for me to imagine I'd been her first choice.

"Wouldn't miss it," I said.

"It's black tie, dude," she said in that metallic voice.

"Can't fake it with a dark suit?"

"I'm afraid not." And she proceeded to rattle off a list of places that rented tuxedos. The girl came prepared.

"Is this gonna be fun?" I asked.

"It's gonna be just like going to the prom," she promised.

It felt good to be in demand again.

I'd forgotten all about the Raynes woman until I went to pick up the morning mail Friday, just before Florine Ransom's birthday party. They sling it through a slot in the door. I retrieved it from the floor and thumbed through it quickly, hoping to find the Georgia money. It should have been coming through the slot any day now. All I found was the usual collection of junk: flyers for Chinese takeout, a stationery supply house catalog, the water bill, a tax notice, and a pair of comp tickets to a club and a disco—don't ask me the difference—which would cost fifty bucks to use. No checks.

Susan Ferrante's note, on Cartier stationery—I know because I've photographed their catalog—separated itself from the pack like pedigree from mutts. It was a formal thank-you note for my efforts on behalf of her sister. Her sister, she explained briefly, had been under the care of a psychiatrist for some time, and was despondent over personal matters. The implication was plain enough, although she never used the word; her sister was a suicide.

I had better things to do than speculate about a suicide. But if her note was intended to put the matter to rest, it did not. It raised more questions than it answered. For instance, how come there had been nothing in the newspapers or on television about it? A woman does a nosedive into the concrete from a Park Avenue building and it goes unreported? You'd think that was news. But there had been nothing about it in the papers. Strange, too, when you consider all those cops at the scene. I also wondered whether they performed autopsies in cases like these. And did her sister leave a suicide note? Don't suicides usually leave a note?

At noon I ducked out to be fitted for a tux. The nearest place on Josephine's list turned out to be Murray "Beau" Brummell's Formalwear, between Madison and Vanderbilt, on Forty-third street, one flight up. A phone call had assured me that Murray carried a full line of evening wear for the sport about town. Adolfo, After Six, Bill Blass, Pierre Cardin, Givenchy, Christian Dior, Lord West, Charles Jourdan, and Ted Lapidus were a few of the names I recognized.

Door chimes sounded as I entered. A short, paunchy, bald, middle-aged man in shirtsleeves, a tape measure draped around his neck, pounced on me. "May I help you?" he asked.

"Murray?"

"No, Manny."

"Oh. I want to rent a tux."

"You've come to the right place. If it's anything to do with formal wear, Murray 'Beau' Brummell's the name when formal wear's your game."

"Great. I thought, for a moment, I had the wrong place, that you did leg waxing and acupuncture."

"Get outta town!" Manny scoffed, stepping back and appraising me with a practiced eye. "Don't tell me," he said theatrically, placing a hand over his eyes. "Lemme guess. You're a forty-two regular, and the only stand-up comic working in a tux, right?"

"Close enough," I said. Before I knew it, he'd whisked my jacket off and replaced it with a tux jacket. Twenty minutes later, after reconciling myself to the fact that I'd never look like Fred Astaire in a tux, I left Beau Brummell's bearing a suit box containing an After Six tux. Manny had sent me packing with the enjoinder to "Enjoy! And try not to get any pecker tracks on the goods."

Sunday night, I arrived at the Thackeray at seven-thirty on the dot. I was directed to the banquet hall, a walnut, polished-brass, and cut-glass dining room on the second floor. Waiters in tuxes just like mine buzzed around the place thick as cluster flies. I found Josephine putting the finishing touches on the floral centerpiece on the head table. She was wearing a cheongsam of watery silk the color of pale jade. The slit skirt and form-fitting dress showed her off to good advantage.

"Very nice." I nodded at the dress.

"Thank you," she said. "I don't think I have to worry anyone else will show up in one of these, do you?"

"I shouldn't think so."

"Wanna give me a hand with these place cards?"

"Okay."

"Follow the chart, and match the card to the seat," she said, handing me a morocco folder with the cards and the seating arrangement.

The cards were in alphabetical order, the seating in order of importance, I noticed, after checking for my name and seat. It was slow going, matching place card to seat, and I was poking along when suddenly everyone seemed to momentarily freeze.

Josephine dropped what she was doing and rushed to greet a wiry man not much taller than herself. Ransom, I thought, my host. He had a full head of steel-gray hair, and a blue shadow for a beard. His complexion was lumpy, like oatmeal. Thick glasses masked his face and reflected the light, making him seem remote and enigmatic. Josephine was only one of many people competing for his attention. He dealt with each one with an economy of words and gestures, and then was gone as suddenly as he had appeared.

"That was Marc," said Josephine, flushed from the brief appearance of the almighty.

"No kidding. The man with the five big ones?"

"Why don't you get yourself a drink," she said. "I'll finish that." She took back the morocco folder.

"Not a bad idea. You want one?"

"I'll wait."

I drifted with the flow of the crowd through a hallway line with mural-size photocopies of modern and impressionist paintings. Facsimiles of the Florine Ransom collection, a wall plaque informed me. To hell with facsimiles, I thought, where's the bar?

I was standing there with a bourbon on the rocks in my hand and feeling like a cigar-store Indian when a waiter passed by with a tray of hors d'oeuvres. "Nice tux," I said, helping myself to what looked like caviar and cream cheese on a wedge of wholewheat bread. "Get it at Murray 'Beau' Brummell's?"

"Scusi?" he said.

"Never mind," I said.

It was dawning on me that I was out of my depth—that I had nothing in common with this crowd. What did these guys know about watching *Monday Night Football,* eating pizza, drinking beer, and matching up your socks? They were out seven nights a week to functions like this, and I'd bet they never wore the same tuxedo two nights running. Machers like these had a closet full of tailor-made monkey suits.

Josephine materialized, ending my wallow in self-pity. "Let me introduce you to the old lady," she said. "She's quite a character." She steered me through the crowd to the receiving line.

The birthday girl, looking alert, though very fragile, was perched on a Hepplewhite chair, or maybe it was a Chippendale. Whatever it was, it was worthy of royalty, and the old lady was regal, and chic, in a simple black dress accented with a string of diamonds.

"Who's her boyfriend?" I asked, pointing with my eyes at the chubby guy with the unruly black hair and twinkly eyes fawning over the old lady.

"Bernard," Josephine whispered, "her secretary."

When our turn came, the old lady regarded Josephine shrewdly for a moment before speaking. Then she said, in a startling, strong voice, "You look lovely tonight, my dear."

"Thank you, Mrs. Ransom," Josephine said demurely. "You look wonderful this evening yourself."

"You are kind, but I've looked better," she said, fixing a pair of bright eyes on me. "And who might you be, sir?"

"This is Charles Byrne, Mrs. Ransom," said Josephine. "He's a well-known photographer."

"A photographer? How interesting," said the old lady, offering her bird's-claw hand as she sized me up. Her features were too sharp for her to have been a beauty when the juice was in her, but, imperious and commanding now, they served her well in old age. "Horst and Cecil Beaton have done my portrait. Are you familiar with their work, Mr. Byrne?"

"Yes, ma'am, I am," I said, surprised by the strength of her grip. "I'd like to see those pictures."

"They're not much to see," she said.

"Now, Florine, don't be modest," chided the secretary. "They're wun-der-ful. Florine is positively glamorous in them."

"Nonsense," chuckled the old lady.

Conscious others were waiting to pay their respects, I said, "Let me wish you a happy birthday, Mrs. Ransom."

She held me firm in her grip and impaled me with a fierce look. "Let me assure you, sir," she said, "when you reach ninety, happiness is a memory."

What was I going to say, have a nice birthday?

She spared me having to say anything. "Do you know what is important when you reach my age, Mr. Byrne?"

"I'd rather know the secret of your longevity." I smiled.

"Longevity, bah! There is no secret. Longevity is in the genes, and a damn nuisance it is, sitting around watching yourself . . . watching yourself . . . dis . . . dis . . ."

"Disintegrate, Florine," the secretary said helpfully.

"Yes, that's right, fall apart," said the old lady. "What's important at ninety is comfort."

"Well, in that case, Mrs. Ransom, let me wish you a comfortable birthday."

"Indeed," she laughed, animating quickly, and flashing a lively personality much younger than her years. "I'm so glad you could come. It was a pleasure meeting you, sir."

"The pleasure was mine," I said.

"Enjoy yourself this evening, Mr. Byrne. You are only young once." Her eyes darted from me to Josephine and back again before she released her grip.

"Charlie, this is Bernard Kiernan," Josephine said as we made way for the next in line.

"Hi, Charlie," Kiernan said.

I said hi and shook his damp hand. Josephine pulled me

away, saying, "Excuse us, Bernard, there's someone I'd like to introduce Charlie to."

Faces familiar from television and gossip columns came in and out of focus as we weaved our way through the crowd. I recognized a diminutive, bald, big-bucks Hollywood agent bumper to bumper with a department store magnate. A movie actress and her consort, a refusenik ballet dancer, were chatting up a former Secretary of State. An obese heir to a media empire was tête-à-tête with a recording industry tycoon, a somnolent Turk with blinking lizard eyes. And there was the doyen of the dance, a contemporary of Florine's and still nimble.

I was gawking at the rich and famous when Josephine began bussing cheeks with a little guy who looked like a gopher in a tuxedo. His name was Nelson Rudd, and he was known as Nellie to his friends. He was Ransom's commercial leasing agent and, coincidentally, cousin, Josephine explained. Nellie's date was a plain, middle-aged blonde named Pam. Josephine introduced me as the photographer of Marc's new tapestry, as though the tapestry were a personality.

"Oh," Pam murmured politely at that piece of information.

"How are things in the photography business?" Rudd asked, peering at me craftily from behind a pair of horn-rimmed glasses.

"Not bad at the moment," I said.

"Real estate is flat," he volunteered sanguinely.

"Too bad," I said.

"It's okay. We're in pretty good shape. We've got five thousand leases, and not a shovel in the ground," he bragged.

"That's good," I said.

"Marc's happy."

The lease on my studio was worth $36,000 a year. And my building was a dump. If Ransom's average lease was only a modest fifty thousand a year, he'd have a cash flow of two hundred and fifty mil a year, minimum. I was no whiz at math, or at making a buck, for that matter, but that number sounded more like the combined gross national product of the Baltic nations than the cash flow of a single man. Marc Ransom was a man with a leg up on his first billion, it appeared.

The dinner bell tinkled just as I'd finished digesting this unappetizing piece of information. We were moving toward the banquet room when someone clapped me on the back. "Moonlighting as a waiter, sport?" said a voice from behind.

I turned to find Henry Stein bouncing on the balls of his feet, grinning at me over a black tie. "Stein? Who let you in here?"

"I was invited," he said equitably.

"I don't suppose you're the only crook in this crowd." I grinned, pleased to find someone I knew at this soiree.

"Highly unlikely," he admitted. "No need to broadcast it, ace. Crooks have feelings too."

"Henry, aren't you going to introduce me to your friend?" said an attractive brunette, several inches taller and a decade younger than Stein.

"Darling, this piece of urban blight is no friend of mine, he's Charlie Byrne."

"Charlie Byrne of Ponzi scam fame?" she said with a dazzling smile.

"The same," said Stein. "As much as it pains me to do this, Byrne, the lady is Marion Stein, my wife and the mother of my children."

"How do you do, Mrs. Stein." I smiled politely. She was about forty and could still break hearts pushing a cart through the aisles of any suburban Foodtown. Her face was a shade too long and narrow, perhaps, but her profile, when she glanced at Stein, was perfect. She had soft brown eyes, and her neck was long, thin, and uncreased. Nothing wrong with that. She was one of those women whose imperfections seemed to make her more beautiful.

"I'm delighted to meet you finally, Mr. Byrne," she said graciously. "Henry has mentioned you so often, I feel as though I know you already."

"The pleasure's mine," I assured her. "Please call me Charlie."

"All right, Charlie."

"And I'll call you Mrs. Stein."

"Good idea," said Stein, grinning.

"Call me Marion," she laughed.

"Marion." I smiled.

"Your turn, Byrne," said Stein, studying Josephine, who'd been patiently standing by.

I introduced them, and she batted her eyes brazenly at Stein, who pretended not to notice. So did his wife, who held herself aloof, viewing the scene with amusement, as though women were forever throwing themselves at her husband.

Henry Stein wasn't much to look at. He only stood five six or seven in stocking feet, and seemed to be little more than gristle and bone. His fifties, whiffle-style haircut sat like a yarmulke on his skull. His mouth was broad, and bent up in a permagrin at the corners, making him appear guileless and simple. Nothing could be further from the truth. It was the eyes that gave him away. They were prankster's eyes, warm and sunny normally, but gray and bleak, too, when it suited his purpose. I don't know what it was he was packing, but I know for a fact women found Stein irresistible. Maybe it was the supreme self-confidence he exuded—a requirement of a good con artist, and Stein was the best—that made him so attractive. Women sense that in a man immediately.

I had met Stein through a mutual friend, a cop named P. C. Strunk. I had appealed to Strunk for help on behalf of a stylist friend of mine who had invested all her money in the Ponzi scheme Marion had alluded to. Strunk was unable to help, but said he knew a guy, one of his snitches, who might be able to do something. The snitch turned out to be Henry Stein. Stein scammed the scammer, and miraculously my lady friend got her money back. Of course, he managed to line his own pocket in the process. And to show her gratitude, the lady dumped me for another guy.

Marion regarded Josephine with a cool smile and said, "Pleased to meet you."

"Nice meeting you," Josephine said. "I think you'll find your places over there," she said, gesturing.

"We'll talk after dinner," said Stein.

"You bet, Henry," I said.

"Well, isn't it a small world?" I remarked, as Josephine steered us toward our seats.

"Sure is," she said, astonished Ransom and I would have a mutual acquaintance.

We had found our places and were about to be seated when I spotted her. She must have felt my eyes on her, because she looked up and stared at me momentarily. In my case it was the bare shoulders, ruffled silk, and sequins that threw me off. In her case it was probably that I looked so dashing in my "Beau" Brummell tux, she failed to recognize me at first. Whatever it was, no sooner had our eyes met than we looked away in embarrassment. Susan Ferrante was seated two tables away from mine.

7

Any fears I might have had about holding up my end of a dinner conversation with a mogul, a czar, or a movie star proved to be a baroque worry. You needed binoculars to see the host table from where we were sitting. Josephine and I had been relegated to a slum of nobodies. The banter at our table wouldn't strain the repartee of a parrot. All I had to worry about now was keeping the cutlery straight.

Nelson Rudd and his date, Pam, were seated at our table. He'd just signed up a new tenant to a million-dollar-a-year lease, or so he said, and I was impressed. But in this crowd he was still a nobody.

Ransom's daughter, Pauline, a fat girl with a sallow complexion and lank brown hair, sat at our table with her date, a terribly bored-with-it-all-looking kid named Paulo. Paulo, a sophomore at Yale from a prominent real estate family south of the border, was preoccupied with the lock of black hair that flopped across his forehead. He was constantly tossing it back, or raking it with his fingers; so often, in fact, that these gestures could be mistaken for tics.

The most interesting character was Dr. Dean Mumminger. Not because of anything he said—he was polite without saying much of anything—but because of who he was and how he behaved. He behaved like a snob. He and his wife were unable to disguise their disappointment with where they were seated; after all, he was Florine's personal physician. The only one, Josephine had joked, who saw the old lady naked these days. The old-timer was rumored to have lived life in the fast lane. She'd had lots of boyfriends, Marc had told Josephine, and outlived them all. Mumminger was a distinguished-looking stud in his early forties, tall, slim, and graying at the temples. He was the type I'd cast for a liquor or luxury car ad. The type who in real life probably couldn't afford the product. His wife, thin and chic, with skin like crepe paper, looked older than he, and like she came from money.

The remaining members of our party were Mr. Joel Lesser and his wife, Lynne. Lesser was Ransom's accountant, and according to Josephine, who seemed to have the hot-skinny on everyone, Lesser was involved in a torrid office romance with someone named Jackie Dhiel. "Jackie's some package," Josephine said from behind her hand. Then, grinning merrily, she hefted her hands, palms up, in front of herself, miming "jugs." It seems this "package," who either wasn't invited or had a previous engagement, was the sales ace of Ransom's residential and co-op entity, Residential Realty.

I had to take another look at Lesser after hearing this bit of scandal. He was about thirty-five, and obviously from the outer boroughs. Queens, most likely, judging from the accent. Probably graduated from Brooklyn College or CCNY. He was of average height and build. Neither handsome nor homely, he had an air about him of resignation and guilt. He seemed like the kind of guy who'd question a gift horse. Other than that, he was an ordinary Joe, or "Joel," right down to the rented tux that looked like mine.

There were party favors at each place setting. We each received a sterling silver gewgaw from Tiffany's that might have been a mint dish or an ashtray. The women got Chanel perfume, the men got Givenchy cologne. We aahed and oohed appropriately, unwrapping them. The table was set for twelve, and there were only ten of us, so there were two extra settings, two extra sets of favors. Pauline Ransom, quick and agile, snatched the favors from one of the empty place settings. Paulo twitched with excitement, tossed back the greasy lock of hair, and grabbed the other favors. They clawed the gift wrapping apart greedily. The rest of us exchanged glances and sour smiles.

The first course was a carrot soup, next came fish, Irish salmon with endive and capers. Flatware clattered and crystal clinked in a cheerful serenade. The salmon was sublime. But then, as my aunt would have said, that was because salmon are top swimmers. For no special reason, unless it was the fish association, I thought of Dolly Varden.

Scanning the hall, I estimated nearly five hundred people, most of them financial top swimmers. I wondered how many units the big fish in this crowd represented. Enough to make a dent in the federal deficit and solve the homeless problem, too. And why not? How much of it had been gotten in tax abatements and dubious tax shelters back in the go-go years?

Sharks are also top swimmers, and the really big fish in the room were great whites. I wondered about my dinner companions. Mumminger might have a little money. A tuna, or a cod, I thought with a smile. Lesser a weakfish, probably. But Rudd, what to make of him? He'd be one of those fish that attach themselves to sharks and clean them. A small fortune feeding off of a big one. A sucker fish. Me, I wasn't even bait.

The appetizer plates were removed, replaced by gilt-edged dinner plates. The waiters circled the table in relays with silver service platters of roast beef, fancy hash browns, peas and carrots, and hearts of artichoke in butter sauce. A superlative burgundy flowed like water. I cut the roast beef with a fork and worried about my cholesterol as it melted in my mouth. I'd have to remember to tell Dolly Varden about the Thackeray's Dumpster. Dessert was a lemon meringue tart in a puff pastry shell. Coffee was poured, and Godiva chocolates followed, along with brandy and Benedictine.

A bell tinkled, asking for silence. All eyes turned to our host's table, where Marc Ransom stood patiently waiting for quiet. "Ladies and gentlemen," he began after clearing his throat several times while the last few shuffles and coughs died down, "welcome to the Thackeray Hotel, the newest, brightest star in the firmament of our town's luxury four-star accommodations. I trust dinner was to everyone's satisfaction?"

Murmurs of assent rippled through the room. Nelson Rudd grinned, and held a small fist to his sternum and burped.

"Nellie?" Josephine squealed.

"As you know," Ransom continued in a light baritone with no discernible accent, "we are gathered here tonight to celebrate a milestone, the ninetieth birthday of a most singular woman, my mother, Florine Ransom. Happy birthday, Mother." He clapped, leading the applause.

"Here, here," someone shouted.

"Is Ransom an only child?" I whispered to Josephine.

"He had a sister, I heard, but she died in infancy."

"How do he and his mother get along?"

She wiggled her hand in the "so-so" sign.

Ransom hushed the crowd. In an unemotional voice he went on to eulogize a woman, "orphaned in her teens, widowed in her twenties, with a child to support, her pluck and courage was more than a match for life's challenges. With little more than brains and grit, she had the temerity to set up shop for herself in the most cutthroat business known to man, Manhattan real estate."

The last line drew a few knowing chuckles from the audience.

"Brains and grit and ten million dollars," Josephine whispered.

"Where'd she get the ten million?"

"Her husband left her a rich widow."

"Today," Ransom went on, "the woman executive is a fixture in American business. This wasn't so in the forties and the fifties. There were no women executives to speak of in those days. And yet, in 1948, according to *Fortune* magazine, Mother was the highest paid executive in the country." Ransom had to pause and wait for a round of applause to die down. "But Mother was more than an executive," he continued, "she was an entrepreneur. After World War Two, when the G.I.'s returned home to find a housing shortage, Mother was the second largest developer —only Levitt built more houses—in the low-cost tract-housing market. And it was she who ramrodded the investment syndicate that developed the first suburban mall in the Northeast. There's a story, apocryphal or otherwise, that attests to the esteem with which her peers in the industry regarded her. When asked once to name the three shrewdest, most hard-nosed businessmen he'd ever had the pleasure of cutting a deal with, canny Teddy Doyle, patriarch of the Doyle family, replied: 'Florine Ransom, Florine Ransom, and Florine Ransom!' "

That got a pretty good laugh from the room.

"She was probably sitting on his face when she popped the question," cracked Nelson Rudd.

Pam poked him with her elbow. The brats, Pauline and Paulo, giggled irreverently. The Lessers reacted uncertainly with expressions frozen somewhere between a smirk and a frown. The doctor smiled faintly. His wife stiffened, pretending not to hear Rudd's blasphemy. Josephine giggled.

"At the time," Ransom said, hushing the crowd, "old Teddy Doyle was pinched for cash, and anxious to sell Mother a piece of property she was interested in. She made him an offer, which he thought too low and foolishly refused. When no other buyers materialized, he was obliged to go back to Mother and seek a second offer. Naturally, this offer was considerably lower. 'Dammit, woman!' Doyle exploded, when Mother wouldn't budge. 'I'll take it. And the devil take you!' "

The crowd roared its approval.

"My tutor, mentor, and inspiration, a legend in her own time, my mother, Florine Ransom. Stand up and take a bow, Mother."

The living legend rose slowly from her chair, beaming and waving to the cheering crowd.

We weren't about to get off that lightly; there were a number of old friends of the family waiting their turn to blow some wind and smoke. I signaled the nearest waiter for a refill on the brandy. Dr. Mumminger requested a refill, too.

The ambassador to, or from, somewhere or other was the first up to lay a wreath at the shrine of the living legend. He was followed by a senator, a judge, and the comptroller of either Delaware or Pennsylvania; I didn't quite catch which, but his name was Randell Elliott. He was a youthful-looking fifty, much younger than the speakers before him, none of whom was exactly a contemporary of the birthday girl. When you are ninety years old, you can't expect to find many of the old crowd at your testimonial, I guess. Anyway, Elliott, the comptroller, told some cockamamie story about how Florine, with a timely loan, had pulled his father's financial chestnuts out of the fire, for which he, as his father's son, was eternally grateful. He composed a verbal nosegay with adjectives such as *visionary, magnanimous, gentle,* and *wise,* and tossed it in the dowager's direction. Having got the job done, he sat down, and that put the capper on the veneration of the ancient mogul.

Ransom explained it was getting past Mom's bedtime. We rose as one and saluted the tiny figure as she tottered out of the hall on the arm of Bernard, her secretary. We were asked to adjourn to the next room and let the waiters clear the hall. Dancing would follow.

8

We stood on the edge of the dance floor listening to a society band, an aggregation of dads and granddads, lumber through their first set. They were having fun with Willie 'n' the Po' Boys when Josephine said, "Let's dance."

The kicks I get from tripping the light fantastic are strictly vicarious, but I took to the floor anyway and gamely shook my booty. Josephine eyed me like I was the circus bear.

Just as I was beginning to get loose, the band segued into a salsa number, and Ransom appeared from nowhere, like a knife in the hand, and tapped my shoulder. Josephine lit up like a hundred-watt bulb as he swept her away. They were good dancers—they looked as though they'd danced together before.

It was the best look at Ransom I'd had all night. His eyes were close-spaced and deep-set, his chin aggressive, his forehead narrow and lined. He had a blunt and prominent nose. His full head of wiry, steel-gray hair was brushed back flat on his head. Superb tailoring created the illusion he was taller than his five foot six or seven. He was lean and fit-looking for a man in his mid- to late-fifties. He wasn't pretty, but with five big units, it was a face that more than Florine Ransom could love.

I drifted over to the bar and consoled myself with a bourbon on the rocks. I noticed Henry Stein chatting with Matty Fallon, the comptroller, and a third man, and wandered over to join the circle. "Marc shouldn't have any trouble with the variance," I heard Fallon saying as our eyes met. I smiled amiably, expecting him to remember me. He gave no sign of recognition. "There's someone I'd like to meet," he said to the comptroller, and dragged him off. The third man suddenly developed a case of happy feet and tangoed off.

"You could empty Madison Square Garden in the middle of a Rolling Stones concert, Byrne." Stein grinned.

"You think it's the tux?"

"It looks like it comes with a bar tray."

"I know Fallon and the comptroller—who's the other guy?"

"He's Karl Sauter, Ransom's architect."

"Is Ransom building?"

"That's what developers do."

"I just heard Nelson Rudd say they didn't have a shovel in the ground."

"Sooner or later that'll change."

"So tell me, Henry, how are things in the bucket shops these days? Or are you working the real estate rackets now?"

He managed to look offended. "You are an insensitive geek, Byrne," he said, "but business couldn't be better, thank you. And I've always had an interest in real estate."

"Uh-huh, 'Give me one weekend of your time at Motel 8, and two hundred dollars a person, charge it on your Visa card, and I'll show you how you can become a millionaire, like me, overnight, and for no money down, through the miracle of leveraging.' Is that the kind of real estate you mean?"

"That's very good, Byrne." He grinned. "I've been to a few of those seminars myself."

"I'll bet you have."

"In answer to your question, though, I have a couple of

irons in the fire. Of course, I'm not at liberty to discuss them with a down-at-the-heels photographer like yourself."

"This is no Motel 8 seminar, Henry. Who do you know?"

"Who do you know, Byrne?"

"I asked you first."

"I was invited by Mrs. Ransom herself."

"The old lady?"

"Is there another?"

"Henry, I'm in awe."

"You ought to be. So, tell me, how'd a disreputable character like you manage to crash such a tony bash?"

"I came as a beard."

"For the China doll?"

"That's right."

"Way to go, Byrne. Be careful, though, I understand that's private stock."

"My eyes are wide open."

Stein was regarding me with his patented bemused expression when his wife glided up and slipped her arm through his. "Excuse us, Charlie," she said, "Henry promised me a dance."

I watched them join the other dancers. Josephine and Ransom had changed partners. He was dancing with a postdeb even younger than his daughter, and she was dancing with Dr. Mumminger.

"Would you like to dance, Mr. Byrne?" I turned to find Susan Ferrante.

"If you don't mind having your toes stepped on," I said.

"I'll take my chances."

As I followed her to the dance floor, the baritone sax was breathing the intro to "Where or When." She turned, paused a beat, and looked me in the eye. Then she moved silently into my arms and we began to sway to the music. She felt supple and vibrant. Just holding her was a thrill.

I was the first to speak. "Well, small world, isn't it?" Not a very original opening line, but serviceable.

"Isn't it," she agreed.

"Although it doesn't come as a complete surprise finding you here."

"And why is that?"

"William recognized your name."

"William?" she said, studying me with eyes so luminescent violet I wondered whether she was wearing contact lenses.

"Ransom's butler. I was photographing a tapestry in his apartment that day."

"I see." We lapsed back into silence.

She was a regular chatterbox. But it was her quarter.

"You're not such a terrible dancer," she said after a while.

"Thanks."

"You must have thought me awfully rude."

"Why's that?"

"Not recognizing you right away."

"Funny, I thought you did."

"I didn't. I was wondering why this strange man was staring at me."

"If I was staring, it's because you look so beautiful." Women always like to hear that—it's the right thing to say. And in this case it was true.

She smiled modestly. "Anyway, I had no idea it was you until somewhere in the middle of dinner. Then I suddenly remembered you were the gentleman in the courtyard. I never would have expected to bump into you again, and certainly not here."

"What a coincidence. What do you suppose the probability of that happening is?"

"What do you mean?" she said warily.

"Nothing. Just what would you guess the odds were that we ever meet again?"

"I haven't a clue."

"Well, they are surprisingly good, fifty-fifty."

"Interesting. Are you a gambler?"

"Only when the odds are a joke, like in Lotto. Can't blame you for being surprised to see me, though. I'd never expect to bump into a guy like me here, either."

"I didn't mean it like that."

"I didn't take it like that. It's a fact—this is not my usual scene. I'm here as a walker. It's a first for me."

"You're a paid escort?"

"No, I'm still an amateur."

"Are you walking Mrs. Cyzeski?"

"Yes, you know her?"

"We've spoken," she conceded neutrally.

"Is there a Mr. Ferrante?"

"I'm divorced."

"Who's your walker?"

She cocked her head and arched an eyebrow. "Perhaps I'm the walker." She smiled.

"Maybe," I said, "but you'd be on my A list if I were Ransom."

She wasn't cool enough to hide her pleasure with that remark. "I came with Matty Fallon."

"I was afraid of that."

"Do you have something against Matty?"

"Just that he's with you, and that he's a politician."

"You have something against politicians, then?"

"Doesn't everyone? Theirs is the world's second oldest profession. The only difference is politicians don't do anything for their money."

"I'll have to tell Matty you said that," she laughed.

"He must have been called worse."

The tune ended, and the band was blowing a signature riff. Time out for a smoke and something wet. Take five.

"Thank you," I murmured. If she hadn't mentioned her sister, I'd be damned if I'd be the one to bring her up. Her chestnut hair fell lustrous against pale skin, and I caught a scent of jasmine.

"If what you say is true"—she smiled enigmatically—"the odds seem pretty good we'll meet again." She gazed at me steadily, her eyes smoky. For a moment I forgot there were blondes, redheads, and lovelies like Josephine in the world.

"I hope so," I said. "I believe in coincidence. If you ever need a walker, I'm in the book."

She laughed, merrily and musically. "I'll keep that in mind," she said, gently disengaging her hand from mine. "Good-bye, Mr. Byrne."

I watched her saunter over to where Fallon and Ransom were standing. At six two and two sixty, and growing, Fallon loomed over the smaller Ransom like a heavyweight over a flyweight. His obsequious manner, however, tipped off who the real heavyweight was. In the newspapers and on television, Fallon photographed like a Warner Bros. second male lead, the big handsome, smiling Irishman type popular in forties B movies, and in recent presidential elections. In real life, though, his curly hair was dyed too dark and he was beginning to get the florid suety look of a boozer and trencherman. Preoccupied as they were, neither of them seemed to pay much attention to Susan Ferrante.

The band break was taken by some as a cue to say good night. The crowd started thinning out. Tomorrow was the start of another business week, and top swimmers needed their rest.

"Wanna go?" said Josephine, materializing suddenly.

I think she meant "Let's go." I'd had enough haute monde for one night, and we went.

The night was warm and sultry. Cabs were stacked up in a line outside the hotel. The chubby princess and the gaucho took the first one. Nelson Rudd and his date took the next one, and we came in third. Josephine thanked the doorman by name as he tucked us inside. I didn't feel it necessary to tip him. What are friends for?

9

I'll drop you, Charlie," she said. "I'm no good tonight . . . I'm out of commission for about a week. . . ."

"Out of commission?"

"It's okay, nothing to worry about . . . only a yeast infection," she explained ruefully.

"Yeast infection, huh? Well, thanks for telling me," I said, looking dumb.

"Have fun tonight?" she asked.

"Not as much fun as the prom."

"I'm sorry."

"Not your fault." I shrugged.

She gave me a significant look, eyes moist and wide as saucers. She made a little mewling sound and pulled me to her suddenly, planting a wet one on my kisser. I groped her politely, playing along, and she moaned with pleasure. We weren't trying to kid ourselves, only each other.

The cab skidded to a stop at the far right corner of Thirty-eighth and Sixth, and we untangled ourselves. "I'll make it up to you, Charlie, soon as I'm off the medication," she promised as I piled out.

"It's a date, and wear your heels." I grinned, slamming the door. The cab lurched off, trying to beat the light. She didn't look back. I started up the block. I couldn't wait to get out of the soup and fish. I felt used and soiled. You can't mingle with Ransom's kind of money and not wonder where it really comes from. Nice guys don't have cash flows of hundreds of millions of dollars a year.

I have my beefs with the photo business, but not getting rich isn't one of them. I didn't go into it to get rich, and so far it hasn't disappointed me. It hasn't treated me badly, though. You can make a decent living at it if you're good. It's strenuous work, but you'll never get a hernia from lifting a Nikon. The work is fairly honest, satisfying, and generally harmless. Which is more than can be said about jobs like developer, takeover lawyer, greenmailer, and junk bond salesman. These guys don't make anything, grow anything, create anything. They don't work for a living—they work to make money. And the world never seems any better after they get done screwing around with it. I'd never have a unit, and I wasn't going to lose any sleep worrying about how to get one, or keep one.

"Sinse, sinse, you man, got some good sinse," chanted a black guy. He was hanging out by the boarded-up subway entrance, dressed in sweats, felony flyers, a Mets baseball cap, and a pair of wraparound plastic shades on a necklace. There was a guy just like him on every corner of the intersection. A month ago, at the height of rush hours, there'd been a shootout at Sixth and Bryant Park, and a commuter caught a stray slug. For a week after that incident, the cops patrolled the strip from Thirty-fourth to Forty-second Street in force. But as soon as the furor died down, the cops were gone, and now the hustlers were back in force. From easy street to mean street in a few brief seconds, only in Manhattan.

"Yo, man, you a cop?" the black asked furtively.

"No, man." I waved him off and passed him by.

"Got sinse, man, good sinse."

Yeah, sure. If he had sense, he'd be doing something else for a living.

The block was poorly lit. There were a couple of bars and an after-hours Korean gambling joint over a kosher restaurant, but other than that, Thirty-eighth Street was as desolate late at night as the dark side of the moon. The clunky metal gates merchants shuttered their shops with were an ominous reminder that the vandals were waiting to sack the city.

Did the block look as ripe for development to the robber barons of Manhattan real estate as it did to my untutored eye? I wondered.

The fine hair on the back of my neck bristled suddenly, and a trickle of adrenaline seeped into my bloodstream. It had seemed, momentarily, there was a pair of silhouettes etched in the cyan glare of the sodium vapor lamp. When I focused on the spot, though, there was nothing there.

Had I imagined it? Wariness was ingrained, watching my back as involuntary as breathing. If there was anyone behind me when I squatted to unlock the plate-glass doors, I wanted to know about it. Only another hundred and fifty yards and I was home.

Shadows flickered on the pavement.

My scrotum shriveled with the second jolt of adrenaline. "Shit," I muttered, staring hard ahead. My imagination hadn't been playing tricks on me. There was a pair of jokers holed up in the doorway next to mine. I thought about crossing the street, but I didn't. I wanted a weapon of some kind, a gun, a knife, a club, a broken bottle even. Don't let them see fear, I told myself, and trooped on, feeling stupid and conspicuous in the damn tux.

Ahead of me, in front of the kosher restaurant, was a Dumpster, the smaller, bucket type. It was jammed to the gunnels with scraps of Sheetrock, splintered wood, and twisted pieces of conduit piping.

I tried to convince myself they were kids, making out or doing drugs, in the doorway. No threat to me, no cause for alarm. No need for a piece of pipe from the Dumpster.

But then there was a flurry of sound, and the shadows on

the pavement seemed to be slam dancing. Two figures shot out of the doorway.

"Sheed!" cried one of them.

"E's uh fuggin' dawg!" cried the other, backpedaling madly and throwing karate kicks at a snarling, snapping Socrates.

Dolly barreled out of the doorway with a demonic shriek, wielding a billy club. She went right after one of them. I rushed for the Dumpster. It took a couple of grabs to come up with the right length of pipe. I charged the nearest mugger.

Dolly mistook me for another hostile and let me have one across the shins. She sent me sprawling on hands and knees, the pipe clattering out of reach.

"Goddamnit, Dolly, it's me, Charlie Byrne," I howled. I scrambled to my feet. My shinbones hurt so bad I was dancing.

Dolly's guy, a black kid, maybe sixteen, was on his toes like Zorro, slicing air like it was white bread with twelve inches of kitchen knife. She didn't waste any time acknowledging me. She was busy clearing swaths of turf with every swing of the billy club. I didn't think this was the first time she'd rumbled in the street.

Socrates was earning his kibble dodging and slashing at my guy, a wiry Hispanic in his twenties. "Good dog, get 'em, Socrates!" I cried.

Socrates had the Latino doing a fandango.

"Yo, call off duh dog, man!" Over his head he held what looked like a plastic water bottle, the kind used by cyclists.

"After he eats your ass, pal."

He fumbled with the bottle cap. "Yo, muthafugger, call off duh dog." He held the open bottle in front of his grinning face. I realized instantly what it was.

"Take it easy, man," I said, backing off, hands in front of me, my nostrils filled with the sweet and pungent fumes. "Dolly, hold it!" I shouted.

The billy club dropped to her side and she retreated. "Socrates, heel!" she commanded sharply. The dog obeyed immediately, and she grabbed him by the collar.

I was very thankful she understood.

The Hispanic was grinning broadly, his teeth green, where he had them. His hair was greasy, his beard scraggly, and his skin boiled with zits. "That's better, homeboy," he said. He had on a pair of baggies, knee-high socks, sneakers, and a nylon tank top. "Jus' chill, muthafugger."

The black kid, to show how bad he was, sneered, and took a gratuitous swipe at Dolly with the blade. Dolly avoided the arc of the blade by casually leaning back. Socrates objected loudly and attempted a lunge, but Dolly clung to his collar.

"Do the dog, Angel. Toast 'im," the black kid jeered. He was iridescent in a cheap polyester orange and black warmup jacket and matching pants.

Angel hopped from foot to foot, then he feinted, menacing us with the contents of the open bottle.

"Go on, man, whatta ya waiting for, douse the dog!" said the black kid.

"Yo, come on, you money, give it up," laughed Angel. "Ya heard wha James say. He say toast the dog."

I held out my wallet. "Don't hurt the dog, whatta you say, Angel?"

It startled him to hear me call him by name. His eyes darted from the wallet to me and back again. "Jus' give it up, man, an no one ged's hurt." He gave me the gimme sign with his free hand.

I tossed him the wallet. "How about letting me have my cards, whatta you say?"

He didn't make me any promises. "Yo, mama, you too, give it up," he demanded.

"Douse the dog," James insisted.

Dolly tossed Angel a billfold.

Grinning wickedly, Angel had a peek in both wallets before passing them to James. He continued to threaten us with the bottle, holding us at bay.

James pawed through the wallets. "Sheed, man, ain' got but fifty bucks between both 'em," he complained, tossing the empty wallets back in our faces. "These peebles don't even be worth takin' off," he scoffed. "These be poor people.

Come'n, man, les have some fun with 'em. Les toast the dog." A butane lighter flickered off and on in his hand, and so did the gleam in his eyes. "Ah wanna watch that fugger fry."

"Ya hear 'em?" Angel grinned. "Don' be holdin' out on us now, unnerneath all them clothes, know wha I mean, mama?"

Dolly flopped her head mutely.

"That all of it, mama?" Angel asked skeptically, doing the gimme again. "Give it up, mama, give it all up."

"That's all of it," Dolly mumbled, eyes downcast. Socrates growled low and steadily.

"Whatta ya waitin' for, muthafugger? Douse the dog," James giggled.

Angel bent over, took aim, and with a smirk, squeezed the bottle. Socrates snarled and leaped for him, jerking Dolly forward. Angel jumped back, barely avoiding the snapping teeth. Gasoline splashed at our feet.

"Yo, ya missed, muthafugger," James laughed.

"Fuggin' dog almost took ma hand off," Angel protested.

Socrates was making a racket, straining to get at our tormentors. I glanced at Dolly, her face a mixture of terror and rage. Where were the cops when you needed them? I couldn't let this thing go on much longer.

Angel juked around, wiggling his hips. Then he lunged, swordsman style.

His arm was at its full extension. So was my leg when my foot met his hand. The bottle went flying, a roostertail of gasoline trailing after it. It was a lucky shot. I don't know karate. I'd never done anything but punt before.

Dolly was a blur of motion.

Crouched and ready, James let the flame touch an errant jet of gasoline.

Socrates yelped and bolted from the eerie rush of sound. A wall of heat and flame divided us. The air was black with sooty smoke.

I was doing the worst thing possible, running. I stopped. My pant leg was on fire. I smacked at the flames with my hands. Not too smart, either. I dropped to the ground and rolled. That did the trick. Sitting on the sidewalk, I inspected the damage. Nothing hurt. I wasn't burned, only scorched.

Dolly was keening softly, holding and rocking a trembling, whimpering dog in her arms. I climbed to my feet and went to them.

Puddles of gasoline were burning themselves out slowly on the concrete. The stench of burnt hair and gasoline hung in the air. James, on his back on the sidewalk, moaned. "Ah'm hurt baad, help me, man," he pleaded as I stepped over him to get to Dolly and the dog.

"Dolly, you all right?"

She was nuzzling the dog and cooing to him. He was licking her sooty face. She didn't answer me.

I tried again. "Dolly, you're not burned, are you?" Her clothes looked as though they'd been singed through with a hot iron, with two or three layers showing in places. Her hair was frazzled and her face was dirty. Other than that, she didn't appear any the worse for wear. Socrates looked like he was going to be a shorthair for a month or so. He could probably use a little ointment on his toes and nose. I tried one more time. "You okay, Dolly?"

She let rip a burst of expletives.

"My bleeping sentiments exactly," I muttered.

"Sheed . . ." James groaned. I turned to see what his problem was. He was on his back, thrashing from side to side, nearly naked, and in pain. "Ah need uh am'lance. Help me, man," he begged.

"No kidding, pal," I murmured, kneeling over him. Dolly had opened a gash on his scalp that would take twenty stitches to close—a pretty sure sign he also had a concussion. But worse than that were the burns. The sateen polyester, when it had ignited, melted and stuck to his flesh as it burned. His arms, legs, and chest were as black as charcoal. The kid looked like barbecue.

"Ya gotta help me, man. Ah need uh am'lance, baad," he moaned.

"What happened to your friend?" I said, searching the empty street for Angel.

"How am I s'pose to know? Gimme uh break . . . help me, man, please."

"Yeah, yeah, sure." Give me a break. I had a free pass on this one. Why shouldn't I leave the son of a bitch lying there? Isn't that what he and his pal meant to do with us?

"Ah need uh am'lance, man . . . real baad," he moaned.

I got to my feet. "You shouldn't play with fire when you're wearing polyester, know what I mean, man?"

"Yo, man, where ya going?" he cried in alarm. "Ya can' leb me . . . Ah need help, baad."

"Ya need help, baad," I mocked him. "Take it easy, I'll call 911."

"Hurry, man."

"Right." I started for the pay phone on the corner.

Angel was strolling down the street as nonchalant as if he were out for the Sunday paper.

I looked around, found the piece of pipe, and braced myself.

Angel approached, pulled up ten feet away, and displayed his rotten teeth in a smirk. "Chill, man. Be cool," he said genially. "An don' move."

"Your friend needs help, fast."

James moaned.

"Don' worry 'bout James, man. Everyting's un'er control."

"I'm calling 911." I showed him the pipe.

He showed me the kitchen knife. "You ain goin' nowhure, frien'," he said, juking from side to side.

Socrates had his back up and was barking. Dolly started swearing.

"Yo, man, wh'sa matter wid dat bitch?" said Angel, easing off a bit.

"What do you think, bright guy? She's upset." I moved closer to him.

"Bitch's crazy," he muttered.

Dolly was daring him to come closer. She crouched silently, glaring at Angel and beating on the pavement with the billy club while restraining the snarling, lunging dog.

I edged closer. The knife didn't scare me. Without James,

the guy was nothing. One guy's shuck, one guy's jive. What bothered me was, why had he come back? "You shouldn't have gotten her mad, Angel."

"Duh bitch's crazy, man," said a wide-eyed Angel, maintaining the gap between us.

A cruiser rolled up the street, gumdrop flashing, and glided to a halt. A warm sensation of relief flooded over me. The cop riding shotgun climbed out of the cruiser and hitched up his pants. Better late than never.

"Here comes the cavalry." I grinned at Angel.

"Don' bed on id, suck'r." He grinned back.

The cop ambled over. He was just a kid, fat and pear-shaped; if he shaved twice a month, once was wishful thinking. "What's going on here?" he demanded.

Angel jabbed a finger at Dolly. "Duh bitch's crazy, man. She wen' off on us. Me an ma frien' was walk'n down duh street an she sicced her dog on us, man. She try'd ta torch us. She's fuggin' crazy, man," he said in a rush of words.

"He's a liar," I said.

The cop gave me the fish-eye.

"These creeps were trying to roll her," I explained.

"Hey, check it out, man, I'm the one called 911," Angel protested.

"Who're you?" demanded the cop, switching his gaze back to me. His eyes were small, dull, and too close together.

"He's with her, man, they're together," interjected Angel. The guy was a magician. He had made the knife disappear, I noticed.

"He's fulla shit," I said.

"Drop the pipe, mister," the cop ordered.

I'd forgotten about the pipe. I let it go. It hit the concrete, bounced and rolled with a staccato, metallic sound that sent Socrates into another barking fit. I held my hands up to show they were empty. Angel grinned.

"You, too, lady, drop the nightstick!" the cop ordered.

"Hey, man, looka what he did to my friend," cried Angel. "He hid 'im wid a pipe, man."

James groaned as if on cue.

Angel gestured to James. "He's fugged up, man. Ya gotta get an am'lance."

James seconded him with a moan.

"There's one on the way," said the cop.

"Hear dat, James?" Angel shouted. "Am'lance be right here, man."

James groaned, he heard.

In a trance, Dolly rocked back and forth, mumbling softly to herself and rapping on the pavement with the billy club.

"I said, drop the nightstick, lady!"

Dolly kept on rocking.

"She's harmless, officer," I said.

"Who asked you?" he said.

"Bitch's crazy," Angel said.

The cop's partner was out of the patrol car, posed, elbow on the roof of the car, foot still inside the door, talking on the radio. He was an even less impressive specimen of New York's finest than his partner. He might go 140 dripping wet, maybe he was five five in lifts. His uniform hung as limp on him as it did on the hanger. He was even more baby-faced than the fat kid. Where'd they get these guys?

The fat cop approached Dolly.

"Watch out, man," warned Angel.

Dolly cranked up the volume on the profanity. Socrates showed his teeth.

The cop's hand went to his holster.

"Shoot duh muthafugger," Angel urged.

"Shut up," snapped the cop. "Lemme have the nightstick, lady." Socrates took a swipe at the extended hand but missed when Dolly yanked his collar. The startled cop jumped back.

"Tol' ya, man, shoot duh fuggin' dog," Angel said.

"She'll be all right, officer. Give her a chance to calm down," I said.

"Both you assholes, shut up!" Skinny ordered.

"You," said Fatso, pointing at me. "What'sa matter with her?"

You had to wonder whether this was their first real job. Had these guys done anything other than flip burgers at McDonald's before they joined the force? "You mean, besides these guys"—I indicated James and Angel— "trying to mug and torch her?"

"Can ya belieb dis sheed? 'E's lyin'," Angel cried.

"Shut the fuck up," Fatso told him.

Angel stomped his foot, as petulant as a tennis player after a bad call.

"The woman's distraught, she needs help," I said.

"What about this guy? How'd he get burned?" said Fatso.

I nodded at Angel. "This clown was splashing gasoline around. They were gonna torch us." I eyed James. "Some of it must have spilled on him. When he went to light it, he slipped and fell and set himself on fire."

"Leesin tuh dis bullsheed," said Angel, holding his head as though he'd come down with a sudden migraine. "She was duh one hid James in duh haid, man, den she doused 'im an' set 'im on fire."

"I told ya ta shut da fuck up," said Fatso, poking Angel's scrawny chest with a sausage finger.

"She hid me," James groaned.

"Din't I tell ya?" Angel exclaimed.

"They can't even get their story straight," I said. "First it was I hit him, now it's she hit him."

Angel started to speak. Skinny made a motion toward him. "Din't say nut'n, man, din't say a ting," he blurted out, crisscrossing his hands in front of his face and shaking his head.

"What's your name, mister?" Fatso asked me.

I gave him my name and address, which he noted on his pad. He squinted at the dark building. "In there?" He nodded. I nodded back. "Is it true he called 911?" He nodded at Angel.

I shrugged. "How would I know?"

"Hey, id was me all right, check id out." Angel grinned.

"How come you didn't call 911?"

It was coming down to my word against Angel's, and Sherlock Holmes was on my case. "There was no time, firchrissake."

His eyes narrowed and flicked in Angel's direction. "He had time."

"Because he was the only one who wasn't burned."

"Sheed," Angel protested.

"You know this woman?"

"Everyone on the block knows her. That's her doorway. That's where she lives." I pointed a finger at Dolly's belongings.

"Undomiciled," Fatso mumbled as he scratched on his pad. "She have a name?"

"She calls herself Dolly Varden."

Fatso moved toward Dolly, then hesitated, thinking better of it. "Is that your name, lady? Dolly Varden?" he shouted.

Dolly answered with a volley of obscenities, choke wide open. Fatso jumped as though stung by pellets. Socrates growled.

Skinny leveled his revolver on the dog.

"Shoot duh fuggin' dog, man. Whatta you waitin' for, e's uh killer," said Angel.

It was apparent Dolly and Socrates were up to nothing nuttier than cursing and howling. "What's your name, asshole?" said Skinny, reluctantly holstering the .38 and ready to take his frustration out on Angel.

"Yo, man, ain' ya gonna arres' 'em? Looka wha da dog done tah me." He held up a bandy leg for inspection. The dirty white tube socks were stained with blood, and his baggies were torn. "Looka wha he done tah ma pants. 'E's a killer, man."

A mix of young Koreans and drunks had started to collect.

"Cut the crap and give us a name," said Fatso.

James moaned, "Mason, Ah'm Mason . . . help me."

"Fuggin' white dudes, man," Angel complained, playing to the onlookers. "Ya be alla time stickin' it ta duh brudders." This got a mix of cheers and jeers from the small crowd.

Skinny sighed. "Just give us a name, asshole."

"Say'd Ah'm Mason, help me, ged me uh am'lance."

"I wanna file uh complain', man," Angel persisted. "I called 911. I reported uh crime, I wan' dese fuggers arres'ed. We was mine'n our own bidnez an duh bitch jumped us. Looka mah legs, man, looka mah frien' James, dere."

"Sure, sure, what's your name?" said Fatso.

"Angel Cruz," he answered with dignity.

"Got an address, Angel?" said Fatso.

"Duh La Fleur," he said defiantly. The La Fleur, a whole other league from the Thackeray, was an infamous SRO (single-room-occupancy) cesspool of crime and crack off Herald Square on Thirty-second Street.

"And your friend's name's James Mason, is that right?" Fatso grinned, his eyes firmly to his pad.

"Say'd Ah'm Mason . . . Ah'm fuggin' dyin' here."

"Hang on, James, the ambulance'll be here any minute," said Fatso.

Sirens whooped, the sound crashing nearer and nearer. The block was spinning like a disco, flashing lights everywhere. Another blue-and-white pulled up and double parked. Two older, economy-size cops, a black and a white, climbed out of the cruiser and bulled their way through the gawkers, scattering them and ordering them to move on.

"Where you live, James?" said Fatso. Skinny briefed the reinforcements.

"Sheed, man . . . same place."

"La Fleur?"

"Dat's right," said Angel.

"Ged me uh fuggin' am'lance," James begged.

It was beginning to look like a disaster scene. An EMS crew from St. Clare's Hospital arrived, siren honking, gumdrop strobing. A powerful-looking black woman hopped out of the driver's seat and went directly to James. Her partner unloaded a gurney from the rear of the van.

"Id'll be all right now, man," Angel reassured James.

The EMS crew scraped James up off the sidewalk, wrapped him in a mylar foil blanket, and gingerly loaded him onto the gurney. The cops cleared a path through the crowd. They hoisted James into the ambulance. The driver slammed the door shut, and lights flashing, siren wailing, they took off. My ears were still ringing and my head spinning when an ASPCA van slid up.

"What's happening?" I asked Fatso.

He turned away, giving me his backside. It only took a moment. The ASPCA guy had Socrates at the end of a pole with a noose around his neck. The two big cops were in a tussle with a kicking, screaming Dolly, wrestling the billy club from her grip. Angel smirked with satisfaction.

"Are you fuckin' guys nuts or something?" I hollered. "The woman was only trying to protect herself."

Fatso turned and bumped me with his stomach. "Let's go for a ride, pal."

10

They took us to Midtown South on West Thirty-fifth Street. There was no sign of Dolly. I wondered where they'd taken her. If I'd thought about Socrates, which I didn't, I'd have guessed they took him to the pound, which was exactly where they'd taken him.

Fatso led me to a table in a corner of the booking room and told me to have a seat. Across the room, Skinny was prodding Angel to another table. I sat down with a groan. My stomach felt queasy. My whole system seemed to be going sixty miles an hour. My hands and knees were skinned. My shins throbbed, and my legs were singed. I felt like shit. But I was giddy at the prospect of sorting this thing out and getting justice.

Fatso began asking questions. He got my answers down in a neat hand with a ballpoint pen. "Come on, Charlie," he said when he was done. He pushed back his chair and got to his feet.

"Mr. Charlie, to you."

"Ha, ha," he said, and shoved toward the desk.

Angel and I stood shoulder to shoulder in front of the desk sergeant, a handsome middle-age guy in an immaculate, hand-tailored uniform. He gazed down at us coolly from behind the Plexiglas barrier with eyes paler than Windex. I looked down at myself. I was a wreck. It dawned on me that I'd just bought my first tuxedo, and that it was in tatters, worthless.

"Whath your complaint?" the sergeant asked Angel.

"Yeah, well, I wanna file a complaint against 'im." Angel gave me the nod.

"A complaint?" I said.

"Wath I thpeaking to you?" said the sergeant. There was enough sibilance in his voice to credit a window dresser, or indicate a speech impediment.

"No . . . sir."

He nodded for Angel to continue.

"But you gotta be kidding," I said.

"Quiet, friend," a strange voice advised. I turned to find a uniformed cop, about my own size and age, staring back at me. His thumbs were hitched in his belt, a cigarette dangled from his lips. He was bad. "Jus' listen to the sergeant, everything'll be all right. Okay?"

"You'll get your turn, mithter," the sergeant promised. "Go ahead," he said to Angel.

Angel was all sweetness and light as he began to tell his version of the story. It was a remarkable transformation, as though an altar boy were trapped inside the scabrous body of a crack addict. Even his speech miraculously improved. It was still liberally peppered with "man," but the verb to "fug" was conspicuously absent. He claimed to have been innocently strolling down the street with his friend James when, out of nowhere, the bag lady sicced her dog on them, and the guy in the tux, me, doused them with gasoline.

I couldn't resist some editorial comment. "Listen to this guy, will you?"

Angel glanced contemptuously in my direction.

"Thaid you'd get your chanthe," the sergeant reminded me.

"C'mon, you don't believe this creep?"

"Look, we got a guy in the hothpital with thecond degree

burnth all over hith body. Lemme get thith man'th thtatement, then we'll take yourth, all right?"

"The guy's filing a complaint. He's a liar. It's not all right."

The sergeant seemed to be looking through me with his Windex eyes. "Take it easy, friend," warned the cop behind me.

"But this scuzz and his pal were trying to mug the woman—"

"Tol' ya, calm down, friend."

"Calm down, bullshit!"

Angel leapcd back, spooked, like I'd scared him.

"Cuff him," the sergeant ordered.

Fatso and the other guy grabbed my wrists and hand-cuffed my hands behind my back. Fatso shook his head and went tsk-tsk.

"He's violent, man," said Angel, having trouble keeping a straight face.

"Another outburth and I'm booking you, mithter," the sergeant warned.

"Me? It's that piece of shit you should be arresting."

Angel looked wounded.

"What'sa matter with you guys, anyway? He a friend of yours?"

The station house sadist wrenched my arms up to my shoulder blades. "Do yourself a favor, asshole," he said in my ear, "take a chill pill an walk outta here. Keep this shit up an you'll be spending the next forty-eight hours in jail." He gave my arm a yank just for emphasis. "Know what I'm saying?"

It was going on two o'clock in the morning. Did I know where I was? I was in a bleeping police station. "I'm beginning to get your drift," I said, relaxing, the fight going out of me suddenly.

"Good boy," he said.

What followed was like a Three Stooges routine, except there were five of us. All right, let's try again, said the sergeant. He asked Angel if he wanted to file a complaint against me. "Damn right," said Angel. The sergeant sighed.

He repeated the question to me. I said that I did. "If you file croth complainths, I'll have to book you both," he explained.

Angel was still a page behind. He looked at me as if to say, "What's going on here?" I grinned and shrugged. "White people's justice," he muttered, catching up to the rest of us. "Wha' about James?" he demanded. "He's haid's cracked open, and he's burnt to a crisp. Wha' about that? Who done that?"

The sergeant, who had been looking at the monitor on his desk, fixed his Windex eyes on Angel and said, "Maybe he tripped and fell, and thet himthelf on fire. I thee here, Mithter Cruth, you have more priorths than Frank Perdue hath chickenth, and your friend Jameths ithn't much better. Thtill wanna file that complaint?"

"Sheet," said the disgusted Angel, and he dropped the complaint.

I walked back to the studio from Midtown South, about seven blocks. A pretty good defense mechanism in the city is to outcrazy the crazies. In the singed and tattered tux, I looked as weird as anything else that was walking the streets at that hour, so I figured I didn't have much to fear.

In the short time that she'd been there, Dolly had become a fixture, so it was strange to see her doorway empty. There were ambiguous glyphs, some carbon, some blood on the sidewalk. It was hard to tell which was which in the bad light. I wondered where they'd taken her and Socrates. I promised myself I'd try to find them in the morning. All I could think of at the moment was a hot bath.

I squatted to unlock the plate-glass door. My neighbors, Hasidic Jews, a father and son who wholesaled cheap watches out of a couple of rooms on my floor, were headed straight for me, pushing a dolly loaded with cardboard cartons. They were an incongruous couple of birds, the patriarch about as big as your thumb, and with his chiseled features and flowing gray beard, handsomer than Moses; the son as bulky as a nose tackle, and homelier than matzo. It wasn't unusual for tenants to come and go at all hours of the night and day. A small businessman's work is never done. But I'd rather not have bumped into them. I once rescued the father, who was trapped in the elevator between floors with a load of cartons. We'd barely acknowledged each other in the halls until then. That broke the ice. "Ah, there's my friend," he exclaimed the next time we met, "the man I was telling you about. He helped me out of the elevator with the cartons." His son glowered at me suspiciously, but from then on we said hello. I got to know them a little better after buying several watches from them wholesale. And better still when Gorbachev first came to town and turned the city on its ear. I had dropped by their place to get a new battery put in a watch.

"Such a fuss they are making over Gorbachev," the old man said disgustedly. "Meanwhile, the Russians are buying up all the electronic equipment the Hasid has in stock. You never saw such a thing."

"Well, they've gotta shop somewhere," I said. "I've never seen anything made in Russia for sale in Lord and Taylor, or Forty-seventh Street Photo."

"Never. Communism," scoffed the old man. He rejected the idea with the wave of his hand. He was in his shirtsleeves, and the tattooed numerals were visible on his pale forearm. "It's no good," he said.

"It's no good," echoed his son. "It's—It's . . ." He searched for the word he wanted. "It's a fraud. That's what it is, a fraud. It's a fraud on the people."

"He's right," the old man agreed. "The old Russia fed all of Europe, now she can't even feed herself."

"Are you from Russia?" I asked.

"Poland, originally. Schlomo"—he nodded at his son—"was born in this country."

"Schlomo?"

"Mo." He smiled.

"I'm Charlie."

"Mordecai, Mort," said the old man, patting himself. We were Mort, Mo, and Charlie after that.

Anyway, I hated having them see their friend looking like he was coming off a three-day drunk.

"Ah, Charlie," said the old man the moment he spotted

me. "How are you this morning?" If he noticed my condition, he was too polite to comment.

"Fine, Mort, just fine. How about yourself?"

"Tip-top." He beamed. The man was an unqualified optimist.

Mo made no pretense of politeness—he examined me as frankly as if I were a piece of dubious goods. Funky black suit, white shirt, put a hat and a beard on me and I might pass for one of them. Well, almost. I could see he recognized the possibility, though.

"Okay, shall I lock up?" I asked.

"We're through, go ahead. And Charlie"—Mo grinned and nodded at me—"I'll have to introduce you to my tailor."

"Thanks, Mo, appreciate that." I held the door for them as they pushed the dolly through.

"Good night, Charlie," the old man waved. They pulled the dolly to the trunk of the twelve-year-old Buick Century wagon waiting at the curb. I locked up after them.

Morbid and Curiosity, the studio cats, were waiting for me by the door, demanding attention. I took a moment to rough them up and feed them. Then I drew a hot bath. The third thing I did was pour three fingers of Early Times over ice. The fourth thing I did was shuck the tux. You're not supposed to do it—booze and bath are a bad mix, I hear—but the fifth thing I did was dive into the tub with glass in hand. I didn't bother turning on the lights. I soaked and sipped—it felt great. I dozed off for maybe half an hour. When the water cooled, I woke with a start. I climbed out, toweled off, slipped on a robe, and padded off to bed without finishing the bourbon.

I slept until ten the next morning, and hobbled out of bed all aches and pains. My shins were black and blue where Dolly had whacked me, and the palms of my hands were raw and burned. While the coffee was brewing, I did what I could for my wounds. By eleven I was ready to face the world.

There was no sign of Tito, which was strange. He was usually in by nine. I found the explanation waiting on the answering machine. He'd left a message saying his grandfather had had a dizzy spell and was in the hospital, and he had to take the day off. His grandparents were in their eighties and spoke no English. Tito took them to the doctor and the clinic, dealt with their landlord, got them the best rate on their CD when it came time to roll it over, and did their grocery shopping. He had been raised by his grandparents, and they'd done a good job. Whatever needed doing, Tito did it, and not just for them, but for his own family and all the nephews and cousins, too. Tito took care of everyone.

There were two junk calls on the machine. One guy selling insurance, another guy selling pork bellies. They don't come right out with it, but you can tell—it's the way they leave their names that's the tip-off. They try to sound authoritative, like they're the boss and you'd better call them back.

"Charles, this is Rodger Pharr," the last caller had intoned. It was the smooth young photographer's agent with the seven-hundred-dollar suit and the forty-dollar haircut. "Wondering whether you'd like to break bread? I'd like to discuss further the possibility of my representing you and your work. Please call me at your earliest convenience." I hadn't expected to hear from him. It was my impression he thought I didn't have the right stuff. I jotted down his number. What did I have to lose? We'd split the check, naturally.

Next, the A.D. with the bank ads had called, barking for model composites to send to his client. That's how it is in the ad business—take your time and hurry up. Casting was a chore I'd happily leave to Tito. Pulling composites from the files, getting new ones from the agents to fill in the gaps, and getting the whole mess over to the agency killed the better part of the day. And when that was finished, my paperback book-cover client called and invited me to dinner that night at his house in Greenwich, Connecticut. Don't take no for an answer, his wife had told him. Seems there was this divorcée they wanted me to meet. I couldn't think of a good reason to decline a client's invitation, so I hopped the six-thirty train out of Grand Central Station. I never did get a chance to track down Dolly and Socrates.

The divorcée was attractive and lively, but she had three

kids and lived in Old Greenwich, which made romance problematical, assuming, that is, she was interested in an unsteady guy like me. Anyway, it was another late night, I didn't get back from Connecticut until after midnight. And wouldn't you know it, I bumped into my Hasidic friends again. Mort and I agreed we were tip-top; well, I was presentable, at least. And Mo said he was fine. Then he said, "There was a woman looking for you today. We tried your door, but you must have been out."

"A model?" I said. It must have been while I was at the agency.

"No, a reporter."

"A reporter? What did she want?"

"Something to do with the bag lady."

"Dolly?"

"Lusk, I think she said."

"I don't know anyone named Lusk. What did you tell her?"

He shrugged his big shoulders and showed me his palms. "What could I tell her?"

"Did you get her name?"

"I remember now, it was Miriam Lusk. Oh, you mean the reporter's name. She left her card. Can you wait until the morning?"

"That'll be soon enough. Want me to lock up?"

"Go ahead."

The message light on the answering machine was winking. I played it back and listened while I fed the cats. "Mr. Byrne, I'm calling regarding Miriam Lusk," said a woman's voice. "You probably know her as Dolly Varden. My name is Diedre Mahoney. I'm with the *Times*. If you can spare a moment, I plan to be in your neighborhood this afternoon, and I'd like to get your version of what happened Sunday night. Hope to see you then. Good-bye."

She must have come by, talked to Mort and Mo, and left her card after this message. I wondered why she was interested in Dolly. Maybe she knew what had happened to Dolly and Socrates.

There was one more message. It was Henry Stein, the little con man. "Hey, Byrne, I know you're there, pick up . . . all right, don't pick up, gimme a call."

Stein and Mahoney would keep until morning.

I was up early the next day with time to spare before Tito got in, so I went out for the paper. Spikes of sunlight, so sharp they hurt my eyes, slanted through the gaps in the buildings. The street was a wash of white light and blue shadows; f8 in the shade, I guessed, f22 in the sun. Warm and sunny, with no humidity, it was going to be a brilliant day. I couldn't help humming "Autumn in New York." The city was at its best this time of year.

Thirty-eighth Street is just another crease in the concrete jungle, another mean street, as Raymond Chandler might have said, but this morning it seemed as good a place to be as any. This morning it was like the opening number in a Broadway musical, with people hurrying about as if they were on stage. Trucks and cabs choked the street. Goods and people, coming and going. Women, dressed for success in tailored business suits, with flat leather attachés under their arms, hustled to work wearing a sensible pair of sneakers, a practical solution held over from a transit strike, until now it looked like fashion. I pictured Susan Ferrante in blue serge and a pair of jogging shoes, and liked what I saw. I wondered why a name designer hadn't come out with fuck-me sneakers for career women. I wondered where Susan Ferrante was at the moment, and what she was doing. Which led me to wonder how much Murray was going to clip me for the tux. I even found myself wondering what that little dirtbag, Angel, was up to this time of day. If he was up at all, he was probably lighting up a crack pipe and contemplating the first mugging of the day.

Passing Dolly's empty doorway was a mute reminder to call the *Times* reporter. Diedre Mahoney had said Dolly's real name was Miriam Lusk. It figured. Dolly Varden was too glitzy to be her real name. So who was Miriam Lusk? And what about her family? Did she have one? And how had she come up with the name Dolly Varden?

I picked up the *Times* at the Korean's around the corner

on Sixth Avenue, and checked the Lotto prize. There were no winners Saturday and the payoff was up to six mil. I blew five bucks on ten games. I stashed the tickets in my wallet as though they were as good as gold. The best I'd ever done was three numbers out of six.

I returned to find the mail had been chucked through the slot. I scooped it up and flipped through it. No sunflower check. A billion-dollar-a-year advertising agency, and you had to beg them for your money. One more call to make.

The answering machine was blinking again. It was the art director who'd introduced me to Pharr. He wanted to know how it was going. A.D.'s are hard to catch at phone tag, and they never return my calls, so any excuse to call is a good one. I returned his call, got a secretary and left a message. I returned Stein's call and got no answer, and no machine. He knew how to live. I dialed Beau Brummell's. No one there, either. My client with the bank ads wasn't in yet. Diedre Mahoney and Dolly could wait another half an hour. I decided to kill time reading the paper and drinking more coffee.

An article in the metro section stopped me cold. It carried the Mahoney byline, and was accompanied by a photo of Dolly, looking as dowdy as a plainclothes nun, standing in court with an ACLU lawyer. There was a garbled police account of Sunday night's fracas, and I was startled to see my name in print. Mahoney said the city was going to make a test case out of Dolly. City Hall wanted her declared mentally incompetent and a menace to herself and society. Society, in this case, meant one James Mason, who refused to file charges even though he was hospitalized with third-degree burns he claimed to have received in an altercation with the homeless woman. Mahoney was sympathetic to Dolly's plight. She'd interviewed everyone on the block who had come in contact with Dolly, and they were all skeptical of the official claim that Dolly presented a threat to herself and society.

Mahoney went on to say that, although diagnosed as schizophrenic, Dolly appeared reasonable and rational in court. Despite protestations from her daughter, who pleaded for psychiatric help for her mother, the judge could find no cause for holding Dolly, and released her in her own recognizance. He set a date for a hearing on her mental competency, and ordered Dolly and Socrates be reunited.

The shocker was, the daughter's name was Susan Ferrante.

11

Only in fiction does coincidence seem incredible. But how often have you discovered, when talking to a stranger, that you have a mutual acquaintance? Or that someone you haven't seen for a while materializes before you on the street just as you were thinking of them? Or you pick up the phone, and before you can dial, or the phone rings, the person you were about to call is on the line? It would be some coincidence if Dolly's daughter turned out to be the same Susan Ferrante.

Tito found me speeding on coffee and shaking my head in disbelief at the story as I computed odds of one in a million. Or were they the same as bumping into her at Ransom's party?

"What's up?" he asked cheerfully.

"Here, read this," I said, handing him the article.

While he was reading it, the phone rang. It was the bank ads. We've made our picks, you can come and get the composites. I told the A.D. Tito'd be right over.

"Leave you alone for forty-eight hours"—Tito grinned, handing the paper back to me—"and you gotta go and be a hero. Is that the same Susan Ferrante as in the courtyard?"

"I think so."

"Man, glad I'm not related to her."

"She's got a few heartaches, huh? That was Carlson on the phone. Get on your pony and pick up the composites. I'd like to get the job booked today, if possible."

Tito left, and I crossed the hall and knocked on Mort and Mo's door. Mo slipped me Mahoney's card, and I thanked him. I tried her number at the *Times* and got a secretary. It figured. I left my name and number.

Couldn't think of anything else to do for the moment, so I thought I'd clean up my business with Murray. He picked up on the first ring. "Murray, Charlie Byrne, about the tux."

"What'sa matter, you don't like it, Charlie?"

"No, nothing like that."

"So, what about the tux?"

"It's just that, well, it's sorta blown out, it's in tatters."

"Uh-huh, whadda ya do, go wilding in it?"

"You might say that."

"You didn't look like the type, but that's why we make you leave a deposit charge slip."

"You can tear up the rental slip and cash the deposit."

"I sell more tuxes that way, but listen, fella . . ."

"What?"

"It shouldn't be a dead loss. Bring it in, lemme have a look at it. You'd be surprised, maybe I could fix it up nice for you."

"It wouldn't be a surprise, it would be a miracle. I'll drop it off first chance I get."

"Might not cost as much as you'd think."

"That'd be a pleasant surprise."

Then I dialed Stein, and connected.

"Schmuck," he laughed, "what's this I see in the paper?"

"My fifteen minutes of fame."

"The Ferrante babe mentioned in the article—wasn't she at Ransom's Sunday with Matty Fallon?"

"I think it's the same Ferrante, why?"

"Just wondering. Listen, I happened to mention to Strunk

that I ran into you at the birthday party, and he says he knows your date, Cyzeski. Says she used to be his girl."

I could see him grinning into the receiver. "Still is, as far as I'm concerned. We all know each other from Pakistan. Strunk was an embassy guard, and Josephine and I were in the press corps." Somehow or other, Strunk, a nineteen-year-old jarhead back then, had gotten it into his head that the cameras were cover and that I was really with the Company, as he liked to call it. He hoped to join the Company himself when his hitch was up. I let him believe I was a spook because he was eager to please and could get me access to the embassy. In fact he helped me get a picture of Ali Bhutto hours before he was overthrown in a coup. The photograph went ballistic. Every newsmagazine in the world wanted reproduction rights. I made a nice enough chunk of change on the picture to buy a handyman's special upstate in a small town named Hobart, for which I was grateful to P. C. Strunk. Unfortunately for Strunk, Langley was less enamored of him than he was of Langley, and he had to settle for a job as a State Police investigator with the Attorney General's Office.

"The guy still believes you're a spy," Stein said.

"I know, but I can't help that. I'd love to chew the fat, Henry, but I've got a shitload of things to do."

"What's your hurry, sport? This is New York, we're all busy. What I really called to say is, Strunk wants us to have lunch."

"Is this a business lunch?"

"Sort of."

"You guys scamming Ransom?"

"Why don't we discuss that over lunch."

"Not Chinese?"

"What else? And the guy isn't even Jewish."

"Is it on the taxpayer?"

"Of course."

"Okay, just give me a day's notice so I can arrange to have my stomach pumped afterward."

"Maybe we could go someplace else," he said, not too hopefully, "an Italian place, or maybe Indian, or Spanish."

"Anything but Chinese."

"I'll see what I can do," he promised, and hung up.

In my gut I knew we'd end up in a Chinese joint. I never saw P. C. Strunk eat anything but Chinese food.

I got to thinking about Mahoney's story and Susan Ferrante again as I waited for Tito to return from the agency. With her mother living in the streets, and her sister's death labeled a suicide, the woman wasn't having an easy time of it lately. I suppose there must be picture-perfect families, like the ones I'm always casting in ads, somewhere, but families like Susan Ferrante's, or for that matter my own, are probably the norm. My own father could be out there on the street somewhere.

When it came to the family history, my aunt held her cards pretty close to the vest. I never did get a straight story from her, which made me think there must have been something to hide. According to my aunt, my parents' courtship was a sort of immigrant romance wrapped in gauze. She worked as a maid, he worked construction. They were both slightly past thirty when they met at an Irish dance hall in Queens and fell in love. The story gets grittier as life begins to crowd them. In order to save money, they were living in Astoria with my uncle, Austin Byrne, and his wife, Maureen, when my mother got pregnant. Austin Byrne was, is—I'm not sure which, I've never actually laid eyes on these people—my father's big brother. Anyway, according to my aunt, Maureen Byrne was a real bitch who made my mother's life miserable. Mom pleaded with my father for him to get them a place of their own, and he kept putting her off, telling her he was working on it. Fed up, finally, with her sister-in-law's abuse, she picked up and left. Expecting my father would eventually come for her when he'd found them a place of their own, she moved in with my aunt, her sister. But he never did come for her.

Instead, his family sent their kid brother back to Ireland, my aunt says, where he met and married another girl. His brothers and that bitch of a wife of his had done everything in their power to break my parents up, she claimed. My aunt was no slouch when it came to the oral tradition, she never let the facts get in the way of a good story. It had lovers, it had villains, it made a great yarn, and I ate it up as a kid. But it was too full of holes for an adult to believe. There was no evidence of a marriage, or a divorce, either; no wedding pictures, gifts, nothing. Patrick John Byrne was listed as father on my birth certificate. My mother was listed as Curran-Byrne. She was pregnant, and he ran out on her, is what I think the real story was. But even when I was grown, my aunt could never bring herself to tell me the real story.

The funny thing was, though, she probably knew my father fairly well because her portrait of him was too shrewd to have been entirely invented. My aunt was a woman who either loved you or hated you, so it always came as a surprise to me when she spared my father the harsh opinions she had of most people. Part of this was an unwillingness to speak ill of him to me, I realized, but part of it also seemed to be a genuine liking for the man. The most she'd say, and then only after I'd done something boneheaded: "You're just like your father, not a lick of common sense." The only other complaint she had against him, and that halfheartedly, was that he liked to play the horses. This was always followed up with the observation that, like him, I too was reckless, a gambler. She held it against me that I hadn't become a doctor or a lawyer, as she'd had in mind for me, and instead had unaccountably become a photographer. A dubious profession at best, she thought. Although if there were any artistic talent in the family, it certainly didn't come from my father's side. From him I got all my bad traits, while all credit accrued unilaterally to her side.

I used to think about my father all the time as a kid. I would imagine us as a family, living together happily, the way I imagined everyone else did. But as time went by, and he never came around, I began to wonder why he wasn't interested, or curious about me. I seldom think of him anymore, but when I do, it's because I'm worried that I might be more like him than I know, weak and ineffectual, a gambler without a lick of common sense. That's how I'd come to think of him in the end. My mother's image is even dimmer and vaguer. She is simply this long-suffering, uncanonized saint martyred in her youth, a myth cultivated by my crusty, ordinarily tough-minded, self-reliant aunt, who was all the role model I'd ever needed.

I have no family now, or at least none that I know of, but from what I learn from personal experience, and that of friends and acquaintances, there are no perfect families. When it comes to family, you take the good with the bad, the joy with the sorrow and, in too many cases, the misery. Which is why, along with the fact I haven't a clue about what being a dad is all about, I haven't started a family of my own, though I'm not at all down on the idea. Being an orphan can be lonesome, but maybe Susan Ferrante wouldn't have minded changing places with me at the moment. The ringing of the phone snapped me out of it.

"Hello, studio," I said.

"This is Rodger Pharr, Charles."

"Hello, Rodger, you got my message?"

"Yes, I did."

"You mentioned something about lunch."

"Yes, Thursday, if that's all right with you, at Rossini's, just east of Park on Thirty-eighth Street. Know the place?"

"I know the place." A little pricey for whatever we'd have to talk about, I thought.

"Meet you there at quarter to one?"

"Fine with me."

"Excellent, and by the way, I see you are a celebrity."

"Are you referring to the article in the *Times?*"

"I am. You came off rather well, I thought, coming to the aid of that bag lady as you did."

"Yeah, well, that and a buck twenty-five'll get me a ride on the subway."

"Believe me, Charles, there's no such thing as bad publicity."

"Just spell the name right, huh?"

"That's it. Well, I'll see you Thursday at Rossini's, then."

"See you then." So that was it, he'd seen my name in the paper. Publicity works.

Tito returned from the agency shortly after Pharr's call, and together we went over the final casting. The ads called for a series of portraits of yuppie types blissfully interfacing with computers while accessing their money through the miracle of electronic banking. The casting was supposed to reflect a cross section of the population—an Asian, a

Hispanic, a black, a couple of women, and that endangered species, the white male. The usual suspects, in other words. We were at least eight deep in each category. Since you couldn't always get the model you wanted, there were first, second, and third picks in each category. For the most part the client's picks conformed pretty closely to ours. The only difference was that he had a thing for redheads, and booked one. Tito spent the rest of the morning on the phone to the various modeling agencies, putting holds on the first-, second-, and third-place talent.

Diedre Mahoney returned my call sometime before lunch. I apologized for not getting back to her sooner. She asked if I'd seen the piece. I told her I had and that I liked it. She said she wished she'd been able to get my account of what had happened. I said I'd be glad to give it to her. It was too late now, she said, the story was done, fini. I asked her if she knew that Dolly had had two daughters. She said no. Her other daughter's name was Sharon Raynes, I said, she died in August in a fall from her apartment. There was a pause on the line, then she said, I wish I'd known that. Was it an accident? I think it was listed as suicide, I said. There was another pause. How do you know about the sister? she asked finally. I told her I was the one who had found the body. You seem to be Johnny-on-the-spot, she said. Just a coincidence, I said. She said she was sorry she hadn't spoken to me sooner. Me, too, I said, and we said our good-byes. It was time to break for lunch.

"I have a nice moussaka today," said Chris. "You know, Greek pasta." He was enjoying his own fifteen minutes of fame. Diedre Mahoney had mentioned him by name in the article. The luncheonette was a mom-and-pop store. Chris, the son-in-law, waited tables. His wife worked the cash register. Pop cooked, and Mom, who was battling the big C, came in when she was feeling up to it and ran the place.

"I'll have the moussaka," said Tito.

"I know." Chris looked at me. "Spinach pie." He was a mind reader.

I worked the *Times* crossword puzzle and Tito read the sports in the *Daily News* while we ate. Chris had thirty or forty small transactions in the air at the same time, and still managed to give points on the Giants-Eagles game and make book on the heavyweight fight. He was busier than the guy in the circus who spins the plates on sticks. When we stood and signaled for our check, it took him a moment to spot us. "You wanna check, I know, just a minute." He dashed for the lunch counter and back again, an order of toast in hand. "Step up, folks, I got a table for four. Who's four?" He slung the toast at a customer, and whipped out a pencil and pad. "Lemme see—one spinach pie, one moussaka, two Miller Lite, right?" he said, slapping down the check on the table as a party of four slipped into the booth. He gave me a nod and beamed at a pretty girl in the party. "This man's Charlie Byrne, darling. He's a hero," he said. She gave me an uncertain smile. Tito grabbed the check—it was his turn—and I left the tip. Chris pocketed the tip as he swabbed the table with a gray rag. We pushed our way toward the cash register. "There he goes, the man who saved the bag lady from the muggers, folks," Chris announced to the crowd waiting in line. "Read all about it in today's *Times.*" Gimme a break.

"Look," said Tito, as we stepped out on the street.

Dolly and Socrates had resumed light housekeeping in their favorite doorway.

We crossed the street, Tito hanging back slightly as I approached them. Socrates spotted me right off. He strained at his leash to greet me, his tail waving happily.

"Dolly, you're back," I said.

She pretended to be engrossed in a paperback.

"Hey, Dolly, it's me, Charlie Byrne, remember?"

"Whatta ya want, a medal or something?"

"How about being polite?"

"Okay, I'm polite."

"Did you see today's *Times?*"

"I don't read newspapers."

"I don't blame you. But you're in it—you, me, Socrates . . . they did an article about us. About what happened the other night."

"Really?"

94

"Really. You're famous. It ought to help you in court. It was a sympathetic article, Dolly."

"Well, I don't give a fat rat's ass what happens in court."

"Bullshit you don't. They put Socrates in the pound again, and your ass in the loony bin, and you're gonna care a whole lot what happens in court."

She considered that a moment. "Charlie?" she said finally.

"Yeah?"

"Got any money?"

I reached for my billfold and pulled out a dollar.

"That's all you got?"

"I don't know that I can afford that much. What'd you have in mind?"

"A ten."

"A ten? Jeez, to know you, Dolly, you gotta pay dues," I said, reluctantly pulling a ten from my wallet.

She snatched the bill. "I'm famous." She grinned, stuffing my ten somewhere in her clothing. "See you, Charlie."

"Yeah, sure." The way she said my name, it sounded like a synonym for sucker.

"You crazy?" said Tito as I rejoined him.

"Just doing my bit to help the homeless."

"Keep it up and you'll be homeless yourself. Man, if there's one thing I hate, it's a greedy beggar."

The afternoon trickled by uneventfully. Tito went home at six, and feeling lethargic, I took the Lejeune out for a spin. It was either that or take a nap. Mo, seeing me with the bike in the elevator one time, observed dryly, "You must be meshugana, Charlie, to ride a bike in Manhattan." I liked the sound of that, Meshugana Charlie. It would make a great name for an electronics store. Seriously, though, you don't have to be meshugana to ride a bike in Manhattan, but it helps. It comes under the heading of cheap thrills. Like when an old lady steps off the curb in front of you without looking, or when someone opens a car door unexpectedly, or changes lanes without signaling and drives you up on the sidewalk. Another thrill is the efficiency with which a bike converts energy into speed. It beats jogging. Traveling twenty-five to thirty-five miles an hour on twelve pounds of aluminum tubing is the nearest sensation to flying that I can think of. I love it. Something else I love is the way the Lejeune looks. It is a beautiful candy-apple red, the logo in white block letters on the frame. It looks delicate, and like an antique, but it is neither. It is balance and precision. Form following function. It is a perfect machine.

I peddled up Madison Avenue, dodging potholes and kamikaze cab drivers, and entered Central Park at Fifth and Fifty-ninth. I have nothing to prove, but when a guy my own age or a girl whizzes by, it's impossible not to accept the challenge and give chase—without letting on, of course. I did three laps and half a dozen chases. When the workout was over, I headed downtown tired, but feeling good.

It was only eight o'clock, and Dolly had already turned in for the night. She was buried under a heap of clothing, the way she had been the first time I saw her. Socrates woofed hello. I stopped to give him a pet, sorry I didn't have anything for him. So was he.

"Leave us alone," said Dolly from beneath the pile of rags.

"It's me, Charlie Byrne, Dolly."

"I don't care if you're the mayor, beat it. I'm trying to get some sleep."

Sure, so you can stay up all night cursing at the moon. "Gotta go, fella," I said, petting the dog.

"Charlie!" Her head poked out of the pile.

I started to shove off, suspecting what was about to come.

"Hey, not so fast. How about some money?"

"I gave already, Dolly, remember?"

"Cheap motherfucker," she muttered, and disappeared again under the rags.

I didn't say anything. This nut case was Susan Ferrante's mom.

Thursday I had lunch with Pharr. I didn't like the vibes I'd been getting off the guy, and lunch was more of the same. He seemed to know the business, though, and be shallow and superficial enough to do well in it. Did I have to like the guy to do business with him? It would help, but it wasn't necessary, I rationalized. Conversation consisted mostly of my listening to him gloat about how well his life was going. I could see for myself the forty-dollar haircut, the seven-hundred-dollar suit, and the manicured nails. I was thrilled to learn he owned a brownstone in Murray Hill, drove a classic car, a '57 Porsche Cabriolet, and dated a Ford model. He mentioned her name. I knew the girl. Used to admire her. He sprinkled his patter with the names of well-known art directors, guys who wouldn't ordinarily give me the time of day. He skied Colorado with them in the winter, and summered in the Hamptons with them. This was an image business, he informed me. He was a natural-born salesman, or so he claimed. He could sell an Eskimo an air conditioner. If he wasn't selling photography, he'd be selling yachts, or estates. He could sell anything just as long as it was expensive.

He had me sold.

"Tell me, Charles . . ." he said, ordering a brandy with his coffee.

Brandy at lunch? What the hell, why not? I ordered one, too. That ought to waste the afternoon.

". . . what are your aspirations?"

That sounded like a trick question. "Aspirations?" I asked, buying time.

"Yes, what do you expect from your career?"

Fame and fortune, what else? I didn't say that, though, for fear of sounding too greedy. "I'd like to have a solid career . . . you know, a reputation for doing good work . . ."

Not to worry how I sounded, he wasn't listening. "Because I'm interested in representing only the very best. I want my photographers to have a fire in their bellies. There's a lot of money to be made in this business, and my photographers have to want to get rich."

Visions of Porsches danced in my head. "I'm your man," I murmured, feeling like I was making a pact with the devil.

"That's important, Charles. That's what I want to hear." He hoisted his brandy glass. "To an auspicious beginning," he proposed.

"I'll drink to that."

"Settled, then. Charles Byrne is now represented by Rodger Pharr. You are my new illustrator, my people guy. You realize, of course, we have our work cut out for us."

"We do?"

"For starters, I'll want to go through your files and assemble the strongest portfolio possible. It has been my experience that photographers seldom are the best judges of their own work. You'll have no objections to that, I hope?"

"I guess not." In truth, I didn't care much for the idea.

"I may even ask you to shoot some new stuff."

I hated that idea—everyone hated shooting samples once they were established—but I could see the necessity for it. The competition is ferocious, and there's no such thing as bad, only good and better. "Okay, but I can only fit that in between bookings."

"I understand. Speaking of which, have I mentioned my commission?"

"Not yet."

"Well, it's twenty-five percent."

"After expenses."

"Of course, and I'll require a small draw against commissions."

"How much?"

"Oh, say three hundred a week."

He had two other photographers, a still-life and a fashion guy. At that rate, each one of us kicking in three bills a week, he'd have almost a grand a week before lifting the telephone. "Let's make it a hundred and fifty a week to start, Rodger," I said recklessly, wondering where the money would come from.

"I can live with that," he said equitably. "Now, I think we should discuss a percentage of the house business. You'll probably want me to service your accounts."

"I don't think so. I'd rather you concentrated on new business." But nice try anyway, Rodger.

"As you wish. Customarily, I handle the business affairs of the artists I represent—"

"Business affairs?"

"Yes, accounts payable, billing, the bookkeeping, that sort of thing," he said with a wave of his manicured hand, as though these were mere trifles. "It's a juggling act, wearing two hats—businessman, artist. My people find it frees them up creatively."

"I prefer doing my own bookkeeping, but thanks anyway."

"Fine—settled, then." He reached for the leather folder containing the tab. It had been sitting there for quite some time. He made an elaborate display of examining it, checking that each item was correct, and doing the math.

"How much is it?"

"Eighty-nine ninety, reasonable," he said, leaning back and patting his breast pocket.

"Lemme see, with tip, that's about a hundred and five, or ten."

"That sounds right." He looked puzzled, still frisking himself.

"Shall we split it?"

"Damn, I seem to have left my platinum card in my other jacket." He shrugged haplessly. "Would you mind getting this one, Charles?"

Auspicious beginning indeed. "Next one's on you, Rodger," I said, slipping a Visa card in the folder.

"Naturally." He reached again for the folder. "I'll take the expense tab on the check, if you don't mind."

"Go ahead, I have my credit card slip."

"Right," he said, tearing the tab off the check and pocketing it. "Oh, one more thing, before I forget."

"What's that?"

"That mention in the *Times*, it was a very good thing. I think we should exploit it. I'd like to hire a press agent. Plant your name in the columns."

Here I was about ready to smack the guy, and he comes up with something intelligent. "What would that cost?" I asked.

"I don't know. I'll have to get back to you on that."

Josephine Cyzeski was sitting in the lounge, dangling a black pump off the end of her foot and flipping through a copy of *Vogue,* when I returned from my power lunch.

She dropped the magazine and jumped to her feet to greet

me. We bussed each other's cheeks. "Josephine! To what do I owe the pleasure?"

"Thought I'd surprise you."

"You did."

"Are you very busy?"

"Well . . ."

"I mean right now, this afternoon."

After a couple of glasses of red wine and a brandy, I didn't envisage accomplishing a whole hell of a lot this afternoon. What did she have in mind? I wondered. "Well . . . I don't know . . ."

"I'm on my way to Sotheby's, and thought you might like to keep me company."

12

~~~

It seemed there was another tapestry, a mate to the one owned by Ransom, and Josephine had been instructed to bid on it. This ought to be interesting, I thought, as we sped uptown in a cab driven by an illegal alien claiming to be Ibreham, Yussef.

"Hey, Joe," I said, "I see you're named for the prophets." It's a habit of mine, reading cab driver's licenses and memorizing their numbers. You never know when you might leave your wallet in a cab.

His glance ricocheted off the rearview mirror.

"I'm Joseph, too." I grinned. "My middle name."

"I didn't know that," said Josephine.

"Yeah, we're three Joe's."

"All my names are prophets' names," the driver said, beaming, displaying one gold tooth. "My middle name's Ishmael."

"You've got it made, huh."

"I'm going to Heaven." He grinned. Josephine and I lurched to one side as he swerved, narrowly avoiding a truck. He let out a stream of expletives in Arabic that sounded suspiciously like Jesus, Mary, and Joseph.

"Don't be in such a hurry to get to Heaven, pal."

"Sorry," he apologized.

Ten minutes later we were nearly tossed from the cab as Ibreham, Yussef came to a sudden stop in front of Sotheby's. Josephine paid the fare.

She seemed familiar with the place. After consulting the directory briefly, she led us straight to the right gallery. The room was nearly full. Josephine mentioned Ransom's name to the usher, and we were shown to our seats and handed a sales catalog.

"Shit!" she whispered from behind her catalog. "It's that creep, Bernard."

My eyes met those of Florine's secretary. We exchanged smiles. "Isn't he supposed to be here?"

"He's supposed to be here."

I couldn't decipher what that was supposed to mean, so I concentrated on the catalog instead. If there was a point of view to the sale, and there probably was, it went over my head. It seemed to me to be a mixed lot of antiquities. The auctioneer, understated, urban, and fiftyish, rapped his gavel for attention. A hush fell over the room and the sale commenced. A set of eight Louis XIV chairs was the first item on the block. Bidding started at fifty thousand, and before you could say supercalifragilisticexpialidocious, someone had made off with them for the paltry sum of 160 simoleons. That seemed like an expensive squat, twenty grand per chair, although it's hard to imagine even Louis placing the royal buns on them at those prices. An armoire went for a quarter of a million, and an equestrian portrait for almost a million. Every rap of the gavel meant big bucks were changing hands, but judging from the decorum and aplomb, you'd never guess this was real money they were playing with. And in a sense, it wasn't. I figured most of these people were dealers, or like Josephine, and possibly Kiernan, nominees for the real money. How else could you explain their cool? They were a mean bunch of poker players.

By the time the tapestry was put on the block, my head

had begun to loll and my chin to droop to my chest. The wine and brandy at lunch were catching up to me. It was nap time. The auctioneer opened the bidding at a nifty hundred and fifty thousand United States dollars. That woke me up like a slap in the face.

"One seventy-five, one seventy-five, who will give me one seventy-five for this outstanding Aubusson tapestry? I have one seventy-five, do I have two hundred, only two hundred for this magnificent tapestry . . ."

Kiernan tugged his earlobe, I noticed.

"I have two hundred. Two fifty, two fifty, the bid is now two fifty, who will give me two fifty? I have two fifty . . ."

I never saw the bid.

"Who will give me two sixty, ladies and gentlemen, two sixty, who will give me two sixty for this truly fabulous tapestry . . . two sixty?"

Josephine touched her nose.

Josephine scratched her nose again at three hundred thousand.

The auctioneer called for three five several times until Kiernan finally obliged with another yank of his lobe.

Josephine was somber.

The auctioneer called for three ten, got no takers, and finalized the sale with a rap of his gavel as the crowd caught its breath.

"Let's get out of here," whispered Josephine, already on her feet.

We bumped into Kiernan in the lobby. "Ah, Charles." He beamed, gliding up to me. "Just the man I've been looking for. I left a message with your assistant for you to call. He said you were out to lunch. Mrs. Ransom would appreciate it if you could pay her a visit, as soon as possible."

"What could she want with me?"

"I haven't the foggiest, I'm sure. You will give her a call, though, won't you?"

"Yes, certainly, I'll call."

"Good, and, Josephine, darling, try not to be too upset about the tapestry. After all, it's in the family, you know."

"Bernard . . ."

"Yes?"

"Fuck off."

"As you wish, ta," he said, wiggling his fingers at us as he swept by on his way to a cab.

"I wonder what Florine wants with you?" said Josephine.

"I see you're anxious to report back to Mr. Big. Well, this has been fun, Josephine. We'll have to do dinner and the wild thing some other time."

"Sorry if I'm acting like a bitch. It's just that I hate to lose. Anyway, I'm still on medication."

"Hey, no problem."

We pecked each other on both cheeks, and I poured her into a cab, glad to see her go. It was nearly five-thirty. Tito would be gone before I got back to the studio. No sense rushing. I decided to walk home. One of the civilized aspects of living in Manhattan is, given time, you can walk most everywhere. I headed east on Seventy-second and turned south on Third Avenue.

I thought about my lunch with Pharr as I made my way downtown. Would he make me rich and famous? Probably not. But he might be able to do a decent repping job, and I'd settle for that. I started to warm to the idea of shooting some new stuff. It might even be good for me. Work for hire isn't the same as your own work. It doesn't stretch you. It's like the tip of the iceberg, it only shows a tenth of what you can do. And the problem with the portfolio was that it consisted mostly of work for hire. I ambled across town on Fifty-seventh Street, continuing downtown on Fifth Avenue. Doubleday Book Shop was still open, and I stopped in. I browsed the best-sellers and the mysteries, working my way slowly toward the photography section. I'd begun to visualize what a new portfolio might look like. The shelves were full of books by Adams, Avedon, Mapplethorpe, Penn, Weston, and others. The masters. Flipping through a few of them, I fantasized about joining their ranks, seeing my own photographs printed and bound alongside the masters of the medium, accessible to anyone off the street, reaching the public, not just the trade. I resumed my stroll back to the studio. By the time I'd reached the Public Library, I'd made up my mind that I was going to do it. I was going to shoot a new portfolio, one worthy of any coffee table, one that made a statement.

The cats were waiting for me at the door. I scratched and fed them, and then I changed my clothes and got to work. I hung a painted canvas backdrop and roughed out my lighting. I got the Hasselblad lenses, bodies, and backs from the safe and laid them out on the camera caddy. I loaded the backs with Tri-X. Six rolls should do the job. When I'd finished with the preparations, I locked up and went out to get the first subject. I was going to photograph the people of Thirty-eighth Street, in all their glory and diversity. I was going to be Pharr's people guy. Who better to begin with than Dolly Varden? Her gaudy costume, the dog, and her props, milk crates, rags, and shopping cart made her a natural photographic subject.

"Hey, Dolly, wake up. It's me, Charlie Byrne." She was tucked in for her early evening nap.

Socrates woofed, and slurped at the back of my hand.

"What do you want?" she said.

"I wanna talk to you."

"I'm sleeping."

"How about I run around the corner and pick up a couple of Big Macs for you and Socrates? Whatta ya say?"

Socrates said yes, woofing and dancing.

"How about you just give me the money?" said Dolly, reluctantly appearing from under the heap.

"Nah, I don't think so. Tell you what I'll do, though—I'll go for the burgers, you get yourself together. When I get back, we'll go upstairs and eat them."

She gazed at me skeptically. "Why would I want to do that?"

"So I can take your picture."

"So take my picture. No one's stopping you."

"I can't, not here."

"Why not?"

"Well, it's just not right. I have to do it in my studio. It's special, a portrait."

"You got something funny in mind?" she asked suspiciously.

"I just want to take your picture, that's all. It's for a project I'm doing."

"What do you want my picture for?"

"Because we're friends . . . I know you, you've got style."

"Bullshit."

"All right, how about if I pay you? Say, twenty bucks."

"You're a photographer?"

"That's right."

"And you take pictures of models?"

"Yes."

"How much do you pay them to take their picture?"

"That depends."

"On what?"

"How long they work, how the picture's used, whatever."

"They don't work for no twenty bucks, do they?"

"They're professionals."

"I don't work for no twenty bucks, either."

"Okay, fifty bucks, and the burgers, whatta ya say?"

"How long is this going to take?"

"An hour, maybe."

"Make it a hundred, then," she said.

"A hundred? Jeez, that's highway robbery, Dolly."

"A hundred or no deal."

"Money, money, money, that's all anyone thinks about these days. Okay, a hundred."

"I don't know, sex seems to be on a lot of people's minds nowadays." She squinted at me. "You sure you've got nothing funny up your sleeve?"

"This is on the level, I swear."

"Because I've got a great body, but I'm not taking my clothes off for no lousy hundred dollars."

For a second I wondered how much she would take her clothes off for, and then remembered she was Susan Ferrante's mom. "I betcha got a great body, Dolly, but you don't have to worry, I'm not gonna try to get you out of your clothes."

"I'm a good girl. I don't go in for no funny stuff."

"Believe me, there isn't gonna be any funny stuff. You want the burgers?"

"Okay."

"I'll be right back. Get your stuff together." I bolted around the corner to McDonald's on Thirty-seventh and Fifth before she changed her mind. When I returned, Dolly was ready to roll.

"No funny business," she cautioned me.

"I promise, Dolly, no funny business," I said, holding the plate-glass door open for her. She had Socrates on a leash. I helped her lift the cart over the doorsill. When I looked up, Mort and Mo were pushing a dolly loaded with cartons in our direction.

"Ah, there's my friend Charlie," said Mort. "How are you, Charlie?"

"Fine, Mort, fine, how about yourself?"

"For an old man? Tip-top, tip-top."

"Glad to hear that. Hello, Mo."

He cast a baleful eye on Dolly. "Hello, Charlie," he said.

These guys had impeccable timing. Next time they'd be catching me with my pants down for sure. "Dolly's going to pose for me," I explained.

"I'm going to be a model," she said.

"You don't say," Mort marveled.

"For money," she added.

"I should hope so," said Mort.

"It's for a book I'm working on," I said, wondering whether I could persuade them to pose for me. They were definitely candidates—they'd be perfect—although this was no time to broach the subject. I held the door for them.

"That should be some book," Mo said in passing. What's he doing with the meshugana bag lady? I could see him asking himself.

The cats, as usual, were waiting at the door. They scattered and hid the second they laid eyes on the dog. I had Dolly wheel her junk right into the shooting area. I set the burgers and fries out on the table, and offered Dolly a stool. "How about a little dinner music?" I asked.

"What have you got?"

"Most everything."

"Got, 'The Rage, Miss Patti Page'?"

"'How Much Is That Doggy in the Window,' right?"

"That's right."

"I'm afraid she's a little before my time."

"Got any Kay Starr? The wheel of fortune . . . goes spinning around . . ." she sang. She had a nice voice. "She's probably before your time, too."

"I think so, but, hey, you're not bad," I said. "You've got a real nice voice."

"I've been told that before," she said. "I used to make my living off my voice."

"Were you a singer?"

"No."

"You did voice-overs?"

"I did phone sex, for jerkoffs like you." She lifted the bun and inspected the burger.

"You're kidding."

"Why should I kid you?" She slathered the burger with catsup. "Mm, baby, I'm so wet and juicy . . . I can't wait for you to take that big, beautiful cock of yours . . . and stick it in my coo . . . zinart." She had a laughing jag over her own joke. For a moment, though, she was very convincing. On the telephone it would sound like she was sixteen. "It was so easy, it was a joke," she said, taking a bite out of the burger. I remembered she was supposed to be a vegetarian, but I guess she'd forgotten. "You didn't even have to leave home. You could sit around the house in your underwear and do it. All you had to do was talk like a little girl, say a few dirty words, and tell them how big their cocks were, and before you knew it, the guy would be grunting like a pig." She took another bite of the burger. "I made good money at it, too," she said, munching. "Had a flock of regulars, lawyers, had a judge, politicians, professors, cops—you name it. You're all alike, pigs, all of you."

I could see her, a fifty-year-old woman, with a cigarette, a can of diet Pepsi, her hair in curlers, sitting at home, filing her nails and talking on the telephone, and some joker, a judge, on the other end of the line, pounding his pud, with visions of Julia Roberts dancing in his head. "If it was so easy, and the money was good, what happened?"

"Burnout," she said matter-of-factly, as though she'd been an arbitrageur, or an air traffic controller, "and I was having trouble with my landlord."

"How would he know what you did, and why should he care?"

"He didn't. He wanted me out. I had a rent-controlled apartment, and he was co-oping the building—it was as simple as that. And there came a point when I just couldn't handle it anymore. I lost it. I started insulting the johns, calling them weenies, and weenie wallopers." She giggled. "Pretty soon the service stopped referring johns to me. I fell behind on my rent, and the next thing I knew, the city marshal came and tossed me out in the street. Been there ever since."

"That's tough, Dolly."

"Whatta ya gonna do?" she said, finally noticing Socrates, who had been sitting patiently at her knee. "Oops, Mommy forgot all about her good doggy," she said, removing the foil from a burger and feeding it to the dog, letting him lick her fingers.

I studied her, searching for a resemblance to Susan Ferrante. It was slight, but it was there. It was the nose, mainly. Susan's was more prominent, but the shape was the same. All I could remember of her other daughter, Sharon Raynes, was she was blond, probably not natural, and well dressed. I had no real basis for comparison there. As we polished off the rest of our burgers in silence, I wondered if Dolly knew she had a dead daughter.

"Say thank you to the nice man, Socrates," said Dolly.

The dog let out a couple of gentle woofs that sent the cats scurrying back into hiding.

"Well, let's go to work, shall we?" I said.

"Where's the dressing room?" Dolly asked, as though she were in and out of photographer's studios all day long.

"You don't need a dressing room. I'll take you just as you are."

"I don't know about this," she balked.

"What's the matter?"

She looked down at herself in dismay. "Like this?" she said.

"Sure, that's the way I want you, just the way you are."

"You can't photograph me like this," she protested.

We got trouble in New York City. It would have been too

much to expect this thing to go off without a hitch, but who'd have guessed vanity would be the problem? I'm not a dictator on the set. I never impose my will on talent—it's not my style. Go ahead, spoil my vision. "Okay," I sighed, showing her the dressing room. "Your dressing room, madam."

"Thank you," she said. "I'll only be a minute." She ran back to the cart, rummaged through her belongings, and, with a pile of garments slung over her arm, retreated to the dressing room and closed the door.

I put on a Wes Montgomery tape and waited—I find Wes soothing at times like these. Socrates was sniffing around the studio, hunting for the cats.

"How do I look?" asked Dolly, emerging from the dressing room. I needn't have worried. She looked like she was ready to march in the Greenwich Village Halloween parade.

"Joo look mahvelous, Dolly," I said. Her arms and legs were encased in green Day-Glo spandex. Her layered skirts and tops came in plaids, checks, stripes, polka dots, solids, and moirés. And they clashed like brass and glass in a hurricane. Her face was smeared with lipstick, and her cheeks with rouge. On her feet were a pair of orange Timberland boots, on her head a felt bush hat, with her hair tucked up in the crown.

"I've been saving this outfit for a special occasion," she said, perfectly deadpan. "Do you want Socrates in the picture?"

"Of course."

"Come on, baby, we're gonna get our pictures taken. He's not as pretty as usual. His coat's not as nice as it should be," she lamented, kneeling and brushing the singed fur. "There," she said, tying a bandanna around the dog's neck, "we're ready when you are."

I arranged them, along with their shopping cart and milk crates, against the canvas backdrop, and fired up the strobes. The studio flooded with light. Dolly and Socrates were enveloped in a defused, Vermeer north light as seemingly natural and soft as a summer's evening, yet contrasty enough to pick out detail in a fabric weave or the texture of skin. I gazed at them on the ground glass of the Hasselblad through a 125mm lens. Dolly wiggled, tugging and pulling at herself. This wasn't quite the effect I'd hoped for. They were a couple of clowns. What happened to the poignancy, the pathos, the plight of the homeless I had hoped to exploit? Too late for that now. I fired the camera and a riot of color exploded in my face.

"That was just a Polaroid," I explained, glancing at the sweep hand of my watch. I tore off the paper backing and studied the black-and-white Polaroid. Leeched of color, the scene had undergone a subtle transmutation. Sometimes a photograph bombs—a lot of times a photograph bombs—and sometimes they exceed your expectations, but seldom do they come out exactly as conceived, especially when people are involved. At least that has been my experience. The Polaroid told me that this picture would work. Dolly and Socrates had registered clearly in all their vulnerability and gallantry. I tweaked my lighting, made a second Polaroid—even better than the first—and we began shooting.

They were naturals, changing poses like pros. I took what they gave me, and occasionally asked for a variation, and they gave me that, too. "You know, Dolly," I said, making conversation, "I've met your daughter."

"I don't have a daughter," she said.

I dropped the subject. Were they estranged, or did she mean that literally? I wondered. We worked swiftly, effortlessly, and in silence after that, and when it was over, I felt confident I had some wonderful pictures. The photo muse had worked her magic. "It's a wrap," I said.

"The hour's up?"

"That's right, we don't want to go over."

"It's your money." She shrugged.

"We did good." I beamed, handing her a pen and the standard release form granting me unlimited rights to the photos. "I'll need you to sign this release form, Dolly."

She squinted suspiciously and pored over the form. Then, to my surprise, she signed it without comment. Probably because it read, in consideration for the sum of one hundred dollars. She signed it Dolly Varden.

"In the *Times* they said your name was Miriam Lusk?"

"What are you, Sherlock Holmes or something?"

"I was just wondering, that's all."

"Well, don't. It's none of your business. The name's Dolly Varden, period."

"Whatever you say." I handed her a hundred-dollar bill and it was prestidigitated into her clothing.

I had a sudden inspiration. "Just a minute, Dolly," I said. "I've got an idea. Give me a couple of more minutes, okay?"

"It'll cost you."

"What else is new? Just hold on a minute." I went back to the storage room, found a small pedestal I'd kept for a prop, and humped it onto the set. I placed the computer for the bank ads on top of it. I seated Dolly at the computer with Socrates at her feet, and cranked two more rolls through the camera. Dolly seemed to be enjoying herself. She mugged shamelessly for the camera. It was a gag shot. The client would get a hoot out of the picture, I thought.

"Okay, we're done," I said. "How much is that going to cost me?"

"Twenty bucks," she replied.

I wouldn't argue with that. I gave her a twenty.

"That's it?"

"That's it," I said.

"Now, how do I get out of this dump?" She had the milk crates stacked on the cart, ready to go.

"This way," I said, showing her to the door.

"Come on, Socrates, time to go," she called to the dog, who looked as though he'd found a home.

"He seems to be dragging his paws," I said.

"Socrates!" she said sharply, pushing the loaded cart. He trotted to her heel.

The thought had crossed my mind that, like the dog, she might decide she preferred my place to the doorway. I was relieved to see her eager to clear out. For the life of me, though, I couldn't figure out what her rush was. Was it to hear voices, hallucinate, and throw fits?

"Thanks, Dolly," I said, putting her in the elevator.

"Anytime," she said reasonably.

There goes Susan Ferrante's mom, I thought.

13

What could the grande dame of Manhattan real estate want with me? I wondered. I was on my first cup of coffee, still brushing sleepers out of my eyes and scratching my butt, when I remembered Kiernan saying Florine Ransom would appreciate a visit from me. I showered, shaved, and dressed, then I had a second cup of coffee and called the Thackeray. The old lady was still in bed, but Kiernan said I should come for tea that afternoon.

I was wondering what to wear, when Josephine called. Marc would like a word with me, she said. Fine, put him on, I told her. No, dummy, she said, he wants you to come to the office. When? I asked. Now, she said, as though it were understood. No can do, I'm busy, I'm still working on my first unit. Hold, she said stiffly, and she consulted with the boss. When Marc Ransom whistled, people usually came running. What about tomorrow morning, eight o'clock, in Marc's office? she said. Fine with me, and I take milk and sugar with my coffee, and a buttered bagel or a prune

Danish would be fine, too. We'll see you then, she confirmed officiously, and hung up.

Tito arrived with the mail. "What's this?" he said when he saw the studio.

"I took Dolly's picture last night."

"What for?"

"The new portfolio."

"Uh-huh," he said.

"I think I got some interesting pictures."

"Can't wait to see 'em. She behave herself?"

"She was no trouble at all."

"They drop you on your head when you were a baby?" he asked, eyeing me dubiously.

"I don't remember."

"Should I strike the set?"

"Go ahead."

Without bothering to call, Pharr showed up a few minutes after Tito. He knew a press agent who, for twenty-five hundred bucks, could get my name dropped three different times in various columns. "Does that sound reasonable?" he wanted to know.

"All depends where, doesn't it?" I said.

"Page six the *Post, Rolling Stone, Avenue, Vanity Fair,* and I forget the other one. How's that sound to you?"

"Sounds like a pretty good deal. What do I know?"

"Shall I go ahead with it?"

"I guess so."

"Excellent. I've lined up a few appointments, so if you've got a couple of minutes, I'd like to go through your files and put together a new book to show."

I said okay, and a couple of minutes pretty much killed the morning, and lunch, too. We had sandwiches sent in.

I see you've got a lot of girlie stuff, he said at one point. Book jackets, I do five or six of them a month, I replied. I've got a publisher of literary smut who feeds me the stuff. He's my anchor account. Very nice, he said, examining a sheet of slides. I can sell this stuff in Europe and Japan. Really? I said. I could get to like this guy. Photographers love to sell stock—it's getting paid twice for the same job. A nature photographer I know retired on a single photograph. It's a picture of a yellow caterpillar on a green leaf that he took twenty years ago and sells a dozen times a year, year in, year out. They eat T and A up in Japan, he said. I told him I'd get together a selection. You're only as good as your last picture, he reminded me, on the way out the door with the new portfolio.

"You gonna let that turkey rep you?" Tito wanted to know.

"What have I got to lose?" I shrugged.

"I don't know. What kind of deal did you make with him?"

"Nothing I can't live with," I said. I was in for a hundred and fifty a week, and a bite of twenty-five hundred, some of which was sure to find its way into Pharr's pocket. That's what I had to lose. Meanwhile, it was teatime. What to wear?

I decided to go as a photographer, and pulled on a pair of wide-waled blue corduroys, a checked shirt, deck shoes, and a suede windbreaker before ambling on over to the Thackeray.

The uniform of the day ranged from Rodeo Drive casual chic to British hand-tailored business suits. My suede jacket and corduroys didn't cut it. I was as conspicuous as a sea gull in a penguin rookery in the lobby of the Thackeray. An unctuous bird in white gloves and formal wear challenged me immediately, shooing me to the desk, where I was obliged to state my business.

I admired the decor while I waited for them to clear me with Kiernan. It was easy to see why the Thackeray was rated one of the best hotels in the world. The lobby was rococo splendor redux. Oriental carpets on the floor, oil paintings on the walls; everywhere you looked, museum quality furniture and fresh-cut flowers. And it didn't hurt the cachet of the place that the staff was so immaculate in their uniforms, and so snotty.

I received a deferential nod from the theatrical type behind the desk. He looked too young to be condemned for life to the hotel business—he was probably working his way through ballet school. He directed me to the elevator, and a few minutes later the maid was showing me into Kiernan's office.

"Charles," he said, coming out to greet me from behind a burled-wood desk that was probably three hundred years old.

"What's up, Bernard?" I said, noting how effortlessly we'd gotten on a first-name basis.

"I'd like a word with you when you're finished with Florine," he said.

"No problem," I said.

"You'll find me at my desk," he said.

"See you later," I said, and followed the maid. She led the way to a pair of walnut doors, threw them open, and bid me enter.

"Mr. Byrne, ma'am," said the maid, and I found myself standing before Florine Ransom.

Erect and slim in a black sheath of couturier design, she was a spector of indeterminate age in the twin shafts of diffused light filtering through the French windows. She certainly knew how to stage a scene, I thought. But then she offered her hand, and I was reminded that this was a very old party. It was thin and bone dry, the hand of a ninety-year-old woman, even if there was still some strength left in it. "Thank you for coming, Mr. Byrne," she said in a voice that made no concession to age. "Please be seated."

I thanked her for inviting me, and took a seat. My gaze wandered as I got my bearings. Several table lamps glowed dimly in the corners of the room. It was done in dark polished wood, Bukhara and Persian carpets, and bronze and porcelain bric-a-brac, and made me think of an exclusive men's club. The ubiquitous fresh-cut flowers were the only feminine touch in the handsome room.

"Well, did you enjoy yourself the other evening?" she inquired politely, folding herself carefully into the recesses of a wing chair.

"Very much, and thank you, Mrs. Ransom," I said. She was nearly invisible in the shadows of the backlit chair.

"I'm pleased to hear that, sir. I understand the evening took a rather unfortunate turn for you." It was disconcerting hearing such a clear voice emanating from an amorphous shadow, a phantom.

"You saw the *Times?*"

"Yes."

The maid was standing by patiently.

"Perhaps Mr. Byrne would prefer a drink rather than tea, Louise," she suggested. "I believe we have most everything, Mr. Byrne."

"In that case, bourbon and ice would be nice."

There was an imperceptible movement in the shadows of the chair, and the maid hurried off. "Do you like to drink, sir?" A table lamp was reflected as a pinhole of light where her eyes would be.

"I do, as a matter of fact."

"Good, I like a man who likes to drink," she chuckled. "They are generally more congenial than teetotalers. One must learn to drink. It takes practice. Real drinkers practice every day."

"I'd say I fit the profile."

"Well, I can tell you, sir, they don't know how to drink like they did when I was a girl."

"Is that right?" I said. A little swift math told me she was a girl before Prohibition.

"Yes, but then that's probably because of the drugs. Terrible thing, the drugs."

"Yes, they are," I agreed.

"Nothing new, though. We had them in my day, of course—marijuana, cocaine, morphine, opium—the lot. But nothing like today, I suppose. Instant gratification, that's what drugs promise, and that's all today's young people seem to be interested in."

The maid had returned with a silver service tea tray, which she placed on a coffee table between us. She poured for her mistress. Florine Ransom's claw reached out from the shadows of the chair and received the cup and saucer. The ice cubes clinked musically in the crystal glass as the maid served me the bourbon on a linen cocktail napkin.

"That unfortunate woman—she's a drug user, I suppose," the old lady said.

"I don't think so," I replied, "I think she's mentally ill."

"Yes, that's what they said in the article. Schizophrenic, I believe?"

"Yes." I swallowed a sandwich in one bite. It tasted fishy. "Very good," I said.

"Beluga. You may leave us now, Louise. If I want you, I'll ring."

"Yes, ma'am."

I sipped the bourbon. It was excellent. A private stock, no doubt, as venerable as its owner. I'd tasted bourbon almost as good once in New Orleans.

"Tell me, sir, are you a brave man?"

"I don't think so."

"Only a fool would claim they were brave," said the old lady. "Still, it was brave of you to come to the defense of that poor woman."

"Maybe, but there wasn't much choice."

"Most people would walk away from a confrontation like that."

"I might have, too, it's the wisest thing to do. But since she wasn't a stranger, I had to do something. You never know how you'll act in a situation like that until you're faced with it. Is that why you've asked me here, to talk about the other night?"

"And to find out what kind of man you are."

"Well, it's your caviar and bourbon, Mrs. Ransom."

"That's correct, sir. There is one other thing, though."

"What's that?"

"I'd like you to arrange for me to meet your friend Dolly Varden."

"May I ask why?"

"You may, but I'm not sure I'll tell you."

"You can meet her anytime you want, you know. She's in her doorway most days. You hardly need me for that." My eyes had grown accustomed to the light, and I could make her out dimly in the gloom of the chair.

"Your candor is refreshing, sir," she said in a flinty tone, "and your suggestion has merit. However, I had in mind a private meeting. I thought, perhaps, at a prearranged time

I'd drop by in a limo and we'd have a chat. Is the woman clean?"

"She's clean, all right—reasonably so, anyway."

"Good. I would appreciate it, then, if you would speak to her and make the necessary arrangements."

"But why would Dolly want to meet with you?"

"You mean, what's in it for her?" It was easy for those sharp features to look hard.

"That's not what I meant, but with Dolly there's always a quid pro quo."

"It's been my experience in life there's always a quid pro quo, sir. How much do you want?" She looked alert, and eager to haggle.

"I don't want anything, Mrs. Ransom."

"No?" There was a note of disappointment in her voice.

"No. But I'll have to be able to promise Dolly something. Dolly wouldn't hold the door for you without expecting something."

"Just tell me how much this is going to cost, Mr. Byrne, and be done with it."

"A hundred dollars," I said.

There was a pause. "And whom do I pay?"

"I'd prefer you give it to Dolly yourself, when you meet her." I helped myself to another sandwich.

"Yes, of course," she said. "It's settled, then, you'll arrange it?"

"I don't think I could refuse you if I wanted to, Mrs. Ransom."

She was cackling to herself as though at some private joke. It was unnerving.

"Did I say something funny?" I asked.

"You are an amusing man, sir. A hundred dollars is what you might leave a waiter."

"Not where I eat."

"No, I suppose not. Being rich is better than being poor, Mr. Byrne."

"I never had any doubts, Mrs. Ransom."

"But it isn't all it's cracked up to be. I expect to pay more for what I want, and am seldom disappointed. I apologize if I've impugned your honesty."

"I hardly noticed."

"I'd like to meet your friend as soon as possible."

"I'll speak to her tonight."

"Wonderful. Perhaps Louise can freshen your drink?" she suggested.

"I don't think so."

"Nonsense," she said, knowing what was best for me, or what I wanted. She rang for the maid. "The papers said her real name is Miriam—Miriam Lusk, I believe. What should I call her, Dolly or Miriam?"

"If you expect to have any kind of conversation with her, I'd call her Dolly. That seems to be how she thinks of herself." As soon as I saw the maid, I drained my glass. It was too good to waste even a single drop.

"Mr. Byrne will have another bourbon, Louise," said the old lady.

"Yes, ma'am," she said, taking my glass.

Elbows propped up on the arms of the wing chair, fingertips touching, forming a pyramid, Florine Ransom peered at me speculatively over her hands while waiting for the maid to exit. "You asked earlier why I wanted to meet your friend," she began, as the doors closed silently.

"I'm still wondering."

"You're a photographer, is that correct?"

"Uh-huh."

"Work for hire?"

"That's right."

"A precarious existence," she commented.

"It's what I'm used to," I said, feeling like pretty small potatoes.

"And you're used to poverty as well, I suppose?" She harrumphed, as though I'd been impertinent.

I might have replied that rich and poor were relative conditions, as in: I cursed myself for having no shoes until I met a man who had no feet. "Actually, most of my energy is spent resisting poverty," I replied mildly.

"No doubt. What I'm getting at, though, is you don't seem the type to be working a fiddle, as we used to say."

"You invited me here, Mrs. Ransom," I reminded her.

"And I have reason for caution, sir."

The maid returned and served my drink. The old lady fixed her gaze on me until the maid left the room, and then a moment longer. I had another slug of bourbon. "You've been frank with me, sir," she began, "so I will be as frank with you as I can, since you do not appear to have an interest in this matter. As you may have heard, I had another child besides my son Marc."

"I've heard that," I said, "a daughter, deceased."

"That's what they say, is it?"

"It's not true?" I gazed at her expectantly.

"I was young, a teenager," she said, her voice deliberate and flat. "I had a child out of wedlock, and was abandoned by the father, a college boy whose family owned a brownstone right here in Murray Hill. It was quite an elegant neighborhood in those days. Well, sir, what was I to do?"

I shrugged.

"I'll tell you what I did. I asked a couple I knew to take care of the child for me, and I went to work. There was no welfare in those days, none of this public assistance stuff you have today," she said scornfully. "I did whatever it took to get along. I scrubbed floors. I worked as a seamstress in the sweatshops on lower Broadway. I was a waitress, a secretary, and a shop girl. And no matter how bad the pay was, I always managed to send a little something to my friends for the care of the baby."

"It must have been difficult," I sympathized.

"It was. I was smart, though, and it didn't take me long to figure out I was going nowhere fast. One day, I bumped into a girl I'd worked with behind the counter at Woolworth's. Well, didn't she look grand. I mean, she was dressed to kill in a fox stole, silk stockings, the works. She looked like her ship had come in. 'What happened, Helen, did you find a rich husband?' I asked. She laughed, thought that was hilarious. 'Come to Schrafft's with me,' she said, 'and I'll tell you what's up.' Well, she treated me to an ice cream soda, and brought me up to date. She had more money than she knew what to do with, she said. She had charge accounts at all the best stores, and her rent was paid each month by generous gentlemen." The old lady chortled at the memory. "She suggested I could do the same thing if I wanted to, and she knew some butter-and-egg men who might like me."

"Mrs. Ransom," I said, enthralled, "you don't need to tell me all this." I had a feeling I was about to hear more than I should.

"Don't be ridiculous, sir," she snapped. "I'm not ashamed of anything I've done. I did what I had to do. Believe me, I know what it is to be poor, dirt poor. I came up on the lower East Side, three and four to a bed in a cold-water flat, the kitchen and bath shared by the other families in the building. I know what it is to be kicked around the streets of New York. . . . I wasn't shocked, or offended, by Helen's proposition. My only concern was men wouldn't find me as attractive as Helen. Well, I needn't have worried on that account. Men liked me well enough. Before long I had more of them than a passenger train could haul." She chuckled. I helped myself to another swallow of her good bourbon.

"The only difference between the rich and everyone else, Mr. Byrne," she confided, "is the rich have the money. Well, sir, I made up my mind that one day I'd have money, too. I saved the money I made. Marc's father, and my future husband, was a client of mine. He helped me invest in real estate, and taught me the ropes. Meanwhile, the woman who was looking out for my baby died suddenly. Her husband had no way of getting in touch with me at the time. He couldn't manage with the baby, and so he put her up for adoption. By the time I found out about it, it was too late. The court had already sealed the adoption papers. Later, of course, with a bribe or two in the right places, I did get access to the adoption papers. Unfortunately, by then her adoptive family had all died off, and there was no trace of what had become of my daughter. I did everything in my power to track her down—private detectives, the works— all to no avail. Then, last summer, I was contacted by a young woman with whom I was casually acquainted, and out of the blue she suddenly claimed she was my grand-daughter. I must tell you, sir, this is not the first time something like this has happened. Of course, the claims have always been spurious, and nothing has ever come of them."

"But this time it was different?"

"Yes, but I'm not prepared to say why. The strange part is, I never heard from the young woman again."

"That's strange. Maybe, though, as you would say, it was a fiddle, and she got cold feet and couldn't go through with it."

"Perhaps."

"But surely you don't think that Dolly is your daughter?"

"No, of course not. She's too young to be my daughter. But she's not too young to be my granddaughter."

"What makes you think that?"

"As I've already said, I'm not prepared to say."

"Well, I hope it's true, for Dolly's sake."

"I wouldn't get my hopes too high, sir."

"Obviously you have some reason for thinking it's possible, otherwise why would you be so eager for this meeting?"

"Let's just say I have a few questions I'd like to ask her."

"There's no guarantee she'll cooperate."

"I understand. Just arrange the meeting, and let's see what happens."

"I'll see what I can do, Mrs. Ransom."

"Very good. Well, sir, you have heard my story, or part of it anyway. As you can see, I've made my share of mistakes, but I make no apologies for the way I've lived my life." She paused, and rang for the maid. I sensed teatime had concluded, and finished my drink. "It's a man's world, Mr. Byrne, and it was even more so when I was young. But I was always convinced I was as good as any man, and I've lived my life like a man. I beat the men at their own game."

I glanced around in admiration. "You certainly have, Mrs. Ransom," I said. When you reach ninety, your future is pretty slim, and the past is everything. The old lady climbed to her feet. I returned my glass to the tray and followed suit. Louise, the maid, parted the sliding doors.

"Thank you for coming, Mr. Byrne," she said, extending her hand. "I've enjoyed our little chat."

"It was my pleasure, Mrs. Ransom," I assured her. I took her hand, and again her strength surprised me.

"How did it go?" Bernard asked, as soon as the walnut doors closed.

"All right, I guess."

"Did she give you the I-did-it-my-way speech?" he asked, eyes flashing.

"Something like that."

"How tiresome."

"What was it you wanted to speak to me about, Bernard?"

"Step into my office," he said, leading the way. "Have a chair. Want another bourbon?" I noticed he had a glass of something on his desk.

"I've had enough, thanks." I took a seat and waited.

He moved behind the desk, sat, and leaned back in his chair, making himself elaborately at home. "Well, I understand you're the man to see about photographing a tapestry," he said, striking a pose, hands folded behind his head. "What do you charge for that sort of thing?"

"Three eight-by-ten chromes for five hundred dollars."

The smile vanished. "So much?"

"That's what I charged young Ransom."

"Really."

"That's right."

"Well, he's richer than we are," he said with a pout. "Er, I was hoping you'd put something on it for me."

"For you?" I stood up to go.

He jumped to his feet. "Never mind," he said quickly, "I'll have to speak to Florine. I'm sure it will be all right."

"You have my number. This way out?" I pointed down the corridor.

"Yes, yes." He wagged his head, a shock of hair in his eyes, his body quivering like a two-hundred-pound sheepdog that didn't know what was expected of him.

The osteopath passed me in the lobby. "Hello, Dr. Mumminger," I said. He looked at me as though I were a germ. "Charles Byrne," I said helpfully. "We were dinner companions the other night."

"Oh, yes, the photographer," he said. "Nice to see you again. Excuse me, I'm in a hurry."

"I understand," I said, sensing I was getting the brush-off.

I wondered if Medicare picked up his tab and decided, nah, rich is when a doctor will make a house call.

The walk back to the studio gave me a few minutes to mull over Florine Ransom's story. It would be a real Cinderella story if Dolly turned out to be the old lady's granddaughter. It would be almost as good as having your number come up in Lotto. The odds were about as long. And if Dolly was the old lady's granddaughter, then Susan Ferrante was the great-granddaughter. Atta girl, Susy. And then a more sobering thought struck me: if that were the case, Sharon Raynes was also a great-granddaughter. Well, as the old lady had said, she wouldn't get her hopes up. Still, if it turned out that they were related, it would make a helluva follow-up story for Diedre Mahoney, the reuniting of grandmother and grandchild. There did seem to be a downside to all of this, though. It seemed cruel, for a hundred bucks, to check Dolly out and discard her if she didn't come up with the right answers. Although, I don't suppose Dolly needed to know why she was being questioned.

I glanced at my watch. It wasn't six yet. If I hurried, I could catch Tito before he went home. I ran into him on the street, in front of my building. "How was tea?" he wanted to know.

"Tea was bourbon."

"You were right at home."

"I mean this was bourbon." I kissed the tips of my fingers and exploded them in a gesture of magnificence. "The rich are different than the rest of us, my man."

"Yeah, they've got all the money."

"That's what the old lady said."

"What did she want?"

"She wants to meet Dolly."

"Really. What for?"

"She thinks Dolly might be a long-lost relative of hers."

"Hey, what about me, man? I could be a long-lost relative of hers, too, bro." He grinned.

"Yeah, right. Did I miss anything while I was gone?"

"We're on for tomorrow with the bank ads. I booked it for three, all right?"

"Sounds good. See you in the morning. I may be a little late. I've got a power breakfast with Marc Ransom, the son."

"If he's looking for any long-lost relatives, I am definitely one of them, okay, bro? And, Charlie, we getting any work outta all this hobnobbing you're doing with these rich people?"

"I think we've got another tapestry to shoot. A guy named Bernard Kiernan should be calling."

"Can't hardly wait."

I hustled upstairs, changed my clothes, hauled the Lejeune down off the ceiling hooks, and headed out for the park. I'd deal with Dolly on my way back from the ride.

I did about ten miles, counting the trip uptown and back—not a lot on a bike, but enough to break a sweat. I never stopped pedaling, and rode steadily at about twenty miles an hour the whole time. I didn't do the big loop all the way up to 110th Street, but instead took the cutoff in the nineties. That circuit's about four miles, maybe more, and I did it twice.

Dolly and Socrates were enjoying a frugal repast from plastic trays when I pulled up to their doorway. Food seemed to have a soothing effect on Dolly; I found her rational, and almost amiable. I told her there was someone I knew who'd read about her in the newspapers and was willing to pay a hundred bucks for the privilege of speaking with her a few minutes. As I'd thought, the mention of money had the desired effect. For a hundred bucks, she'd talk to a lamppost, she said. Why not, I thought—so far she's been doing it for nothing. She asked when this interview was likely to take place, and I said I'd try and set it up for the day after tomorrow. I had a full day tomorrow. She said fine, go ahead and set it up, she had nothing on her calendar for that day.

"Okay, I'll get back to you," I said, petting the dog before departing.

"Gimme a dollar, Charlie!" she said, palm extended.

14

By seven-thirty the next morning, I'd showered, shaved, dressed, fueled up on coffee, and was ready to rumble in the asphalt jungle. I dressed for success, in my Brooksgate suit. The day was sunny and bright, the sky cloudless. The streets belonged to the achievers. I strode off purposefully to my eight o'clock meeting with the man with the five big units.

Ransom's office was on Park Avenue and Fifty-fifth Street, a pleasant fifteen-minute walk from the studio. Checking the number, I noticed, with mild surprise, Ransom neither owned nor managed the building. We had something in common: he rented, too. There had to be an angle, of course, and I wondered what it was. Maybe it was as simple as writing off the rent and having more space to let. Whatever the reasons, I sure would like to be a fly on the wall when he made a lease with his landlord. The elevator dropped me off in a hallway that was impersonal, bland, and cramped. There were other offices on the floor, entities like a holding company, a fund, an import-export business, all concealed discreetly behind plain, painted metal doors.

Ransom's door opened into a sparsely furnished holding area where there was no sign of life. I glanced at my watch. I was right on time. I poked my head through the receptionist's window and pinged the hand bell on the desk. "Anyone home?" I called.

Josephine darted past an open doorway and reappeared holding open the door for me. "Good morning," she said. "Come on in. Marc's busy at the moment. Follow me . . . can I get you a coffee?"

"No thanks," I said, trailing after her into a large room with more than a dozen desks, most of them already occupied at this early hour.

"Wait here," she said, indicating a plastic straight-back chair beside one of the few empty desks. "I'll let Marc know you're here."

"Fine," I said, and took a seat. Smiling, I glanced around the room. Several people smiled back curiously. I don't know what I expected, but I was definitely underwhelmed. After Ransom's apartment, and the hotel, and the old lady's suite, I guess I expected some kind of display. Most of the advertising agencies I dealt with went in for flashy decor: blond wood floors, suede walls, simulated leather and chrome furniture, neon, and high-tech glitz—these were practically de rigueur. They tried too hard. But Ransom didn't seem to be trying at all. His office was about as pretentious as a fly-by-night operation selling vacation homes in the Poconos.

A woman at the far end of the room rose from her desk and sashayed to the door. She was about my age, and wore a tailored skirt and a silk blouse that showed her off to good advantage. Her jewelry jangled as she walked, and one of the Chanel perfume numbers trailed her, like a spoor, as she exited the room.

"How's business, Charlie?"

I looked back, and Nelson Rudd was sitting behind the desk in his shirtsleeves, grinning like he'd just popped up out of a gopher hole. "Oh, Nelson, hello. I didn't see you there. How are you?"

"Jackie Dhiel, our co-op salesperson." He smiled at the door.

"Very nice." I smiled, man-to-man.

"If that's what you like."

What's not to like? I remembered Josephine saying that that was what the accountant, Joel Lesser, liked.

"Are you busy these days?" said Rudd.

"I've got some work, but I'm always looking for more."

"I'll bet. Pretty competitive business, photography, huh?"

"There's a lot of good guys out there. Any idea what Ransom has in mind?"

"We may have a job for you."

"Really?"

"I think so. I better let Marc handle this, though—he's the one—"

"Marc will see you now," Josephine interrupted, beckoning from the doorway. "You, too, Nellie."

I bounced to my feet. "This could be my big break." I grinned at Rudd.

He frowned at my attempt at levity. Funny, I thought the guy was quite a little kidder himself. He had cracked a very irreverent joke at the matriarch's expense the other night, but then he didn't work for her. Well, Marc Ransom was probably no joking matter.

Josephine ushered me into a corner office thrown together with the same casualness as the rest of the place, except that it was thrown together with good stuff, on a par with the Thackeray and Ransom's own pad. Ransom and Joel Lesser had their heads together, poring over spread sheets. My pal, Matty Fallon, beefy and florid, overflowed a dainty chair. "How are you, Byrne?" he said, offering a beefy hand without getting up.

"Good," I said, squeezing his hand briefly.

Karl Sauter, the architect, in shirtsleeves and suspenders, leaned against a table supporting an architectural model of a high rise or office tower, I couldn't tell which. His gaze was neutral, his arms folded across his chest.

Ransom looked up from the spread sheet he and Joel Lesser had been pouring over. I had an eerie sensation of being able to look right through him, because his eyes were opaqued out by reflected light off the lenses of his wire-rimmed glasses. "Thank you for coming, Mr. Byrne," he said after a slight hesitation.

"My pleasure."

"That'll be all for now, Joel," he said, and the accountant gathered up his materials and silently withdrew. Like Sauter, Ransom was also in shirtsleeves and suspenders. Josephine said he worked out to Jane Fonda exercise videos, and it showed. His stomach was flat, and he seemed as spare and hard as extruded steel. Only Rudd was smaller than he, but Ransom's presence easily filled and dominated the room. "Do you know everyone?" he asked.

"Yes." I nodded.

"Good, have a seat, then," he said, gesturing to an antique chair next to Rudd. He waited for me to get settled before continuing. "Perhaps this is not your sort of work, but we'd like to have pictures taken of the neighborhood surrounding the La Fleur Hotel. Are you familiar with the area?"

"I know it well, quite a few of my suppliers are located in the area."

"Good. Are you interested in the job?"

"I'm always interested in work."

"Very good. I assume you are aware, then, of the condition of the neighborhood?"

"Of course."

"Well, we'd like you to document it."

"You mean the street people, the crack dealers, panhandlers, purse snatchers . . . the people living in cardboard cartons?"

"That's the general idea," Fallon interjected, "the soaped-up storefronts, the grunginess of the hotel, the filth and dirt on the streets, the whole nine yards. Rip open a Glad bag or two and spill some garbage if you have to."

"We'd like the photographs to look as grimy and squalid as possible," said Ransom.

"Color, or black and white?" I asked.

"Black and white, Marc," Sauter advised. "It'll look far worse in black and white."

I agreed. Usually I'm asked to make things look better than they are. "How soon do you need the photos?" I asked.

Ransom looked at Fallon. "Within the month," said Fallon.

"No problem," I said. "It might be helpful, though, to know how the photographs will be used." Actually, I knew all I needed to know to do the job, but since fee and usage are linked in my business—you wouldn't want to see a picture in a national magazine when you'd been paid trade publication prices for it—I was fishing to get an idea of what the job was worth. The wider the usage, the larger the fee. "You know, where will the photos appear?" I added, as they stared at me blankly.

"They won't appear anywhere," said Fallon. "We wanna use them to get the city to commit to a clean-up, like they did in Union Square, that's all."

"Presentation only," I said. "We should talk money."

Ransom looked as stunned as if I'd told him his fly was open. "Take that up with Nellie," he said curtly. "Anything else?" he asked, glancing at the others.

They shook their heads.

"Nellie?"

"I think we covered everything," said Rudd.

"That's all for now, then," said Ransom, and he turned his attention to papers on his desk.

"Come with me, Charlie," said Rudd as we prepared to leave, "we'll talk money."

"My pleasure."

"Just a moment, Mr. Byrne," said Ransom, looking up from the papers, his eyeglass lenses opaque again. "I'd like a word with you in private."

"You know where to find me when you're done," Rudd said to me, and he filed out with the others.

"I understand you met with my mother yesterday."

Josephine must have told him. "She asked me to drop by," I admitted. "She's quite a woman."

"How so?" he said bluntly, his gaze intent from behind the thick lenses.

"She's a very old lady, and her mind's so clear," I said, fumbling. "She's as sharp as a tack."

"She asked to meet you because of the *Times* article, correct?"

"Yes."

"I thought so," he said pensively, "and I suppose she wants to meet the bag lady?"

"It's already arranged. Is there a problem?"

"No, no," he said, shaking his head in resignation, "it's quite all right." He dropped his eyes back down to the desk. "That's all, Mr. Byrne," he said abruptly, dismissing me.

The old lady hadn't sworn me to secrecy; still, I felt as though I'd betrayed her confidence. Was Ransom's job real, or merely a pretext to get me there to pump me for information about his mother? I wondered. It would be easy to get caught sideways between these two. The old lady was some piece of work. If she was busting sonny's balls—I'd lay odds she could be a world-class bitch when she put her mind to it—it was nothing to me, she wasn't my mother. I kind of liked her. Feisty old folks are cute when they're not your own. On the other hand, Marc Ransom would be forever opaque to me. It wasn't his fault. He was just too smart and too rich, that's all. He'd caught me off guard with his bluntness.

On second thought, the job was probably legit. Ransom, as I recalled, had wanted to meet with me before I went to his mother's. That didn't mean he wasn't keeping tabs on her, though. The thought that he and Dolly could possibly be related made me smile. One thing was sure—as seductive as the smell of Ransom money was, they weren't giving any of it away. No one ever put together a unit working for rich people.

I plunked myself down in the chair beside Rudd's desk.

"How do you guys work?" said Rudd.

"What do you mean?"

"Do you charge by the photograph, by the hour, the day, or what?" He was real innocent, like asking if he could sit in on the next hand, claiming nickels and dimes were his usual limits, and then asking if someone could change a yard.

"That depends," I said. "Why don't you tell me how much you've got to spend?"

"Why don't I give you my credit cards?" He smiled.

"Well, how much would you like to spend?" I was getting the feeling we were playing in different ballparks.

"I wouldn't like to spend a dime. This is Marc's idea. We could make just as good a case without pictures, as far as I'm concerned."

That was his brushback pitch. "All right, let's say fifteen hundred dollars, and film and processing, and prints." I could play hardball, too.

"Let's say five hundred dollars for the works." He grinned.

"Let's say good-bye," I said, standing.

"Hey, wait a minute," he said.

I waited.

"Seven fifty." He grinned.

"I'm outta here, Nellie. Tell Marc thanks, but no thanks."

"Don't go," he pleaded, grabbing my arm. "I can't tell him that. What's the matter with you? Don't they haggle in your business?"

"You want to haggle?"

He shrugged. "Nothing's engraved in stone. Everything's negotiable."

"Okay, how about twenty-five hundred dollars?" How'd he like that chin music? If they refused the first offer, make the next higher. According to Josephine, that was Ransom's technique.

"All right, fifteen," Rudd said sourly.

I offered him my hand. "You've got yourself a photographer, Nellie."

"And you photograph the model, too," he said, gripping my hand.

"What model?"

"The architectural model in Marc's office. We're gonna need pictures of that, too."

"No one said anything about a model."

"I just did."

"Okay, Nellie, send it over to the studio, and I'll shoot it." If it was important for the little guy to think he'd gotten over on me, what did I care?

That noon I met Stein and Strunk for lunch.

"What's the occasion, why the lunch, P.C.?"

"Because we want your help, Byrne," the big black cop said, shoveling in another mouthful of noodles.

I called him P.C., he called me Byrne. Stein looked on with bemused indifference. We were twirling chopsticks in bowls of subgum chow fun in a joint called Wok Man, P. C. Strunk's Szechuan restaurant de jour.

"Since you're hanging out with JoJo, we'd like you to stay in touch," Strunk went on, without looking up from his bowl. The man was a glutton for MSG. "For instance, what's she do for this guy Ransom?"

"She's an errand girl," Stein said.

"Let's hear it from Byrne, Henry. You guys through with this?" He indicated the remains in the serving bowls. We nodded. He emptied the leftovers into his bowl. "She give you her job definition, Byrne?"

"Henry said it, she's an executive errand girl."

"How'd she get the Polish name?" Stein asked.

"She was married to a guy named Cyzeski," said Strunk.

"And she's a friend of yours, P.C.?" said Stein.

"Was, in the old days."

"She cop the big bamboo?" Stein grinned.

"You'll never know, Henry," Strunk said primly. He glanced over at me. "Think she'll be helpful, Byrne?"

"For old times' sake, you mean?" I asked, wondering what he had in mind.

"Yeah, for old times' sake."

"I don't know how you remember her, P.C., but she doesn't strike me as the sentimental type."

"You're probably right," he said solemnly. "Maybe she's a disgruntled employee—anything in that angle?"

"I don't think so, P.C.," I said. "It's my impression our old friend JoJo is as happy as a pig in shit, being so close to five hundred million dollars."

"Loyalty is one thing money can buy, P.C.," said Stein. "And besides, by the time the Cyzeski babe knew anything, it would be a done deal. Marc Ransom's not going to run off at the mouth to some broad he's been tumbling, if that's what you're thinking, P.C."

"Just looking for an angle, fellows," said the cop, pushing his bowl away and wiping his mouth.

"You still haven't told me what this is all about. Is Ransom under investigation?" I said.

"Did I say that?" Strunk grinned.

"The Attorney General's Office has had an anonymous tip that Ransom's been ripping off his investors," Stein explained. "Ransom-owned companies service the buildings his syndicates control, and they overcharge for cleaning, maintenance, or whatever it is that they do, thus transferring millions of dollars from the investors' pockets to Ransom's pockets. It's an old landlord trick."

"And that's only the tip of the iceberg," said Strunk.

"He writes off millions in personal living expenses against the Thackeray," said Stein, "but they all do that."

"I'll let the tax boys worry about that," Strunk said. "What interests me is, 'them that gives, gets,' if you know what I mean?"

"I don't know what you mean," I said.

"Illegal campaign contributions," said Stein. "But, hell, P.C., that's business."

"Dirty business," said Strunk.

"Without contributing to a politician's campaign, you couldn't build a birdhouse in this town, P.C.," Stein said. "It isn't as though Ransom gives a damn who gets elected— he probably doesn't even bother to vote—but what's he gonna do when he needs a code violation overlooked, or a building permit, or a variance?"

"Yeah, but he does it illegally through dummy corporations set up expressly for the purpose," said Strunk.

Stein shrugged. "It's the quid pro quo for doing business. Ransom didn't invent the system."

"Maybe not," said Strunk, "but the situation is one elected official has sole control over billions of dollars of government workers' pension funds. It's an invitation to steal, a system ripe for corruption. You and I both know he ain't letting out a dime of that money to a guy like Ransom unless Ransom has kicked into the war chest, Henry." He popped his eyes, showing the whites, to emphasize his point.

"Who is this guy?" I asked.

"He's talking about Randell Elliott, the comptroller at Ransom's party the other night," Stein explained. "Someone leaked a memo in which he supposedly instructed his top staff that only them that gives, gets."

"And Ransom gives," I said.

"We think so. What we'd like to know is how," said Strunk.

"Lemme get this straight," I said. "Ransom gets around the campaign contributions law by giving, and giving big, through dummy corporations. In a show of gratitude, the comptroller invests pension funds in a Ransom syndicate. Ransom then milks the syndicate like a cash cow through his service businesses."

"That's the general idea, Byrne."

Stein toyed with a pair of chopsticks. "You're gonna have a hard time proving it, P.C."

"It's gonna be a challenge. Sounds like your heart's not in this thing, Henry."

"I know the family a long time, and the old lady's always been on the level with me. I wouldn't want to see her get hurt."

"I understand," said Strunk.

"But Marc Ransom isn't holding any of my markers," said Stein.

"Glad to hear that, Henry."

"Then Ransom is under investigation," I said.

"You didn't hear me say that," said Strunk.

"I see, you're neither confirming nor denying Ransom's under investigation, is that correct?"

"That's correct."

"But you'd like me to be a snitch?" I saw Stein wince, and realized that had been a bad choice of words.

"I'm appealing to your sense of civic duty. Besides, I don't have anything I can use on you to make you snitch."

Strunk was holding a couple of my markers. I still owed him big-time for the Ali Bhutto photograph, and then, as I have said, there was the Ponzi scheme business. "Since you put it that way, P.C., I don't see how I can refuse."

"See, I told you we could count on him, Henry," Strunk beamed.

"Swell," said Stein, without enthusiasm.

"Don't get your hopes up, P.C. JoJo and I aren't exactly a

hot item, and I'm hardly an insider when it comes to Marc Ransom."

"No kidding," Stein added sarcastically.

"Just keep your ears open and let me know what you hear."

"I don't know if this is of any interest to you, but I think Ransom's cranking up to build on the site of the old La Fleur Hotel."

"Where'd you hear that?" said Stein, perking up.

"I just came from Ransom's office. They offered me a job shooting a documentary of Herald Square."

"See how helpful he is already, Henry?" Strunk grinned.

"But that property belongs to his mother," said Stein. "Ransom's been after her for years to let him develop it, and she's always turned him down. She's got some cockamamie attachment to the place. It was one of her first properties."

"Maybe he's come into his inheritance early," said Strunk, "maybe his mother has finally relented and transferred the hotel over to him."

"In a blue moon," said Stein. "If anything, it's in the name of one of Marc's holding companies. But let's say she was willing to sell and he had clear title, he still couldn't do anything with the place. The Landmarks Commission has to rule on the site first, and if that's not enough, there's a new law going into effect soon that says, in essence, SROs are untouchable. If a developer razes an SRO, he can't build on the site for eighteen months, and he is creamed with fines."

"Well, Nelson Rudd asked me to photograph an architectural model that was sitting in Ransom's office. I got the impression it was part of the job."

"I still don't see how Ransom can develop the property," said Stein stubbornly.

"Isn't it Matty Fallon's job to figure out the angles?" said Strunk.

"He's Ransom's Mr. Fixit at City Hall," Stein conceded.

"Seems I can't turn around these days without bumping into Matty Fallon," I said.

"Where have you been running into Fallon?" Strunk asked.

"Well, he was at the meeting this morning. He was at Florine Ransom's birthday party . . ."

"So were you and Henry, so what?" said Strunk.

"So this—the first time I ran into him was in the courtyard in back of Ransom's apartment. Did you hear about the jumper?"

Their blank stares told me they hadn't. I told them how Tito and I heard the breaking glass, and the scream, and how we found the body in the courtyard below.

"When was this?" said Strunk.

"It was the day of the blackout."

"And Fallon was there?"

"He showed up with Susan Ferrante right after it happened."

"Susan Ferrante?" said Stein. "That's a familiar name. . . ."

I reminded him of Diedre Mahoney's article in the *Times*.

"The bag lady's daughter?"

"Uh-huh, the bag lady's daughter," I repeated. "She identified the body. She is the dead woman's sister."

"Phew," said Stein, "talk about a dysfunctional family."

"You guys have lost me," Strunk complained.

Stein did me the favor of explaining it to Strunk.

"Okay, I get it, they're a family. But I still don't see what the hell the bag lady has to do with Ransom," he grumbled.

"Patience, P.C.," I advised, "there is a connection."

"Well, hurry up and cut to the chase."

"Okay, Mahoney also mentioned my name in her article, and because Florine Ransom had just met me, and the incident happened the night of her party, and whatever other reasons she might have had, she invited me to tea."

"How nice," said Strunk.

"She asked me to arrange a meeting for her with Dolly."

"Dolly Varden?" Stein mused. "What kind of name is that?"

"Dolly Varden's a rather colorful character in a Dickens novel titled *Barnaby Rudge,*" said Strunk, and then, seeing our astonishment at this surprising display of erudition, added, "I've read everything the man wrote."

"I thought a Dolly Varden was a fish," said Stein.

"A trout, actually," said Strunk. "They took the name from the Dickens character."

"Fascinating," said Stein, and he switched his gaze to me. "So Florine had you to tea, huh?"

"That's right."

"I suppose she said she thinks Dolly Varden is her long-lost daughter?"

"No, she said she thought it was possible Dolly might be her granddaughter."

Stein rolled his eyes. "That's a new twist."

"You've heard the story?"

"I've heard it," he sighed.

"You've lost me again, fellas," said Strunk.

"Forget about it, P.C.," said Stein, "it's not important."

"Why are we talking about it, then?"

"Here's the thing," I said. "Would a suicide jump through a closed window or would she open it first?"

"We're back to what's-her-name, the sky diver?" said Strunk.

"Raynes, Sharon Raynes," I said. "The point is, she was a friend of Marc's. She got her apartment through him. JoJo says she was a girlfriend, that Marc used to call her Acid Raynes behind her back."

"Sounds like he was crazy about her." Strunk grinned. "But are you saying she was pushed?"

"What I'm trying to say is, I think she would have opened the window first if she was going to jump."

"You'd think so," Stein agreed. "Was there a note? Suicides usually leave a note."

"I don't know. You might want to ask Fallon that question."

"Man, you're turning out to be a regular blabbermouth, Byrne," said Strunk.

"Just doing my civic duty, P.C. It seems strange to me, though, that Fallon and Ferrante were on the scene as quickly as they were. And it also seems strange there was nothing in the papers about a jumper on Park Avenue."

"Fallon must have had it hushed up," said Stein.

"Yeah, but why? Something isn't kosher."

"I appreciate your trying to help, Byrne," said Strunk, calling for the check.

"You asked for it."

"Okay, but if Ransom gave his girlfriend flying lessons without a parachute, that's homicide's problem. All I wanna do is nail the guy for fraud. Keep me posted, though."

"My ears are your ears, P.C."

"Good man." He beamed.

"Hey," said Stein, "you guys know the difference between a condom and a condominium?"

"I'll bite, Henry. What's the difference between a condo and condominium?" said Strunk.

"A condom only holds one schmuck at a time."

"Shall we split the check?" Strunk suggested, stone-faced.

"Trouble with cops is they have no sense of humor, and they're cheap," Stein bitched.

15

The intermittent flashing of the strobes, the steady whir of the fans cooling the strobe heads and inflating the billowing fabric bank lights, the rustle of strangers—agency people, their clients, the talent—milling about, the stylists, makeup artists, and assistants moving purposely about their business, the scattered muted conversations, the rock-music-pulsing-beneath-the-room tone, the anticipation, the charged atmosphere—it's always like this just before a shoot. That's what I stepped into after lunch. It was time to make pictures. For the next two hours I'd seek perfection on the ground glass, and find it because I was a pro. That's how I earned my money.

"Where's Carlson?" I asked Tito, glancing around.

"He called, said he was on his way."

"Okay, let's start without him." I've never known an art director to be on time for a shooting. They love to make an entrance. Not too late, just late enough to be the last one on the set. It's latent resentment at having to take a backseat to a photographer.

The stylist had the first model on the set, plucking and pulling at the sleeves and collar of his sport shirt and crew-neck sweater. He was a clean-cut young black, an actor impersonating a college student. There were six of these ads in all, and the casting, like a foxhole in a WWII movie, reflected every major ethnic group and all the genders. A freckle-faced, redheaded actress in medical whites imitating an obstetrician waited on deck.

We made a couple of Polaroids. Tito tweaked the lighting and, to the consternation of the account executive, who wanted us to wait for Carlson, we began shooting.

I was changing backs on the Hasselblad when our tardy A.D. shuffled onto the set. Carlson was an avuncular guy with an incipient paunch, a red beard streaked liberally with gray, and a habit of peering at you from over a pair of horn-rims perched on the end of his nose, which he was doing at the moment. "How you doing, funky draws?" he said.

"Fine, wanna see some 'roids?"

He shifted his gaze to the set. "Looks good," he commented. The model smiled demurely. Tito handed the Polaroids to him, and he pushed his glasses up on his nose and scrutinized them.

"How's the wardrobe?" I asked anxiously. The stylist hovered even more anxiously over his shoulder.

"The clothes are fine," he said to her, and motioned for us to huddle out of earshot. "This guy look a little fruity to you?"

"A little, but he's got a good look. He'll be all right."

"Hey, pal!" he called.

"Me?" said the model, hand on chest.

"Yeah, what's your name?"

"Robert."

"Robert, huh. Looking good, Robert," he said amiably.

"Thank you." Robert squirmed with pleasure.

Turning to me, he said, "Make sure he comes off like a Robert, and not a Roberta. Got a beer?"

"Is the Pope Polish? You know where to find them."

He shuffled off in quest of a cool one, only to be waylaid by the account exec, who began chewing his ear sotto voce.

"I'm the only one allowed to whisper in this studio," I announced. "If you've got something to say, I want to hear it now, not later."

She glared at me momentarily, then turned her eyes imploringly to Carlson. He grinned at me over the top of his glass. "It's nothing, ace," he said, and brushed past her.

The account exec sulked through the session with Robert, then occupied herself by getting on the phone and reaching out and bugging someone else for the duration of the shoot. Carlson, beer can in hand, took an extravagant interest in the redhead, regaling her with biker stories. He's a weekend easy rider, a Norton 750, and he's partial to redheads—he's got one at home.

It has been my experience that there are two kinds of art directors. There are the gerbils who nibble the photographer to death with their own insecurities, and for whom Dr. Land invented Polaroid, and then there are the A.D.'s like Carlson, who know their job and leave you alone and let you do yours. These are the guys who can sell the chromes to their clients and for whom it is a pleasure to shoot.

The models came and went, taking turns making love to the computer, the real star of the ad. We'd staggered the bookings at half-hour intervals so we always had one on the set and one dressing. By five-thirty, right on time, we wrapped the shoot.

Carlson had some time to kill before his train to Norwalk, so we adjourned to a trendy neighborhood bar, a regular spawning bed for Associated Dry Goods buyers and Seventh Avenue types. It was three deep at the bar, and people were still piling in. A lounge musician beat on an electric keyboard, accompanied by synthesized percussion, and belted out an idiosyncratic rendition of "The Piña Colada Song." After picking up a couple of Beck's, a bourbon on the rocks, and a Martell we positioned ourselves next to the hot table. They advertised a Thai chef in the kitchen. The chicken wings were crispy, the way I like them, and the meatballs were spicy. With the decibel-level needle in the red zone, and our mouths full of food, small talk was impossible.

"I've just hooked up with a new rep," I shouted.

"Oh yeah," Carlson yelled, peering back at me from over his glasses. "What's his name?"

"Rodger Pharr. Ever hear of him?"

"Nope—doesn't mean anything, though."

"He's got a still-life and a fashion guy. Guys I never heard of."

"You do still life."

"Yeah, but he's gonna sell the people."

"Send him around, let me have a look at him. I'll tell you what I think of him."

"I'd like to know."

It was pointless fighting the racket, and we lapsed into silence. We had another round, and while we gawked at the crowd, I made supper of the hors d'oeuvres. Everyone seemed desperate to convince themselves and their friends they were really having a good time. The men were middle-aged lady-killers, jowly and oily, who dressed too loud and talked too loud. Their hairdos and jewelry were contrived and clunky, and they all looked like guys who knew a guy who knew a guy. The women couldn't keep their hands off them, screaming at anything they said, as though they were stand-up comics. Aside from the occasional twenty-something blond stunner, who looked as though she could use a little help with the rent, or the coke habit, most of the women were closer to thirty-something, with one eye on the spritzer they were nursing and the other on the biological clock.

I was wondering whether Susan Ferrante was in the telephone book, and if I dared call, when Carlson finally turned to me. "I gotta get outta here, Charlie, before I go blind from all the gold jewelry and deaf from the noise."

"I know what you mean, I'm right behind you."

"I'll give you a call in the morning. Thanks for the drinks."

The following afternoon, Dolly and I stood on the side-walk waiting for Florine Ransom's limo.

"What time's your friend supposed to come?" Dolly asked, looking up from a paperback that claimed to possess the secret of *How to Get Rich in Real Estate with No Money Down,* or some such nonsense.

"They should be here any minute now," I said anxiously. I was damp, the afternoon humid and oppressive. The sky hung low overhead like a dingy aluminum lid on a cheap pot.

"You oughta read this book, Charlie," she said, brandishing the paperback. The costume was outlandish, of course—that was Dolly—otherwise she was presentable. A week's time had made some improvements in Socrates' coat, the burn spots not quite as noticeable as they had been. "You can have it when I'm through with it."

"That's all right, Dolly."

"Wouldn't you like to have money?" she asked reasonably.

"As much as the next person, but when it comes to fiction, I like a good plot."

"This isn't fiction," she protested.

"Dolly"—I sighed; this was the wrong time to get into a hassle with her—"if the author had the slightest idea how to make money in real estate, he'd be doing it, not writing books about it."

"That's a strange attitude," she said. "I don't see you riding around in a limousine. You might learn a thing or two from a book like this."

I glanced at my watch. It was nearly two-thirty, the appointed time. Limos were fairly common on the block—the carriage trade arrived at Lord & Taylor's in them as frequently as taxis. At the moment, though, there wasn't a limo in sight.

"For instance," Dolly persisted, "here's something about debt-equity swaps that's rather interesting. Wanna hear how it's done?"

"Go ahead, shoot."

"Well, say you wanted to buy a photography studio in Mexico. The first thing you do is buy a Mexican IOU from a U.S. bank."

"Uh-huh." My eyes were glued on the Sixth Avenue intersection.

"The bank will sell the IOU to you for, oh, say, fifty percent of face value because there's the chance Mexico may not make good on it, and fifty percent is better than nothing. You following me so far?"

"I hear you."

"Okay, so let's say this IOU is worth a million dollars. That means you've only paid five hundred thousand for it."

"Wait a minute—I thought you were supposed to do this with no money down?"

"You don't use your own money, stupid. You form a syndicate—you borrow the money . . . you use your gold card."

"Right, why didn't I think of that? Then what?"

"Then you return the IOU to Mexico in exchange for a million dollars' worth of pesos, and use them to buy the studio. Presto, you've got a studio worth a million dollars for half price. Good deal, huh?"

"That'd be some studio, but why wouldn't the moneymen cut me out and do the deal themselves, if it's that good?"

"Because they haven't read the book," she answered blithely, licking her finger and turning the page.

I was about to ask why, if Mexico could afford to buy the IOU from me for a million pesos, they didn't just pay the bank, when Dolly said, dreamily, as if to herself, "I wish I'd read this book when I was young. It might have made all the difference in the world for Freddy and me."

"Freddy? Who's Freddy, Dolly?"

"My husband."

"What happened to Freddy?"

"Oh, Freddy's dead."

She'd never mentioned family before. "And what about Susan, Dolly?" I pressed.

"Susan who?" She seemed genuinely interested.

"Your daughter, Susan Ferrante."

"You must be mistaken." She smiled. "I don't have a daughter."

There was no time to pursue this; a black stretch limo with smoked-glass windows drew alongside the curb. "She's here, Dolly," I said.

"A limo," Dolly observed.

"Yeah, she's in real estate."

The chauffeur got out and opened the rear door. Kiernan and Mumminger piled out.

"Who are they?" Dolly said from the corner of her mouth.

"The hired help."

"Hello, Charles," Kiernan said with a fatuous grin. "Well, this must be Cinderella." He put a hand on his hip and gave Dolly the once-over.

Mumminger looked on with an annoyingly superior smile. He was a regular clothes horse, I noticed. Today it was a neat, gray double-breasted glen plaid, a club tie, and the ubiquitous blue shirt with the white collar. He probably had on a pair of yellow suspenders as well. You don't see many men in double-breasted suits these days, but Mumminger, tall and snake-hipped, had the figure for one.

"Yes, well, why don't you make the introductions, Charles," said Kiernan finally, slightly flustered from Dolly's stare. He gestured to the door the chauffeur held patiently.

"All right," I said, guiding Dolly toward the limo.

"Do you believe that outfit?" said Kiernan behind our backs.

Dolly balked and began to turn. Crazy she might be, but stupid she wasn't. "Who does that faggot think he is?" she muttered.

"Never mind," I said, sensing imminent disaster and keeping a firm grip on her.

Mumminger took it upon himself to block our path. He poked his head inside the backseat of the limo. "Florine, I must protest," he said.

"I wish to meet the woman. Stand aside, Dean."

"But not alone, surely," he implored her.

"You're blocking the door, Dean."

Reluctantly, Mumminger withdrew, and I propelled Dolly forward. The old lady sat in the corner of the seat, dressed in black, as usual, looking as somber as a bird on its perch. Even in the flat light of an overcast day, her skin seemed pale to the point of transparency. "Hello, Mr. Byrne," she said in that incongruously strong voice of hers.

I answered with a polite hello of my own.

"And you must be Dolly Varden," she said, extending a gloved hand.

Dolly hesitated, glancing momentarily at me.

"Is there something the matter?" asked the old lady.

"You watch my stuff, Charlie," said Dolly.

"Sure, and maybe I'd better take Socrates," I suggested. She handed me the dog's leash. "Dolly, this is Florine Ransom, the lady I've been telling you about," I said by way of introduction. I gently urged her into the limo with my free hand. Sullen and suspicious, she climbed in. Thanks to Kiernan and Mumminger, we were not off to a very good start.

"Driver, you may close the door," said the old lady.

He did as instructed, then, leaning against the side of the car, became instantly absorbed in doping out the OTB scratch sheet he produced from a pocket.

I lingered near the car door, half expecting it to explode open any second and either Dolly or the old lady to come flying out. Socrates sat on his haunches with that anxious look common to dogs and children when they are temporarily abandoned and told not to move, to stand and wait.

Mumminger stood on the curb, one hand in his pants pocket, looking as though he were doing a spread for *Gentlemen's Quarterly.* "This is fantastic," he said to no one in particular.

"What's that?" I asked.

"One of the wealthiest women in Manhattan in the backseat of a limo with a derelict," he said in disgust.

"They're called homeless nowadays," Kiernan corrected him.

"I don't care what they're called," Mumminger said, "the woman's a street crazy."

"It's kinky," Kiernan simpered.

"And just when you thought you'd seen it all," I said to Mumminger. Not that I thought Dolly would get physical, but I was concerned for the old lady's safety as much as he was. I was worried Florine might say something that would set Dolly off and start her ranting. A blast from Dolly could send that frail old lady to her reward. To my relief, nothing like that seemed to be happening. The door stayed closed, and all was calm. What offended Mumminger, I thought, was fraternization between the classes. His problem was, he wasn't rich enough, and the poor rich made the worse snobs of all, or so my aunt had always said. I felt a sudden desire to put some space between the two of us, and gave Socrates a tug on the leash. He trotted off with me, happy to explore.

When Socrates had finished freshening his territorial markers, we returned to the doorway. I sat down on Dolly's crate like I owned the place, and Socrates and I played with his leash.

Five minutes stretched into ten, and ten into fifteen. Mumminger, I could see, was getting fidgety. He and Kiernan had run out of small talk.

"I'm going to look for a necktie in Lord and Taylor's, since we're in the neighborhood," he said finally. "I'll only be a couple of minutes."

"Take your time," I said.

He gave me a cool look, and strolled off like the cock-of-the-walk. An attractive woman actually gave him a second glance as he made his way to the side entrance of the store.

Kiernan, who probably couldn't keep his mouth shut if he had lockjaw, drifted over to strike up a conversation with me. He had no other choice—the chauffeur wanted none of him, occupied as he was with the permutations of parimutuel calculations.

"Florine okayed the money for the tapestry," he said. "When can you shoot it?"

"Shoot whenever you like, just make sure I have it tomorrow, you mean?"

"You know how it is, the insurance," he said apologetically.

"You tell me, when's a good time?"

"Anytime, we're always there. All you have to do is call."

"Okay, we'll get to it sometime this week," I promised.

"What do you suppose is going on in there?" he said,

glancing at his watch. "They've been at it for twenty minutes now."

"They're probably discovering how much they have in common, what a small world it is," I said.

"Please, that's all we need, a bag lady at the Thackeray."

"Marc'd like that, I'll bet."

He rolled his eyes.

"Bernard, what's the deal with the tapestries anyway?"

"You mean, why'd we buy it?" I loved his use of the editorial *we*.

"Yes, I'd think they'd be more valuable as a pair."

"That's right."

"So what's the big idea?"

"Well," he said, eyes dancing at the chance to gossip, "Marc may be an only child, and then again he may not, but he's certainly not her favorite son."

"There are more kids?"

"No, no, silly boy, I mean she bought it to spite him. It's as simple as that. Marc and his mother don't see eye to eye on anything. She thinks his business practices are suspect. He relies too heavily on borrowed money, and everything's mortgaged to the hilt. He's a gambler, she says."

"Where have I heard that before? But that's how business is done these days."

"Tell me. When she gets on the rag, there's no stopping her, though. She says she knows what it is to be poor and he doesn't. She saw to it that he always had the best of everything. I hear 'em on the phone once or twice a week," he confided.

"You can't win with your parents."

"Not if you're Marc Ransom anyway."

"You'd think the old lady'd be proud of him. He made it on his own, didn't he? He's a regular chip-off-the-old-block."

"I think she's actually pissed off he made it on his own. He's been after her for the longest time now to let him develop some of her properties—the La Fleur Hotel in particular—but she won't hear of it. Real estate prices are inflated, they're sky high, she says, and what goes up must come down. The money's no damn good, it's only paper. It can all disappear overnight, and we're all going to hell in a handcart." He laughed.

"She could be right," I said. "She seemed reasonable enough to me."

"She's not your mother," he pointed out, "and she can be very reasonable when she wants something."

"You gotta give the guy some credit. He doesn't need to work. He could be a playboy if he wanted."

"It's Florine's opinion that he is a playboy. I mean, all those women. She hates that."

"He could be a mama's boy—is that what she wants?"

"Absolutely," he said with a smirk. "Florine smiles in their faces, but she's definitely jealous of all his girlfriends. Behind their backs, they're all sluts and bitches. She even hates his politics."

"Well, I'd never have guessed, judging from the other night, that there was any rancor or dissension in House of Ransom."

"Appearances can be deceiving, but make no mistake about it, if the Indians look the least bit hostile, the Ransoms will circle the wagons. Anyway, what I really think is Florine's waiting and hoping Marc's going to stumble and fall."

"And Mama will be there to pick him up?"

"Right—nothing would give her greater pleasure than for one of his deals to sour."

"She wouldn't hang him out to dry?"

"Not at all—she'd bail him out, all right. She'd be thrilled to death to do it. Then she could say I told you so, and poor Marc would never hear the end of it."

"Well, you've got to have a dream, I suppose. Speaking of girlfriends, did either you or Florine ever hear of a woman named Raynes?"

"Hmm, there was a Sharon Raynes," he said after a moment's thought, "a dreadful person. She worked for Florine's designer. She came with the alterations once in a while."

"Did you know she died?"

"The Raynes woman?"

"No, Barbara Stanwyck."

"Witty," he said, arching an eyebrow. "What happened to her? She wasn't so old."

"In her thirties, I'd guess. They say it was suicide."

"Ohmigod, no. But why?"

"I wouldn't know." I shrugged.

"Now that I think of it, Florine did mention how strange it was we never heard back from the woman."

The chauffeur suddenly snapped to attention, cramming the scratch sheet in his pocket and catching the car door as it swung open. Dolly stepped out like she was being dropped at the ball.

I bent, anxious for a glimpse of the old lady, curious to see how she'd weathered the encounter. She appeared unruffled. She motioned for Kiernan to climb in and for the driver to move on.

"Well, how'd it go?" I asked Dolly, handing her the dog's leash.

Socrates bounded happily all over his mistress, planting a wet one on her cheek. "Did you miss your mama, huh?" She cooed and nuzzled, ignoring me.

The limo reversed, then glided forward smoothly into traffic.

"Dolly, what'd the old lady want to see you about?" I tried again.

"That's none of your business, but if you must know, she wanted to know how I got my name, Dolly Varden."

"What'd you tell her?"

"What I'm telling you, it's none of her business."

"Dolly, this lady could help you."

"Help me what?"

She had me there. If it turned out she wasn't a Ransom, she could sit on her crate and rot, for all anyone would care.

"I'll help myself," she said, sounding just like a Ransom —Florine.

"Did you get your money, at least?"

"What do you think?" She grinned impishly. "Feel like making a contribution?"

"No thanks, Dolly. See ya."

"So long, cheapskate."

Mumminger came hustling down the block, a Lord & Taylor shopping bag in his hand, looking in all directions at once. "Where are they? Where'd they go?" he demanded.

"You missed the bus, Doc." I grinned. "They left without you."

Scowling, he muttered what sounded like a screw you, and pivoted back to Fifth, walking east at a brisk clip.

16

Let's make the trip count and take the Nikons for a walk," Tito said.

We were off to scope out the vermin infesting the real estate values in the neighborhood of the La Fleur Hotel.

Tito tossed me a couple of rolls of Tri-X. I stuffed them in my pants pocket. He handed me an F2 camera body with a motor drive and an f3.5, 150mm lens. He had another F2 fitted with an f1.4, 105mm lens hanging around his neck. We were going to keep our distance from whatever we aimed at.

I hate walking around with cameras strapped to me. They're cumbersome, conspicuous, and an invitation to a mugging. Having lost a few, and bought a few—trying to stay even—on the thieves' market, I speak from experience. Advertising photographs, whatever else you may think of them, are created, not found, like reportage pictures. I must confess, though, that there were plenty of times as a photojournalist when I did the former. A perk of advertising photography is you never have to wear a camera unless you want to, unless it completes the image. This, however, was one of those times when it made perfect sense to strap on the old Nikon. Why not make the trip count?

The weather had stayed in character. The sky emitted an eerie blue light through low-lying clouds run aground on shoals of concrete, steel, and glass.

F4 at 125th of a second, was my guess, which was confirmed by a quick reading through the camera meter. We could always push the Tri-X to 800 or 1600 ASA, if necessary. Like most things in life, in photography there's always a trade-off. In this instance, what we'd lose in shutter speed and aperture, we'd gain in rendition. It was a gorgeous light, perfectly even and shadowless, the kind you wanted to photograph metal—an automobile, for instance. I'd practiced handholding a 200mm lens wide open at a sixtieth and a thirtieth of a second, which is a little like shooting a gun: inhale, exhale, hold it, then squeeze the trigger or release the button.

The lull between lunch and the evening rush hours was ending, the action on the streets beginning to quicken. The Big Apple is a kaleidoscopic feast for the eye, and the short walk to the La Fleur was filled with dozens of stunning images. I felt like a slug for not packing a camera more often.

The minute you raise a camera to your eye and focus, people react to you. As I've said, cameras are conspicuous. I suggested we walk around the block once before we did any shooting.

"We could miss a shot," said Tito.

"I missed a dozen of them on the way over here. Let's get the feel of the block first—we'll have a better idea where the pictures are."

"You're the boss, boss."

Like SoHo before it, it had happened between Fourteenth and Twenty-third streets, between Second and Tenth avenues. First came the artists and the photographers, then architects, galleries, fancy restaurants, trendy clubs, boutiques, publishing houses, and advertising agencies. Above Twenty-third Street was another matter. Manhattan South was still grungier than a gorilla's armpit and deader than Kelsey's nuts after seven o'clock at night. Aside from

Korean gambling parlors, and the padded cells that kids called studios and rented by the hour to study the nuances of heavy metal, gentrification had yet to reach Manhattan South.

Here are a few of the signs to look for when an old industrial neighborhood is about to molt and get new feathers. First come the sporadic pops of strobe lights spilling out on the cobblestones after dark. The photographers have arrived. It's time to grease the old folks, come into your inheritance, buy a building and sponsor a co-op conversion plan. Next comes a no-name after-hours dyke club in the basement of a loft building. If you haven't been able to get your hands on the old-timers' nest egg and buy the building, you'd better hurry up and get friendly with your loan officer and nail your place down at the insider's price. Because after the dyke club comes the restaurant with a single name, like Odile's or Nona's, but not out front, only on the matchbooks, and the limos are double parked and lined up around the block. If you haven't cut your deal by then, you can fa-gedda-bout-it—unless you're a trust fund baby, you can't afford it. And it ain't worth it. The prices are inflated. All through the seventies and eighties, that was the way it went. Jerks without a pot to piss in got rich playing the game. There seemed to be no end to it, but things had cooled off considerably the last few years. Real estate was flat. I doubt that made much difference to Ransom, though. Bull market or bear, he made money. And if he were to tip me that this was the next neighborhood to happen, it still wouldn't do me much good.

"Check it out, Charlie," said Tito. "There's a deal going down." He was looking directly at the entrance to the hotel.

It figured, though I hadn't expected it. "I know those guys," I laughed. They hadn't been there on our first pass.

"Been buying your shit at the La Fleur, huh?" said Tito, glassing them and cranking half a dozen frames through the camera.

I stepped in front of the lens.

"Hey, isn't this what we came here for?"

"Yeah, but I don't want to spook them. Let's keep moving," I said. "That's Angel Cruz, one of the guys who tried to torch Dolly." Pretending to window-shop a computer store, we drifted up the block. A black van, with bubble windows and sporting a flame-motif paint job up front and wrapping around the sides, screened us from view. Cars with Jersey plates paused, waited for the runner, got their parcel and continued on to the Lincoln Tunnel. It was a takeout window where the bridge and tunnel crowd could pick up their drugs on the way home. And it was the peak time of day.

"What'd you see, exactly?" I asked Tito.

"Cruz was buying, I could see the money in his hand. The tall dude was selling, but he wasn't holding. Shit, it was a deal, all right."

I had no reason to doubt him. "Stand over there for me," I said. "Make like I'm taking your picture."

Tito stood and grinned for the camera. I cranked a few frames of the cars and runners, then I found Angel and the tall Spanish guy in my frame of view and focused on them. Tito continued to mug and mime for me. A third guy came into the frame. There was an elaborate display of high and low fives, during which the merchandise changed hands. Then the guy was gone. The tall Spanish guy in the silk suit watched the charade impassively.

"He just took delivery of the goods," I said, and motioned for Tito to follow me.

"Did you get it?" he wanted to know.

"Wanna ask 'em to do it again for the camera?"

We crossed over to the La Fleur side of the street. The rear doors of the van were open. A bumper sticker on the fender said, SHIT HAPPENS! Two men, both in hard hats and tool belts, one young, one older and paunchy, were unloading spools of cable from the truck. We continued on up the block toward Fifth Avenue and did another lap.

"I don't see 'em," said Tito as we rounded the corner for the third time.

"Where'd they go?"

"Well, your pal, Cruz, probably went to step on the blow before he put it out on the street."

"And have a toot."

All kinds of hustlers were working the cars. The squeegee

brigade was attacking windshields like they were on Normandy Beach. Guys hawked Walkmans, wristwatches, telephones, and sets of carving knives car to car. You could get anything you wanted. They'd probably take orders and steal on demand. Was this how R. H. Macy got started? With our backs to a building, and using rush-hour pedestrian traffic as a blind, we caught some of the action on film. Eventually we began working our way up the block again. We strolled past the entrance of the La Fleur and gave the lobby a good, long, casual look. It was bleak and dismal inside, stripped of every vestige of its former glory. Well, almost. There was one old relic. A contemporary of Florine Ransom, the old geezer looked like a leftover from a forties screwball comedy gone horribly to seed. An actor, maybe, about two decades between jobs, he was dressed in a badly stained double-breasted blazer, an open shirt collar, and ascot. His liver-spotted hands rested on the crook of the cane that was placed between his feet, which were shod in bedroom slippers. His sparse hair was swept back on his head and yellow with bleach and age. His jowls were shiny and razor-nicked. A half a dozen black kids raced around him playing tag. His gaze was vacant and rheumy. The mothers, strung out and worn, drifted listlessly in the background.

The camera finds squalor irresistible, and Tito automatically started to bring the Nikon to his eye. I put a hand on his arm. "I've seen enough," I said. "Let's get outta here."

"Did you see the old guy?"

"I saw him."

"Let me get the shot."

"It's too easy, a cheap shot, you hadda be there's all."

"Man, I have film in the camera."

"Me, too." But I wanted to get out of there. Angel could come back any minute. I scanned the opposite side of the street. There were several vacancy signs. "Come on," I said finally, "we'll shoot out the film in Herald Square. The winos and crackheads are easy meat."

The film was ready, and I was waiting for Tito to return with it. I flipped through the white pages. There was an S. Ferrante with an East Side address. I dialed the number and got a machine. It was early, she must have been at work. I left my name and number and asked her to give me a call.

When I hung up, Carlson called, hot for his pictures. I told him Tito was on the way. I didn't say which way. Tito finally showed with a fourteen-by-seventeen envelope under his arm.

"What's that?" I asked. "Where's Carlson's stuff?"

"It's in here, relax."

"He's yanking our chain, wants his film. Leave your coat on, you've got to fly right over there." I took the envelope. Inside, I found the contacts of the bank shoot, forty-two sheets of two-and-a-quarter film, including the six rolls I'd done of Dolly at the computer. Photography is still a mystery to me. Whatever happens happens in complete darkness inside a little black box. I flipped through the contact sheets anxiously, amazed and relieved to see that it had worked again; I had an image. Looking good, if I say so myself. No comebacks—Carlson should have been happy with them. Even the stuff of Dolly worked like dynamite. She was a real ham. Schizophrenia probably isn't much of a handicap for an actor. She looked like a sister of the Three Stooges. I packed them up, slapped a label on the envelope, and sent Tito off to the agency with them.

While he was gone, I poured over the 35mm blowup contact sheets we'd done of the La Fleur. We'd only shot four rolls between the two of us, but they seemed to tell the story. We'd captured the street scene with the beeper brigade working the cars. The hard hats with the flaming van and spools of cable were there. So was Angel Cruz and the tall Spanish guy, money changing hands clearly visible. There was even one cockeyed frame of the old gent with the ascot. Then there was a short roll, only about a dozen frames, of something I hadn't expected to see. I put the loupe to my eye and studied them frame by frame. I saw myself in the last frame, bending over her.

The phone rang, interrupting me. "Hello, studio," I said.

"Mr. Byrne?"

"Yes."

"Susan Ferrante," she said. "I saw your name in *WWD*

today and thought it's about time I called and thanked you for coming to my mother's aid. Please forgive me for not calling sooner."

"You saw my name in *WWD?*" I didn't remember Pharr mentioning *Woman's Wear Daily.*

"Yes. It said, lensman, Charles Byrne, at the Seventh Avenue Fashion Hall of Fame Awards with an unidentified brunette, is getting hot on Madison Avenue. That is you, isn't it?"

"I don't know, I wasn't there. I've got a new agent, and he's trying to get a few miles out of the *Times* story. Unless there's another Charles Byrne, it's probably a plant of a press agent he's hired."

"It's not true?" she asked. "You're not getting hot on Madison Avenue?"

"As the champ says, don't believe the hype." I laughed. "I'm about as hot as I ever was, which is not so hot. But I'm glad you called. I'd like to talk to you about your mother, if I might. Could we meet for a drink, maybe?"

"When?"

"This afternoon, if that's convenient. Just tell me where and when."

"Do you know J. G. Melon on the East Side?"

"I know the place."

"I'll see you there after six."

"Great, see you then." I hung up. *WWD,* she'd said. I was damned if I could see the point of appearing in *WWD.* I wasn't a fashion photographer. I punched Pharr's number and got a machine. I asked him to call.

Tito returned from the agency before I had a chance to get back to the contact sheet. "How'd it go with Carlson? Did he like his pictures?" I asked.

"Dunno, he was in a meeting. I had to leave them at the reception desk."

"Hey, look what I found," I said, holding up the contact sheet of the short roll. "What's this?" It was obvious what it was—it was just that their existence took me completely by surprise.

"So that's what it was," he said, glancing at the sheet. "I found the roll in the camera the other day and I couldn't figure out what it was. It must have been the camera I packed when we went to shoot the tapestry. We haven't used that Nikon since, and I forgot about it. How'd they come out?"

"You're about three quarters of a stop under—they're corrected contacts—otherwise they're fine."

"Lemme have a look at them," he said, snatching the sheet from my hand. "Man, look at that," he murmured, staring at a frame through the loupe. Then he suddenly thrust the sheet and the loupe back at me.

"What is it?" I asked, putting the loupe and the sheet to my eye. "Did you see something?" Sharon Raynes's corpse stared up at me from the courtyard.

"I dunno. She's lying on her back, like she'd been pushed. Seems to me she'd be lying facedown if she jumped."

"Yeah, that's what I thought, too. But there's something else. Here, have another look."

Reluctantly, he took the loupe and reexamined the contact sheet.

"Notice anything?"

It took a moment, but he got it. "Hey, someone messed with the body! It's moved. Her hands, her arms, are in different positions."

"Notice anything else?"

"There's no shoe except in the frames you're in."

"These shots aren't in sequence, are they?"

"I was back and forth on the phone, and with William. There were time lapses, if that's what you mean. You can tell where I stopped and started by the different framing."

"That means someone was tampering with the body while you were shooting, and just before I got there. How else could the shoe have gotten there? It's a wonder you didn't catch them in the act. We must have just missed them."

We stared at each other in silence. "What are you gonna do?" he asked finally.

"I should go to the cops with it, huh? Hey, whatta ya mean, what am I gonna do? You're the one who took the pictures."

"I should have thrown the roll out."

"I wish you had," I said. "Either she got up and got her

shoe and then lay down and died, or there was someone else down there besides Raynes and me."

"What about the doorman?"

"I don't think so."

"How about Fallon, then?"

"That's what I was thinking. He and Susan Ferrante got there mighty quick."

"The cops could think these pictures incriminate you, Charlie."

"Why would I go to the police with incriminating evidence? It wouldn't make any sense."

"The system makes no sense."

"Besides, I've got a witness—you."

"I'll go along with whatever you say, but I don't trust the cops."

"Someone oughta see these pictures."

"Maybe, but let's make sure our asses are covered."

"I'm with you. Meanwhile, we've got another tapestry to shoot. Just for spite, old lady Ransom bought the mate to the one we photographed for her son. Is tomorrow all right?"

"It's all right. Same equipment as last time?"

"Yes, but leave the Nikon in the studio," I joked.

"Hey, no problem. Is that it?"

"One more thing. I want you to start calling around the rental places, F&B/CeCo, Camera Service Center, and the like, see what kind of a deal we can get on a month's rental of a video surveillance camera and a VCR."

"Uh-oh, what's up?"

"I'm going fishing. I wanna catch a piranha—Angel dealing dope on videotape."

"So you catch him, what then?"

I shrugged. "Maybe Ransom can use it in his presentation."

17

I was nursing a Grand-Dad on the rocks at a window table in the dining room of J. G. Melon, waiting for Susan Ferrante, and suddenly there she was. She gave me a brief smile and made her way to the table. She was dressed in black and shades of gray, a loose blazer over a cashmere sweater, and a skirt to the knees. She had an inch or two on me in her heels. We exchanged pleasantries and sat down. She ordered a glass of red wine and I had a refill on Grand-Dad. The light that filtered through the window put her in relief, separating her from the background shadows of the room. It put a luster in her chestnut hair, highlights in her violet eyes, and accented her prominent nose. I stared at her a bit too appreciatively. You don't find women like this anywhere else but in Manhattan.

"So?" she began, with a lopsided grin, returning my gaze with an expression of frank curiosity.

"The odds were fifty-fifty we'd meet again," I said.

"I'd have thought they were higher." She smiled. "But once again, I seem to be in your debt."

"Because of Dolly?"

"Yes."

"I hadn't thought of it that way. Sorry, I don't mean to stare," I said, "but I'm having trouble getting it into my head you're Dolly's daughter."

"Why is that?"

"Well, you're as different as chalk and cheese," I said.

"Really," she chuckled. "And which am I, chalk or cheese?"

"I was speaking figuratively, of course."

"Of course."

"Since you asked, though, you're not the chalk." I grinned.

"Well, we are mother and daughter," she said, eyes dancing away from mine. "What do you suppose the odds are that it would be you who'd come to my mother's rescue?"

"At least as good as those we'd meet again."

"Fifty-fifty."

"You'd expect them to be longer, I'll grant you, but I did meet her first. What would you say the odds are that Miriam Lusk, aka Dolly Varden, was related to Florine Ransom?"

When she crinkled her face at the hilarity of that notion, I realized I'd fallen in love with her. "Slim to none, I'd say," she laughed.

"That's what I'd say, but Florine might give you better odds. She saw the *Times* story and asked me to arrange a meeting with your mother."

"And have you?"

"They met yesterday. Whatever Florine Ransom wants, Florine Ransom gets."

"And fell into each other's arms, no doubt," she said.

"Not exactly, but the meeting wasn't a disaster, either. They seemed to hit it off, in fact."

"Thank God for small favors."

"Dolly wouldn't tell me what happened. What I'm wondering, though, is how did the old lady get the idea that Dolly could be related to her?"

"I haven't the faintest idea, I'm sure. Aside from being a

poor relation, what kind of relation does Mrs. Ransom suspect my mother is?"

"She told me a story about having had a daughter out of wedlock when she was a teenager."

"My mother'd be too young to be her daughter."

"I realized that, and so does the old lady, but is there a chance Dolly could be her granddaughter? I've tried broaching the subject of family with your mother, and she's brushed me off. She has alluded to a husband, but flatly denies any family."

The look of pain was palpable. She lowered her eyes. "My mother is sick," she said mechanically. "She was always shaky, even when I was a kid. When Dad died, she lost it altogether, she just seemed to flip out into her own orbit. But there's no reason for her to be living in the street."

"She told me she lost her job and was evicted from her apartment when she fell behind in the rent."

"Even so, do you think I wouldn't take her in?"

"I'm sure you would," I murmured.

"I've done everything I can to try and help her." She sighed. "I've even hauled her into court and tried to have her declared legally insane. She won't have anything to do with me ever since then." She lifted her eyes. They were moist. "She may be crazy, but she isn't stupid. Get her in front of a judge, and she's as normal as you or I; the minute she leaves the courtroom, she turns into a fruitcake again. And the courts," she said, with a look of futility. "Well, they're worthless. They make it impossible to take care of your own."

"The courts are a crapshoot," I said.

"If she'd take her medication, she could function. But there's no way to get her to do that, short of force-feeding her."

"It must be awful. Why do you think it's so unlikely your mother and the old lady are related, though? What about Dolly's parents—are they living?"

"My mother's an orphan."

"Parents unknown?"

"Yes."

"Well, there you go." I smiled. "It's possible they could be related."

"Anything's possible if you believe in fairy tales."

"The old lady must have some reason for thinking Dolly could be her granddaughter, though. Could it be the name?"

"Dolly Varden?"

"Yes. Do you think it means something to the old lady? Does it mean anything to Dolly, or to you?"

"Not really. Dolly Varden's a Dickens character, isn't she?"

"That's right—a novel called *Barnaby Rudge,* I believe." I had P. C. Strunk to thank for that bit of arcane knowledge.

"I can't speak for Florine, but I doubt it means anything to my mother, although you never know. Next week she's just as likely to call herself Oprah Winfrey or Bella Abzug. I think she'd rather be almost anyone but herself."

"How long has she been Dolly Varden?"

"Going on a year now. It started when she was in Bellevue."

"But why Dolly Varden, and not Oprah or Bella?"

She shrugged. "Who knows? She reads a lot. Maybe she read Dickens when she was in the hospital."

"I don't mean to be coming on like the Inquisition. If I'm out of line, just tell me to bleep off, okay?"

She smiled sadly. "Just say whatever it is you want to say."

"Okay, is it possible your sister was murdered?"

"The thought has occurred to me," she replied bleakly.

"Don't you want to know who killed her?"

"What difference would it make? She'd still be dead. What do you know about my sister?"

"Nothing," I admitted.

"Did you know she was a whore?" she said matter-of-factly. "You look surprised. Am I being too candid for you?"

"No."

"Some family, huh? Mom's a nut, and sis's a hooker," she said with a cruel smile.

"How'd Sharon meet Ransom?"

"Through me, actually. She worked for me occasionally as

a showroom model. I'm a designer, and Florine Ransom's a client of mine. One day Marc came by with his mother, and Sharon happened to be working in the showroom. Evidently, he liked what he saw. And Sharon, well, she took one look at him and saw pay dirt. The rest, as they say, is history."

"Pay dirt is what would cross the minds of most women the first time they meet a Marc Ransom."

"The first thing that crossed my mind," she said with a smile, "was how short he was."

"Do you think Ransom had anything to do with the death of your sister?"

"No comment," she said.

"Was there an autopsy?"

"Why are you so interested in Sharon?"

"I was the one who found her, remember?"

"The medical examiner said, probable cause of death, suicide."

"I don't buy it."

"Look, it isn't that I don't care," she said gravely, "it's that there's nothing to be gained by making waves. Suppose there was an investigation, and an arrest. Can you imagine the field day the media would have? It would be a feeding frenzy. And for what? Sharon would still be dead. I'd be put through the ringer. God knows, Dolly doesn't need any more publicity. No, the sensible thing to do is forget about it, put it behind us, and turn the page."

"So you think Ransom did have something to do with Sharon's death?"

"I didn't say that. What I'm saying is, what difference does it make? She's dead."

"Maybe you're right," I said mildly.

"I know I'm right."

"There's sure to be publicity, though, if Dolly and the old lady turn out to be related."

"That at least is no crime," she said.

"If it's true, that'd make you a great-granddaughter. You'd be Marc's what? Grandniece? He'd be Uncle Marc."

Her eyes glanced off me and out the window.

"Seriously, though," I continued, "Florine must know

you're Dolly's daughter. It was in the *Times* story. I wonder why she didn't ask you to introduce her to your mother."

"I wouldn't know," she said idly.

"It's no secret. Marc knows she's met with Dolly."

She switched her gaze back to me. "Marc knows everything his mother's up to."

"How, Kiernan?"

"Mumminger, more likely."

"Tell me, does Dolly know about Sharon?"

"I told her, although God only knows if it registered."

"I'm sorry," I murmured.

"No need to be, she didn't kill the messenger," she said with a lopsided grin.

"How did you happen to be on the scene so soon that day?"

"You did say to tell you when to bleep off," she said, her face darkening.

"That's right," I said quickly. "Enough about you. Let's talk about me. What would you like to know? Latest book read? *Den of Thieves* by James B. Stewart. Latest achievement? Shooting some bank ads. Drug of choice? Alcohol. Sexual preference? Women. Anything else you'd like to know, just ask. My life's an open book."

She smiled. "All right, since you asked, and since I don't wish to seem evasive, Sharon asked me to meet her at her apartment that day. It was important, she said. That's how I happened to be there so soon."

"How about a refill?" I asked, nodding at her empty glass.

"I don't think so. I should be running along soon."

"Don't go," I pleaded. "I'll put the Ziploc on my lip, no more questions, I promise. Are you hungry? How about dinner?"

She waggled two fingers at me, grinning.

"What's that?"

She popped up a third finger. "You just asked me three more questions."

"I did? Oops, there I go again. Listen, if you don't like this place, we can go somewhere else. What do you say? Strike that last question."

She laughed. "We only agreed to meet for a drink. Another time, perhaps."

I signaled for the waiter. "The regular man, huh, Fallon," I said.

"Here, let me pay for mine," she said, reaching for her bag.

I waved her off. "I invited you."

"Fallon's a friend," she said.

That covered a lot of territory these days. Still, I took it as encouraging. "When can I see you again?" I left the money on the table, and we made our way to the door.

"I don't know," she said.

"Do I stand a chance?"

"You never know," she said, smiling, "the odds are fifty-fifty, aren't they?" She turned and walked away.

I headed west toward Fifth Avenue. There was no doubt about it, we moved in different circles, I was thinking. She probably had lots of rich old ladies like Florine for clients, while I had a handful of scary art directors. She went to dinner parties at Ransom's, and I ate at B.B.'s Ribs. She traveled first class, and I rode coach. It could never work. By the time I'd reached Madison Avenue, I'd checked off a dozen reasons why a romance with her could never work.

I hailed a cab and headed back to the studio.

The cats heard the key in the door and were waiting for me. I stroked them and fed them Tender Vittles, then I changed my clothes and hopped on the Lejeune. I did ten laps in the park, took a hot shower, and a cold shower, but it didn't help. I couldn't stop thinking about Susan Ferrante.

Carlson was the first caller next morning. "Hey, dork, about that new rep of yours . . ."

"Pharr? What about him?"

"He was in the agency yesterday to see another art director, a friend of mine. I was in my friend's office when Pharr called from reception, and we looked at the book he was showing together."

"Mine?"

"No, a fashion guy. My friend's flipping through the

work, and there's one of our ads. The face-cream thing with Miss What's-her-name . . ."

"North Carolina," I said helpfully.

"That's the one. I thought you ought to know, your rep's passing off our ad as the work of the fashion guy."

"Are you sure?"

"Sure I'm sure. My friend picked up on it, too. He was just about to say something when I caught his eye and silenced him."

"What did you say?"

"I didn't say anything, I let it slide. I wanted to talk to you first."

"I'm glad you did. Why would he go and do a dumb thing like that?"

"My friend's got a layout to shoot. Pharr was hustling the job for his fashion guy."

"But for all Pharr knows, I might have done the job for your friend."

"It was a bonehead play. He should have been hustling the job for you—you had a leg up on the account."

"Yeah, well, thanks for telling me, Al."

"You're welcome."

"How'd you like your pictures?"

"They're fine. Oh, that's another thing, what were those shots with the zany broad? We didn't shoot those pictures."

"It was a gag."

"My writer loves them. Suppose we wanted to use one, for a fee, of course . . ."

"Of course," I said. "Keep talking."

"Could we get a release?"

"I don't see why not."

"Okay, I'll stat one up and present it with the rest of the ads. We'll see who salutes it. I'll have a print order for you in a couple of days," he said, and hung up.

I should have known the guy was a phony from the suits, the haircut, and the name dropping. I dialed his number, cursing myself for going against my better instincts. The machine picked up, and Pharr's unctuous voice explained he was sorry, but he was unable to come to the phone at the moment, and to please leave a brief message. In the calmest voice I could muster, I asked him to please return my call, it was urgent.

We were back in the studio before noon, after a trip to the Thackeray to photograph the dowager's tapestry. Louise, the maid, and Kiernan moved the furniture for us. The old girl was getting her bones massaged by the good doctor Mumminger, and did not emerge from her boudoir. While Tito unpacked and put the film in the lab, I paid a visit to the La Fleur. The Shit Happens van was there again, but there was no sign of Angel. It was a little early for the drug trade. A building across the street had a Vacancy sign hanging out. I found the super, and we haggled. He asked for a grand and settled for five bills, in exchange for which I got the key to a twelve-by-twenty room on the third floor overlooking the hotel for a month—no lease, and no questions asked.

Pharr trotted into the studio at six, after Tito had gone for the day. I'd given him a line about having to air-freight the portfolio to a Chicago advertising agency. I flipped through the book. Sure enough, no face-cream ad. "There's an ad missing," I said evenly.

"The face-cream ad," he said, beating me to the punch. "I haven't been showing that particular ad."

"Why not?"

"I thought it looked dated. Here," he said, changing gears smoothly, "take a look at these, and give me a price." He produced three Magic Marker layouts from an eleven-by-fourteen envelope and placed them in front of me.

It was like pulling a rabbit out of a hat. I'm ready to cut the guy loose, and he asks me for a price on three ads. "Where are they going to run?" I asked, wondering if he'd guessed what was up. "Trade publications, home furnishing magazines, and similar publications."

They were carpet ads. I studied them carefully, one at a time. One called for a shot of a mom admiring her carpet, another was to be a shot of a kid tracking mud on Mom's new carpet, and the third was the all-American family, Mom, Pop, and the kids, and sheepdog, on the sofa in the living room. It was a nice job, if it was real, and ordinarily I'd be happy to get it; now I wasn't so sure. "Five grand an ad," I said, "plus expenses, of course." Thirty-five hundred was a more realistic number.

"Of course, plus expenses," he said. "I'll bounce it off of them. We'll see if they go for it."

"Fine," I said. "Meanwhile, I want the face-cream ad, the one you haven't been showing."

"As you wish. Is something the matter?"

"I got a call from Al Carlson the other day. He said he saw the ad in your fashion guy's book."

"So that's it. Purely unintentional, let me assure you," he said, avoiding my eyes. "It got mixed up somehow with his work when I was editing the portfolios. I didn't catch the mistake until I was showing his book."

"You might have pulled the ad, or said something."

"It would have been awkward to do that in the middle of the presentation."

"How come you weren't showing my book? I've worked on that account."

"It was a fashion job. Look, Charles, I regret the mix-up, it was unfortunate, but that's all it was, a mix-up."

"I won't argue with that, Rodger, but I can't afford another mix-up like that. We're through."

"Hold on now, let's not be hasty. I'd never do a thing like that on purpose. It was a mistake."

"Yeah, yours, Rodger. I want the ad in the studio tomorrow before the end of the day, or I'll take the matter up with the ASMP's grievance committee."

"What about these ads?" he asked, indicating the Magic Marker comps.

"If I get the job, you get the commission."

"You're throwing away a promising collaboration because of a relatively minor mistake."

"I don't see anything minor about it. I'll give you the benefit of the doubt—the ad got in the other guy's book by mistake. But I won't give you it would have been awkward to correct the mistake when you were making the presentation."

"That was a judgment call."

"And yours was bad. You were willing to let the guy think the shot was the work of your fashion guy. I wonder what else you're willing to do for a job?"

He was adjusting his tie and shirt collar. "Well, your mind's made up, I see," he said.

"You're right."

"Very well," he said airily, stroking the seven-hundred-dollar suit like a bird smoothing its feathers. "Perhaps it's just as well we part now. I would find it impossible to work with someone without their complete confidence."

"Just get the ad to me right away, and we'll forget about the whole thing," I said.

"As you wish."

"So long, Rodger."

"Good-bye," he said.

"You know the way out," I said.

18

Friday morning Tito and I set up the video camera and VCR. There wasn't much doing, so we closed shop early, and by three o'clock that afternoon I was on the road to my handyman's special upstate in Hobart with the Lejeune on a bike rack on the trunk of a Dodge Aries rental. When I returned Sunday night, just after midnight, a gauntlet of hustlers was lined up around the block. One clean-cut guy in jeans, windbreaker, hundred-and-fifty-dollar sneakers, and a Mets cap, got to me first. "Whadda ya need, man? I got smoke, crack, blow, whatever."

"I'm all right, man." I waved him off.

"Have a nice day anyway," he said philosophically.

Day, night, whatever, I was paying a visit to the electric eye to change cassettes. There should have been about four hours of the La Fleur follies on video. Viewing it was going to be like reading the phone book, a little short on plot, but long on cast and repetition. But that's why they made fast forward. I didn't waste any time changing the tapes, because the Lejeune was on the Dodge and I was anxious to get back to the car before it got ripped off. Mission accomplished, I dropped my stuff off at the studio. Morbid and Curiosity rushed me at the door, mewing and rubbing against my legs. They get lonesome and bored when I leave them alone for a weekend. I tried taking them to the country, but they didn't travel well, and when they got to the house, they hid under the floorboards. It took the weekend to coax them out. They were city cats. Now I left them in the studio when I went away. I changed their food and cleaned up the countertop where I'd let the faucet drip for them. Then I returned the car. When I got back to the studio again, I noticed the message light on the answering machine was blinking. It was too late to do anything about it, so I let it blink—it would keep until morning. I took a quick shower, threw on a robe, fixed myself a bourbon, popped the cassette into the VCR, and settled back to view the tape.

It was Friday evening; the time frame was from five to nine P.M. The scene was the entrance to the La Fleur. Remote in hand, finger at the ready on the fast forward button, I let the tape roll for a minute or so to get the feel of it. The featured players gradually distinguished themselves from the cast of thousands.

The hard hats with the Shit Happens van, which was parked in front of the hotel, were the first people I recognized. They made several trips between the hotel and van, lugging desks and file cabinets. The old guy Tito had wanted to photograph scuttled back and forth with the help of his cane. Long after it had grown dark, small children darted around the frame while their glassy-eyed mothers stumbled around like the living dead.

Angel and his gang couldn't have performed any better for the camera if they'd been making a rap video. The surveillance camera was working like a charm. It was the height of rush hour and business was brisk. Angel was restocking his string of runners. Friday night in America, prime time, and drugs were moving right along with lite beer and pizza. One dope deal looks pretty much like another, and I began to feel like I was watching a loop. I pressed the fast forward button, stopping occasionally to check out scenes when the cast seemed to change. There was still better than three hours of tape left, and what I'd hoped to get I'd already gotten twenty minutes into the tape.

Angel was ricocheting around the TV screen like he'd smoked an ounce of crack as the tape sped ahead. A pair of strange figures appeared suddenly. I backed up the tape and then switched to play. Nelson Rudd and Joel Lesser, in real time, gave the brother high and low fives, real chummy-like. Look at that, I thought, Ransom's management. Are they looking to score? I estimated the time as somewhere between six and seven Friday night. They huddled for quite a while, and before the meeting broke up, Rudd slipped an envelope to Angel. Angel folded the envelope and stashed it in the cuff of his knee sock. Rudd didn't get anything in return. He and Lesser then disappeared inside the hotel. Angel continued to hang out on the street. I skipped ahead on the tape, but slower now. Twenty minutes must have elapsed before Rudd and Lesser emerged from the La Fleur. They were accompanied by the two hard hats. As Angel looked on, the four men held a brief sidewalk conference. Heads shook affirmatively, indicating they'd come to an understanding, then the hard hats climbed into their truck and drove off. Rudd and Angel waved good-bye, and Angel, looking as lonesome as a coyote, was left alone on the screen. There was still quite a bit of tape left, and I'd seen more than I could have hoped for, and more than I should have, I sensed. I glanced at the clock. It was nearly two o'clock. Should I scan the rest of the tape, or should I go to sleep? Easy. I should go to sleep. Right. I pressed fast forward and let the tape roll. Angel eventually abandoned his post, and there was nothing of interest on the last three quarters of an hour of tape. I polished off the bourbon, flicked off the TV and the lights, and lay in the dark thinking. If Rudd and Lesser weren't at the La Fleur to buy or sell drugs—and I wouldn't rule out either of those possibilities—what were they doing there? As managing agents for the building, they had a legitimate reason to be there. But I had my doubts that they were there on business, slipping a character like Angel an envelope at six or seven o'clock on a Friday night. And what about the hard hats? Who were those guys? Two guys might do some electrical work, or repair a boiler or an elevator, I suppose, but nothing much in the way of major construction. Besides, the La Fleur had no future. Ransom had plans for the site.

"See today's *Newsday?*" said Tito as he walked in the next morning.

"Something I should know?"

"See for yourself." He passed me the paper, opened to Liz Smith's column, his finger on the item.

"Lemme see that." I focused on the blurb. "Don't tell City Hall," it said, "but lensman Charles Byrne and fashion luminary Susan Ferrante were tête-à-tête the other night at the East Side J. G. Melon bistro." My first reaction was, I liked seeing our names linked in print like that. And then I thought it felt creepy, an invasion of privacy, like being spied on. Where did they get that item? I wondered. It couldn't have come from Pharr, could it? I wondered whether Susan had seen it.

"You and Dolly's daughter," said Tito, eyeing me speculatively. "Anything to it?"

"I'm not in a position to confirm or deny it." I grinned.

"Uh-huh. Lensman Charles Byrne, I like that. You're a star, boss." He beamed.

"Yeah, sure. Twenty-five hundred bucks'll get you mentioned in the column—you can be a star, too. It was a promotion idea of Pharr's."

"Show's to go, no one's all bad," he said grudgingly.

"I don't hear the phone ringing off the hook, do you?" That reminded me, I hadn't played back the answering machine yet.

"It's early."

"Don't hold your breath."

There were only two calls on the machine, Kiernan and Rudd, both from Friday. I returned Rudd's call first. He wanted to send over the architectural model to be photographed. I told him we'd be expecting it. He asked whether I'd made any progress on the La Fleur job. Not much, I told him. Well, get on the stick, he said, Fallon's had the meeting bumped up on him. It's always like that, take your time, but get it to me yesterday.

Kiernan was calling to inquire about the tapestry transparencies. I told him I could come over with them now, if he'd like. That'll be fine, he said, and twenty minutes later I was being ushered into the presence of the dowager. She looked chic, as always, in a basic black frock, presumably by Susan Ferrante, and about as good as you could hope to look at ninety. She dismissed Kiernan with an imperious wave of the hand, and gestured for me to be seated on an antique chair covered in raw silk. I'd say a Hepplewhite, but the truth is I wouldn't know a Hepplewhite from a ham sandwich. All I know for sure is it was covered in raw silk, was more than a hundred years old, and had less wear and tear than its owner.

"Nice to see you again, Mrs. Ransom," I said politely.

"A pleasure to see you again, sir," she said, roosting on a matching chair.

"Was your meeting with Dolly satisfactory?" I asked cautiously.

"Interesting," she conceded, "interesting."

"I hope she wasn't too difficult?"

"I'm not used to being talked to in that manner . . . but she's a genuine character." She chuckled.

"That she is, but I take it she's not your granddaughter."

"I haven't decided yet."

"Well, the suspense is killing me."

"Why is the woman living in the streets? Surely there must be other alternatives."

"There are. Dolly has a daughter, Susan Ferrante—I believe you know her—who'd gladly take her in."

"Ah, yes," said the old lady thoughtfully, "she was mentioned in the *Times* article."

"There were two daughters, actually. The other daughter's name was Sharon Raynes—"

The old lady shot forward in her chair, her face fierce enough to light kindling, her eyes bright as coals. "Did you say Sharon Raynes, sir?"

"Yes. She died a month or so ago in a fall. Did you know her?"

She collapsed back into the chair, seemingly spent and

confused. "Yes, I knew Sharon. Well, that explains that," she mumbled to herself.

"Explains what?" I asked.

"Never mind. Go on with what you were saying."

"Well," I continued, "I was about to say that I've discussed the situation with Susan Ferrante, and she tells me she's done everything in her power to get her mother off the streets, but to no avail. She's been stymied at every turn, by the courts, and even by Dolly herself. We live in a democracy, and it seems if Dolly wishes to live in the streets, well, that's her right and choice."

"What kind of choice is that?" snapped the old lady. "Did you mention to Susan that I was interested in her mother?"

"The subject came up."

"What was her reaction?"

"She was astonished, to say the least. She said Dolly was an orphan, and she seemed to think it highly unlikely that her mother could be your granddaughter. I also asked her how her mother happened to come up with the name Dolly Varden."

"And what did she say?" the old woman asked, watching me keenly.

"She said she didn't know. Her mother could be one character one day, and a completely different one the next. I wonder, Mrs. Ransom, does the name Dolly Varden mean anything to you?"

"Why do you ask, Mr. Byrne?"

"Because it seems to me, all that distinguishes Dolly from the rest of the orphans her age is her name."

"You are observant, sir. But that is what names are for."

"All the same, it's not a common name."

"I'd like to confide in you, sir, but I think it's wiser I keep a few of the pieces of this puzzle to myself."

"I've also been wondering why you haven't spoken directly to Susan Ferrante about her mother."

"I'm unaccustomed to being interrogated, sir," she said testily.

"Sorry," I murmured.

"I suppose you mean well. I was hoping to make my

inquiries discreetly. I see now that that is impossible. I've been reluctant to speak to Susan for fear of embarrassing her, and, more important, because I wouldn't want to raise any false expectations."

"Concerning your estate?"

"Yes."

"I understand. Still, it seems to be the simplest way to clear the matter up once and for all."

She gave me a tolerant smile. "This is not a simple matter, Mr. Byrne. There's a great deal at stake here, and I'm one woman, alone, and trying to cope."

"But you have your son, Mrs. Ransom."

"And he has his own interests."

"I see what you mean. Does Marc have an interest in the La Fleur, Mrs. Ransom?"

"He is the CEO of a limited partnership, and he manages the building, but I control the major interest. Why do you ask?"

"I'd heard it was a Ransom property, and it seems ripe for development."

"Not while I'm alive," she said, eyes blazing. She rose from the chair, signaling an end to the audience. I stood immediately. Kiernan appeared like an obedient genie. "Bernard, see to it that Mr. Byrne is paid for his services."

"Yes, Florine."

She extended her bony hand. "If you'll excuse me, sir, I'll say good-bye now."

"Thank you. Good-bye, Mrs. Ransom," I said. Bernard waited by the door. I turned to follow him.

"One moment please, Mr. Byrne," the old lady called after me.

"Yes, ma'am?" I hesitated.

"Did you say Sharon died in a fall?"

"Yes, ma'am."

"Was it an accident?"

"It's my understanding it was ruled a suicide."

"How is it you happen to be so well informed, if I may ask?"

I told her, briefly, how I happened to be working in her son's apartment at the time, and was present when the body was identified. "I see," she said. "Thank you for coming, Mr. Byrne."

I murmured, you're welcome, and followed Kiernan. I waited while he cut me a check. "Are you a gambling man, Bernard?" I asked.

"I like to go to Atlantic City now and then."

"What kind of odds would you give me Dolly's the old lady's granddaughter?"

"God, I hope I don't look like Jimmy the Greek," he said, tearing off the check and handing it to me.

"I'd say they're pretty long, wouldn't you?"

"I like long shots, myself."

"Did Sharon Raynes visit the old lady privately during the summer?"

"It's possible. I don't remember."

On my way back to the studio, I recalled the last meeting with the dowager. She'd told me she'd been approached by an acquaintance, a young woman claiming to be her granddaughter. The mention of Sharon Raynes's name seemed to have touched a nerve. What if Sharon Raynes had been the young woman, and had had the right idea but the wrong chronology? She had Dolly pegged as Florine's daughter, instead of granddaughter. Florine said she never heard from the woman after that. If it was Raynes, the reason was obvious. Because of the mix-up in chronology, the old lady would have had to suspect a fiddle. But she was just cute enough to play along with Raynes. What else did she have to do? After all, when the days dwindle down to a precious few, they probably tend to drag a bit. Then, just when she was beginning to wonder why she hadn't heard from Sharon Raynes, and dismiss the incident as another hustle, along comes the *Times* piece, and with it, a renewal of interest. What was it about the article that fired her up again? Although there was no mention of a connection between Dolly and Raynes, or even Susan and Raynes, for that matter, the old lady could figure it out for herself. But so what? Neither Dolly nor Susan had applied for membership in the Ransom clan. If Raynes was the unnamed woman who had approached the old lady during the summer, she was dead. That should have been the end of the matter. Case closed. It was easy to see that Marc Ransom came by his opaqueness naturally. And that you don't put together a unit by being transparent. I wondered just what pieces of the puzzle Florine was keeping to herself.

Later that day, Tito and I returned to the La Fleur. It didn't perturb me any that Rudd and Fallon were suddenly in a rush for their pictures. I'd had about enough of the Ransoms and their money. It's a funny thing about money —it has a gravitational pull all its own, like the sun. If you're not careful, it sucks you into its orbit. Look at Josephine and Fallon, Mumminger and Kiernan. Luckily, the Ransoms hadn't put my scruples to the test yet, and advertising still paid better. Until they upped the ante, there was little danger of me becoming just another one of their satellites. I was anxious to wrap the job and move on. I could live with being a nova more easily than being a dead planet.

19

The La Fleur looked benign and tranquil under the flat and failing light. The days were growing shorter, and there was a bite in the air.

Angel wasn't in his usual spot. Either it was too cold for him or it was siesta time. No one seemed to be around. It was too early for the rush-hour drug traffic, the kids were still in school, and their mothers were wasting another day at the welfare office.

"What do you say we go inside?" I suggested.

"You nuts?" Tito said, as if I'd asked him how he'd like a stick in the eye.

"Come on, the coast is clear."

"I want combat pay, I go in there."

I tried appealing to the photographer in him. "Might get some good pictures," I said.

"Might get your cameras liberated," he countered.

I tried shaming him. "What's the matter, no *huevos?*"

"I got 'em, all right," he insisted, "and I don't want 'em scrambled."

"Hey, no problem." I grinned. "Anything happens, we'll sue the Ransoms for all they're worth. It's a piece o'cake. Come on, I'm going in."

"You're crazy, Byrne, you know that?" he said stubbornly, and followed like a good soldier.

Daylight leached through the bare, grime-encrusted French windows facing the street. The only other light source was a dismal sixty-watt bulb where a chandelier had once hung. The once stately walls with their dilapidated, ornate plaster moldings, a relic of happier, more elegant times, were painted over with flaking layers of landlord green. Off in one corner, a plastic potted palm looked as if it had died. There were several orange stack chairs scattered about on the industrial carpet, which was patched and badly stained and tacky underfoot. The place stank of decay and Pine Sol.

An obese desk clerk with a pineapple face looked up from his newspaper and blinked, taking a second look. I smiled and nodded amiably as we continued through the lobby to the elevators. His sleepy eyes followed us. I had a line ready. We were from the office. It had the advantage of being true, but he never challenged us. This wasn't the Thackeray. This place was a landfill for human debris.

"Maybe he thinks we're here to cop some drugs or get a blow job," said Tito.

"Maybe."

We stepped into a war-scarred elevator. I pressed sixteen and the door stuttered shut. The motor whined, the slack snickered out of the cable, and the cab lurched up the shaft.

"I'm suing for whiplash," Tito muttered sourly. "Where're we going anyway?"

"To the top," I said. "We'll work our way down floor by floor."

"I can hardly wait."

The elevator came to a halt, dropped suddenly, and then slowly crept up about six inches. After a while the door opened reluctantly. "Watch your step." I grinned. Tito scowled. It was still a full six inches short of the mark.

We peered up and down the hallway, getting our bearings. There was no one in sight. A mixture of sounds and smells indicated the presence of humans. Radio talk shows and TV game shows toyed with their audiences' fears and greed. Rap music thumped from a boogie box, and dribbled your brain like a basketball. Oregano, garlic, and roach spray were a few of the more familiar smells.

"This way," I said, picking a direction, any direction.

Some people had left their doors ajar for cross ventilation, and we caught a glimpse of their rooms—cells, really—as we passed. The bed took up sixty percent of the floor space. The windows were covered with bed sheets, shower curtains, or whatever could be improvised. Milk, sugar, coffee, tea, beer or booze were just a few of the items stored on the windowsills. There was usually a hot plate, and there might be a TV or Mr. Coffee for the more affluent. Electrical outlets sprouted extension cords. Laundry was strung up. Clutter and confusion ruled. Eight pairs of soft brown eyes, a mother and three small children, gazed at us soulfully from one room. We looked away and kept walking.

"Think this door leads to the roof?" I asked.

"Probably," said Tito, "but you don't want to go up there."

"Why not?"

"'Cause surer'n shit, someone's up there."

"Let's have a look."

"Man," he muttered in exasperation.

I pulled open the door and we piled up the stairs. Tito was right. There were three of them passing around a crack pipe, two guys and a girl, young Hispanics. "You guys cops?" said one of the guys.

Tito answered him in Spanish and they relaxed. The first guy said something in Spanish. "They wanna know if we'd like to get high?" Tito said.

"Another time, maybe, tell him," I said, doing my best to appear friendly.

There was a rapid-fire exchange in Spanish. Tito turned back to me. "They wanna know if we'd like to buy some drugs, they've got some good shit." He grinned.

Before I could answer, the girl let out a rapid-fire burst, also in Spanish.

"She wants to know, would we like to party?"

"Tell them it's nice of them to ask, we'd really love to, but unfortunately we don't have the time right now. Maybe later."

Tito relayed our apologies. They'd begun circling us. The second guy, who'd remained silent until now, said, in plain English, "You ain't cops, you ain't buyers, what the fuck you doing here?"

"We're scouting a location," I said, and Tito translated.

"For a movie?" the girl asked in English. All cameras were movie cameras to some people.

"For 'Wiseguys,' the TV show," said Tito.

"Yo, bro, that show ain't been on for years," said the belligerent one.

"They're bringing it back," Tito said.

"I seen that show," said the first guy, "it's cool."

"Yo, man, take my picture," demanded the belligerent one.

A photographer foolishly said no in a similar situation a few years ago and got himself stabbed to death. What does it hurt to pop off a couple of frames? "What do you think?" I asked Tito, pretending to consider the ugly son of a bitch.

"I like him," said Tito thoughtfully. "They're all good," he added.

I arranged the three of them, and stepped back admiringly. Tito was focusing on them. The girl tried to look seductively into the lens, the guys tried to look bad. "Lookin' good," I lied, and cranked off a few shots. They broke up laughing, too pleased with themselves to hold the pose for long. They'd been validated. They were happy. We said good-bye and they went back to their crack pipe.

"Satisfied?" said Tito as we clamored down the stairs.

"Hey, was that a great shot or what?"

We didn't waste any time on the eleventh floor, it was pretty much a repeat of twelve. Stepping over a pair of derelicts sleeping off a wine drunk as we made our way down to ten, it crossed my mind that the stairwell was a perfect spot for a mugging.

"Seen enough?" Tito asked hopefully.

"Yeah, I think so." I scanned the corridors, satisfied ten

was running true to form. "Come on, we'll skip the rest and take the elevator down."

"All right," Tito said, brightening considerably.

I pressed the elevator button hard, beginning to feel some of Tito's anxiety. If the stairwell was a good place to get mugged, the elevator was even better. The indicator showed both cabs on the ground floor. I leaned on the button continuously. "Come on," I pleaded.

A woman's scream pierced the ambient sound of TVs and ghetto blasters. "He's an old man, leave him alone!" Smack! Then a baby was bawling. We interrupt this program to bring you a news special.

Tito and I swapped looks. We bolted down the corridor. A spindly black girl, a bawling child on her hip, sobbed into her hand. Four goons were working someone over.

Tito leveled the Nikon to his eye and fired. They froze like statues. The flash etched them on my retina. One was Angel. The bandaged one was James. The other two were strangers. An old man was lying on the floor.

"Yo, James, lookee 'ere." Angel grinned, his vision clearing.

"Duh dude dat burnt me," said James, advancing slowly, like a mummy.

One of them flicked open a switchblade. The four of them advanced.

Tito and I began backpedaling. I sighted my camera and let them have a blast of strobe. The flashes took forty seconds to recharge, an eternity. We'd shot our load.

"Man, I knew something like this was gonna happen," Tito complained. While they blinked and saw spots, he ripped the fire extinguisher off the wall.

"Get the fuckers," Angel barked.

Tito aimed the nozzle at one and then the other as they circled, juking and feinting.

Then the bomb seemed to go off. The explosion was deafening. I could see fear in the eyes of the goon in front of me, but it wasn't caused by Tito or me. The woman was screaming, her baby bawling. My ears were ringing from the gunshot. Angel and James and their pals were staring into the barrel of a .38 Police Special.

"Chill, bro. Okay?" Angel pleaded. "We jus' tryin' tuh help da ol' guy up is all. . . ."

"Fuck you were."

"We din't mean no harm, man."

"Get yo asses outta here 'fore I blow 'em off."

A rugged-looking black in his forties recocked the .38.

"Steady, man," said one of the goons.

"Move it," said the black man.

"Be seein' ya, homes," Angel said through his green teeth. "We know where yuh lib."

"Thas two ah owe ya, whitey," said James, smelling of camphor as he pimp-rolled by.

"You be shittin' in a bag, you don't move it," said the gunman. He aimed the weapon at Angel's ass. Angel scurried out of sight.

The old man, the same one Tito had wanted to photograph, was crawling on all fours, unable to stand, and mumbling incoherently.

"You all right?" I asked.

"Help me to my feet."

Tito and I hoisted him to his feet, supporting him on either side. "Anything broken?" I asked anxiously.

"Don't think so," he said gamely. He seemed more shaken than anything else.

"They was beatin' on 'im fo' nut'n," the woman sobbed. "They animals."

"It'll be all right now, sister," said the gunman, comforting her.

"Where do you live, pop?" Tito asked.

The old man nodded at an open door.

I hesitated. "Maybe we should take you to the emergency room and let them have a look at you," I said.

"No you don't. I won't go there." He was shaking his head decisively. "If you'll help me to my room, I'll be all right."

We helped him into a hovel of a room and onto the bed. The old man lay on his back, trembling slightly.

"Can we get you something?" I asked.

"No, no, just let me rest. Thank you, thank you."

"You want us to call anyone?"

"There's no one," he said.

Remarkably, all he seemed to have suffered in the scuffle was a cut lip. Tito found a washrag, wet it in the tiny sink, and placed it on the old man's lip. The old man promptly removed the compress, placing it on his forehead. Hands folded across his chest, he looked as stoic as a corpse.

Our protector appeared in the doorway. "How're ya doin', ol' man?" he asked.

"Fine, fine," the old man answered.

"Dey get you money?"

"Didn't have any on me," said the old man.

Tito nudged me. He'd been thumbing through a scrapbook on the bureau. It was full of theatrical clippings, playbills, and reviews from the forties and fifties. Aldo Fabrizi was the old man's name. In his salad days he'd been a tenor with the City Center Opera Company.

"Mr. Fabrizi," I said, "do you have money to eat?"

"Yes, yes, but I'm not hungry."

"Is there anything we can do for you?"

"No, nothing, thank you," he said. The washrag shielded his eyes and his humiliation from us. "Leave me now. I'll be fine," he said.

"Ah'll look in on ya later, ol' man," said the black man. He motioned for us to follow him.

"Fine, that'll be fine," the old man murmured.

"Mah room's jus' down the hall," he said, closing the door softly after us.

Tito shot me a skeptical glance, and we trailed after the black man. Before opening the door to his room, he offered me a callused mitt. "Mah name's Sonny," he declared.

"Pleased to meet you, Sonny," I said, shaking his hand. I introduced Tito and myself.

"Ya'll look like ya could use a short one." He grinned, and ushered us into an austere but neat room. There was a cot, a steamer trunk, a couple of pieces of cheap luggage, some cartons, and a stack chair like those in the lobby. There was a roll shade on the window, which had a view of the street. "Be it ever so humble," he apologized. "Flop wherever you can." Tito took the chair. I sat next to Sonny on the cot. He tossed the gun between us, bent over and felt around underneath the cot. He produced a bottle, of Alexi vodka

189

and medicinal-size paper cups. He handed us each a cup, uncapped the bottle, and poured. "'Ere's to ya," he proposed.

We nodded, and tossed the vodka down in one swallow.

"'Ere," said Sonny, refilling our cups. "Whatcha'll doing in this shithole?"

"Taking pictures for the landlord," I said, figuring it was best to be straight with him.

"Landlawd? Sheet." He snorted in disgust.

"It's a job," I said.

"Ah only been 'ere since Friday, bud dat wo'man wid dah baby say dose fuggers been hasslin' duh tenants alla time."

"Angel and his pals?"

"Da fuggers down duh hall. Dey on duh landlawd's pad. Dey wan' everybuddy out."

"She say that?" I asked, wondering if that explained the envelope Rudd passed Angel.

"'S wha' she say."

"What are you gonna do, Sonny?"

"Me? Sheet, don' make no diff'rence tuh me. Ah'll find a place. Ah'm not like dese peebles, Ah can work."

"What do you do?"

"Was workin' fo' a contract'r inna Village, bud he got slow and hadda lay me off."

"Where were you living before here?"

He grinned ruefully. "Riker's Island." Tito fidgeted in his chair. "Before dat Ah hadda place in Washin'ton Heights." He proceeded to tell us about how the day he'd been laid off he'd come home to find no woman and no supper, so he got drunk. As luck would have it, the Pakistani landlord had to pick that time to come looking for two months' rent. Sonny took his frustration out on the landlord, and the judge gave him thirty days in the cooler.

"What happened to your woman?" I asked.

"Duh Pakie threw 'er ass outta duh apartment, motherfugger. She young, had nowhere tuh go, so she hopped duh bus home tah Georgia."

"Sorry to hear that."

"Sheet, she be back," he said philosophically. "Soon's

Ah'm back on mah feet, Ah'll send 'er a ticket. Ain't nuttin' fo' a woman like dat in Georgia."

"Glad to hear that," I said, sipping vodka.

"Ya know how wimmens be." He grinned.

Tito and I agreed we did. "How you fixed for cash?" I asked.

"Ah'm all right."

I had four twenties in my wallet. "Got a couple of twenties?" I asked Tito.

"Hey, Ah don' wan' no charity," Sonny said indignantly.

Tito gave me the money, and I offered Sonny a hundred bucks. "It's not charity, it's a loan, till you're back on your feet," I said. "And maybe the old guy could use a couple of bucks."

"All right den, thanks, man," he said, accepting the bills reluctantly.

I finished my vodka and got to my feet. "Gotta bolt, Sonny," I said, handing him a business card. "You need a hand with anything, gimme a call."

"Thanks again, man," he said with a smile.

We weren't home free yet. We had to pass Angel and James as we left the hotel. "Yo, whitebread," James called, the minute he spotted us, "we be lookin' fo' ya, me an mah Bic."

"Say it, James." Angel grinned.

"We gonna light you fire, know what Ah mean?" James taunted.

"Oh, yeah, try it, asshole," I said lamely. James and I were in each other's faces, doing the stare. Unadulterated malevolence. They hated me. I hated them. I hated them because the streets belonged to them. Because they were predators. Because they made me dream of being Charles Bronson, or Bernie Goetz. I hated them because they made me hate.

"Who ya callin' asshole, faggot?"

"Tell 'em, bro." Angel grinned, juking behind him.

Tito gave me a shove. "Come on, let's go."

The drugstore was open, and they had prescriptions to fill instead of wasting time with us. Tito gave me another shove. James got the last word in. "You toast, honky," he called.

"You hear what he called me?"

Tito kept on prodding me down the block. "What, whitebread, faggot, or honky?"

"All of them. Where's their sensitivity? You can't go around calling people names. That's a crime nowadays." I grinned. "We ought to turn that asshole in to the Bias Crimes Unit."

"They gotta be beating on you when they call you a name."

"Maybe you're right."

"Since we're here, maybe we should have a look at the surveillance camera," he suggested.

"Not a good idea at the moment. Besides, I changed the tapes last night."

"Anything on it?"

"About what you'd expect, and then some." I told him about Rudd and Lesser, and the hard hats with the van.

By this time we were standing in the triangle in front of Macy's. "So, what do you want to do?" said Tito. He glanced at the camera around his neck. "I've only taken half a dozen shots."

"Angel and James in the hallway?"

"A couple of those, and the kids on the roof."

"Forgot about those."

"We were gonna wrap the job, remember?"

"Yeah, but I think we've had enough fun for one day. Why don't you hop the train here."

"You sure?"

"Sure, lets call it a day. Give me your camera, I'll shoot out these rolls first thing in the morning."

"You're the boss," he said, handing over the Nikon.

20

I was lobbing darts and trying to decide whether or not to call Susan Ferrante when the phone rang. "Hi, Charlie, what are you up to?" asked the abrasive voice of Josephine Cyzeski.

"Right now? I'm working," I lied, chucking a dart. It hit the board with a thunk.

"Can I lure you away?"

"What's up?"

"I wanna show you my new place."

"New place?"

"The Raynes apartment."

"You got the Raynes apartment?"

"That's right. Wanna see it?"

This I had to see. "Sure," I said, putting a little more zip on the next dart.

"Okay, I'll meet you there in an hour. You know the address, right?"

"Right."

193

"Oh, and Charlie," she said, her voice softening, "I'm off the medication, dude."

"Great," I lied. I threw the last dart in a straight line. It hit the bull's-eye with a satisfying thwack!

"What's that sound I keep hearing?"

"Nothing, I'm working on a shot."

The Afghani cabdriver wasn't named for any prophets, but he was a believer. After a discussion of the differences between Urdu and English—it's written from right to left, and is similar to Arabic—we agreed that Salman Rushdie was probably a wiseguy. I didn't ask, but I didn't get the impression he was eager to whack Rushdie. He dropped me at 211 East Sixty-seventh.

Raynes's building, a prewar, art deco affair, was more upscale, or higher-end residential, than Josephine's other co-op primarily because of location. Location, location, location, as they say. I noticed the Residential Realty sign, which was the name of Ransom's residential entity. The doorman was the same donkey I'd had trouble with the last time I was there. I pretended not to remember him, and he returned the favor. "I'm here to see Miss Cyzeski," I said. "My name's Charles Byrne."

Without a word, he buzzed and announced me. I heard Josephine tell him to send me up. "Go ahead," he said in a surly tone. "Ten B."

I rode up to the tenth floor. There were four apartments to a floor, and Josephine had left the door of 10B ajar. I entered, and not seeing anyone, called, "Anyone home?"

"In here."

"Where?"

"Here," she repeated.

I traced her voice like a bat on sonar until I found her in a dingy, bare room in the rear of the apartment. "There you are."

"Well, how do you like it?" she asked excitedly.

"Real nice. What's the maintenance on a crib like this?"

"Don't ask," she laughed. "This is a servant's room, or a utility room," she explained, as though I were a potential buyer. "Come on, I'll show you the rest of the place." She slipped her arm through mine.

"I think I've seen most of it searching for you."

"Let's look at it together." She gave me the guided tour of the six rooms, two baths. "Nellie says he'll paint and do the floors. I think I can get him to put in a new bath and kitchen, too, if I work on him a little."

"Can't beat that," I said, noticing the new window frame and glass with the manufacturer's stickers still on them in the master bedroom. I disengaged myself from her for a look at the courtyard below, where Raynes's body had fallen. "This must be where she jumped from," I said.

"Uh-huh," she murmured, hugging herself.

I glanced over at the discreet windows of Ransom's apartment. "Real handy." I smiled. "You can put a show on for the boss."

"Marc didn't need to peep at Sharon," she said.

"Anyone'll look in a window if there's something to see." I gazed down at the courtyard again, trying to imagine how she must have looked from this perspective. It seemed to me she'd landed quite a distance from the building.

"I've got a bottle of champagne in the fridge," she said, pulling me away from the window.

"What are we celebrating?"

"My new apartment . . . and I'm back in commission. I'd say that calls for a small celebration, wouldn't you? Be right back," she said, and ran off.

I put my palm against the window frame and pushed; there was no give to it. It was hard to imagine Sharon Raynes taking a running jump at a window like this, although the old window might have been different. I gazed down into the courtyard again. How could she have landed on her back if she'd jumped? She would have had to do half a revolution in the air. Josephine was about the same size as Raynes. I tried to imagine throwing her out the window. I'm probably stronger than average, but it wouldn't be easy, especially if she put up a fight. There was something else: if she had jumped, or been pushed, from the window, why hadn't she been cut by glass?

"Hey, what are you doing in there?" said Josephine. She had a bottle of Kristal in one hand and a pair of chilled stemmed glasses in the other. "Let's go to the living room. The movers left a couple of chairs."

We sat on a pair of cheap tubular-chrome kitchen chairs facing a window that also looked out on the courtyard. It was a rear apartment. The angle was too oblique, though, to see Ransom's apartment. Josephine hiked up her skirt and gripped the bottle between her knees. She unwrapped the wire and popped the cork like an expert. She squealed with delight when the champagne sprayed her face and foamed over on her hand. She poured quickly and deftly, not spilling another drop.

"To your new place," I said, raising my glass.

"I'll drink to that," she said, touching glasses. She took a long sip before kicking off her heels, putting her feet up on the windowsill, and making herself comfortable. She wiggled her toes in pleasure.

"Can you afford this place?"

"Nope."

"What are you gonna do, sublet it?"

"I'm gonna flip it. The sooner I do it, the more I make. I could net as much as two hundred thousand dollars after I pay off Marc."

"Does he know you intend to flip it?"

"Why do you think he let me have it?"

"You must have been an awfully good girl for Daddy to slip you two hundred grand just like that."

"Marc's very generous with his employees," she said pretentiously.

"Don't mind me, I'm just jealous. Think he could use a full-time photographer?"

"I don't think so, but you're first in line," she laughed, refilling our glasses. "Besides, Marc's not doing it purely out of the goodness of his heart."

"There's always a catch, isn't there?"

"Yep."

"Let me guess—the reason you're getting the place so cheap is because he needs to sell a certain number of apartments to satisfy the co-op conversion plan, and your vote is in his pocket at board meetings?"

"Anything wrong with that?"

"Yeah, it stinks."

"You wouldn't do it?"

"I didn't say that." I don't think the moral nuances of speculating in the housing market held much interest for her.

"How often do you get a chance to make that kind of money for almost nothing?" she asked.

"Me? Never, so far. How much is 'almost nothing'?"

"All I can put up is twenty thousand."

"And how much is Marc selling it to you for?"

"One fifty."

"An insider's insider, huh?"

"Much less," she replied, with a wickedly greedy grin.

"You have to put up twenty percent, or thirty grand, don't you?"

"That's right. Marc's loaning me the difference."

"Sharon Raynes must have had a similar deal, huh?"

"She was a renter—the co-op conversion plan hadn't kicked in yet—but I'm sure Marc would have done something for her. Why?"

"Just wondering," I said. "Here's looking at you, kid— I'd say you're golden." I raised my glass to her. Two hundred grand was a lot of money. Why was Ransom being so generous with her? Could Josephine have polished off Sharon Raynes for the apartment? I wondered. Nah.

"Thank you," she said, getting up suddenly, "and it couldn't happen to a nicer person. All this talk about money turns me on, how about you?" She grinned.

"It has the opposite effect on me."

"Well, let's see if we can't do something about that, dude," she said, crouching.

"Hey, it isn't up to me," I said, glancing down ruefully.

"Don't worry. That's one dictator I can lick any day in the week."

"Forget about it," I said, gripping her wrists.

"Got another girl?"

"Yeah," I said lamely.

"I don't mind."

"Look, I've gotta be the one who makes the moves," I apologized, standing up, "otherwise I'm a dud."

She jumped up, too. She wasn't going to take no for an answer, and neither was the dictator. "Okay, make your move, stud," she dared me, rubbing against me. "Trust me, no way are you gonna be a dud. You can tie me up with my own panty hose if you want to."

"That's an idea."

"I've got a better idea," she said, her eyes moist and shining. "Whaddya say we move it to the bedroom and give Marc a show?"

"Is he home?"

"Who knows, who cares?"

"What about the neighbors?"

"Let 'em watch . . . you chicken?"

"Whatta you say we go get something to eat?"

"Let's eat in." She grinned lasciviously.

"Eat, like in food, I mean."

"All right, let's get something to eat," she said, slipping into her heels and straightening her skirt.

Believe me, it's not like I'm so successful with the ladies I can afford to turn down a sure thing, but Josephine made me feel about as special as a vibrator.

We were headed for Third Avenue when she suddenly remembered a call she had to make and ducked into a phone booth. Our eyes met while she was on the phone, and she looked away. She hung up, said she was sorry but something had come up. She'd call me, she said, and left me standing on the sidewalk feeling like a real wussy.

A woman like Josephine must get more than her share of unwelcomed propositions, and as a result, be more practiced fending off men. I've been turned down more often than the bed sheets, and most women have been smooth enough not to leave a wrinkle. They'll usually say something like, I'm seeing someone, I'm living with someone, I'm engaged, or I'm married, none of which seem to be impediments when they're interested. If the situation had been reversed, Josephine, I'm sure, would have let me down easy. It takes practice to turn someone down gracefully, more practice than the average man is likely to get in a lifetime. And I botched it. I wasn't expecting to lose much sleep over it, though. It's just I hate giving my gender a bad name. What would Dashiell Hammett have said?

I needed cat food and half-and-half, so I stopped by the Korean's before going home. Socrates was tied to a signpost outside the store. I picked up the items I'd come for and brought them to the cash register. Dolly hadn't noticed me—she was busy hassling with the clerk, who refused to take the Hefty bag full of tin cans she was returning.

"Dolly, what's up?" I said.

She wheeled and glared at me. "Oh, it's you," she said, when it dawned on her who I was.

"What's the matter?" I asked.

"Aw, the gook won't take my cans."

"Have you tried to say 'please'?"

The Korean shook his head, no, as he rang up my purchases.

"He has to take 'em, it's the law," Dolly insisted.

"Maybe he doesn't like to be called a gook."

The Korean's head was bobbing affirmatively. "You rerry rude person," he scolded Dolly.

"Hear that?" I said to her.

"He doesn't want to be bothered counting 'em," she complained.

"How about it?" I asked the Korean. "You've got to take them, it's the law."

"Gimme cans," he said.

Dolly handed over the Hefty bag, and we watched him count out the cans. He pulled a five and a dime from the cash register and slapped them down on the countertop.

"Say thank you, Dolly," I said.

"Thank you, Dolly," she said, scooping up the money.

I gave the Korean an apologetic shrug. He twirled a finger at his temple.

We walked up the block together, Socrates squirting here and there, posting his boundaries. She hit me up for the usual dollar. It had become an entitlement. I was beginning to regard her as my charity of choice. If Florine Ransom decided Dolly was her long-lost granddaughter, I wanted to be in her good graces. Maybe she'd remember my kindness.

Mort and Mo were loading cartons of cheap wristwatches into the Buick Century wagon. The old man spotted me and lit up like a kid at the circus. Mo'd seen me give Dolly the buck and tactfully averted his doleful gaze.

21

Suddenly, the pictures of Sharon Raynes's corpse blazed across the vidicon tube of my subconscious. The corpse moved, this way and that, jerky at first, like the sunflowers as they bloomed and died in time-lapse photography. Then it twisted and coiled into a serpent trying to trip me up.

I bolted upright from the bed. The LCD numerals on the clock bathed the room in an eerie green light. It was six-thirty, time to get up—that much I knew. I was damned if I knew why, though. I flopped back on the damp sheets, too spooked to think. I promised myself I'd do something about those pictures of Sharon Raynes. Stein or Strunk would know what to do, I thought, waiting for the fog to lift from my brain. What was it I was supposed to do at this ungodly hour of the morning? Except for the afterimages of the dream, my mind was a blank. I didn't have a clue what it meant, if anything. It was probably nothing more than a symptom of unspecified ambient anxiety, or in plain English, stress. It would go away eventually. But when? When I had a new agent, a million bucks, a Porsche, and Susan Ferrante, maybe. Those would do for starters.

All right, now I remembered—I had to finish shooting out those rolls of film and wrap the La Fleur job. I hauled myself out of bed, brewed the coffee, showered, shaved, dressed, and was out of there.

Good morning, America's wretched refuse, rise and shine! Give my regards to Broadway, remember me to Herald Square, because you won't be there ere long if Marc Ransom has his way. There seemed to be bodies everywhere, in the maze of tunnels that meet under the square, over airshafts, and on every park bench. It was as though a neutron bomb—a weapon that could only have been developed with the real estate interests in mind—had been dropped, killing the people and leaving the buildings standing.

I photographed people in sleeping bags or under cheap polyester blankets. I photographed the meanest and worst off under newspapers and cardboard. I photographed the better off in their refrigerator-carton pieds-à-terre, wondering where they had got them. Were that many refrigerators sold every day? I photographed them in doorways, huddling by the dozen for warmth. And the real cold weather was yet to come. What would they do then? Go underground like moles, most likely, or freeze to death. I shot out the two rolls and reloaded a couple of times, and it wasn't even seven-thirty yet. A few of the more enterprising homeless were up and on their feet now, in time to catch the first wave of commuters as they flooded out of Penn Station. I got pictures of them scrounging Dumpsters for breakfast and making nuisances of themselves panhandling the working stiffs on the way to another boring day on the job. God, how the camera loved this kind of stuff. Ransom couldn't ask for more. I had some sensational pictures.

By nine o'clock I'd shot half a dozen rolls of Tri-X and decided the La Fleur job was in the bag. While I was in the neighborhood, I changed the tapes on the surveillance camera. I already had what I wanted there, too, but I had the rental equipment and the space until the end of the month. I wouldn't save any money by striking the setup, I figured, so I might as well let it stand. This tape and the first tape I'd made were both in the four-hour-record mode, straight time from five P.M. to nine P.M.—nothing fancy. I switched the mode to six hours' recording time, and changed the timer to record from twelve noon to two P.M., from six P.M. to eight P.M., and from eleven P.M. to one A.M. That would give me a more complete picture of the day. Then I changed the angle of view by a degree or so, and zoomed in on the spot where Angel usually posted himself. Now I had a larger and slightly different image.

As I left the electronic eye, the kids from the La Fleur were on their way to school, a few of them even accompanied by their mothers. It was too early for Angel and his crew. I wouldn't expect them to show much before noon.

By the time Tito got in, I was back in the studio, drinking coffee and in the middle of the *Times.*

"Did you shoot out those rolls?" Tito asked, handing me the morning mail.

"Yep."

"Whaddaya know," he marveled. "Didn't think you could get up that early in the morning."

"Piece o' cake." I yawned. I had a gulp of coffee and pawed through the mail. "Shit," I muttered.

"No check, huh?"

"Nope. I gotta get on the horn to those mothers."

"Be cool," he advised.

"Don't worry, it's been a pretty good day so far. I'll be patient and reasonable."

"Meanwhile, what would you like me to do?"

"Well, you could block out the shot of the architectural model—we should knock that out."

"Okay."

I called the art director. He didn't know what was going on—all his suppliers were bitching, he said. Cold consolation. I should call the account guy. I did. It was out of his hands, he said. Call accounting. Right. I asked for accounts payable. I'd foolishly believed the last guy I'd spoken to, and neglected to write down his name. This time I got a woman. I explained patiently and politely what had been going on, and gave her the purchase order and invoice numbers. She

ran it through her computer, and yes, they'd received a copy
of the bill. So far so good. Next question. When do you
intend to pay it? She did not know that. Could you please
find out? I asked politely. She put me on hold. Maxine
Nightingale came on the line belting out, "Right Back
Where We Started From." She was followed by Olivia
Newton-John warbling "Have You Ever Been Mellow"—
you talking to me?—and then "Bad Blood" by Neil Sedaka.
I wondered who was doing the music score for my life.

I had the *Times* crossword puzzle half licked before
Accounts Payable picked up again. We'll be cutting checks at
the end of the week, she said. You should have your check by
next week. Where have I heard that before? I asked for her
name, and this time I noted it on my copy of the bill, along
with the date. Then I informed her, as gently as possible,
that if I didn't get my check by next week, I'd be obliged to
take matters into my own hands. Oh yeah, she said, genuinely curious, whatta ya gonna do? I said I had her name and
knew where she worked, and that I'd seek her out, bind,
blindfold, and gag her, and force her to listen to Neil Sedaka
until I was paid. Well, she said stiffly, it's in the computer.
And it's been there for nearly ninety days now, I rejoined.

It was going to be called Manor's Tower, get it? An
anagram for Ransom. Sooner or later all real estate moguls
get a boner to build a monument to themselves, and
Manor's Tower was apparently designed to satisfy Ransom's
edifice complex. If the architectural model was any indication, Manor's Tower would be all glitz and smoked glass
sixty-nine stories high—take that Trump Tower, mine's
bigger than yours by a whole story. The elevators would be
on the outside facing west, overlooking Herald Square and
the Hudson River. An upscale department store chain
would be the anchor tenant in the atrium. Whatever happened to lobbies? Plans called for a Broadway theater
complete with revolving stage and seating a thousand. There
would be swimming pools, tennis courts, driving and putting greens, as well as an electronically simulated eighteen-
hole golf course, along with the usual amenities like gyms,
saunas, jogging track, discos, and what have you. Not just

for out-of-towners; the place would be irresistible to New Yorkers in search of a mini-weekend vacation, too. That was the concept, anyway. A getaway city in the city. No travel hassles. It was no threat to the sedate Thackeray, though. It was strictly for novelty seekers, and there are plenty of those in New York.

Tito had dug up a painted backdrop of a cloudscape and placed it behind the model. From a low angle the effect was very realistic. The camera doesn't know the difference between a good scale model and the real thing, which makes shooting one fun. We'd been playing around with it for an hour, and I was timing a Polaroid, when the phone rang.

Surprise! It was Pharr's art director, the guy with the carpet ads. Had Rodger spoken to me about the ads? He mentioned them, I've seen the layouts. Good, how's your availability? Er, was the price okay? Sure, no problem, didn't Rodger tell you? I've been out of town, I lied. Well, we'd like to get cracking. Well, I'm available, soon as I get a purchase order, we'll start prepping. Okay, but first we have to have a pre-pro meeting with the client and account people. Okay, as soon as I have a purchase order. He said he'd messenger one right over. I told him I thought the ads were winners and I'd shoot my brains out for him. Well, Rodger spoke very highly of you, I'm looking forward to working with you, he said.

"Maybe I misjudged Pharr, maybe I was too hasty," I said, hanging up. Then I said, "Nah."

"Work," said Tito.

"The carpet ads."

"All right." He almost shouted, swinging a cocked arm and a clenched fist.

"Wait'll we get a P.O.," I advised, "then we'll celebrate."

I hadn't been quite truthful when I told Josephine talking about money didn't turn me on. If I'd have been the one talking about a quick $200,000 profit flipping an apartment, I'd have been randier than a televangelist. The anticipation of a purchase order worth fifteen grand was all the stimulation I needed to pick up the phone and call Susan Ferrante. Things seemed to be going my way today. How lucky could I get? Why not push it and find out?

"Susan Ferrante, please," I said to the voice that said, Susan Ferrante Designs.

"Whom shall I say is calling?"

"Charles Byrne."

"What is this in regard to, Mr. Byrne?"

This is in regard to my fervent desire to please your employer any way I can. To take her anywhere she wants to go, to tickle her fancy, and her pink, to kiss her brains out, and so on ad infinitum. "It's personal, I'm a friend of hers," I said.

"Just a minute, I'll see if Miss Ferrante's available." There was a long pause, no Musak, mercifully, and then, "I'm sorry, Miss Ferrante is unable to come to the phone at the moment. If you'll leave your name and number, Miss Ferrante will return your call as soon as possible."

Okay, so I wasn't going to get so lucky she'd take my call. I left my name and number, wondering whether I should have claimed to be Matty Fallon.

Tito made a run to the lab with the film, and when he got back, we ordered sandwiches and watched the surveillance tape while we ate lunch. Most of it was a repeat of what I already had, but there was one scene that took us by surprise. Tito had me run it back and forth several times, getting a kick out of it at first, and then growing more somber with each viewing. The electronic peeper had caught Tito and me on tape. It wasn't like the movies, though, where a blind man could tell the difference between the good guys and the bad guys. They didn't look that bad, we didn't look that good.

"Looks like four assholes in a fuck-you, fuck-you contest," said Tito. "You gonna show 'em the tape?"

"I don't think so."

"Why not? Isn't this what they're looking for?"

"Yeah, but they didn't ask for tape. That was my idea. We just photographed the model of what Ransom wants to put on that site. He wants the La Fleur empty. Sonny says these guys work for Ransom. They get paid to terrorize tenants. And the tape seems to back him up. Remember, Rudd and Lesser are on tape schmoozing with Angel and the guys with the van."

"Yeah, but Rudd's management, he has business there."

"Maybe, but what kind of business would he have with a couple of punks like Angel and James?"

"I see what you mean."

"Something's up. If Ransom wants to build his tower, he better get a move on. According to Stein, come the end of the month, the Landmark Preservation Committee votes on whether or not to grant the La Fleur landmark status. If they designate it a landmark, there goes Ransom's tower."

"So they designate the La Fleur as a landmark, what's the big deal? Ransom, or his boy Rudd, hires a torch. Oops, they say, the place burned down. May I build my hotel now?"

"You're a devious enough son of a bitch. Sure you're not a landlord?"

"You don't think it's happened?"

"For sure, Ransom's not going to let a little thing like a landmark designation stand in the way of building his tower. The trouble with arson, though, is the fire department might put out the blaze."

"Okay, then he's gotta pay off the Buildings Department inspectors and get the building condemned, or better yet, blow it up."

"Or implode it, make it look like a collapse."

"Yeah." He grinned. "That's the ticket. You're pretty devious yourself. How long have you had it figured out?"

"How long does it take? As soon as I saw the model, it was fairly obvious the La Fleur's days were numbered. He's gotta clear the site if he wants to build. Anyway, you and I are just talking trash. For all we know, Fallon's got the fix in—everything'll be done nice and legal. The La Fleur won't be designated a landmark. The Buildings Department will condemn, and Ransom'll get a permit to tear down and build."

"Sure." He smiled cynically. "What about the pictures in the hallway, with the old man—you gonna show those?"

"I don't see why not—that's what they commissioned us to shoot."

"But they're Rudd's goons, Angel and James and their playmates."

"They're also the riffraff that makes the neighborhood so

dangerous, and an eyesore. How were we supposed to know they're Rudd's goon squad? Besides, there's no reason for Rudd to suspect anything from a still photo."

"It'd be like those guys to get Angel and James to do their dirty work and then sell 'em out."

"Hey, how much you want to empty the building? Here's your money, see ya around. That's all there's to it. It's work for hire. Like us."

"Man, seems like we oughta tell someone about this."

"Who?"

"I dunno, the police, maybe?"

For him to suggest going to the police indicated an alarming level of concern. Tito was a card-carrying minority member, and as such had an even greater antipathy for the police than I did. "What would we tell them? We've got a suspicion Ransom's about to commit a crime? You know what they'll say, don't you, when they're through laughing in our faces?"

"They'll say he's a real estate guy, you knuckleheads, whatta ya expect—they're all crooked. Talk to us when you got something real."

"Anyway, what's the big deal? So he razes an old building without a permit—one he owns, or his mother owns— where's the harm in that?"

"He's destroying a part of our heritage."

"Go on, ged outta 'ere."

"Seriously, Charlie, don't you think we oughta do something about those pictures I took of the Raynes woman?"

"You know, I had a dream about those pictures last night. Yeah, I think you're right, we oughta do something about them. They're the real thing, at least." I dialed Strunk's number. "Lemme interface with our friend, the good cop," I said as I waited for someone to pick up.

"Message center," said a voice.

"P. C. Strunk, please."

"He's not at his desk. Would you like to leave a message?"

"Ask him to give Charlie Byrne a call," I said, and hung up.

"Not in?"

"It's still lunch—he's probably got his face in a bowl of

subgum wonton," I said. "Anyway, he's gonna say homicide's not his business."

"What about that cop, you know, the one that used to come around when you and Stein were running the sting on the Ponzie guy?"

"Detective Hannibal, you mean?"

"That's him."

I'd thought about calling Hannibal, but was reluctant to because of what had happened the last time. It was unfortunate, but an actor Stein and I had hired overplayed his part and got murdered for it. I still feel guilty about what happened. I let the guy get in over his head. Anyway, that's the reason I'd been dragging my feet and not making the call. "Let's see what Strunk says first," I said.

"He's gonna say, call homicide."

"Mañana." I grinned.

22

Stein called later that afternoon to pass along another request for a meeting of the odd fellows' club.

"Master Wok's the name of the place."

"Wiseguys, those Chinese. Doesn't Strunk eat anything else?"

"Not for lunch, apparently. See you tomorrow at twelve-thirty, sport," he said, and gave me the address and was gone.

Tito and I had wrapped for the day, and I was contemplating a bike ride when Susan Ferrante returned my call. She asked if I would like to attend a dramatist's workshop with her that evening. Three one-act plays by up-and-coming playwrights. Sure, I said without hesitation. I'd rather take her to the movies, but I'd attend a supermarket opening if that was the best shot I had at her. Seven-thirty, she said, and gave me an address way over in Hell's Kitchen, or Clinton, as it's now called by the gentry.

I had two hours before magic time. A nap would be nice, I decided. I wanted to be at my best tonight. I trucked upstairs and flopped on the bed. I closed my eyes, and visions of Susan Ferrante danced in my head. I was too excited to sleep. I pulled on the sweats and Nikes, pulled the Lejeune down off the rack, and lit out for the park. Forty-five minutes later, after an invigorating sprint around the short loop, I was back in the studio. I showered, shaved, and splashed liberal amounts of Givenchy cologne, a party favor from Florine's birthday bash, on my person, public and private parts. The next question was, what to wear? She'd look swell even though she'd be coming from the showroom and dressed for business. This was only a workshop, though. Casual, was called for, nothing too fancy—fat chance anyway. I had some latitude. Since I don't own any black leather and don't wear designer jeans or anything else with a designer label on it—let them buy space if they want to advertise—and since I'm not slim enough to pull off a "photographer chic" look, which gets them every time, I had to opt for a pair of gray slacks, a blue oxford cloth button-down, rep tie, blue blazer, and black loafers. No one's image of how a photographer should dress, but if clothes make the man, I'm in trouble.

It was a novelty to see me in a necktie, and I got the wide eye from Mort and Mo when I bumped into them in the hall.

"You look like you owe a million bucks," Dolly cracked as I passed her door. "What's the occasion—got a date with Ivana Trump?"

"Actually, I've got a date with your daughter."

"Do tell. Lemme have a dollar."

I donated to my favorite charity.

She snatched the bill from me and stuffed it into her clothing. "You oughta dress up more often," she advised. "It'd be good for the career."

"Think so, huh? I'll have to remember that. Well, see ya, Dolly." She didn't deny having a daughter. Was that progress, I wondered, or was her body chemistry momentarily in harmony?

"Have fun," she said.

I hoped to.

I set out for Clinton at a trot. The temperature had reached the sixties during the day, and now it was starting to drop. Looking west, across town to the Hudson River, I could see a glow of hazy salmon pink where the sun had just set. Aside from that, the sky was moody and overcast.

The address Susan had given me was west of Ninth Avenue. "The New Playwrights," it said on the announcement board of what had formerly been a Moravian church. Climbing the limestone steps, I tried to remember when I'd been inside a church last. A handful of people chatted excitedly in what had formerly been God's anteroom, if that's what you'd call it. There was a lull in the conversation as all eyes turned momentarily to me. I made an amiable face, and recognized Pauline Ransom's friend Paulo. He showed no sign of recognition, and the group resumed their chat. I looked for Susan. She wasn't there. It was early, so I plucked a piece of literature about the New Playwrights from a display rack and stepped outside to wait for Susan.

Browsing the pamphlet, I learned a New Playwright wasn't necessarily a young playwright—one of them was pushing fifty. A New Playwright was a beginner playwright, and one of the beginner playwrights was Pauline Ransom. Only Susan Ferrante could have lured me to this event, I thought, as the midnight-blue Mercedes sedan rolled up to the curb. Ransom was the first to emerge, and after him, Nelson Rudd. Josephine came in third, and Pam, Rudd's drag, finished out of the money. Ransom and Rudd shot their cuffs and stroked the blue serge, looking for all the world like bad imitations of Little Caesar. Ransom looked up, and the lenses of his glasses went blank, reflecting the last light in the sky. He trotted up the steps, Josephine at his side. "Nice to see you," he said.

"Same here," I replied, and smiled at Josephine. She nodded curtly, and they passed.

"Hi, Charlie," said Rudd, grinning slyly as he and Pam went by.

They'd shown no surprise at finding me there, which seemed curious to me. What had happened to Fallon? I wondered. I didn't really belong in this crowd. I glanced apprehensively at my watch. It was getting close to curtain time. I looked up and spotted Susan hurrying down the street. "Hi," she called out cheerfully. "Am I late?"

"Hi! You're right on time."

"Good," she said, and we hustled inside. Thirty or forty of us theater lovers filed into the nave of the church. A girl apprentice playwright ushered us to a row of folding chairs, handed us playbills, and told us to enjoy.

"You didn't tell me this was going to be a Ransom show."

"There are two other playwrights," she said, avoiding my eyes.

As the room went dark, Ransom cast a furtive glance my way.

Spotlighted center stage, a solitary figure delivered a rambling soliloquy. It was a guy with a glued-on gray beard, pedal pushers, sandals, and a torn short-sleeve shirt. We were asked to believe we were south of La Paz in a sleepy fishing village. The town hellion, it seems, had just returned from the States swearing to murder his father, rape his mother, and marry his half sister. Well, I wanna tell ya, the villagers knew how to deal with a rotten guacamole like that. They shredded him like he was rope cheese and fed him to the fishes. It drew a nice round of applause. Fasten your seat belt, I thought, we're in for a bumpy ride.

The next opus was set somewhere south of Savannah. The prodigal daughter returns home only to be beaten by her father for deserting him, raped by her uncle for exciting him, and murdered by her brother for the hell of it. These New Playwrights weren't fooling around—they took no hostages. The audience seemed to be eating it up, though. The play got a hardy round of applause.

Our gang stood in a tight circle during a cruelly short intermission, smiles frozen on our faces, murmuring words like "gripping," "powerful," and "riveting." Then the buzzer sounded and we drifted back to our seats.

"This is gonna be good," Rudd leaned over to assure me.

"They always save the best for last, don't they?" I said. "Have you seen it?"

"I've seen other plays of Pauline's," he said as the lights dimmed.

From the corner of my eye, I thought I saw Ransom measuring me again.

This time we were in the middle of the Mojave Desert.

The New Playwrights seemed to have a thing for the warmer climes. I know they made me sweat. A ripe Susan Sarandon type runs a trading post on the fringe of the reservation. She's got the hots for a handsome half-breed half her age who's been hanging around the store. Unbeknownst to the two of them, he's the baby she gave up for adoption after an unwanted teenage pregnancy. Now where have I heard that tune before? Anyway, the little papoose was adopted by his father, the chief. Now, it hasn't rained for many moons, and the rain man has been chanting and dancing for hours, to no avail. But then the babe seduces the young brave, and as they are doing the wild thing, the rains come and the desert blooms. No sooner is he a buck well spent than he discovers who he has been sleeping with. Ugh! You've ruined my life, he declares, turning hostile, and going on the warpath. When he tries to scalp Mom, she levels him with a frying pan, killing him in self-defense. Inconsolable with grief, she smokes and dries him, preserving him like beef jerky, and entombs him in a hogan in the backyard. Now they will be together forever. Man alive, lighten up, New Playwrights. Dickens, Faulkner, and Tennessee Williams have already mined this ore.

Our row did its job. We clapped wildly, grinning and bobbing our heads knowingly at each other, as though we'd just witnessed the second coming of Eugene O'Neill. The cast took their bows, and Rudd actually called out, "Author, author." The three New Playwrights took a bow. Cast and playwrights took a bow together, and it was over.

I was on my feet as soon as the applause died down.

"Marc's taking us all to dinner," said Rudd.

I looked for Ransom, but he'd slipped out while the house was still dark.

"He's gone to see Pauline," Rudd said. "We'll meet outside."

I touched the arm of the usherette. "Is there a men's room?"

"Downstairs, in the basement," she said.

Excusing myself, I peeled off from our party as they made their way toward the exit. Bellying up to the porcelain, I began rehearsing what to say to Ms. Ransom when we met.

"Moving," or "so intense," perhaps? I didn't think so. That approach was too vague to come across as sincere. I'd have to do better than that. "It was wonderful, I enjoyed it immensely." That sounded dopey, not to mention faggy. This was a tricky proposition, and I was going to earn my supper. Maybe I should put it in the form of a question? Something like "How'd you ever come up with the image of the desert as metaphor for death, rebirth, and death again? It was brilliant, simply brilliant." Yeah, I thought, zipping up, that's the ticket, something like that.

Confident I'd found a way to flatter the new playwright without seeming insincere, I pushed open the bathroom door. Voices came from across the hall, and Ransom and Josephine emerged from what appeared to be the actor's dressing room. They closed the door carefully after themselves, acting as though they thought they were alone. I hesitated, reluctant to intrude on them. There was some sort of exchange between them. Josephine stepped back suddenly, looking provocative, or provoked, or both, I couldn't tell which, and flung her shawl on the floor with a theatrical gesture.

"Pick it up!" I heard her command him.

Certain I didn't want to intrude upon them, I let the door close, continuing to observe them through the crack.

Ransom, his back to me, mumbled something I couldn't hear.

Wham! She hauls off and lets him have one right across the chops. His steel-rimmed eyeglasses were dangling off one ear. "I said, pick it up, wimp!" she repeated distinctly. She stood feet apart, hands on hips. I couldn't see her face, but I had the impression she was acting.

Ransom mumbled again, adjusting his glasses. Then, kneeling meekly, he retrieved the shawl, which lay on the ground where she'd flung it.

"Good boy," she praised him gaily, giving his cheek a pinch. "Let's go, mustn't keep the others waiting."

I waited a decent interval, to be sure they'd gone, before easing open the door. Ransom and Rudd were waiting for me in the street. Ransom's cheek was crimson where he'd been smacked, I noticed. His eyes narrowed to lasers behind the thick lenses when he saw me. Great, I thought, he knows I witnessed the scene in the basement.

"I'm afraid we can't all fit in," Ransom said. "The car's brand new, and I don't want to take a chance of scuffing the upholstery. If you don't mind walking, the name of the place is Orsini's. It's only a few blocks away, between Eighth and Ninth on Forty-sixth Street."

"I don't mind," I said, bending to catch a glimpse of Susan. She was busy chatting up the playwright. I watched Rudd climb into the front seat, and Ransom get in the back with the women. The sedan pulled away from the curb, and I began to walk.

They were in the restaurant waiting to be seated when I caught up to them again. Orsini's, very haute Italian, a bustling place after the theater, was on the ground floor of a brownstone. It was done in tones of peach and mauve, which contrasted nicely with the white linen. The waiters, in white also, were a youthful bunch, as quick in their movements and light on their feet as a soccer club. Orsini's sold pastas and pizziolas at extravagant prices. I checked the menu at the door.

Susan was still engaged with Pauline, and Rudd and Pam were absorbed with each other. Ransom, always watchful, seemed to be waiting for me to say something.

"Smells good in here," I offered. From a distance, with his rough complexion, wiry steel-gray hair, and lean build, he seemed taller, more menacing. Up close, though, his slimness and lack of height made him seem almost fragile, until you felt the raw power and raw energy that pulsed invisibly from the man. Constant exposure to Ransom must have been like living under high tension wires; after a while every bump and mole must seem malignant.

"Northern Italian cooking," he said.

"Come here often?" I asked inanely.

"Once in a while," he admitted. Why did I have the impression he had me figured out to the nickel and dime, and had concluded I wasn't worth much effort?

"Your table's ready, Mr. Ransom," said the maître d', "this way, please."

Ransom led the way. Relieved not to be going one-on-one

with a man I had nothing in common with, I ran a balance sheet of my own. Ransom's clothes were English-tailored. Mine were off the rack. Ransom rode in a Mercedes. I rode a Lejeune. He had a friend at Chase Manhattan Bank, and at Manny Hanny, and at Chemical, and at Salomon Brothers, and ad nauseam. And I had a dubious TRW report. Those were a few things in his favor. But I had a couple of things going for me. I was younger than he was. And I was taller than he was.

The first order of business, once we were settled, was the wine. Ransom asked around, and we agreed, a red wine to start.

"May I recommend the Amaroni de Tomasi," the maître d' suggested.

The Amaroni went for seventy dollars a bottle.

"We'll have two of those," said Ransom without hesitation.

A hundred and fifty bucks for grape juice? This must be some wine, I thought.

I was perusing the menu, and about to ask Susan what she was going to have, when Pam said, "Pauline, that was marvelous the way you used the image of the desert blooming as a metaphor for rebirth. How in the world did you ever come up with something like that?"

Rudd beamed with pride at Pam's brilliant question.

"The play was originally set in Forest Hills," Pauline said.

"Forest Hills, Queens?" said Pam. "No."

"Yes, she ran a bodega, and he was the son of a real estate developer," said Pauline. I couldn't tell if she was putting us on.

"No," scoffed Pam.

"It's true," said Pauline. "But the play wasn't working. And then I had this dream, and it was my play, set in the desert. Voilà, it worked, and that was all there was to it."

"Isn't that interesting," said Pam, in awe.

The wine arrived, and after Ransom had tasted it, he turned to me and said, "What did you think of the play, Charlie?"

"Me?" I stalled, silently cursing Pam.

The playwright studied me avidly, expecting nothing less

than extravagant praise. With the exception of Paulo, who seemed more involved with his hair than the group, the others seemed to be enjoying my discomfort. Josephine regarded me coolly, hoping, no doubt, I was about to put my foot in my mouth. She didn't mind me seeing her with Ransom; on the contrary, she flaunted it, giving him soulful looks, brushing against him and touching him. If she was dominant when they were alone, in public she was totally submissive. At the same time, though, it annoyed her seeing me with Susan.

"Yes, what did you think?" Ransom repeated.

"Well, I'm no critic, but frankly I was disappointed . . ." I said, pausing for effect.

Father and daughter frowned. The others looked apprehensive. Rudd looking as though he would have a bird. But Josephine favored me with a faint and sanguine smile.

". . . in the production. I thought you deserved better, Pauline."

"It's only a workshop," she said, relieved.

"Still, I was impressed," I went on. "The writing had weight, I thought." Not the happiest choice of words there, but a natural association. "I agree with what Pam had to say about the atmosphere, and the imagery of the desert and all. Have the Public Theater people seen it?"

Father and daughter beamed with pleasure. Josephine looked away in disgust. "We sent out invitations," said Pauline, "but it's impossible to get people like that to attend a workshop."

"I can imagine. Perhaps your father can help," I said, leaning back to let the waiter pour. "The Public Theater must accept contributions."

The glance Pauline gave her father told me I wasn't the first to think of this. "That's a thought," Ransom agreed.

"To Pauline and her success," Rudd proposed, raising his glass, and deflecting the thought.

We toasted the new playwright, and then there was a pause in the bootlicking while we took time to order. Susan had sautéed sole, and I had a pizziola from an Italian province I'd never heard of. Ransom ordered a club steak and a salad, and Josephine had an omelette. Pauline claimed she was too excited to eat, and had a salad. Paulo, however, made up for her, ordering an antipasto, two pastas, and a surf, turf, sky combination. Rudd ordered linguine in white clam sauce, and Pam a scampi.

"Buono," said the waiter, and he darted off.

The brownnosing resumed in earnest. While we ate, the new playwright stuffed herself on obsequiousness, and morsels from Paulo's plate. Susan said she found the play compelling and profound. Rudd pronounced it fabulous, and not to be outdone, Josephine said it was poignant and riveting, and gave it five stars. Paulo never stopped masticating long enough to offer an opinion. Pauline was glowing, but her father, whose art was the deal, took it with a sardonic smile, and for what it was: ass-kissing.

When the fat girl had swiped the last scrap from Paulo's plate, she suddenly remembered a party downtown at which they were expected. "Sorry to eat and run, Daddy," she said, and they ran.

"Well, anyone for dessert? Coffee and brandy, perhaps?" Daddy inquired after they'd gone.

The conversation drifted from the evening's dramas to personal dramas, and how, one way or another, we were all children of abuse. Pam told of how her father used to beat her mother and herself. And how she left home as fast as she could and hadn't been back since.

Josephine told of what it had been like growing up in a second-generation Chinese family, no longer Chinese, yet not quite American, either. Her mother had had a brief acting career before settling down to grow sprouts and water chestnuts with a man twice her age. She wasn't growing old gracefully, and was always putting the moves on the boys Josephine brought home.

"Did she ever score?" Rudd asked.

Ransom turned his gaze on him.

"Just kidding," Rudd said with a nervous laugh.

Josephine didn't seem to mind the question, though. "Not if I could help it." She smiled bitterly. "Like Pam, I couldn't wait to leave, and when Cyzeski came along, he was my ticket out of there. I was only sixteen when I married him."

There was an awkward moment, and then Susan spoke. "My story is practically in the public domain," she said quietly.

"You don't have to say anything, Susan," said Ransom.

"I don't mind, Marc," she said. "My mother's problems began while I was a teenager. Those were not the happiest years."

Ransom listened solemnly. We all did.

"Dad meant well, but he couldn't cope. He couldn't afford the kind of care my mother needed. He barely made enough to get by. Like Pam and Josephine, I got out of the house as soon as possible. I had to, for my own sanity. When Dad died, Mother lost it completely. I wish I could help her. . . ."

"Of course you do," Ransom murmured.

"But she won't let me. It worries me that I might be like my parents, that someday I might end up like my mother."

"I doubt that," Ransom said reassuringly.

"Aren't we a bunch of misfits," Pam giggled.

It seemed curious Susan hadn't mentioned her sister. Everyone at the table, with the possible exception of Pam, must have known Sharon Raynes. Susan was willing to call it suicide and let it go at that, but she had her doubts. She'd said as much at J. G. Melon.

"What's your story, Charlie?" said Josephine.

"Me? Well, there's not much to tell. My father went out for cigarettes when I was a baby and forgot to come back. My mother died young."

"Didn't you have any family?" Pam asked.

"I had an aunt. She was my guardian. But she worked as a cook, for rich people, like Marc, and couldn't look out for me full-time, so I was placed in a boarding school."

"Boarding schools don't come cheap," said Rudd. "There must have been some money."

"These were charity schools, for kids from broken homes. Some were Catholic, some Protestant. I imagine they must have been partially funded by the state."

"There are lots of good boarding-school stories," said Pam.

"Tom Brown's School Days," said Ransom.

"I was thinking of *A Separate Peace,*" said Pam.

"How about *Bad Boys?*" Rudd grinned.

"Or *Oliver Twist,*" I said.

"Tell us what it was like growing up in boarding school," said Susan.

"Yes, make up a story if you have to," said Josephine.

"That won't be necessary," I said. I told them about the summer of '69 and Pop Mugovero, a houseparent I'd had in boarding school. He was a retired cop with a young wife thirty adolescent boys called Mom and had wet dreams about. It was in the spring, and every evening after supper, Mom Mugovero'd go out for a stroll. Curious where she went every night, three of us decided to follow her. We trailed her to the old gravel pit, where she sat down on a boulder and waited. Eventually, a car came along, the door opened, she hopped in, and off they went. We were disillusioned and dismayed. Now we had to face the old cop, knowing where his pretty young wife went every night, and whom she met. We liked Pop Mugovero. He'd always treated us right, which was more than could be said for some of the staff. There was no way we could tell Pop what was going on. We were forced to share his wife's secret, and it felt like we were betraying him as surely as his wife was. Then, one night, she didn't bother coming back. She'd run off with her boyfriend, the son of a staff couple. The boyfriend had been hanging around school, sponging off his parents. At first we thought he was a cool guy. An ex-Marine, twenty-six or -seven years old, he'd seen action in Nam and been to Japan. But as we got to know him better, we began to see him for what he was, a braggart, a drunkard, and a liar. Indifference toward him turned to contempt when we learned he was sleeping with Mom Mugovero. We couldn't see what she saw in him.

"He was young," Josephine said.

"I guess that was it. Anyway, the old cop took it hard. They divorced, and she got a piece of his pension in the settlement. To make a long story short, about a year later, Pop Mugovero ate his revolver in the same motel his wife and her boyfriend used to shack up in."

"What a sad story," said Susan.

"You oughta join the New Playwrights," Rudd cracked.

"You were at an impressionable age. What did you learn from the experience?" Ransom asked, his face a mask.

"I learned to mind my own business."

"Always a wise policy." He smiled faintly.

"Nellie, we haven't heard from you yet," said Josephine. "Tell us how you got twisted the way you are?"

"What's to tell?" He shrugged. "Unlike the rest of you, I had a happy childhood."

"And look how you turned out," Pam laughed.

"Ask Marc to tell you a story." He grinned. "He's got some doozies."

"Yes, tell us about when you were a little landlord, Marc," Pam begged. The girl was starting to grow on me.

"Very well," said Ransom obligingly, and had a sip of espresso. "Nellie knows the story, but here goes . . ."

"When you were collecting the rents for Grandpa?" said Rudd.

"Yes."

"This is a good one," Rudd assured us. "You were what, Marc, seventeen?"

"Sixteen."

"His mother decided it was about time he got some experience in the business, so she sent him to work for my grandfather one summer."

"Let Marc tell it," said Josephine.

"Nellie's grandfather was my uncle," Ransom explained amiably. "He had some property up in Harlem, and that's where I had to go to collect the rents."

"Sixteen years old," Pam cried in disbelief.

Ransom smiled. "Yes, my mother wanted to see if I had the right stuff, I suppose."

"That's crazy," said Josephine.

"Nevertheless, I had to do it. It was dangerous, but nothing like today, with the crack. I used to carry a sap, though, for protection."

"You were a sap," said Josephine.

"The trick was to be there when the welfare checks came." Ransom smiled. "Because if you weren't, you didn't get paid. Even so, there was always a wiseguy who didn't want to part with the check. I'd had trouble with this particular fellow before. He always gave me a hard time, especially when he was drunk. And I never saw him any other way. I asked him politely for the check, and he said come and get it."

"How big was he?" Pam asked.

"Big enough, six feet, a hundred and ninety. I couldn't have weighed much more than one twenty." He didn't look like he weighed any more now.

"What did you do?" asked Susan.

"I went and got it."

"Ohmigod," Pam murmured.

"I couldn't go back to the office without it."

"Why not, for God's sake?" Josephine demanded.

"Because Grandpa would have kicked his butt out of there, and told him to go and get it. He was one tough son of a bitch, that old man." Rudd chuckled fondly, in memory of his ancestor.

"You took it from the man, just like that?" said Susan.

"It wasn't that easy. He pulled a Saturday night special and popped me," said Ransom, making a gun with his thumb and index finger.

"He shot you?" Pam gasped.

Ransom leaned back, opened his jacket, and pointed to his left side, just above the waistline. "In and out," he said, leaning forward slightly and pointing to the exit wound.

"I wondered about that," said Josephine.

"I broke his hand with the sap, and disarmed him." Ransom smiled.

I swallowed some brandy and felt the burn as it went down. It wasn't hard to visualize the scene. I glanced from uncle to nephew and back again, thinking about the peeper tape, and the misery in the La Fleur. These were guys who hired thugs to beat up women and old people. Beneath the veneer of society, these guys were gangsters. Would Sharon Raynes be alive today if that drunk had had better aim? I wondered. If I were a cop, I'd want to know where both these guys had been the night she took up flying. After that story, there was no question in my mind Ransom had the right stuff. Nellie, too, for that matter.

"And you got the check?" Josephine asked.

"I got the check," Ransom said laconically.

"That was the first thing Grandpa wanted to know," laughed Rudd.

"Before are you hurt, or are you all right?" Pam asked incredulously.

"Yep."

"Unbelievable," she murmured.

"What did your mother say when she heard about it?" Susan asked.

"Did you get the check?" Ransom grinned mordantly. "Speaking of which." He hailed the waiter.

"Grazie, grazie, signore," said the waiter, bowing and scraping after Ransom paid the check with an AX platinum card. Evidently he was a good tipper.

The maître d' followed us to the door. "Good night, Mr. Ransom, come again," he said, holding the door. He gave both Rudd and me perfunctory nods. "Come again," he repeated.

"When am I gonna see the pictures?" Rudd said abruptly, the moment we were on the street.

"You'll have them Thursday, Nellie."

"Any later and you can forget about them."

"Gotcha, Nellie," I said. Susan and I thanked Ransom for his hospitality. Josephine clung possessively to him and made a point of ignoring me. We said good night and went to look for a cab.

23

We hailed a cab on Eighth Avenue. Susan gave the driver, Horatius Diderot Gauguin, an address in the East Sixties.

"You're awfully quiet," she said.

"Just thinking. You didn't tell me Ransom would be there."

"Would it have made a difference?"

"Probably not."

"Is that what's bothering you, seeing Marc?"

"What's bothering me is seeing more of Ransom and Rudd lately than I care to."

She smiled. "It's about time you met a better class of people."

"You mean a better-off class of people. I can't help wondering, though, is it an accident, or is it on purpose? What happened to Fallon?"

"I told you, he's just a friend."

"Uh-huh. Has Ransom ever come on to you?"

"That's what's really bothering you, isn't it? Well, you can relax, he hasn't. I'm not his type."

I didn't believe that. According to Josephine, he had no type. "Did Sharon ever talk about him?"

"Here we go again," she said, turning her face away from me. "No, Sharon never talked about him, okay?"

I sensed I couldn't pick a fight with her if I wanted to. "She never said anything about getting rough with him?"

"Rough with him?" she said, turning back to me.

"Did she ever say anything about playing games with him?"

"What sort of games?"

"S and M games?"

"No, never, she never talked about . . . ah, her professional life. What a question to ask. Whatever gave you the idea that Marc would be interested in that sort of thing?"

"I don't know, I've heard guys like Marc, powerful guys, who boss people around all day long, sometimes go in for being bossed around themselves at night." I told her about seeing Josephine hauling off and walloping him one, and how meekly he reacted.

"I wondered about that mark on his cheek," she said.

We rode the rest of the way in silence.

"Do you want to come up for a drink?"

I said okay. Her place was on the top floor of a town house that had been co-oped. It was a walk-up. "This a 'Residential' property?"

"No," she answered, with a smile that said she understood the question. "You are suspicious, aren't you?"

She unlocked a Medeco and a Fox lock, and threw on the lights. It looked like the set of a successful career woman's apartment. A *House & Garden* photographer could have shot it as it was. "Very nice," I said.

"I did it myself."

It was done in shades of blue and yellow, with lots of prints and patterns. The room was alive with plants and fresh-cut flowers. It looked casually elegant, and at the same time, warm and inviting.

"Brandy?" she asked.

"That'll be fine."

"It's in the cabinet." She gestured. "Make yourself comfortable, I'll only be a minute."

I poured a snifter of brandy and browsed the wall of books. I settled down on the sofa with a lush edition on architecture. This was nice—a good book, a drink, and alone at last with Susan Ferrante.

Except something was wrong with this picture. I couldn't quite put a finger on it, but it was there—a feeling that I was being jerked around like the blindman in a game of blindman's buff. The anticipation I had been feeling when I first sat down turned to a prickle of paranoia. This wasn't so different from being at Josephine's, I thought. It was running into Ransom unexpectedly that had put me on edge. Was it coincidence or chance? He hadn't seemed surprised to see me with Susan. He must have known she'd invited me. I wondered if he'd asked her to invite me, and if so, why? Had he suddenly decided he'd like to have a photographer for a friend? I didn't think so. Maybe he thought there was something I could tell him about Dolly and his mother that he didn't already know. Maybe that was the reason he was cozying up to me, if that was what he was doing.

Or maybe—and this one was a reach, but that's what paranoia is—it had something to do with Sharon Raynes. Maybe it was the fact that I had been there the day she had her one and only flying lesson. Or maybe I just had a suspicious mind. Of course, Ransom couldn't have known I was suspicious of Sharon's death, not unless Susan told him. And if he had had nothing to do with it, why should he care? On the other hand, Raynes had been his girlfriend. It had been one of his buildings, one of his apartments, she fell from. And there was the suddenness with which both Fallon and Susan arrived on the scene. It was almost as though they'd been waiting for her to jump. And Tito's photos clinched it—they were convincing evidence there had been someone else at the scene when Sharon Raynes went out the window.

I stared at the book, an Ionic column indistinguishable from a Doric column, the pictures Greek to me. Susan returned wearing a silk dressing robe. "I needed to freshen up." She smiled, and poured herself some brandy. She perched on a love seat and crossed her legs. I told myself to relax, finish the drink, and go home.

"I see we made Liz Smith's column," she said.

"Sorry about that, it was my agent's idea."

"Did you pay to have my name mentioned?"

"Just my own, but I would have if that's what prompted you to call. I don't know where they got the item. Hope you don't mind."

"I don't mind." She smiled. "I've been meaning to call—"

The doorbell rang.

"Who could that be?" she said anxiously. She went to the intercom. "Hello?"

A blast of static came from the speaker, then Matty Fallon's voice. "Susan, it's me, Matty. Can I come up?"

"Have you any idea what time it is?"

"It's late, I know—can I come up for a little while?" he said in a thick voice.

I clenched my jaw. She glanced at me apprehensively. "I'm with someone, Matty."

"Just for a minute, please."

She gave me a what-should-I-do look, and I shrugged, although I would have liked to tell him to get lost.

"For a minute, Susan, that's all," he begged.

She looked at me helplessly. "Okay, for a minute," she relented, and buzzed him in.

"Checking up on you?" I said. "It's okay, I'll finish this and be on my way."

"No, don't go."

Fallon lumbered into the small apartment and dumped his bulk in the nearest chair. He was panting and sweating from the exertion of four flights of stairs. He didn't seem surprised to find me there. "The photographer," he said. "Take any good pictures lately?"

"The politician," I replied. "Fix any parking tickets lately?"

Susan's eyes darted nervously from one of us to the other.

"Where ya been?" he demanded. "Been calling all night."

"We went to Pauline's play."

"Bet it sucked. Saw one of her plays and it sucked."

"Can I get you anything?" she asked politely.

"I'll have one of those," he said, nodding at her glass.

"Been drinking all night at Doran's," he explained needlessly.

"What's the occasion?" she asked, pouring a brandy.

"What occasion?" he said over his shoulder, as though I wasn't there.

"For celebrating at Doran's," she said, handing him the snifter and resuming her seat. Swell, I thought, now the son of a bitch'll never leave.

He seemed to have trouble remembering; finally he said, "My brother just made captain in the NYPD."

"That's wonderful," said Susan.

"Yeah, well, there's more to life than the NYPD and a pension," he said, eyeing me dully.

Yeah, like being a mick fixer at City Hall, I thought. "I don't see anything wrong with it," I said.

He looked away from me and gazed at the amber liquid in his glass. "I'm different than the rest of them," he said. "That's all they can think of, a civil service job and a pension. I've always wanted more. One of these days, I'm gonna have some real money. Not as much as that little prick Ransom, maybe, but plenty. And I won't have to take his crap, and clean up after him anymore."

"Like with Susan's sister," I said, without thinking.

"Think you're smart, don't you?" he said, with a canny grin.

"Matty," Susan protested.

"'S all right," he said.

"I never heard whether she left a note," I said.

"There was no note," Susan answered. "Matty's drunk, and I don't want to talk about Sharon."

"Sorry," I said. I would like to have asked him if he had been the one who tampered with Sharon's body, if that was what he meant by cleaning up after Ransom. Instead I said, "Have you heard? Susan might be related to Ransom."

Susan didn't say anything, although she didn't seem any more comfortable with that than suicide notes.

Fallon focused glazed eyes on me as though noticing me for the first time. "Not a chance," he said, after we'd done the stare.

"Florine Ransom seems to think so," I said amiably.

"The old lady's senile," he said.

"Tell her that."

"What's it to you anyway?"

"It's nothing to me.

"I saw that piece in the paper Deidre Mahoney wrote about you and the bag lady. . . . What's your angle? Lookin' for a piece of the action?"

"What action is that?"

"Don't get cute. The old lady's estate, that's what action."

"There's nothing in it for me."

"Better believe it. Ransom'd have you measured for a cement overcoat ina heartbeat, pal."

"That's enough, Matty. You said a minute," Susan reminded him. "I think you'd better go now."

The seedier the hack, the trashier his rap, I thought, looking at him wedged in the chair, his beefy hands gripping the arms. "All right," he said grudgingly, and hoisted himself to his feet. He lumbered after her to the door. I didn't budge, my riparian rights having been established.

I could hear their earnest voices on the landing, but not what was being said. "He's gone," she said, returning finally. "I apologize for that."

"It wasn't your fault. I'll push off in a minute myself. I've got an early call tomorrow. And you must be tired." The early call was always a handy excuse. If something was going to happen between us, it wasn't going to be tonight. Rekindling the mood would take too long. And besides, I was in no hurry to get to know her. I could get serious about this one.

"I am a little tired," she admitted, collapsing in the chair just vacated by Fallon. The silk robe poured over her body, the vee expanding and revealing an expanse of smooth skin. "Perhaps Pauline's play wasn't such a hot idea," she said ruefully. "I shouldn't try to mix business with pleasure."

"Ransom?"

"I dress his mother, why not the daughter? God knows she could use some help."

"I see what you mean. What about Josephine?"

"No class." She smiled. "And she can't afford me. Marc isn't that generous. He'll never take her anywhere important. There are women, though, for whom he's willing to pick up the tab. So, as you can see, I had an ulterior motive for dragging you to Pauline's play. Hope you didn't mind— you did offer your services as a walker."

"It was my pleasure," I said, getting to my feet. "Hope I didn't say or do anything to queer the deal for you."

"You were fine," she said, rising. "Next time let's make it a movie and dinner, shall we?"

"It's a date." We were at the door. Her gaze was steady, searching. I took a chance, leaning toward her. She pulled me to her impulsively and twisted against me, her body slippery in the water-silk fabric robe. She kissed me with a moist open mouth. Static electricity crackled between us. Startled, we broke it off abruptly, laughing.

"Good night," she whispered.

"Good night," I said hoarsely.

She watched me descend the stairs with an enigmatic smile.

Twelve-thirty Wednesday I stepped into the Master Wok looking for Strunk. He was usually the first to arrive, Stein usually the last. This establishment was about as pretentious as the rest of the kind that P.C. seemed so partial to. The wallpaper had a bamboo pattern. Rustic scenes of China decorated the walls. The palms were plastic, the tables and chairs Formica and tubular chrome. The place mats were paper. I spotted Strunk with his back to the wall at a table for four in the rear.

"What's happening, P.C.?" I greeted him.

"How you, Byrne?" he replied. Both questions rhetorical.

"Stein's late, as usual," I observed, sliding into a chair.

"Here he comes," said Strunk, his eyes on the middle distance.

"The quest for the perfect spare rib goes on," said Stein, falling into the chair next to mine. He picked up the menu. "So, what's good in this dump?"

"I thought we might start with the hacked chicken with sesame hot sauce," said Strunk, "and then progress to the Mongolian-style beef with snow peas and mushrooms, served over crispy silver cloud noodles."

"Mongolian beef and silver cloud noodles? Where do you see that?" Stein asked, searching the menu.

"There," said Strunk, reaching across the table and pointing.

"Sounds like marinated yak," said Stein. "You going along with that, Charlie?"

"I think I'll have the pan-fried flounder with ginger and scallions," I said.

"Pussy, Byrne," said Strunk. He thought the world of me. "We're sharing, anyway."

"I dunno, P.C., is that a whole yak? Because if it is . . ." Stein smiled.

"You're a hole, Stein. That's marinated beef, Mongolian style."

"Well, I gotta see those silver cloud noodles," said Stein, putting down the menu.

As usual, we let Strunk do the ordering, and when he was done, he turned his gaze to me. "It's your lunch, Byrne," he said. "What's on your mind? Got something for me?"

That wasn't the way I recalled it, but why argue? It always seemed to be my lunch.

"I don't know," I said. I told them about the roll of film Tito found in the camera.

Strunk's reaction was predictable. "Can't help you," he said. "You want homicide, or the D.A.'s office. Told you, I'm strictly financial scams and boiler rooms."

"I know, but Sharon Raynes was a girlfriend of Ransom's," I reminded him.

"He kill her?"

"I don't know, it's possible."

"Uh-huh, what was his motive?"

"I don't know."

"What do you know?"

"I know she wasn't a suicide."

"How do you know that?"

"Well, the pictures show someone else had to be there."

"Maybe they do, maybe they don't."

"I bumped into Fallon last night . . . he was drunk."

The cop and the con man exchanged glances. "Yeah, go on," said Strunk.

"He said he was tired of cleaning up after that little prick, Ransom."

"What's that suppose to mean?"

"Fallon was there, in the courtyard, before the cops got there."

"You think he killed her?"

"I don't know, but it could have been Fallon who messed with the body."

"Did you see him messing with the body?"

"No."

"You're some eyewitness, Byrne."

"He also said he was going to have money, soon."

"What he's gonna have is a shitload of trouble, and soon"—Strunk grinned—"compliments of our conniving friend Henry."

I looked at Stein. "You running a sting on the guy?"

The waiter arrived ladened with platters of food. Strunk, always an eager trencherman, helped unburden him, placing the serving dishes in the center of the table. "Three more beers," he said, taking a spoon to the Mongolian beef.

Stein poked the noodles. "They call this silver cloud?" he said skeptically.

"Dig in, Byrne," Strunk ordered.

"What's happening with the La Fleur?" asked Stein. "You take those pictures?"

"I'm delivering them tomorrow," I said. I told them about the surveillance camera and tapes.

Strunk winked at Stein. "What'd I tell you, Henry, the guy's a spook," he said with a nod in my direction. "Don't think it'll help your case much with the muggers, Byrne, but I'd like to see what you've got—the photos, too. Might be able to use 'em."

"No problem, P.C."

"Is the camera still there?" he asked through a mouthful of noodles.

"Until the end of the month."

"If the tapes look promising," said Strunk, "we might

want to keep the camera in place. We'll pick up the expense, naturally." He picked up a forkful of noodles and beef and shoveled it into his mouth.

"Whatever you say, P.C.," I said, "but if you ask me, the La Fleur's days are numbered."

"What can Ransom do?" said Stein. "It's practically a sure thing for landmark status."

"All I know is, he's got plans for the site," I said.

"No crime in that," said Stein. "Suppose the Landmarks Commission votes against landmark status?"

"Fallon's fixed it, is that what you're saying?" I asked.

"They might vote against it on their own," said Stein with that bemused expression of his, which suggested he didn't believe it for a minute. "It's perfectly reasonable for him to have a contingency plan in that event. The architectural model proves nothing."

"Yeah, and it's just as reasonable to assume Ransom's planned for the contingency of the vote going against him, Henry," I pointed out.

Stein turned his gaze to the big black cop. "P.C.," he said, "it might be worthwhile doing a title search on the property."

"I like that idea," said Strunk, chewing thoughtfully on a cube of Mongolian beef. "We'll do it."

"Maybe I should pay the old lady a visit," Stein said. "Wanna tag along?" he asked me.

"All right," I said. "But you never told me what you have on Fallon."

"It's a long story," said Stein. "But he's facing an indictment for defrauding an S and L in Queens."

"Is that what he meant when he said he was going to have money?"

Stein shrugged.

"Does he know about the indictment?"

"I don't believe he does," said Stein, "but the bank's in trouble, so he might be expecting it."

"It was that investigation, and the tip Ransom was ripping off his investors, that triggered our interest in the guy," Strunk uncharacteristically volunteered.

"But it's the comptroller you're really after," I said.

"I don't remember saying that," said Strunk.

"Them that gives, gets," I reminded him.

"This is a broad investigation," he said, pushing aside the clean plate and wiping his chin. "We're gonna catch a lot of fish before we're done. How's our girlfriend, JoJo?"

"Taking care of business," I said. "Ransom sold her the Raynes apartment way below the insider's price. She expects to flip it and make a killing."

"Always knew that girl'd make out." Strunk grinned.

"In this market? Lots o' luck," said Stein skeptically.

"Maybe I should pretend to be a buyer. What do you think, Henry?" Strunk asked.

"She know you're a cop?"

"Hasn't seen me since Pakistan."

"Just so long as she can't connect you to Charlie or me."

"Wouldn't mind haggling with that little fox," said Strunk.

When I returned to the studio, I found Tito with a grin broad enough to eat a taco sideways. "We've got the carpet business," he announced.

We slapped high and low fives in exaltation.

"And Susan Ferrante called," he said, wiggling his eyebrows significantly.

I dialed her business number and was put right through. "Charlie," she said brightly, "the reason I called is, I need your services as a walker again."

"Repeat trade means a satisfied customer."

"An intrigued customer," she countered. "It's rather short notice, but Marc's giving a dinner party next Friday. Are you available?"

"We will make ourselves available," I promised.

"Wonderful. You'll need a tuxedo, of course."

"Of course. My tailor, Manny, will see that I'm properly attired." Friday was a week off.

"And Charlie . . ."

"Yes."

"I haven't forgotten—we've got a movie date."

"Sure thing," I said, hoping suddenly we might get together sooner.

Tito brought me the comps for the carpet ads. A definite booking meant a production schedule and a deadline. There were sets to build, propping and styling to consider, and logistics. I tried to concentrate on the layouts, but all I could think of was Friday night and Susan Ferrante.

24

Thursday morning the Lotto jackpot was six million, petty cash to a guy like Ransom, but enough to make me happy. I was feeling lucky, so I bought a ticket with my morning paper. On my way back to the studio, I stopped at the Greek's for coffee and bagels. I paid a visit to Dolly's doorway, and she let me feed Socrates a bagel. He slobbered over me with gratitude.

"So, how'd it go with Susan?" she wanted to know, squinting in the morning light.

"We had a nice time." For one brief second I considered calling her Mom.

"Uh-huh. You didn't find her a snob?"

"No, I didn't. Give her a break, Dolly. She only wants what's best for you."

"You gonna see her again?"

"Susan?"

"No, stupid, Madonna. Of course, Susan."

"I'll see her again, yes."

"I want you to give her something." Before I had a chance to agree, she'd fumbled in the layers of her clothing and produced an envelope. "Her name's on this. Changed it the other day," she said, handing me the envelope. "Tell her to hang on to this just in case."

"In case of what?"

"Something happens," she said vaguely.

"Like what?" I persisted.

"You never know," she said, surveying the street distractedly.

"You haven't been bothered, have you . . . by our friends?" I said, trying to gauge her level of paranoia.

"No, I just want her to have it. Anything wrong with that?"

"I guess not. Is it valuable?"

"It's stuff she'll want."

"I'll bring her 'round, you can give it to her yourself," I promised rashly.

"That won't be necessary, I trust you," she said.

"Listen, Dolly, if you've got a problem, come to me. You know where I am."

"How'm I gonna come to you at three o'clock in the morning?"

She had a point there. "You can always call me," I said.

"Sure."

"I gotta run. I'll see Susan gets this," I said, waving the envelope.

"Where's my dollar?"

"Sorry, forgot." I forked over a buck.

At ten-thirty I was standing in Ransom's reception room, a sixteen-by-twenty envelope of prints under my arm.

Nellie Rudd met me and escorted me to what looked like the conference room of a seedy law office. Real estate reference books lined one wall, floor to ceiling. Poorly framed pictures of Ransom's commercial properties hung on the other walls. A twelve-foot oval table filled the center of the room, and a water cooler and a coffee machine shared a corner of the room.

"Want a coffee?" Rudd offered perfunctorily.

"No thanks."

"Let's see what you've got," he said, pulling up a chair.

I stood by his side. First I showed him the sixteen-by-twenty prints of the architectural model. He looked at them without comment, and I wondered what was eating him.

When he was finished with the model pictures, I placed a stack of eleven-by-fourteen prints in front of him, the pictures of the La Fleur. I pulled up a chair beside him to get a better look at his face. He began flipping through the stack silently, pausing to examine a shot of Angel and James, beepers visible, dealing in the street. His face was impassive. He lingered again on a shot of the Shit Happens van, and a later print of the two hard hats. The shot of Angel and James and company attacking the old man inside the hotel brought him to a full stop. It was a very scary picture, every New Yorker's nightmare.

"What's this? Who told you to go inside the hotel?" He flared.

"No one told me not to go in the hotel," I said.

"You could have been ripped off, or worse, in there," he complained, realizing he'd displayed more emotion than he meant to.

"I thought that was what I was supposed to document," I said innocently.

"Lemme get Marc. Wait here."

I was sitting there, twiddling my thumbs and admiring the print that had ticked Rudd off, when Josephine stuck her nose in the door.

She gazed at me contemptuously. "Byrne, you are a shit," she said succinctly, and departed.

What was that all about? I wondered, stunned. Then Ransom marched into the room followed by the architect, Karl Sauter, and a sullen-looking Fallon and Rudd. I seemed to be sideways with most of the firm today.

"Good morning, Charlie," said Ransom.

"Good morning, Marc," I said. It was a strange feeling being on a first-name basis with a man with five big units. I nodded to the others.

Sauter nodded curtly. Fallon ignored me.

Ransom stood, knuckles on the table, gazing down at a

print of the architectural model. "Uh-huh," he said. I switched prints. He gave me another uh-huh, and I switched prints again. In this manner we went through the six different views of the architectural model. The others looked over Ransom's shoulder.

"What do you think, Karl?" he asked eventually.

"Very nice," said Sauter, nodding approvingly in my direction.

"Yes, I think so," said Ransom.

I put the sixteen-twenties to one side and presented the stack of eleven-fourteens. I'd shot nearly a brick of film, more than seven hundred exposures, of which I'd printed up twenty-five, what I considered the cream.

"Uh-huh, uh-huh," said Ransom, turning over the pictures slowly at first, and then picking up speed.

Angel and James and the hard hats with the Shit Happens van drew no special comment from either Ransom or Fallon, which didn't surprise me. It was remarkable enough Nellie was on such good terms with scum like Angel and James. Ransom certainly wouldn't be dealing with guys like that, though, nor would Fallon. When Ransom came to the print of Angel and James attacking the old man, he stopped.

"What's this?" he asked, puzzled.

Nervous Nellie's gaze shifted from Ransom to me.

"Those are the guys who mugged Dolly Varden and me," I said.

"Interesting," said Ransom, studying the photo. "What I meant was, where was this one taken?"

"Inside the hotel," I said. "Makes the point of how dangerous the hotel is rather well, don't you think?"

Ransom's head jerked in my direction. His expression was as opaque as the lenses of his glasses. "Dangerous for you, I should think," he said.

"I didn't ask him to go in there," Rudd added quickly.

Ransom's eyes returned to the picture. "Let me see one of the earlier pictures," he said.

I flashed them for him one at a time. "That's the one," he said. It was a shot of Angel and James on the street, in front of the hotel. "Aren't these the same guys?" he asked.

"They're the same guys," I assured him.

Fallon, Sauter, and Rudd compared the pictures and concurred that they were indeed the same guys.

Ransom glanced briefly at Rudd and then back at the photographs. "Thought so," he mused. Placing the prints facedown on the stack of photos, he turned his attention to Fallon. "These should do nicely, don't you think, Matty?" he said.

"They're okay," he answered curtly.

"Well," said Ransom, turning to me, "you seem to have covered it."

"It's a wrap?" I said.

"It's a wrap," he said. "Nellie, have Joel get Mr. Byrne a check."

Ransom may have had his faults, but unlike some advertising agencies I know, not paying his bills wasn't one of them.

"See me before you leave," said Rudd, and he left the room.

Fallon drifted out of the room after him without saying a word.

Before leaving, Sauter shook my hand warmly and said, "Nice job."

"Thanks," I said, pleased, and mildly surprised.

Ransom was drumming his fingernails on the table, a restless dynamo that seemed to leak energy. "Susan confirmed this morning, Josephine tells me," he said, gazing at me speculatively and slightly wall-eyed behind the thick lenses. "I understand we'll have the pleasure of your company on Friday."

"Looking forward to it." I smiled. That explained Josephine's warm welcome. She probably wasn't invited.

"Well, we'll see you then," Ransom said with a thin smile, giving the tabletop a last a-rump-a-tump with the fingernails before departing, leaving me alone with my photographs.

If I had to run into Ransom from time to time in order to see Susan Ferrante, I thought, well, it was an imperfect world—I'd have to take the bad with the sublime.

I gathered up the pictures and put them back in the large

manila envelope. I brought them with me to Rudd's desk. He wasn't there.

"It's a two-bedroom, river view," said the voluptuous Jackie Dhiel on the phone with a prospective client. She flashed me a winning smile from her desk. I smiled back—it didn't cost anything.

Rudd materialized with what I assumed was my check in hand. "What about the negatives?" he asked.

"What about them?" I said.

"Don't we get them?"

This guy didn't miss a trick. "It's my work, Nellie. The negatives belong to me."

"It's our work. We commissioned you."

"The ASMP doesn't see it that way. You should have thought about the negatives when you commissioned me, although the answer would have been the same."

"I have to discuss this with Marc," he said, holding up the check as though I could wave it 'bye.

"Fine, straighten it out with the boss," I said, getting to my feet and taking the print envelope, "and give me a call."

"Hold on, not so fast," he sighed. "Here, take it," he said, thrusting the check at me.

I placed the envelope of prints on his desk. "Thank you, Nellie," I said, accepting the check.

"You know, you're a real hard-on," he said, shaking his head.

"And you're a regular dick." I smiled.

"Would you like to be alone, boys?" Jackie Dhiel asked.

"I was just leaving," I said.

"So soon?" she moued, batting her lashes. "I've got a co-op I'd like to show you."

Rudd grinned.

Isn't that always the way, just when you have eyes for one woman, and she seems to have eyes for you, it seems they all want you. Where was Jackie Dhiel before my dance card was full? "Another time, maybe," I said. If, as Josephine says, Jackie Dhiel was having an office romance with Joel Lesser, the lugubrious accountant had his hands full with this motor scooter.

Josephine blew by me, mute and chilly, as I was on my

way out the door. I smiled affably, but to no avail. Oh well, unless the evil eye counted, not all of them had eyes for me.

Thinking it was a good idea, I went straight to the bank with Ransom's check before Rudd changed his mind again. Then I decided it was as good a time as any to change the surveillance tapes. I'd gotten lax about changing the tapes. It was a nuisance to have to visit the camera once a day, and if it hadn't been for Strunk, I'd have struck the setup.

I found Stein sitting in the lounge, smoking, drinking coffee, and browsing a copy of the *Photo District News,* when I returned to the studio. "You were at Ransom's, huh?" he said, stabbing out the cigarette and getting to his feet.

"I delivered the photos, and I also changed surveillance tapes," I said, showing him the cassette.

"How'd it go? You get a rise outta any of the pictures?" he asked.

"They seemed to make Rudd nervous when he recognized a couple of friends of his. Ransom was as hard to read as always. I don't think he was too happy we photographed inside the hotel, though."

"I'm sure. What about Fallon, was he there?"

"He was there."

"What'd he think of the pictures?"

"He barely glanced at them."

"Tito showed me the contact sheet," Stein said, that bemused look on his face. "I'd like to have a look at those surveillance tapes."

"Sure," I said. "I've got more than nine hours' worth of tape. Haven't seen it all myself."

"I don't have a day to kill, just a couple of hours. Lemme see what you've got on Rudd and the accountant, and I'll fast forward it from there."

"Okay, the VCR's upstairs." I led the way to the bedroom.

He glanced around the room, taking in my digs. "Look's like a lonely guy's place," he observed wryly. "Get many women up here?"

"I get lucky once in a while," I said, gesturing for him to sit on the bed. I racked up the first cassette, featuring Rudd and Lesser. A few seconds of fast forward and I hit the spot and pressed play.

Stein furrowed his brow and watched intently as the vignette unfolded. "Looks suspicious," he observed. "Doesn't prove anything, though."

I let the tape continue to roll.

"Who are those guys?" said Stein.

"The hard hats I told you about."

He squinted hard. "Rudd seems to be pretty palsy-walsy with them, doesn't he?"

"He's the managing agent. If they're working on the building, it's with Nellie's knowledge. Anyway, that's the most interesting stuff on this tape."

"There's more, right?"

"That's right, but I don't have time to look at them now."

He glanced at his watch. "I've got a two o'clock appointment with old lady Ransom. I'd like you to come along, if you can break away for an hour or so?"

"I think I can manage that. What's up?"

"Strunk did the title search on the La Fleur."

"The old lady doesn't own it anymore?"

"I didn't say that. Let's wait until we hear from Florine before we jump to any conclusions. I'm hungry. Can I get a sandwich?"

"What would you like?"

"Tuna on wholewheat and a Perrier would be fine. I'll scan those cassettes until it's time to go, if that's all right with you."

"Make yourself at home. I'll order up the sandwiches, then I've got some business with Tito." I left him with the remote in his hand, staring at the television set.

Quarter to two, Stein and I trooped over to the Thackeray.

"Find anything on the tapes?" I asked him.

"Just street people and crackheads mostly. The hard hats walked past the camera a couple of times—that was about it."

"I'd yank the camera if it wasn't for Strunk."

"Surveillance is tedious. Be thankful the camera's doing the donkey work."

Louise, the maid, received us, beaming at the sight of Stein.

He lathered her with compliments—you get better-looking every time I see you, doll, love the way you pack your uniform, have I told you I'm crazy about girls in uniforms? If I wasn't a married man, and old enough to be your father, I'd be on you like flies on honey."

I cringed, but Louise blushed prettily.

"I like older men, Mr. Stein," she said demurely.

"Be still, my foolish heart," said Stein, clutching his chest.

She laughed. "This way. Mrs. Ransom's expecting you."

We followed her down the hall. Kiernan waved hello from his desk as Louise opened the door to the dowager's study.

Florine Ransom stood to greet us, a spector in the defused afternoon light. Mumminger, a murky figure, lurked in the shadows, like Rasputin.

"Henry," the old woman said warmly.

"Florine, darling," Stein replied with an easy familiarity, cupping her hand in both of his, "you look wonderful. Whatta ya say you hop into your high-heel sneakers and we go dancing?"

The old girl shook with delight at his impudence. "I'd say you are a liar, Henry Stein," she cackled. Then, regaining her composure, she took notice of me. "You've brought Mr. Byrne with you, Henry."

"I believe you know one another," said Stein.

"Good afternoon, Mrs. Ransom," I murmured with a polite nod.

"Yes, Mr. Byrne's been most helpful. Good afternoon, sir." She nodded. "Please be seated, gentlemen."

Stein went to help her to her chair, but she good-naturedly waved him off.

Stein and I made ourselves comfortable. Mumminger did, too, seating himself behind and to the left of the old lady. He leaned an elbow on a nearby table, resting his head in his hand, and crossed his legs.

Stein's cold blue eyes flickered disapprovingly in his direction. That was all it took. The dowager turned her imperious gaze on the doctor. "Not you, Dean. This is a private meeting," she said, making a shooing motion with her hand.

Mumminger swiftly slithered off the chair. "Try not to excite her," he warned Stein.

Stein regarded him impassively.

"Out!" said the old lady, pointing a bony finger at the door.

"I'll be outside if you need me, Florine," said Mumminger, retreating with as much dignity as he could muster.

"The man has ears like satellite dishes," she said. "He's probably made a fortune from what he's overheard around here."

"No doubt," said Stein dryly.

"Now, gentlemen," said the old lady congenially, "how about something to drink?"

"Only if you'll join us, darling," said Stein.

"Maybe I'll have a little sherry," she said. "What'll you have?"

"What have you got?" said Stein expansively.

"I've got everything," she said gravely. "Mr. Byrne is rather fond of my bourbon, I believe," she said with the practiced smile of an old coquette. The effect was both grotesque and touching, but it left little doubt that she was a woman who preferred the company of men.

"Bourbon's fine," said Stein, shooting me a look that said, humor her.

"Make it two," I said to Louise, who looked on with suppressed glee.

The old lady settled back into her chair, her bony hands on the armrests. "What prompted this sudden visit, Henry?" she said, as Louise left the room.

"Well," Stein began cautiously, "as you may be aware, there's a chance the La Fleur—"

"Ah, it's the La Fleur, is it?"

"Yes . . . as I was saying," Stein continued, "there's a chance the La Fleur will be designated an official landmark."

"I'm aware of the fact."

"You are also aware, I presume, that Marc has plans for the site?"

"That's been obvious for some time, but as long as I'm alive, the La Fleur shall remain as is. I shall not see the hotel torn down, and that's final."

"If the hotel is designated a landmark, Marc will be prohibited from tearing it down—you realize that, don't you?"

"Of course," she snapped, "but that's his problem, although I doubt it'll stop him. Where there's a will, there's a way." She paused for a knowing smile. "But you're not suggesting, Henry, I transfer ownership of the La Fleur to Marc before landmark status can be granted, are you?"

"Not at all."

"Because I have no intention of doing that. Marc will have to wait until I die before he gets his hands on the La Fleur."

"Suppose, Florine, he's not willing to wait until you die?"

Her face knotted, she was gripping the armrest and leaning forward in her chair as though about to spring from it, when the doors opened and Louise appeared. Seeing her presence was unwanted, she served the drinks quickly and left.

"What do you mean?" the dowager demanded the moment we were alone again.

I gulped some bourbon, wondering what Stein was leading up to.

"Does the name Renfoil Limited mean anything to you?" Stein asked.

"No, it doesn't mean anything to me. Should it?"

"I don't know," said Stein.

"Unless . . . ?" She hesitated.

"Yes," Stein encouraged, "unless what?"

"Well, Renfoil's an anagram for my name."

"You're as sharp as you ever were, Florine." Stein beamed. "How could I have missed that?"

The notion of Stein missing anything was hard to believe. First Manor's Towers, now Renfoil Limited. Real estate developers seemed to like anagrams, or maybe it was just Ransom.

The old lady allowed herself a faint smile. "What is this Renfoil Limited?"

"It's an offshore holding company that appears to be the owner of record of the La Fleur Hotel," Stein answered.

The news was greeted with an interminable silence as the bony fingers of one hand drummed mutely on the fabric of the armrest. It was a gesture reminiscent of Marc's drumming on the conference table.

"I thought you ought to know," Stein said quietly.

"Thank you for informing me, Henry," she said calmly.

"Would Marc have any reason to believe he might not come into the La Fleur after you've gone?" Stein asked gently.

The old lady ignored the question. "How did you happen to find out about Renfoil?" she said.

"Through a client," Stein lied. "He wanted my advice about a syndicate of Marc's. Thinking the La Fleur might be involved, I had a title search done on the property."

"I see," she said solemnly.

I peered at the old lady intently. The desiccated ruin that was Florine Ransom was giving nothing away to the curious. Aside from the nervous fingers, she showed no emotion. She was a cool hand.

"Of course, we both know a title search means nothing, Henry," she added after a pause.

"Florine," said Stein, "why the change? It's significant of something."

"Perhaps Marc wanted another buffer company," she suggested.

"Perhaps," said Stein, unconvinced.

Her gaze traveled from Stein to me and back again. "How is it you two are acquainted?" she asked suddenly.

I looked to Stein, letting him explain. "You know how it is, Florine," he said with his most charming smile, "you meet all kinds of people in my business."

"Indeed, sir. However, what I'm really wondering is why Mr. Byrne is privy to our conversation?"

"I've been wondering the same thing," I said.

"Mr. Byrne wouldn't happen to be your mythical client, would he, Henry?"

"I ask you, Florine"—Stein grinned—"does Charlie look like an investor to you?"

She gave me a fleeting smile and switched her gaze to the little swindler.

"My guess is," Stein continued, "that the La Fleur and this Dolly Varden business are somehow linked."

"Dolly Varden?" said the old lady, mildly surprised.

"Yes, this homeless woman Charlie's befriended."

"I know who she is," said the old lady stiffly, "but I fail to see what one has to do with the other."

"So do I," Stein admitted. "It's just a hunch, but I smell a scam."

"Well, Henry," she said, "you certainly have a nose for these things."

"Tell me, Florine, what's the significance of the name Dolly Varden?"

"I'd prefer to keep that to myself."

"But it's the name, isn't it, that makes you think this woman might be your granddaughter?"

"That's true, and when and if I decide she is my granddaughter, I'll let you know the significance of Dolly Varden. Until then, it's a piece of the puzzle, as I've told Mr. Byrne, I intend to keep to myself."

"Fair enough, but who else knows the significance of the name?"

"No one," she said flatly.

"How can you be so sure?"

"Because I've outlived everyone who might know," she said with considerable pride.

"Are you sure Marc doesn't know?"

"Positive."

"Or Nelson Rudd, or someone around here"—he gestured with a sweep of his hand—"Bernard, maybe, or even Louise, the maid?"

"No one knows but me."

Stein looked unconvinced.

"No one," she repeated.

"Doesn't it strike you as a remarkable coincidence that Dolly Varden should be the mother of Sharon Raynes?" he said.

"It would strike me as an even more remarkable coincidence if she, in fact, turned out to be my granddaughter." The old lady smiled.

"Exactly," said Stein, taking a long swallow of bourbon. "Charlie has told you, Florine, that the Raynes woman died under questionable circumstances, hasn't he?"

"Mr. Byrne has brought that to my attention."

"And that she was very good friends with Marc?"

"I'm sure I couldn't possibly keep track of my son's good friends."

"Probably not." Stein grinned. He took another long pull at the bourbon, then, placing the glass on an end table, he climbed to his feet. Taking my cue from Stein, I finished my drink and stood up.

"Is that all?" asked the dowager, disappointed the visit had come to an end.

"That's what I had to say," Stein replied, lending the old lady a helping hand to totter to her feet. When she was standing, he rewarded her with a peck on the cheek. "As always, dear lady," he said, "I see you are on top of things, in control."

"Thank you for coming, Henry, and thank you for the information."

"You're welcome, darling."

Louise threw open the door, and Mumminger slunk into the room like a dog that had made a mistake on the rug.

The old lady gripped Stein's sleeve suddenly. "Marc's not in any trouble, is he, Henry?" she whispered, a glint in her fierce eyes.

"Not that I'm aware of, dear"—Stein smiled, stroking her hand—"unless it's with you?"

The old lady snorted. "Sir," she said, addressing me. "How is our friend, Dolly Varden?"

"She's fine, Mrs. Ransom."

"Good—well, it was nice seeing you again. Thank you for coming."

"Thank you, it was a pleasure drinking your bourbon again."

"Come again."

25

Stein glanced at his watch and picked up the pace. He had a train to catch. We were walking up Park Avenue toward Grand Central Station under a gray sky. The barometer was falling, and so was the temperature. It was going to rain, or snow. The ground ivy in the divider islands looked brown and brittle, the plane and ginkgo trees were bare. Dried leaves and paper debris scudded underfoot. The air smelled of carbon monoxide and decay.

"Henry, what happened back there?"

"You play pool?"

"When I was a kid."

"Well, that was a break shot. I was just trying to separate a couple of balls from the pack."

"You mean put a scare into the old lady?"

"You think Florine scares?"

"Is she in danger?"

He gave me a glance that asked if I was serious. "She's ninety years old, with heirs and a pile of money. I'd say that's living dangerously, wouldn't you?"

"It looked as though you were playing her against Marc."

"Did it?"

"Why'd you tell her about the title search?"

"Don't you think she has a right to know?"

"It's her property."

"That's right."

"What did she mean when she said the title search meant nothing?"

"It's the old shell game. There are more ways to disguise ownership than there are slight-of-hand tricks. Look at all the real estate around Manhattan that the Marcoses are supposed to own, and yet no one can prove it."

"Okay, but if you were Ransom, how would you do it?"

"Well, one way to do it would be through a limited partnership. Florine might even go for something like that. Marc would take her into one of his syndicates; in return for her shares, she'd pledge the La Fleur."

"Why would she do that? She's determined to hang on to the La Fleur until the end."

"She wouldn't do it unless she held the controlling shares in the partnership."

"I get it—that way she'd have her cake and eat it, too."

"Right, she'd still have her hotel and be making a profit from her son's syndicate, of which Marc would be the CEO."

"And as CEO, he decides how to use the assets of the partnership."

"Something like that."

"Maybe, as she said, he switched it to Renfoil as a buffer, or better yet, to ensure it wasn't part of her estate when she kicks. You know, just in case she has a change of heart about leaving him the hotel."

"You're catching on, Sherlock."

"I don't get it, though. All he wants to do is develop the dump and make a shitload of money. Why doesn't she just give him the hotel and be done with it?"

"Maybe she doesn't want to give it to him outright because he wants it. Maybe she wants her ass kissed a little."

"And he won't do it."

"Something like that. Anyway, SROs may not be pretty,

but they're profitable. The dump, as you call it, is fully amortized, and making money. If she doesn't want to, she doesn't have to develop the La Fleur."

"What makes you think there's a link between Dolly Varden and Marc's plans for the La Fleur?"

"It's just a hunch, as I said. If we knew why the old lady's so attached to the hotel, we might know what the name Dolly Varden means to her."

"But Dolly couldn't be scamming anyone. She didn't know the old lady existed until Florine asked to meet her."

"We don't know that for sure. But the sisters, Ferrante and the dead one . . . what did you say Marc called her?"

"Acid Raynes."

"Yeah, Acid Raynes—they knew the old lady existed."

We'd reached Thirty-eighth Street. "This is where I peel off, Henry," I said.

"Okay," he said, pausing, "let me leave you with this thought."

"What's that?"

"Marc Ransom's not into sharing."

"Really?"

"Keep changing those tapes, sport, and I'll be seeing you." He hurried off.

Tito said good night as soon as I got back to the studio, and I was left alone.

I got the Sharon Raynes contact sheet from the files. I should have made prints, I thought, studying the 35mm frames again through a loupe. Looking at them one more time didn't tell me anything new, only that death was immutable. But the pictures did remind me I ought to call Hannibal, the homicide cop. I found his number in the Rolodex and dialed. He was out. I left my name and number.

A photographer's life isn't all glamour and tall, cool, easy blondes. It has its mundane side, chores such as bookkeeping and billing, filing negatives and transparencies, updating client lists, and maintaining the equipment. There's always plenty to do around the studio after business hours. I was too antsy, though, for any of that, and decided to blow off steam with a bike ride.

I was changing clothes when Sonny called.

"Charlie, dey be empt'n duh place," he said, his tongue thick with vodka.

"You need a place to stay?"

"Not me. Ah mean dey be hasslin' people tuh muv, Angel an' es frien'."

"You're all right, though?"

"Dey wood'n mess wid me."

I imagined not. "What about the old man?"

"Aldo? Ah'm lookin' out for 'im, he okay."

"How you fixed for cash, Sonny?"

"Ah'm all right, man," he said, a note of indignation in his voice. "Jus' wanna let ya know what's happenin', s'all. Yuh said call."

"Appreciate that, Sonny. Stay in touch."

"Yuh got id," he said, and hung up.

Regardless of what the old guy had wanted, I wondered whether calling an ambulance wouldn't have been the right thing to do after the mugging. Where was Aldo Fabrizi going to go when they emptied the La Fleur? Robert Frost said, "Provide, provide." Two old people at the finish line, one rich, one broke. Florine Ransom had provided handsomely. She was on Easy Street. The old opera singer, though, was about to find his ass out on Mean Street. Who's to say which one had the better life? I finished tying my sneakers and got the Lejeune off the rack.

Tito hadn't come in yet, and I hadn't had my first cup of coffee, when the buzzer sounded. "Detective!" I said, opening the door.

Hannibal's ruddy face grinned at me. He was a jaunty middleweight of medium height, light on his feet, and forty something. "You called, Mr. Byrne."

"Yes, come in. How about some coffee?"

"Why not," he said amiably, trailing after me to the kitchen. "Is this a professional visit?" he asked, in a faint New England lilt.

"I'm afraid so. I've got something I'd like to show you." His ice-blue eyes turned skeptical. He had the naturally suspicious mind of a good cop. He had only known me in a professional context, and not long enough to regard me as anything but shady. Innocent until proven guilty was an abstraction to him. I steered him to the lounge and excused myself briefly, returning with a loupe and the contact sheet of Sharon Raynes. "Have a look at these," I said.

He put the loupe to his eye, and pressed the contact sheet to the loupe. "She dead?" he said, studying the pictures.

"Doesn't she look dead?"

"I dunno, you're a photographer. These pictures could be staged."

"Why would I do that?"

"I don't know, you tell me." He put down the eight-by-ten sheet and placed the loupe on top of it. The pictures hadn't made much of an impression. Photos of dead people were as common to him as corn plasters.

"They're not staged."

"The question was rhetorical." He smiled. "What do you expect me to do?"

"I don't know"—I nodded at the pictures—"I just wanted to put them on the record, and thought you were the guy to see. You're a homicide cop, aren't you?"

"We need more concerned citizens like you, Mr. Byrne," he said warily. "Why don't you tell me who she is, and where this happened?"

When I'd finished telling him about Sharon Raynes and what had happened the day of the blackout in the courtyard behind Marc Ransom's apartment, all he said was, "What took you so long to call?"

"We just discovered the film the other day. It was in a camera we hadn't used in a while."

"But you had your doubts she was a suicide from the get-go?"

"Yes. Would you jump through a closed window, or would you open it first, if you were going to commit suicide?"

"I suppose I'd open it."

"And don't suicides usually leave a note?"

"Usually."

"Well, not this one."

"How do you know that?"

"Her sister said so. And another thing," I said, handing him the contacts again, "look at the way she's dressed. She's not wearing a bra, or stockings . . . well, you can't see that so well in the photos, but her skirt's on backward, and the buttons on her blouse don't line up. It looks like she was dressed by someone else, and in a hurry."

"Maybe she was drunk, or stoned when she put her clothes on." He put the sheet and loupe back down.

"Maybe, but do you think she got up and retrieved her shoe, and then laid down and died? Don't these pictures prove there was someone else there when she fell?"

"You?"

"You think I tampered with the body?"

"I think all sorts of nasty things about people, Mr. Byrne. It's my job."

"Do you think it was a coincidence that Matty Fallon just happened to show up moments later?"

"Matty 'The Fixer' Fallon?" he said, showing a little more interest.

"Yeah, the one whose brother just made captain."

"I know his brother," Hannibal said matter-of-factly. He drained his coffee cup and got to his feet. "What makes you think the death wasn't thoroughly investigated at the time?"

"I don't know how it was handled. All I know is what I hear—it was a suicide. Maybe it was, but I don't believe it."

"I'll look into the status of the case," he promised. "Can I take these?" He indicated the contact sheet.

"Go ahead, and I'll make you a set of prints." I walked him to the door.

He folded the contact sheet and tucked it inside his blazer. "Her name's Sharon Raynes, you say?"

"Sharon Raynes," I confirmed.

"Call me when you have the blowups," he said, and left.

We were doing the final casting of the carpet ads. Moms, pops, kids, and dogs trooped in and out of the studio to be Polaroided. Sorry, Socrates. English sheepdogs, not German shepherds. Stylists, truckers, messengers, and carpenters came and went. Lumber, props, and wardrobe were delivered. The studio was in chaos and confusion, and Tito and I were in our element.

Tuesday afternoon I ducked out of the studio for a visit to my tailor, Manny. He was delighted to see me again so soon. This time he outfitted me in a designer-name tux. It was a slight improvement. I'd never be as superduper as Mr. Gary Cooper in a tux, but at least no one would flag me for seconds on the fish eggs.

Al Carlson called and said they were running the photo of Dolly full page in the *New York Times* the next week, and he needed a release ASAP. No problem, I assured him, and it promptly slipped my mind. A day or so later Tito said Carlson had called, wondering when he was going to get the release. "Right!" I banged the heel of my hand against my forehead. I dropped what I was doing and made a dash for Dolly's doorway, pen and release form in hand.

But Dolly wasn't home.

Not unusual—she wandered around during the day like a stray cat. I asked at the Greek's if they'd seen her, and Chris said, now that he thought about it, he hadn't seen her around the last few days. I bumped into Mort and Mo on my way back to the studio, and they hadn't seen her, either.

Damn, where were the homeless when you needed them? I'd have to get by with the release I had and straighten up with Dolly later.

The morning of Ransom's dinner party, as I turned the corner on my way to the newsstand, I noticed a shopping cart on it's side, and a Hefty bag full of rags stuffed into the wastebasket. There was a well-worn paperback copy of *Fools Die* by Mario Puzo, and I thought I recognized a striped sweater I'd seen Dolly wear. I righted the cart, retrieved the Hefty bag from the garbage, and pushed the stuff back to the studio.

"Ah, my friend, Charlie." The pint-sized patriarch, Mort, beamed when he spotted me wheeling the cart off the elevator. "How are you today, Charlie?" he inquired.

"I'm fine, Mort. How about yourself?"

"Tip-top, tip-top," he assured me.

Mo and I acknowledged each other with somber nods.

"Say, have you fellas seen the bag lady?" I asked them.

"Funny thing you should ask," said the old man, shaking his head sadly.

"Why? What's happened?" I said.

"You tell him, Schlomo," said the patriarch.

I turned to the big man, foreboding turning to alarm.

"Our friend Moshe found the dog," Mo said gravely.

"Found the dog? Moshe who?" I demanded.

"Moshe who has the Israeli restaurant," said Mo. "Yesterday morning, when he was opening up, he noticed a smell. A stink to high heaven. When he looked, he found the dog in the Dumpster parked in front of the restaurant."

"Its skull was smashed," said Mort.

"The rats had been at it," added Mo.

I felt my gut wrench and gripped the handle of the cart. "Did he report it to the police?"

"I don't know," said Mort. "I don't think so."

"Thanks for telling me," I said, pushing the cart.

"Sorry, Charlie," murmured Mort as they stepped aside.

"What's that?" said Tito, eyeing me fearfully as I pushed the cart into the studio.

"It's Dolly's stuff. Something's happened to her. She's missing, and the dog's been found dead in the Dumpster in front of the Israeli restaurant."

"Aw, no," Tito murmured.

"I think I better report it to the police."

"Do what you have to do," Tito said solemnly. "I'll take care of things at this end."

I called 911 and told them I wanted to report a missing person. They asked where I was calling from, and when I told them, switched me over to Manhattan South. Manhattan South told me to come in and file a report.

I jogged over to the precinct house, checking off in my mind the possibilities. If Dolly's disappearance wasn't accidental, then Angel and James were prime suspects in my book. And if there was a chance she was still alive, a good place to start looking for her was in the La Fleur. Naturally, I thought of the surveillance camera, silently thanking Strunk for insisting I keep it in place. And I cursed myself for being slack about changing tapes. In the crush of work the past few days, I'd let the electronic peeper slide. Maybe something had been recorded. I'd visit the camera as soon as I finished at the station house.

The desk sergeant was the same one who was on duty on my last visit to Manhattan South. Be nice now, I cautioned myself, approaching the desk.

If he remembered me, he didn't show it in those Windex-colored eyes of his. "What can I do for you?" he said.

"I'd like to report a missing person," I said politely.

"How long have they been mithing?" he asked in his sibilant voice.

"I'm not sure."

"They have to be mithing for forty-eight hourth," he said impatiently.

"She's been missing forty-eight hours, maybe longer."

He stared at me suspiciously.

"Remember me?" I said helpfully.

"The name of the mithing perthon?"

"It's the bag lady I was arrested with."

"Doth she have a name?"

I gave her real name, and her alias, and as he questioned me, I gave a physical description of Dolly, her approximate age, next of kin, and usual haunts. I also suggested that the La Fleur might be a good place to look for her.

"That plathe is all but out of bithnith," he lisped. "Welfare hath relocated moth of their clienth. There are only a handful of people left in the plathe."

I told him about Socrates and Angel and James.

"I'll thend a car around," he said.

I thanked him profusely and left.

Next stop, the electronic eye. The VCR had run out of tape twenty-four hours ago. I changed tapes and gathered up the previous tapes that I hadn't viewed yet. I hesitated at the door. Maybe I should change the timing mode, I thought. This was the city that never sleeps, right? Why not have a look at what the night people were up to? I went back to the VCR and reset it to record a straight six hours from ten P.M. to four A.M. I locked up, and left with the tapes under my arm.

The next thought that popped into my head was, I should probably look in on Sonny while I was in the neighborhood.

As soon as I laid eyes on Angel, I rejected that idea. He was hanging out in his usual spot in front of the hotel.

I wished there was some way to get in touch with Sonny. I should have asked him to check in at regular intervals. Nothing like hindsight. Reluctantly, I turned to go. It didn't seem right leaving when there was a possibility Dolly was somewhere inside the La Fleur.

A blue-and-white cruised down the street, pulled over, and stopped under the hotel marquee. Fatso rolled out of the patrol car and ambled over to Angel. Skinny remained in the car.

Even from a distance it was possible to get the gist of the conversation from their body language.

Fatso: Hey, don't I know you?

Angel, grinning: Yo, bro, from duh udder day.

Fatso: That's what I thought. You seen this person? (He reads off a description of Dolly from the pad in his hand.)

Angel: Dat duh crazy bitch?

Fatso nods affirmative.

Angel: Ain' seen her. Duh place almos' empty. See fo' you self, bro.

Fatso trudges inside the hotel.

I decided to wait and see what happened.

Fatso comes back a few minutes later, waves so long to Angel, climbs in the patrol car, and they're gone.

Well, the desk sergeant was as good as his word—he'd sent a patrol car around.

I hurried back to the studio.

Tito was busy with the carpenters, who were constructing a two-flat, windows and door, suburban living room set.

"Stein called," Tito shouted.

I dialed Stein's number and his wife answered. We exchanged pleasantries before she put the con man on.

"Hey, sport," he said, "just wanted to apprise you of the fact that the Landmarks Commission ruled against Ransom. As of midnight tonight, the La Fleur Hotel is officially designated a historical landmark."

"You know what that means, Henry."

"It was coming down, one way or another," he said.

"I've got some news for you," I said. "Dolly's missing. I

checked around the neighborhood and no one's seen her lately."

"Maybe she moved out of the neighborhood."

"I don't think so. A restaurant owner on the block found her dog in a Dumpster with its head bashed in."

There was silence on his end of the line.

"Hello?" I said.

"I'm here. Did you report her missing?"

"Just got back from the station house. Listen, Henry, I've got this gut feeling she's in the La Fleur."

"If she's alive."

"Yeah, if she's alive."

"You tell the cops that?"

"Yeah, and the sergeant sent a pair of the lamest dicks on the force around to the hotel for a look-see." I told him what had happened at the La Fleur. "Hell, Henry, the place has over five hundred rooms. It would take a squad of cops an hour or more to search it thoroughly."

"Looks like you're gonna have to do it yourself. What about the tapes? Anything on them?"

"I'm gonna look at them now. But even if I don't see her dragged into the hotel screaming and kicking, it doesn't mean she isn't there."

"If she's alive," he repeated. "Well, good luck, sport."

Should I call Susan and tell her what was happening? Actually, I had no choice. I'd given her as next of kin when I filed the missing-persons report. I dialed her number.

"Charlie, I was just about to call you," she exclaimed cheerfully, coming on the line. "What time are you going to pick me up tonight?"

"For Ransom's?"

"It's tonight, my dear. Don't tell me you forgot?"

"Susan, Dolly's missing." It was blunt, but there was no easy way. "No one's seen her for the past few days." Before she could suggest the obvious, that maybe Dolly'd drifted to another neighborhood, I told her about the dog.

"Ohmigod!" she moaned.

"I filed a missing-persons report with the police, and gave you as next of kin. Maybe I should have spoken with you first."

"No, no, I'm sure you did the right thing."

"I thought you ought to know. You'll probably be hearing from them."

"Uh-huh, I suppose so," she said numbly. "Thank you."

After a long pause, I said, "What do you want to do about tonight?"

"Damnit!" she snapped. "This is so unfair. Wasn't something like this bound to happen?"

"I don't know," I said inanely.

"So, now it's finally happened."

"We don't know that anything's happened yet," I said, trying to sound hopeful.

"Pick me up at seven," she said. "Dinner's at eight."

"If that's what you want."

"It's what I want," she said flatly. Then in a softer voice, she said, "Charlie . . ."

"Yes?"

"Don't think me a bitch."

"I understand. You've got your own life. It might seem cold, but you've got to take care of yourself first before you can help others. That's just the way it is."

"Thanks for understanding."

I didn't mention the La Fleur because it was just a hunch I had—Dolly might not be there. I might not find her on the tapes. Thousands of people disappear every year and are never heard of again. I just hoped Dolly wasn't one of them.

I fed the first tape into the maw of the VCR, and flicked on the TV with the remote. I eyed the tube warily with my finger on the fast forward button. The tape was a forgettable succession of drug deals, and I skipped through it quickly.

The second tape had a sequence of Angel and James fondling a teenage girl in front of her mother and kid brother. The boy was knocked down and kicked for coming to his sister's defense. The frantic mother was ineffectual in protecting either child. By half submitting and half resisting, the girl defused the situation, and eventually her tormentors lost interest and left the family in search of fresh sport.

The third tape showed the exodus. Welfare clients, their belongings in cheap suitcases and Hefty bags, were being herded into minivans to be bused to the next flophouse.

Sonny appeared occasionally, sometimes with Aldo Fabrizi. In one scene, Angel actually turned and walked the other way when he spotted Sonny.

I was rewinding the tape when Tito poked his head in to say Hannibal was on the phone.

"Mr. Byrne," said the homicide cop, "I wanted to let you know, I checked up on the Raynes case. Our files show probable cause of death as suicide."

"What about an autopsy?"

"The medical examiner's report says her injuries were consistent with a fall."

"But that doesn't mean she wasn't dropped on her head somewhere else, and then dumped in the courtyard, does it?"

"It's possible," he conceded. "Look, I can't promise anything, but I'm gonna return her folder to the active file."

"That's good enough for me. And, Detective, I've got an idea for you. You might want to talk to the doorman who was on duty the night Raynes took the plunge."

"Uh-huh."

"And don't forget Matty Fallon."

"Will see."

"He knew Raynes, and he was Matty-on-the-spot when she was dropped."

"When am I gonna get those blow ups you promised?"

"You'll have them tomorrow. Another person you might want to question is Marc Ransom. She was one of his girlfriends."

"Be talking to you," he said, and hung up.

There was one last tape to scan, and I slipped it in the slot of the VCR. The exodus from the hotel had slowed to a trickle, but the drug dealing continued full flood. There was a scene with Angel and Rudd that, although not particularly incriminating, was interesting for the chumminess between the two it displayed. I noted the place on the tape counter. More curious was a shot of the hard hats lugging what appeared to be an ordinary office file cabinet into the hotel. Several minutes later they returned and repeated the procedure, humping a second file cabinet into the building. Who were these guys, and what were they doing? I stopped the tape and noted the scene on the counter. I went to my own negative file and pulled the contact sheets of the La Fleur shoot. I found the frame, peered through the loupe, and jotted down the license plate number of the Shit Happens van. I returned the contacts to the files and punched play on the remote. I got lucky—it was fast forward from there on out.

But there'd been no sign of Dolly, not on any of the tapes.

The VCR only recorded six hours out of twenty-four, and intermittently at that. So it proved nothing. She might have been brought to the hotel when the VCR wasn't recording, or when, through my own laziness, it had been down for want of tape.

Mea culpa, Dolly.

I was still left with this uneasy feeling that she was in the Hotel La Fleur.

I wrote a job order for two sets of sixteen-by-twenty prints, packed it in an envelope with the negative and contact sheet of Sharon Raynes, and sent Tito to the lab with it.

Next, I gave Strunk a call. "Need a favor, P.C.," I said when he picked up the phone.

"What is it, Byrne?" he demanded.

"A license plate check."

"What's the number?"

I read the number off to him. The van had Jersey plates.

"Wanna tell me why I'm doing this?" Strunk asked.

"It's probably nothing—maybe they're workmen—but these guys with the van keep turning up on the surveillance tape."

"Anything I ought to know about on those tapes?"

"Not unless you're DEA and about to do a street sweep."

"Okay, I'll get back to you in the morning, Byrne." He hung up.

"Hey, Charlie! Pick up the phone," Tito yelled later, above the construction din. I'd been sitting in a funk since calling Strunk.

"Hello?" I said into the receiver.

"Id me, Sonny."

"Sonny, the man I want to speak to," I said, brightening.

"Me? Wad's up?" he said, puzzled.

"Have you seen a woman, a bag lady about your age? You'd notice her if you saw her, she dresses very colorfully. Her name's Dolly Varden."

"Wur Ah'm s'pose tuh seen 'er?"

"At the hotel, with Angel and his buddies maybe?"

"Ain' seen 'er."

"You sure?"

"Sure Ah'm sure."

"Too bad," I murmured, disheartened.

"Wad Ah called tuh tell ya was, welfare muved me an Aldo. We at duh Kenmo' now."

"Twenty-third, between Lex and Third?"

"Dat's duh place."

"You have a phone there?"

"Ya think dis is duh Plazuh?" he said with a hollow laugh.

"What about Angel and James—did they get moved there?"

"Dunno, ain' seen 'em."

"Well, if you see them, or the bag lady, let me know right away, will you?"

"Don' wurry, Ah'll keep an eye out fo' 'em, an Ah'll stay in touch," he promised.

"Thanks, and holler if you need anything."

"Be in touch," he promised again.

I showered and shaved while Tito and his crew went at it for another half hour or so. When I was dressed and ready to leave, they decided to knock off for the day. The living room was pretty well roughed out.

Tito eyed the tux.

"Don't say anything," I warned him.

"Me?" He grinned.

26

It was eight o'clock when William received us with a susurrus of approval at Ransom's apartment. "You look stunning this evening, Mrs. Ferrante, if I may say so," he murmured, as though she were his favorite guest.

"Thank you, William," she said.

She wore a knee-length, bare-shouldered, black satin number of her own design that shimmered with reflected light. Her hair and makeup were flawless. The hairdresser was prancing out the door, tackle box in hand, as I arrived.

"Tarted up, and ready to go," she'd joked.

"You look beautiful," I told her.

That was the truth, even though it seemed her eyes were smaller and less luminous, her lips not quite so full, and her skin, seamless and downy as it was, seemed taut over less flesh. It might have been an illusion, or it might have been calculated, the mischief of a malicious hairdresser, but I thought I detected the beginnings of that gaunt look so many rich women confuse with being thin.

We didn't talk much on the way over in the cab, but Dolly had to be on her mind. I know she was all I could think about. The envelope she'd given me to give to Susan was tucked in my breast pocket, waiting for the right moment. First let's get through this thing, I thought, and I'll give it to her on the way home.

I scanned the crowd, looking for a familiar face, and recognized Sauter, the architect, and Jackie Dhiel, the co-op agent. I was surprised to see Mumminger and his wife, and I half expected to find Stein's bemused mug among the guests, but I guess he was the old lady's friend, not Marc's. I noticed Randell Elliott, the comptroller, and hardly surprising, Nellie Rudd and the ubiquitous Pam. That was it for the familiar. We drifted from the great hall to the room with the tapestry and Bosendorfer piano. Another couple was admiring the tapestry, saying it was new since they'd been there last.

"Is this the B list or the C list?" I asked Susan.

"It ain't the A list, it's safe to say." She smiled.

A young woman in a maid's uniform passed by offering champagne from a silver serving tray. We helped ourselves to a couple of glasses, and so did the other couple.

"I haven't seen Ransom," I said, "have you?"

"Not yet, but I'm sure he's around somewhere," she said, sipping champagne. Then, flicking her head toward the tapestry, she said, "You've been here before, haven't you?"

"Once." I didn't think it necessary to elaborate.

She looked natural in a setting like this; she belonged. But me, well, I felt ill at ease. I could never feel comfortable near Ransom's kind of money.

"How we doing tonight?" It was Rudd, beaming like a beaver over his bow tie.

Shitty was the first thing that came to mind. I exchanged smiles with Pam and said, "Fine, Nellie, how about you?"

"Fine, fine," he said, bouncing on the balls of his feet. "We never used your photographs."

"Oh." As though I gave a damn.

The women chatted with each other, paying no attention to us.

"The hotel was ruled a landmark."

"So I've heard, too bad. Fallon couldn't fix it?"

"Not with the Landmarks Commission."

"Well, you don't seem too upset. How's the boss taking it?"

He shrugged, and grinned.

"But now he can't build."

"Where'd you hear that?"

"Not unless he hires a torch."

"Please," he chided, "Marc's a major developer, not some Bronx slumlord hustling a cheap insurance scam. Besides, who benefits from the landmark status? Think of the tax revenues the city will lose."

"Think of the tax abatements Marc will lose."

"Nobody's gonna lose," he said with a cunning grin.

"But you've got to clear the site before you can build," I said, puzzled, "and you can't do that without breaking the law. Although I guess it's hard not to break the law in your business—there must be a million of them."

"It's a game. You've got to take the chance, they've got to catch you."

"And a developer in Marc's league can afford to take the chance."

"He can't afford not to take the chance. It must be like that in your business," he said cynically. "Don't tell me advertising people are all on the up and up."

"I've heard a few stories about what goes on at the agency-client level."

"There you go, it's all over. Money makes the world go 'round."

"I don't see much of that sort of thing, though—it's fairly clean at my level of the food chain."

"Too bad, but don't get discouraged—you'll move up, or it'll move down." He started to move off.

"Wait a minute, Nellie."

He paused.

"What's with the La Fleur? When's it history?"

"It's already history, according to the Landmarks Preservation Commission."

"I mean, when's it a memory?"

"How should I know?" he laughed. "Our engineers tell us that structurally it's not very sound."

Engineers? The hard hats, maybe? "So that's it, it's gonna collapse."

He smiled. "Excuse me." He collected Pam and they wandered into the adjoining room.

A few years ago, in the dead of the night and without a single city permit, a developer bulldozed an SRO hotel off Times Square before a law calling for a moratorium on the alteration and demolition of SROs could go into effect. Editorial writers and columnists were outraged at the brazenness of the crime, condemning the developer for his arrogance and avarice. The mayor fulminated, saying he was going to throw the book at the perpetrators—maximum fees, civil damages, and felony charges. The developer agreed to pay two million dollars in fines—which the mayor claimed sent a loud and clear message to real estate developers. The furor died down eventually, the developer contributed to hizzoner's reelection campaign, and today a forty-three-story luxury hotel—named for the developer, naturally—stands on the site of the former SRO.

It's safe to say Ransom got the message, all right. He didn't need the mayor's help. Like the other guy, he was smart enough to figure it out all by himself: do the crime and pay the fines. What's another million or two, more or less, factored into the cost of doing business? And as wily Nellie Rudd pointed out, first they've got to catch you. Stein had it figured, but he had it figured wrong. The law wasn't strong enough to save the La Fleur.

Ransom wasn't going to do anything so crude as go in there with a wrecking ball and a bulldozer, like the other guy did. But the dead of night was a possibility.

And even though he didn't have to beat the clock, time is money.

It was going to happen soon.

Tonight, even.

"What were you and Nellie talking about?" Susan asked.

"About the photos I took for Marc." As I spoke, I realized I was going to go into the La Fleur, tonight. I had to.

"Oh," she murmured.

She was a mystery to me. I wondered what was going on inside that beautiful head of hers. What was she feeling? If she was worried about her mother, she was doing a hell of a job keeping it in. With a mother like Dolly, though, she probably had a lot of practice hiding her fears. Let's get out of here and find her, I wanted to say, but she didn't want to hear that, I was sure. I doubted she wanted to hear about her mother at all, and I don't know as I blamed her.

"Be right back," I said, excusing myself.

I made my way back through the great hall toward the rear of the apartment. I passed up the john, continuing down the long hallway until I found myself in the room where William had parked us when the lights went out.

I stood at the window and gazed down into the courtyard where the body of Susan's sister had lain. I tried recalling that night. Some details were clearer than others. There was a brownout, and the storm. We heard a crash, then a scream, and the sound of broken glass, I remembered. We ran to the window. I don't remember the lights coming back on, but when they did, Sharon Raynes was lying in the courtyard on the wet concrete.

Tito's photos proved there was more to it than that.

Suppose the smashed window and the scream were for show, and she was already colder than the last slice of pizza in the box when she was dumped in the courtyard?

I glanced over at Josephine's apartment. Ransom had a good view, five windows at a right angle to his apartment. The lights flicked on as two figures passed from room to room. Josephine must have a prospective buyer, I thought.

"Not much of a view," said a voice behind me.

I wheeled around and faced Marc Ransom.

"Hello, Charlie, may I help you?"

"I was looking for the bathroom."

"You passed it."

"Yes, I know. But I couldn't resist having a look. The last time I was here was when . . . well, you know. Hope you don't mind."

"Not at all," he said unconvincingly. "It was an unfortunate thing. A suicide, you know . . . or hasn't Susan told you?"

"So I've heard." I nodded at Josephine's apartment. "That was her apartment, wasn't it?"

"Yes, it was."

"It's one of your buildings, right?"

"That's right."

"You must have been shocked to hear the news."

"I was, but then suicide's supposed to be shocking, otherwise what's the point? Sharon was very theatrical, she enjoyed shocking people."

"You knew her pretty well?"

"It's no secret we saw quite a bit of each other for a time," he said with elaborate casualness. "Why don't we join the others?" he suggested, checking his watch. "It's almost dinnertime."

He began shepherding me back to the fold. "I wonder why she didn't open the window before taking the plunge, don't you?"

"I haven't given it much thought. Two and two didn't necessarily add up to four for Sharon. There's no explaining the things she did. She was out of control."

"Why do you suppose Sharon Raynes jumped?"

He shrugged. "Anything might have set her off."

"Like an unhappy love affair?" I said helpfully.

"Perhaps. She was extremely suggestible, and impulsive," he said, eyes stony slits behind the thick lenses, a reminder he was a guy who took a gut shot collecting the rent. A guy with five big units. A guy who hired goons to beat up on welfare mothers and eighty-year-old men. A guy who could hurt me. Not a guy to poke a stick at.

"But suicides usually leave a note, don't they?" I said, my scalp tingling.

"I'm not an expert on the subject," he said, staring at me incredulously, uncertain whether to make me for a fool or if there was a purpose to my boneheadedness.

"Oops!" I beamed, slamming on the brakes. "The john, excuse me."

"Be my guest." He nodded curtly.

There were thirty of us, three tables of ten each. Susan was seated at Ransom's table, as was Elliott, the comptroller. Rudd was at the second table, along with Mumminger, and I sat at the third table, between Mumminger's anorexic wife and the well-upholstered Jackie Dhiel. Karl Sauter, Ransom's architect, was at our table, and so was Pam. I didn't bother catching the names of the rest of the guests.

William presided over the help as they flew around the tables removing service plates, delivering smoked salmon and capers and pouring Ransom's good wine.

I said hello to Mrs. Mumminger, reminding her we'd met at Florine's party.

"I remember, Mr. Byrne, you were with that Chinese woman," she said.

"Josephine Cyzeski." I smiled.

"Nice to see you again," she said, turning to the person on her right.

"What's the matter with her?" said Jackie Dhiel, who'd observed the exchange.

"I think she suffers from high self-esteem."

"She's got nothing to be stuck-up about, poor rich," she scoffed. "The board at Two Eleven turned them down."

"Two Eleven East Seventy-seven? Where Josephine Cyzeski is?"

"A special case." She laughed.

"And Sharon Raynes, did you know her?"

"Another special case."

"Marc's string, huh?"

"He's got them all over town."

"I'll bet. Who's he with tonight?"

"The cupcake at Nellie's table." She indicated a diminutive blonde in her early twenties.

"I'd call that statutory rape," I said.

"My lips are sealed." She grinned.

"How are things in the co-op business?"

"Got any money?"

"Nope."

"Then I don't know if I wanna talk to you, either." She laughed. "Since you asked, though, now's the time to buy."

"You guys are hurting, in other words?"

"The commission's aren't so hot," she admitted candidly, "but Marc's never hurting."

I glanced over at Susan as the waiter removed the appetizer plate. She was only a hard roll's throw away, but she might as well have been in Bensonhurst. She didn't return my glance. Randell Elliott, in the midst of a story, held her attention. There was a sudden burst of laughter from his audience as he delivered the punch line and Susan's face crinkled with glee. She was radiant, and I was miserable. I didn't want anyone else to make her laugh.

"Didn't I see Susan's and your names in Liz Smith's column?" said Jackie Dhiel, as though reading my mind. "Are you an item?"

"I don't know," I said. "Who are you with tonight?" I asked, anxious to change the subject but unable to keep my eyes off Susan. She seemed to be having a wonderful time. There wasn't a trace of concern for Dolly. I wondered how she did it.

"See the bald-headed guy?" said Dhiel, indicating Ransom's table. "He's my date."

"Anyone important?" I asked, as the main course arrived.

"Enrique Salazar," she said, as though it was a name I ought to recognize.

"What's this?" I said to the waiter.

"It's roast pheasant, sir. Enjoy!"

"Enjoy?"

"Enjoy!" grinned Jackie Dhiel. "Enrique's a real estate honcho from Argentina."

"Oh, that Enrique Salazar," I said, enjoying. "I think I met his son Paulo. Lots of hair."

"I wouldn't know. I'm doing it as a favor for Marc. You know, business."

"You're a walker."

"Escort." She smiled.

"Whatever," I said, glancing over at Susan.

"Half the crowd at these affairs can't afford to be seen in public with the people they shack up with—they need escorts. Although," she chuckled, "I'm sure the gaucho's gonna wanna tango before the night's over."

"Who could blame him?" I said. She blushed prettily. "Tell me, who are some of the other escorts?"

"Pam's one," she whispered.

"You're kidding."

"Uh-huh," she said solemnly. "Nellie likes little Puerto Rican boys," she whispered behind her hand. "But you knew that, didn't you?"

My gaze shifted to Rudd. Short and pudgy and nerdy, he seemed as innocuous as a gopher. "You could have fooled me," I said.

Jackie Dhiel gave me an indulgent up-from-under-the-mascaraed-eyelashes look.

Maybe that explained Nellie's chumminess with Angel? No way, I thought. Even if Angel swung that way, he was too skanky to give it away. Anyway, I saw Nellie with a pretty boy.

Jackie Dhiel wasn't too hard to take as a dinner companion, and things progressed smoothly from pheasant to chocolate mousse and cookies, from wine to coffee and brandy.

On the off chance he had a piece to the puzzle, I tweaked Sauter on the La Fleur. When did they expect to break ground? I asked. In his opinion the project was deader than last year's election campaign promises. The Landmarks Preservation Commission had put the whammy on it. They'd made a mistake, though; in his judgment, the La Fleur's architecture was mediocre at best. Sauter came across as a sincere guy to me, and I believed him. If what he was saying wasn't exactly true, it was because Ransom didn't tell him everything. Ransom didn't tell anyone everything, not even Nellie Rudd, close as they were. I asked Sauter about the engineer's reports. What reports? he said. That the La Fleur was unsound, I said. He laughed. It would take a bomb to knock the La Fleur down. Now why hadn't I thought of that?

Ransom chimed the crystal for attention. We should adjourn to the music room, he announced, where Cupcake would favor us with a selection of piano favorites on the Bosendorfer.

I groaned.

"You don't like the concert piano?" said Dhiel.

"Almost as much as the glockenspiel. Is the kid any good?"

"She wouldn't be playing if she wasn't. There's nothing second-rate about Marc."

"The last time I was wined and dined by Marc I had to sit through an evening of one-act plays. It was worse than group therapy."

"You've met Pauline, and you're not a theater lover?" She smiled.

We drifted into the music room, and I reattached myself to Susan. "How much longer, do you think?" I asked, checking my watch. It wasn't ten yet, but the evening was dragging. It seemed we'd been there an eternity.

"It'll break up around eleven," she said. "Aren't you having a good time?"

How could I be having a good time when your mother's missing, maybe dead, and we're screwing around listening to Ransom's girlfriend play the piano? "I'm having a ball," I said.

When we were seated, William and his minions passed among us offering more coffee and brandy. I had another cup of coffee.

Cupcake waited like a pro for the foot shuffling and throat clearing of the audience to die down. Ransom stood poised beside the piano, slim as a fillet knife in an English-tailored tux, ready to turn the pages of the sheet music for his protégé. After a dramatic silence, Cupcake pounced on the keyboard. A lilting Chopin polonaise cascaded from the Bosendorfer as enchantingly as the sound of mountain water gurgling downhill.

Cupcake knew her way around the eighty-eights. She polished off the polonaise with a flourish, acknowledged an enthusiastic round of applause, and segued into Bach's Suite in E minor.

The knights and blackamoors, nymphs and unicorns, seemed to be looking down at us from the lonesome tapestry with worldly eyes, as though they'd seen it all before. The posh setting, the fresh-cut flowers on the piano, the women in silk and satin, the men in their tuxedos, all gilded in amber light, brought to mind the paintings of Sargent and Whistler, or a scene from a Mafia opera by Francis Ford Coppola.

I scanned the room.

Randell Elliott's clean-cut WASP features were impassive, his eyes half closed. A plump, ruddy woman sat next to him, fanning herself as though she were having a hot flash. Still on his first wife, I thought. Jackie Dhiel didn't seem to mind being nuzzled by the Argentine. If she knew what was good for business, and really wanted to do Marc a favor—and my guess was she did, and would—the gaucho was going to tango. Rudd and Pam sat side by side, as impersonal as subway riders with little more than a token in common. Rudd wore his trademark patently silly look meant to pass for pleasant. Sauter's eyes were closed, a trace of a smile on his lips, his head keeping time with the music.

Cupcake wrapped up the Bach piece. There was more of the same unrestrained acclaim, which was graciously received. Sensing, though, that she ought to share some more of her success with her patron, she beamed and gestured to Ransom. He took her hand and kissed it, which got a hand. Smiling modestly, he waved for us to settle down. Cupcake announced she would play a Rachmaninoff étude next.

As she was gathering herself, waiting for complete silence, William swept into the room, conferred briefly with Mumminger, and then approached an impatient-looking Ransom. He motioned Ransom aside.

Rudd joined the huddle.

Susan and I exchanged quizzical glances.

I looked at my watch. Whatever the emergency, I hoped it meant an end to the fun. It was going on eleven o'clock, and I was itching to split.

Ransom said something to Cupcake, and she nodded affirmatively.

"Ladies and gentlemen," he said finally, "I apologize for the interruption. Regrettably, I must excuse myself from your charming company."

Murmurs of disappointment went through the audience.

Mumminger and his wife were on their feet, heading for the door.

"Please remain seated, friends. I must say good night, but there's no reason you shouldn't enjoy yourselves. Miss Deshaies will continue with her program, and Nellie will fill in for me. Good night." Ransom exited to applause.

Miss Deshaies, or Cupcake, as I'd come to think of her, attacked Rachmaninoff like a barroom piano player attempting to play over the pandemonium of a brawl. Distracted, the audience twisted and turned, craning their necks to see what was going on in back of the room.

"The Mummingers marched right out of here?" I said to Susan.

"What do you suppose has happened?"

The room buzzed with speculation.

"It might have something to do with Florine."

Miss Deshaies did the best she could under the circumstances, laboring through the piece crescendo. But the mood of the evening had been shattered. When she received only scattered applause, she threw in the towel, sparing us the several encores I suspect she had planned.

"Well, that's it," I said, "let's go." The guests had begun streaming for the door.

"Shouldn't we pay our respects?" said Susan, nodding at the dejected pianist, who was being consoled by Rudd and Pam.

"I guess," I said halfheartedly.

A few of the guests, thinking it was politic, had a similar idea, and we found ourselves in a receiving line. "Move it," I muttered impatiently under my breath at the windbag at the head of the line.

"What's your hurry?" said Susan.

"I've got an early call tomorrow."

Our turn came, and we drooled our compliments for the piano player, and I dragged Susan out of there. Before I did, though, Nellie Rudd admitted that Florine had indeed been the emergency, joking she probably had had a stroke because Marc hadn't invited her.

27

"You don't have to go," she said.

The Sikh driver was watching in the rearview mirror. We were parked in front of her house, the cab's meter running.

"It's late."

"I don't want to be alone tonight."

"Neither do I."

"Then stay."

"I can't." I reached inside the breast pocket of the tux and produced the envelope. "I almost forgot, Dolly asked me to give you this."

She looked startled momentarily, then she clawed open the envelope. There was a key Scotch-taped to a note. She read it hurriedly, before stuffing the note, key, and envelope into her purse.

"What was it?" I said.

"It's nothing."

"I saw a key. Did she say where she was?"

"It's a key to a locker where she keeps a few things. She didn't say where she was." She gazed at me with liquid eyes.

Then she threw her arms around me and kissed me hotly. "Hold me, Charlie," she murmured.

I held her. She seemed overwhelmed. I wanted to help.

"Stay," she pleaded.

"I want to stay," I said, feeling myself weaken, "but I can't. I've got an early call."

"So do I."

"Really, I'd like to. . . ." I wanted to reassure her everything would be all right.

"As you wish, then," she said, suddenly very cool, and slightly schizo. She opened the cab door.

"Tomorrow night?" I said.

"Call me," she said. I reached for her, but she was gone.

I hated leaving her like that, feeling misunderstood and as though I'd misunderstood her, but if there was any chance her mother was alive at the La Fleur, and I didn't make an effort to find her, I'd never be able to face her again.

I gave the driver the address of the La Fleur.

His wary glance bounced off the rearview mirror as he hauled the cab west across town toward Fifth Avenue.

It was hurricane season, and the night was windy and spitting rain. Store signs, awnings, and pendants flapped madly. Debris blew across the cab's windshield. Steam hissed and escaped from excavations and manhole covers as the cab rattled over steel construction plates and potholes large enough to swallow a bus. Somewhere in the dark a car alarm wailed.

The Sikh dropped me on the corner. I paid the fare and slammed the door. He peeled out like it was *Escape From New York,* abandoning me on the desolate street. The La Fleur looked as dazed and forlorn as a strung-out street walker. The building was dark, except for the entrance, which was lit and as open as an invitation. I removed my bow tie and stuffed it in my pocket. I took a deep breath and exhaled. It didn't look promising, but I walked inside anyway.

The basement seemed the logical place to begin, or at least it seemed as good as any other. I heard the elevator motor began to whine, and I ducked out of sight behind what had been the front desk.

The hard hats emerged.

"We've got a little time to kill," I heard the younger guy say.

"One drink," said the older guy.

"That's what I was thinking."

"Wanna be back in time for the drop."

"Wouldn't miss it for the world."

The lights went out and the front doors slammed shut.

Great, I'm locked in, I thought.

I went to the elevator and punched the button. The doors stuttered open. I stepped in, pressed B, and descended slowly to the basement.

A dingy bare bulb was the only illumination. I was facing a brick wall. I turned right, drawn by the hum of the furnace, or boiler, or whatever was humming. Then right again, and I was up against a floor-to-ceiling wire-mesh cage with a Fox lock. I wasn't going any farther. Beyond the security cage were the bowels of the building. The elevator motor and drum that spooled the cable. The maze of pipes and conduits for steam, water, waste, and electricity. The boiler. What you'd expect to find in the basement of a building like the La Fleur.

My first thought was that the security cage made a great holding cell. "Dolly!" I called out. "Are you in here?" I felt foolish, my voice reverberating back to me.

The machine went on humming.

"Dolly! You here?" I tried again, louder. I peered into the darkness, searching the shadows. A whole herd of homeless could hide in here if they could get past the cage.

There was no response, only the rumblings of the machinery.

Then I noticed it. You didn't have to be a Nobel prize winner in chemistry to know what it was. It didn't look the way I'd have imagined it would, but it was close enough. It was chevron-shaped and wrapped around a column. All the columns on the other side of the cage were similarly wrapped. The tip-off was the wire. Each wrapping had a wire leading off of it. I traced the visible wires. They seemed to come together, but I couldn't see where. And it didn't matter because I couldn't reach it.

I replayed the hard hats' conversation.

"We've got a little time to kill," the one guy said.

"Wanna be back in time for the drop," the second guy said.

How much time was a little?

There must be a timing device in there somewhere, I thought. If I could find it, it would tell me how much time was left. I tried tracing the wires again. They had to connect. Time enough for a drink? Twenty minutes? Half an hour, maybe? It was useless. I couldn't see where they connected. I couldn't find the timer. I was wasting time.

My watch had one o'clock.

I dashed for the elevator. I punched the button for sixteen, and cursed the slow climb as the seconds ticked away lapsed time.

A thorough search of the building would take hours to complete. "Wanna be back in time for the drop," kept ringing in my ears. I had fifteen, maybe twenty, minutes before this place blew, or to be more precise, imploded. Those charges were wired to kick out a ten-foot section of steel pillar like it was a beer can. The building was going to collapse upon itself, just "drop," like you see on TV.

I rocketed out of the elevator and charged down the empty hall, bellowing at the top of my lungs, "Dolly! Dolly Varden! Where are you, goddamnit?"

The only answer I heard was the echo of my own voice.

I ran down the stairwell and tried again on the next floor.

"Dolly! Dolly Varden! Can you hear me? It's me, Charlie Byrne!"

Nothing.

It occurred to me she might already be dead, or unconscious.

I ran down to the next floor.

"Dolly!" I screamed. "Say something if you hear me!"

The silence was deafening.

It was like that for the next six flights.

There were eight more flights to go. I glanced at my watch. If I was lucky, I had five more minutes. There was no way I was going to be able to check out all the floors, and I might have already missed her on one of the upper floors.

It was like being trapped in that nightmare where you're wearing lead sneakers and the maniac with the chain saw is after you. I swallowed hard but the lump in my throat wouldn't go down. My clothes clung to me. I was drenched in sweat and glazed with fright. I wanted out of there so bad my flesh was crawling, but I had to keep trying to find her.

"Come on, Dolly! Please talk to me!" I begged.

I held my breath and listened. All I could hear was the panic of my heart.

But then . . .

"Motherfucking, cocksucking—"

For a moment I thought I was hallucinating.

"Shit-eating, ass-licking—" it went on.

I could hardly believe my ears.

Well, hello, Dolly!

It was magic, the cry of the loon. Dolly Varden at her prayers.

"Son-of-a-bitchin', cunt-lapping—"

"Atta girl," I urged. "Keep talking to me! Don't stop now."

The litany of obscenities led me right to her door. I clutched the doorknob and twisted. The door was locked.

And she clammed up on me the moment the knob turned.

"Dolly, it's me, Charlie Byrne," I yelled, rattling the doorknob.

"How do I know it's you?" she said after a moment's hesitation.

"Your daughters' names are Sharon Raynes and Susan Ferrante. You live on Thirty-eighth Street. Your real name's Miriam Lusk," I cried. "Jesus, Dolly, this is no time for Trivial Pursuit. We've gotta get outta here."

Nothing, nada, zip, zilch, silence.

"Goddamnit, Dolly," I exploded, banging on the door with my fist, "don't fuck with me! Open the door! We're rat food if we're not outta here in two minutes!"

"Okay, okay," she said finally, "I'm gonna open the door."

"Hurry, Dolly."

"Stand back where I can get a good look at you."

"Please hurry."

She shot the bolt, and the knob turned. The door seemed to swing open like my sunflowers blooming in time-lapse photography. Her head poked out from behind the door.

"It's you," she said, her eyes wild, the billy club in her hand.

"Right," I said, extending a hand to her. "Come on, we've gotta get outta here. This place is gonna blow any minute now."

I must have looked crazy myself, because she gazed at me with a mixture of awe and respect, as though conceding the presence of madness transcendent. I was credible in her eyes, and she gave me her hand without a murmur.

Almost casually, my mind considered the problem of how we were going to exit the La Fleur as we tumbled down the stairwell as fast as our feet would carry us.

We staggered into the lobby dizzy from running around in circles for seven flights. We were going out the way I'd come in, through the front door; I'd decided it was our only chance. We rushed for the entrance. I grabbed the handles and pulled. Nothing happened. The doors were locked.

Dolly shot me a panicky look as I searched for something, but not knowing what. I laid eyes on the ashtray resting near the registration desk. It was about two feet high, a pottery cylinder filled with sand. It must have weighed fifty pounds. I picked it up and lifted it over my head like it was a beach ball. I rammed the doors, aiming for the lock where the double doors met. The doors buckled, and held. The ashtray shattered. I was on my ass, in despair, covered with sand and cigarette butts.

Dolly, perched on one leg, kicked at the doors. They gave some and snapped back into position. I was on my feet, kicking at the door. Dolly jammed the billy club in the gap and began working it. I kicked again, and again. Dolly levered the club. Together, we put our shoulders to the doors, they gave, and sprung open suddenly, dumping us out on the street under the marquee.

"Run!" I shouted.

It was a footrace to the corner, where we huddled in a doorway. I bent over, head down, hands on knees, as a sudden wave of nausea overcame me. When I looked up again at the La Fleur, it appeared as benign and innocent as its name, standing dark against the moody night skyline. We stared, gasping for breath, our ears ringing with the sound of our own machinery, and then a blue-white light, about the duration of a burst of strobe, flashed at street level, searing architectural detail into our retinas. The sidewalk under our feet felt like a trampoline, and a sonic boom rolled out of the basement of the building.

Suspended in space momentarily, the stately old hotel seemed to hang there, as proud and serene as she'd ever been, in good times and bad; then, with a groan and a shudder, she dropped, slipping to the ground as gracefully as falling silk. A shower of broken glass and plaster followed. Parked cars got dinged, their alarms began to wail, and nearby buildings had their windows shattered. A puff of dust rose from the rubble like a ghost leaving a body.

A moment later the Shit Happens van sped by, headed the wrong way, north on Broadway, the shortest way to the Lincoln Tunnel.

28

Dolly paraded past me in an old bathrobe of mine on her way from the bathroom to the dressing room.

"How about some breakfast?" I asked.

"Scrambled eggs, toast, and bacon would be nice."

I phoned the order into the Greek's, and made the coffee. Then I tried Susan's number. I'd left a message on her machine last night when Dolly and I got in, but she never returned the call. I left another message at home, and tried her office, but she hadn't gotten in yet. The buzzer sounded, and thinking it was the Greek's, I went to the door. Aldo Fabrizi and Sonny were standing there, grinning wolfishly at me.

"Come in, fellas," I said.

The old man, toddling in on his cane, looked the place over and said, "I was photographed by Steichen and Karsh."

"Two of my idols."

"They photographed all the important people of the day."

"You were a star, Mr. Fabrizi."

"Well, that was a long time ago," he said modestly.

"Have you fellows had breakfast?"

"We split ah bagel," said Sonny.

"Are you hungry?"

"Sho, how 'bout you, Aldo?"

"I could eat something."

"How's scrambled eggs, toast, and bacon sound?"

"Jus' fine," Sonny said, beaming.

"I'd like my eggs over easy," said the old man.

I phoned the order in. While I was on the phone, Dolly emerged from the dressing room. She'd managed to come up with a completely different outfit from yesterday by rotating the layers of clothing. She was probably packing a week's worth of wardrobe on her back.

"Dolly, this is Sonny and Mr. Fabrizi," I said, hanging up the phone. "Sonny and Mr. Fabrizi, Dolly."

Everyone made like birds and bobbed their heads.

"I once knew a girl named Dolly," the old man remarked.

"Really?" said Dolly.

"Yes, Dolly Varden was her name," he recalled fondly.

"That's funny," said Dolly, "that's my name."

"Go on," scoffed the old man.

"Really, that's my name."

"Can't be," said the old man, confused. "I knew Dolly Varden, and you're no Dolly Varden."

"I don't see why I can't be Dolly Varden if I wanna be," said Dolly, appealing to me.

"You can be Scarlet O'Hara if you wanna be," I said, giving her a reassuring pat.

"I don't wanna be Scarlet O'Hara, I wanna be Dolly Varden."

Fabrizi snorted in contempt.

"Lighten up, ol' man," Sonny advised. "If duh lady say she Dolly Varden, den she Dolly Varden. Wad's wrong wid dat? Mebbe dere's mo' 'en one of 'em, ever think ah dat?"

"Shall I make some more coffee?" I asked, hoping to nip a possible misunderstanding in the bud.

Everyone wanted coffee.

Unbending slightly, Fabrizi reconsidered Dolly. "I suppose there could be another Dolly Varden," he said.

"Dat's better, ol' man." Sonny beamed. In an aside to me, he explained, "Aldo loses it sometimes. You know how ol' peoples be."

"Of course, the Dolly Varden I knew," the old man reminisced, his eyes moister than usual, "was petite . . . not like you."

Dolly frowned.

"No offense, child," he said gallantly. "She would be a much older woman than you, also. . . . She'd be more my age."

"Were you in love with her?" asked Dolly, reasonably.

I stopped pouring water into the coffee machine, waiting for the answer.

Aldo Fabrizi flashed a dreamy smile. For a nanosecond, in spite of his ridiculous appearance, he seemed young and dashing again, a successful singer, a boulevardier.

"My name isn't really Dolly Varden," Dolly confessed.

"Neither was hers," said Fabrizi. "She just went by that name."

"Miriam Lusk's my real name. I hate it."

"Nuttin' wrong wid dat name," said Sonny, trying to be friendly.

Dolly frowned and shook her head.

"What was your friend's real name, Mr. Fabrizi?" I asked.

"I never did know what her real name was," he said.

"She never told you?" said Dolly.

"No, she never did. But I did see her picture in the paper once, after she'd gone and become respectable. They said her name was Ransom, I believe . . . ah, that was it, Florine Ransom." He flashed the dreamy smile again, pleased just to remember the name. "Of course, that might not be her real name, either," he added thoughtfully.

Dolly looked at me quizzically. "Don't I know her? Isn't she the lady in the limo?"

"Uh-huh," was as much as I could manage. I'd guessed right, it was the name that had made Florine take notice.

"Imagine that—small world, isn't it?" said Dolly.

And getting smaller.

"You know Dolly Varden?" Fabrizi glared suspiciously at Dolly.

"Now don' get eggsided, Aldo," Sonny cautioned.

I put mugs and sugar and milk on the table.

"Florine Ransom, or Dolly Varden . . . the original Dolly Varden, that is," I said with deference to Dolly, "owns the La Fleur, or at least she did until last night."

They'd heard the news. Sonny'd had the *Daily News* under his arm when they walked in. It was the excuse for the visit. And it was all over the morning radio.

"'Ear dat, Aldo?" said Sonny. "Yo' ol' girlfrien' own'd duh hoe-tel."

"Dolly's still alive?" the old man marveled. "Imagine."

I had to wonder about that. She might have crashed with the La Fleur last night, for all I knew.

"Well," Fabrizi snorted, "I'm not surprised."

"That she's alive?" I asked.

"No, that she owned the hotel."

"Why do you say that?"

"Because she used to say she was going to buy the place one day, that's why. And once Dolly Varden made up her mind to do something, she did it."

"But why would she want to buy the hotel?"

"Oh, she had her reasons, I suppose."

"What reasons?" I persisted.

"She worked there. It was where we used to go," he said brusquely.

"Now don' go geddin' you-self in an uproar, Aldo," Sonny warned. "Man don' mean no 'arm wid es questions, an' id ain' good fo' you blood pressure." Turning and grinning at me, he said, "Ain' 'e sump'n?"

"Why, you should have seen the hotel back then," said the old man, with a faraway look. "Oh, there might have been bigger hotels—the Ritz, the Astor—but there were none more elegant. It was grand, a beautiful hotel, and profitable, too. A real good investment—you bet. Dolly always was a shrewd one with a buck. Not like me. With me it was always easy come, easy go," he said matter-of-factly. "The three loves of my life were singing"—he held up a bony finger— "number one, the ponies, and the ladies, in that order," he said, flipping digits two and three.

"Mah man," said Sonny approvingly, and patting the old man gently on the back.

"Yes, easy come, easy go . . . slow horses and fast women . . . that's all it takes," the old man continued with a dreamy smile. "It's come down to Welfare, Goodwill, and Meals-on-Wheels, but I've had a wonderful life, I've got no complaints, and only a few regrets. I had my share of good times."

"Jus' add some aged sour mash tuh dat list, Aldo, an' you be mah main man," Sonny said solemnly.

The old guy wagged his finger at Sonny. "I never planned on living this long, Sonny. You better take care of yourself."

"Don' worry 'bout me, Aldo."

"How does she look?" Fabrizi asked, serious a moment. Then he chuckled softly and went dreamy again. "I bet she's sitting pretty, waited on hand and foot."

I heard Tito's key in the lock.

"She look's real good, for her age," said Dolly.

The old tenor didn't seem to hear her.

Tito entered with the delivery from the Greek's. "Met the kid downstairs," he explained.

"How much?" I asked, taking the food.

"Fifteen with tip. Hey, you hear about the La Fleur?" He had a copy of the *Post* under his arm.

"Why do you think they're all here?" I said, gesturing to the homeless sitting around my kitchen table waiting for breakfast.

"Because we're running a soup kitchen?" he muttered. "Anyway, what did I tell you?"

"I don't know, what did you tell me?" I placed the carton of food on the table, three pairs of hungry eyes watching me.

He acknowledged the group with a nod and a grin.

"Didn't I tell you they were going to blow the place up?"

"Scrambled," I said, opening the lid of the top tray and handing it to Dolly. "Yeah, you did, and you were right." I inspected the next tray. Scrambled also. I dealt the trays to Sonny and the old man. "They dropped it with explosives, all right, just as you predicted."

"The guys with the van, the hard hats, right?"

"That's right."

The full realization of what had happened slowly dawned on Tito. Looking at Dolly, he said, "Is that where she was?"

"Uh-huh," I said, glancing at Dolly's bowed head and noticing for the first time a barely conspicuous gash beneath her matted hair.

"What happened?"

"Later," I said. "How about we climb all over our own case right now?"

"You're the boss," he said, and poured himself some coffee. "But how'd you find her?" he said.

"Later."

He shrugged. "Just asking," he said, and as a parting shot, "This better be worth waiting for." He took his coffee to the set.

I checked the morning mail.

When they'd finished eating, Sonny pulled me aside and put the bite on me for a yard, twenty of which I had to borrow from Tito, my in-house ATM. I watched as the old man toddled out on Sonny's arm. They were in a hurry to get to the nearest OTB office; Aldo wanted to get a bet down on a long shot.

That left me with Dolly.

The good news was, she could sign the release for the bank ad now.

The bad news was, I'd totaled another Beau Brummell tuxedo. I dialed Susan's number at work again, wondering whether Murray would be interested in selling me a piece of the business.

"Mrs. Ferrante's in a meeting," said the girl when I told her who I was.

"Tell her I've got her mama," I said. "Ask her what she wants me to do with her, okay?"

"I'll tell her, Mr. Byrne," she promised.

"Shit," I muttered, slamming down the phone.

I wanted to go get the surveillance tape from last night, but I didn't want to leave until I'd heard from Susan. I dialed Florine Ransom's number at the Thackeray and got Bernard Kiernan.

"Bernard, what's with the old lady?" I asked.

"She's had a stroke," he confirmed. "She's alive, but comatose."

"She in the hospital?"

"She's here, at home. There's a private duty nurse around the clock. Her bedroom looks like a hospital room."

"Is Mumminger looking after her?"

"Yes, he's her physician. He comes and goes. But she's been examined by a neurologist."

"She gonna pull through?"

"Only time will tell."

"How'd it happen?"

"How'd it happen? She's a very old lady. It just happened. Yesterday morning, after Mr. Stein left—"

"Henry Stein?"

"Yes, Florine asked him to pay her a visit early yesterday, and it was after he left that she began to complain about feeling strange. I asked if there was anything she wanted me to do. She said no, she'd be okay. She seemed all right to me. But then, last night, Louise and I noticed that her speech was slurred and she couldn't move her arm. That's when I called Marc's house, and he and Mumminger rushed right over."

"Did Stein notice anything wrong with her?"

"If he did, he didn't say anything."

"Does he know she's had a stroke?"

"He hasn't heard it from me."

"If you hear from him, will you have him give me a call?"

"Of course."

"Thanks. Should I send flowers?"

"God, no, we're up to our armpits in flowers. A card will do."

"Okay, see you, Bernard," I said, hanging up. Dolly was standing over my shoulder.

"I gotta go. Thank you for last night, and the bed and breakfast."

"What do you mean, you gotta go?"

"I gotta go," she repeated, as though that should be perfectly obvious. "I've got things to do."

She had things to do? Like what, scrounge for nickel returns, go panhandling with a paper cup, take a nap in a doorway? "But, Dolly, I'm waiting to hear from Susan. She's been worried sick about you."

"Yeah, sure," she said. "Look, Charlie, I appreciate all you've done, but I've gotta go."

"Dolly, you can't go until we speak to Susan."

"You gonna stop me?"

Man, how is it she can be reasonable one minute and a fruitcake the next? Was it because she was crazy? Nah, crazy was what she made everyone else. "No, of course not, Dolly. But don't you think you should let Susan know you're okay?"

"You can tell her."

I tried another tack, anything to keep her from walking. "But, Dolly, it's dangerous out there. If I hadn't found you, you'd be dead. Someone wants you dead." I hadn't thought of it that way before, it just came out that way. It made sense to me, though, but then maybe I'm crazy.

"Angel and James, maybe?"

"Well, yeah, Angel and James."

"They're not gonna hurt anyone anymore."

"Did they hurt you? Is that where you got that gash on your head?"

She nodded solemnly.

"Did they kill Socrates?"

"They're not gonna hurt anyone anymore," she repeated, the billy club appearing without warning in her hand. She tapped the palm of her hand with it a couple of times, and it disappeared as quickly as it had appeared.

"I see." I decided not to pursue the subject.

"Thanks again," she said. "I gotta go."

"Where you going?"

"I gotta go to my locker."

"Locker?"

"Yeah, Chelsea Storage. I gave you the key to give to Susan, remember? You gave it to her, didn't you?" she said, moving for the door.

"Last night, just before I found you. Hey, wait a minute, I'll go with you."

"Why?"

Why? Why not? I wasn't about to let her out of my sight

until I handed her over to Susan. "I've got an errand to run downtown," I lied, "we can share a cab."

"I don't take cabs."

"My treat, jus' gimme a minute to get straightened out here, okay?"

"Okay." She shrugged.

I told Tito where I was going. He looked at me like I was crazy. I told him I was expecting a call from Susan, it was important, and to tell her I found her mother.

"Uh-huh, uh-huh," he said, "when will you be back?"

"Soon as possible."

We hopped a cab on Fifth Avenue. The cabbie was a young woman, Elena Ionescu, the hack license said.

The radio was tuned to an all-news station. Avoid Herald Square if you can, the announcer advised. Water mains are ruptured, subway tunnels flooded, and power lines are shorted out. The morning rush-hour traffic was a mess, and several streets in the area were closed to traffic. It would be days before the neighborhood was back to normal, he predicted.

Dolly had withdrawn into her own world, gazing blankly out the window at the pedestrians hurrying along the avenue.

"They say what caused the hotel to collapse?" I asked the driver.

"They think it was structural, but they don't really know," she answered in a slight Middle European accent.

"So they think it was an accident?"

"Listen," she said, turning the radio up.

"'At this point in time we have no knowledge of what might have caused the La Fleur Hotel to collapse,'" said a familiar voice. "'However, the Buildings Department will be investigating the matter thoroughly, and I can assure you that if it is determined there is even the slightest evidence of a crime having been committed, the perpetrators will have the book thrown at them. This mayor will not tolerate flagrant disregard for the law.'"

"'Isn't it true,'" a reporter asked, "'that the La Fleur had just been granted landmark status, Mr. Fallon? And that the sudden—'"

"'You have just heard mayoral aide, Matthew X. Fallon,'" the radio reporter intoned, drowning out the complete question. "'And now back to you, Harley.'"

Tired words. Nice try, Matty. I wondered why hizzoner hadn't done the sound bite himself. Ordinarily, the mayor would trample his grandmother to death in his haste to get in front of a camera or microphone.

Dolly muttered an obscenity. I hoped she wasn't about to go off on me. It was a little early in the day for that. I peered out the window and saw what had triggered it. A blind man was tapping his way down the street with a guide dog that was a ringer for Socrates.

"Easy," I said, patting her knee, "everything's gonna be all right."

"Like hell it is," she said, and lapsed back into silence.

"You're Romanian, aren't you?" I said to the driver.

"How did you know that?" she said, giving me a wary backward glance.

"Romanian names end in E-S-C-U, I've noticed."

She had nothing to say to that.

"You've got a famous name, Ionescu, the playwright."

"No relation."

"Been in the country long?"

"Six months."

"What did you do in the old country?"

"I was a lawyer."

Lawyers like to talk, but this one was no conversationalist. We rode the rest of the way in silence. "This seems to be the place," the driver said, pulling up to the loading bay of an old warehouse overlooking the Hudson.

"This is it," Dolly confirmed, climbing out of the cab immediately.

I gave the driver six dollars and told her to keep the change. She thanked me politely and sped away. From lawyer to cab driver—that was some comedown. You had to do whatever it took to get along, though. But I knew one thing, if I had to drive a cab for a living, I'd rather do it in Bucharest than in this town.

29

Chelsea Storage is the perpendicular equivalent of those sprawling U-Stores that have mushroomed along the interstates these days. Storage space is a growth industry. Nobody stays in one place anymore, as the song goes. College kids, people between jobs and apartments, flea market operators and street vendors, old book and magazine dealers, drug dealers, and apparently the homeless—these are just a few of the types that find these places handy. I buy smoke and mist bombs occasionally from a guy I've never met who lives upstate, in Downsville, where he manufactures the stuff. He sells to photographers, movie and video people, and rock concert producers out of a storage place, midtown on the West Side. There probably isn't much call for theatrical effects in a town called Downsville.

Dolly seemed to be a familiar figure because the bent nose behind the Plexiglas gave her a big hello. He consulted the log and said a Susan Ferrante was visiting the room. She'd gone up only moments before. That was all right, wasn't it?

Her name was on the registration. "She's my daughter," Dolly said noncommittally.

Perfect, I thought, I can hand Dolly over to Susan and be on my way.

Dolly and an elderly black man exchanged greetings as we rode up to the fifth floor in the freight elevator. The thought crossed my mind that Dolly's possessions lived better than she did. They were high and dry and safe under lock and key while Dolly was chancing it out on the street. The elevator glided up to the floor and stopped. We got out and wandered through a labyrinth of wire-mesh corridors, like in the basement of the La Fleur, until we finally came to Dolly's cage.

Susan was standing in the corridor, the door to the storage cage ajar. Someone was inside the cage. I could hear grunts and things being moved about.

Susan was stacking cardboard cartons on a freight dolly when she looked up and spotted her mother and me. "Mama," she said, her jaw dropping.

"What's going on here?" Dolly demanded, sounding just like a parent.

Matty Fallon poked his head out from the cage. Hadn't I just heard the guy on the radio? Could he be in two places at the same time? He must have been on tape, I realized.

For one sickening moment Susan's glance met mine, and I wanted to believe that this wasn't happening, that it was a horrible mistake.

It was a horrible mistake. Hers. They were cleaning out her mother's goods, and Dolly and I had walked in on them while they were doing it. My dull brain zeroed in on the fact it was too soon. Susan had no way of knowing whether her mother was dead or alive. Or had she?

"I can explain, Mama," she said.

I prayed that she could explain. But Dolly cut her off before she could offer a word in her own defense.

"Put my things back!"

Susan hesitated, uncertain and confused.

"Put 'em back!" Dolly said flatly.

Fallon glared impatiently at Susan, as though expecting

her to take charge. She seemed helpless, and unable to confront her mother.

"You heard the lady," I said to Fallon.

He stepped over the cartons, going bumper to bumper with me. "Stay outta this, Byrne," he said.

"Matty, please," said Susan. "Leave us alone . . . the both of you."

"You sure?" he said.

"Yes. Wait downstairs for me."

"You heard the lady—move it, pal," he said, mocking me out of the side of his mouth.

"Want me to stay?" I asked Dolly. Somehow, this was not the way I'd imagined mother and daughter being reunited.

"It's all right, you can go."

"I'll wait for you downstairs."

I glanced at Susan before turning to go. Her eyes were sullen and resentful as they met mine.

I gestured for Fallon to lead the way, feeling as empty as a gutted deer. Fallon moved off truculently. I wanted to slug him. I had no reason to feel as I did, yet I couldn't have felt more betrayed if I'd caught them in bed together. Mercifully, the elevator came quickly. There was enough room in it for us to distance ourselves in neutral corners and studiously ignore one another. When we landed, he crossed the street and climbed into a waiting Hertz-Penske rental van. I paced the loading dock.

Why the hurry to clean out her mother's locker? I wondered. What did they hope to find there? What were they looking for? Had Ransom's dinner been a setup? While we were listening to Cupcake tickle the ivories, did Susan know her mother was trapped in the Hotel La Fleur? Dolly was an embarrassment to her, she'd said as much. Wouldn't it be nice if she were gone, missing?

Could that be? I wondered, my mind rank with suspicion, and feeling guilty for having such nasty thoughts.

Susan suddenly stepped off the freight elevator and strode past me. She hadn't once called me by name. I watched as she climbed in next to Fallon and they drove off.

I hustled upstairs to find Dolly padlocking her space.

"What happened?" I asked.

"We put the stuff back," she said calmly.

"Everything all right?"

"Everything's fine."

"She didn't take anything?"

"She was going to take everything, clean the place out."

"Why? What were they looking for?"

"She was looking to get her hands on my stuff. I've got some nice things stored here, and she knows it."

As usual, Dolly wasn't on the same page of the script as everyone else. "I'm sure you have some very nice things," I said.

"I have," she asserted, "I've even got all their dolls and stuffed animals from when they were little girls. . . ."

"Think, Dolly, did Sharon ever give you anything to hold for her—you know, just in case?"

"Susan asked the same question," she said, startled.

"What did you tell her?"

"I told her no, Sharon never gave me anything but trouble."

For a second there I'd begun to feel foolish, like I'd jumped to conclusions and that this had all been a misunderstanding. That Susan had a logical explanation for attempting to clean out her mother's locker. But when Dolly said Susan had asked the same question—and I had been only grasping at straws when I popped that one—I knew there'd been no misunderstanding. Even dead, Sharon Raynes was a problem for someone.

"Did Susan say what it was she thought Sharon might have asked you to hold for her?"

"She didn't say. You think this had something to do with Sharon's death?" she said, suddenly lucid.

"Yeah . . . ah, I dunno," I answered. "I gotta get back to the studio, Dolly, want a ride uptown?"

"No thanks, you go on ahead," she said pensively.

"What are you gonna do?"

"I'll think of something."

"You're welcome to sleep on the futon tonight."

She didn't say anything for a few moments. "Maybe, we'll see."

"Look, I want you to stay with me." I didn't like the idea of her roaming around loose.

"Don't worry about me," she said. "I can take care of myself. I've been doing it for a long time now."

Right, and what a wonderful job of it you've been doing, I thought. Why couldn't she just be reasonable? But if she were reasonable, she wouldn't be Dolly. "You don't have Socrates to protect you anymore," I pointed out.

"No one's gonna bother me," she said, frowning. "Leave me alone now, I'll be all right."

I was getting so I could spot her mood swings, and she was getting edgy. Time to back off. "You sure?" I asked.

"Yeah, I'm sure."

Perhaps it was paranoia, but it seemed to me that someone had just tried to kill her, and damn near succeeded. It also seemed to me this had failed to make much of an impression on her. Which I guess was one of the symptoms of her illness. If I was right, the next time they might succeed.

What could I do? I repeated my offer of a place to stay, and reluctantly said good-bye.

On the way back to the studio, I paid a visit to the surveillance camera to pick up the tapes. In the light of day it was an awesome sight, the jagged shapes of masonry, brick and mortar, the twisted pipes and beams. Where yesterday, on this spot, there'd been a beautiful old hotel—where a young woman who called herself Dolly Varden had played those love scenes that still made an old tenor sing—today there was a pile of friable rubble. Tomorrow there'd be a hole in the ground, and the day after that a new skyscraper. If change, sudden and cold, makes you uneasy, New York's not the place for you. New York's not a sentimental town. The La Fleur's only offense had been getting old.

I returned to the studio not feeling any younger myself. Tito handed me a list of calls. He'd also picked up the blowups of Sharon Raynes.

I called Strunk first.

"Get it on tape, Byrne?" were the first words out of his mouth.

"I don't know."

"Whatta ya mean, ya don't know?"

"Just picked up the tape. What did you find out about the van?"

"Belongs to a small contractor in Jersey, registered to the business. Sent a man out there this morning to find out more, soon as I heard the news. Have more information later in the day."

"Listen, P.C., I just had a run-in with Matty Fallon. He wanted something he thought the bag lady had."

"What?"

"If I knew, I'd tell you."

"Man, you don't know diddly."

"Tell me. Hey, didn't you mention there was something up with the guy?"

"'Bout to be indicted, why?"

"Well, it sure would be nice if you could pick him up."

"You mean arrest him?"

"Whatever, I'd feel better knowing where the guy is. Know what I mean?"

"I can't do that. We're gonna haul his ass into court, though. If you have anything on him we can use on Ransom, I can offer him a deal."

I told him about last night and the La Fleur.

"I need more than that, Byrne."

"I know, P.C. Listen, maybe you should hold on to these tapes?"

"Good idea, Byrne. I'll call ya, an' pick 'em up later myself," he said, and hung up.

I returned Hannibal's call, didn't get him, and left a message. Same thing with Stein.

I went to the VCR and slipped the tape into the machine. Tito drifted into the room to watch. The tape went from black to the La Fleur, dark and quiet. It was ten P.M. Nothing moved. I pressed the fast forward until there was a blip of activity, backed up and pressed play. The hard hats entered the picture, going into the hotel. This was probably around eleven o'clock. The picture was static for a considerable period of time after that, so I went to the fast forward button.

Another blip. Stop, back up, play.

The hard hats exited and reentered the building, and there was another dull spot. Finally, there I was, going into the hotel.

"Here comes the cavalry," Tito said. "Man, you were loco to go in there."

It was about one o'clock then, I figured.

"Uh-oh, the bad guys are in there," Tito remembered, getting as caught up in it as if it were a slasher movie. "I can't watch." He covered his eyes.

The buzzer sounded.

Tito jumped. "Who's that?"

"Why don't you go see?"

"Hold the tape."

He returned with Henry Stein.

"Just tried to call you."

"I was at the old lady's."

"How is she?"

"Hanging in there. What's this?" He nodded at the TV.

"It's last night at the hotel," said Tito. "Charlie's in there with the bad guys."

"This I gotta see," said Stein.

I let the tape roll. The bad guys strolled out the door, turned, pulled claw hammers from their tool belts and proceeded to board up the joint.

I could have sworn I was in there five, maybe ten minutes, tops. Strangely, nothing seems to happen for quite a while. In my panicked state, with the clock ticking and not knowing precisely how much time I had, I lost all sense of time. Five or ten minutes had actually been more like twenty or thirty minutes. Time flies when you're having fun, they say.

"This is riveting," said Stein.

"It gets better, Henry." I forwarded the tape.

The door quaked and burst open and Dolly and I tumbled out, ass over teakettle.

"They made it!" Tito said.

"What did you think?" laughed Stein.

Dolly and I picked ourselves up and ran like hell. The

camera began to shake. The camera microphone picked up the sound of the blast, and then a dull, sustained roar.

We stared solemnly at the TV.

The facade of the La Fleur shimmied and wavered. The picture dissolved into a tumbling, descending blur. Then the screen went gray, until eventually, like a ghost ship emerging from a fog bank, the ruins of the La Fleur appeared as the dust settled.

"Whatta finish," said Stein, "just like in the movies."

"Wait a minute, it's not over yet."

Right then the Shit Happens van streaked across the screen, rubber squealing, as bold as the signature on a bum check.

"That's great," laughed Tito.

"No sign of Nellie Rudd on the tape, huh?" said Stein.

"Not on this one. I've got a couple of shots of him with the bad guys on the other tapes."

"Got a shot of the bag lady being dragged into the hotel?"

"No."

"That's really too bad. Where is she now?"

I told him about Chelsea Storage and how she wanted to be left alone. "There wasn't much I could do but leave. I don't know where she is now."

He massaged his chin thoughtfully. "Did you know the old lady recognized her as an heir?"

"No."

"Well, she did."

"So Dolly was supposed to get it in the La Fleur."

Stein rocked on his heels, his expression both knowing and bemused.

"I don't get it, though, why she would recognize Dolly. They weren't related, and Florine knew it."

"You know that, I know that, Marc knows that, and Florine knows that. . . ."

"Even Dolly knows it."

"Everyone knows it."

"So what's the big idea?"

"It's the old lady's idea of a joke, maybe."

"But Sharon Raynes was scamming the old lady."

"Look's like it worked." He grinned.

"Yeah, but how did Raynes know about Dolly Varden?"

"Maybe Mumminger or Kiernan were in on it with her. The Raynes babe must have learned of Dolly Varden from one of them."

"Can the old lady talk?"

"We discussed the situation before she had the stroke."

"But they got it all wrong, Dolly Varden was just an alias, not the name of Florine's lost daughter."

"And your friend Dolly . . . what's her real name?"

"Miriam, Miriam Lusk."

"Right, Miriam. She's too young to be the old lady's daughter. It was so lame, the old lady was wise to the scam from the beginning. But it was something to do, it amused her. The Raynes babe suddenly appears from out of nowhere—well, nearly out of nowhere—and claims to be her granddaughter. The old lady, however, knows she's one of her son's bimbos. Florine's days are pretty dull. Marc doesn't pay much attention to her. Now, suddenly, she's got a reason to get out of bed in the morning. There's intrigue in the palace. But when she doesn't hear again from Raynes, it's a bit of a letdown. She thinks the game's over. Then the article about you and the bag lady appears in the *Times,* and she realizes she's got a problem. Either Mumminger or Kiernan is a fink."

"Okay, but how did they find out about Dolly Varden?"

"That's easy to explain. Florine likes to talk, and she can be pretty candid."

"Yes, I know."

"Like most old people, she lives in the past, and although she's still fairly sharp for her age, she can be aphasic. You know, forgetful. It may be, while in a slightly muddled state, the name Dolly Varden came up conversationally, and whoever it was, Mumminger or Kiernan, got it wrong and thought she was talking about her daughter, when she really meant herself."

"I suppose it's possible."

"It's also possible Mumminger got it out of her while she was drugged, or in her sleep. He gives her pills when she asks for them. If it was Kiernan, he may have stumbled on it in her papers. The old girl has her secrets; unfortunately, though, secrets have a way of coming out."

"I still don't get it. Why would she include Dolly in her will?"

"She's angry with Marc. She's still his mother, and she wants to punish him for neglecting her, and stealing the La Fleur. Marc made a serious mistake in underestimating his mother's attachment to that old hotel."

"I guess so. Now he's got to share his mother's estate with a bag lady who isn't even a relative."

"It appears that way."

"What's the estate worth, approximately?"

"With all those fully amortized, prewar apartment buildings waiting to be co-oped and condoed, the art, and securities, I'd guess conservatively somewhere in the neighborhood of three hundred million dollars."

"That's some neighborhood."

"It's not too shabby. Cinderella stories do happen."

"Sure, if Dolly lives long enough to collect. What about her daughter Susan—does she share in the estate?"

"Only, as you point out, if Dolly lives to collect."

"Let me get this straight. If Dolly dies before the old lady, Susan's up the proverbial creek without a paddle?"

"That's how it's set up. Should Dolly die first, that's the end of it. In that event, the only way an heir of Dolly's could hope to share in the estate would be if Florine adopted Dolly, which she hasn't done. She's only recognized her as an heir. Her will calls for a per stirpes distribution, or through direct descent. Marc is a blood relative, Dolly is not. Therefore, the only way Dolly's family can come into anything is for Florine to die first and Dolly inherit."

"But once Dolly has inherited, her share can be passed along to her daughter Susan."

"That's right, assuming Dolly's in a sound mind, and that's her will."

"A couple of wild assumptions. But Dolly's worth more to Susan alive than dead."

"At least a hundred million dollars' worth. The bad news is she's worth more dead than alive to Marc," Stein said with his bemused grin. "I think we've just seen some evidence of that," he added with a nod at the television.

"Try and prove it," I said, wondering whether Susan knew about the old lady's will, and if I'd misjudged her.

"Hey," said Tito, sticking his head in the door, "they just pulled a couple of bodies out of the La Fleur rubble. It was on the radio."

"Any ID?"

"They must know who they are. They said they're not releasing any names pending notice of next of kin."

"Probably ID'd them from what was in their pockets," said Stein.

"Wouldn't bother me any if it were those two assholes that hassled us," said Tito before he disappeared.

"The plot thickens," said Stein with a grin. "Looks like the bad guys are facing a manslaughter rap now."

"Yeah, but who are the bad guys?" I wondered.

"The guys in the van, for starters," said Stein.

"Yeah, them, but they're just a couple of guys doing a demolition job."

Stein shrugged. "You gotta start somewhere. If, as you say, it was just a demolition job, a couple of bodies in the building are probably two more than they bargained for. The cops should have no problem finding and leaning on a couple of guys like that."

"But, Henry, the tapes don't show them setting the charges."

"That's where you come in, ace," he said, giving me that bemused look of his, "witness for the prosecution."

"Swell. Henry, what kind of guy knows how to implode a building, and has access to the kind of explosives needed to do the job?"

"Lemme see—I'd guess a rogue in the demolition business," he said, "or possibly someone who picked it up in the military, a soldier-of-fortune type who'd been in the Rangers, or Special Forces."

"In other words, a pussy, huh? What if these guys don't give a damn how many bodies they find in the rubble, they just don't want it to get around that they blow up buildings?"

"I'd start thinking about going into the witness protection program."

"You're a regular comedian, Henry. The point is, the tape I have proves nothing. And even if I had taped confessions, there's no guarantee of a conviction nowadays."

"The courts are a crapshoot. What are you gonna do?" he asked, seeming genuinely concerned.

"They must have seen us exiting the building, and Rudd can identify us for them, but aside from my crew, and you and Strunk, no one knows about the tapes. Unless the old lady's included me in her will, I don't think I have anything to worry about at the moment. I promised Strunk I'd turn the tapes over to him this afternoon."

"It's your duty as a citizen to cooperate with the law," Stein said solemnly. "I do all the time."

It seemed smart to make copies of the tapes. After Stein left, we found a place in the neighborhood, and I sent Tito to have dupes made.

When Strunk showed up, I offered him a beer, and he accepted. We skipped over the highlights of the surveillance tapes. He said it was boneheaded of me to have gone into the La Fleur alone as I did, but then P.C. always managed to have a kind word for me. When we finished viewing the tapes, he was noncommittal about their value, but he said to send him a bill for the extra expense on the camera and for the tape stock.

"What did you find out about the guys with the van?" I asked him.

"I told you, the van's registered to the business of a small contractor in Lodi. His name's Michael Beisler."

"That all?" I said, disappointed.

"We told him we had an eyewitness who spotted the van at the scene of last night's bomb blast."

"What did he say?"

"No way, he says."

"And do you believe him?"

"Listen, Byrne, I wouldn't believe George Washington, and he couldn't tell a lie."

"Those guys knew what they were doing. Stein thought

they might have picked it up in the military—you know, like the Rangers, or Special Forces."

"We're checking out Mr. Beisler thoroughly," he said, waving the tapes in his big hand. "Got a bag for these?"

Tito brought him a manila envelope. On the back of a scrap of paper that looked suspiciously like a check from a Chinese restaurant, he scribbled out a receipt for the tapes. I'd given him the originals and kept the copies.

"Oh, P.C., one more thing," I said, as he was about to step into the elevator.

"What's that?" he said impatiently.

"What about Dolly Varden, the bag lady? Can't you pick her up and put her in protective custody? It's not safe for her on the street."

"And have the ACLU on our backs? Get real, Byrne."

"Yeah, but, P.C.," I pleaded.

"You know where she is?"

"No."

"Then how we gonna find her?"

"You can't arrest Fallon, and you can't protect a bag lady, what good are you?"

"Look, Byrne, we don't prevent crime, we fight crime. I'll be in touch."

30

~~~~~~

It was about eight o'clock that evening when I rolled the Lejeune off the elevator and found Dolly sitting on the floor outside my door. She had her back to the wall, legs crossed, and was reading a paperback titled *New Hope for the Dead* by Charles Williford.

"Mutt and Jeff let me in. The Jewish fellows," she explained, getting to her feet.

"Well, I'm real glad to see you, come in," I said, unlocking the door. The cats were right there to greet me. I leaned the bike against the wall and ushered her into the kitchen. "You hungry?"

"No," she said, bending to stroke the cats as they twined around her legs.

"My offer still stands," I said, gesturing to the lounge and the futon.

"I can't stay." She straightened up and began fumbling in her clothing. "I just came by to drop this off."

"What is it?"

From a secret place on her person she produced what

appeared to be a videotape cassette box and presented it to me. "I think it's something to do with Sharon's death. I lied when you asked whether she gave me anything to hold for her. It was in my safe-deposit box."

"Any idea what's on it?"

"How would I know, I don't own a VCR."

I couldn't imagine why not, she seemed to have everything else—storage space, a safe-deposit box. "Let's have a look at it."

Her face clouded over. "I don't want to see it. You look at it."

"Whatever you say." I was searching for a way to persuade her to spend the night without frightening her. "Dolly, you remember the old lady that came to see you in the limo?"

"Of course."

"Well, it turns out she wants to leave you some money."

"Why would she want to do that?"

"That's what I've been wondering."

"How much money?"

"Lots of money."

"She must be crazier than I am."

I wasn't going to touch that line with a ten-foot pole. "Dolly, maybe you could tell me what happened that day in the limo?"

"Not much—mostly she asked a whole lot of questions about who I was, where I came from, and how I got the name Dolly Varden."

"And what did you say?"

"I told her the truth. I said I was an orphan, I came from Queens, and that Dolly Varden was an alias. My daughter, Sharon, said I should call myself Dolly Varden after a character in a Dickens novel. I'd been calling myself Billie Budd. I liked the idea of a new name. I don't know my real name because I was adopted. And Miriam Lusk's such a boring name."

"What's in a name?" I said idly, wondering whether Gertrude and Henry Stein were related.

"They don't call roses rutabagas," Dolly was quick to point out.

"Anyway, what did the old lady say?"

"She said she wanted to meet the person she'd read about who called herself Dolly Varden because a very long time ago, when she was still poor, she went by that alias herself."

"Did she mention the possibility of the two of you being related?"

"No, but she said she'd lost a daughter she'd had out of wedlock. I said I was too young to be her daughter. She said she realized that. She said she'd enjoyed meeting me, I said the pleasure was mine, and that was pretty much it."

"I'm afraid that's not quite it. Not everyone is happy about seeing you come into a share of the old lady's money. It was no accident you were taken to the La Fleur, Dolly. And I'm not talking about Angel and James now, do you understand?"

She stared at me somberly. I had no idea what she was thinking.

"It's not safe for you out on the street."

"It's not safe for anyone."

I sensed I wasn't being very persuasive. "They found two bodies in the rubble of the hotel."

"Really?"

"They were Angel and James, weren't they?"

"They weren't the Righteous Brothers. They got what they deserved."

"Yeah, but how?"

"They killed Socrates," she said, her voice choked.

"Yes, I know."

"They hit me in the head and took me to the hotel. When I came to, they took turns raping me. When they were finished, and weren't looking, I cracked their skulls open with my billy club."

"Why didn't you get out of the hotel?"

"Because those other men were there."

"What men?"

"The construction workers. I didn't know who they were, so I hid where they wouldn't find me. I must have fallen asleep or something. How was I to know they meant to blow the place up? It was a good thing for me you came along when you did."

She wasn't asleep when I came along, otherwise I'd never have found her, but why quibble? "Dolly, what can I say to make you change your mind and stay?"

"Nothing," she said, shaking her head firmly.

"You sure? It was okay last night."

"Last night was different."

"But you'll be safe here."

"How'll I be safe here? They saw us coming out of the building. Susan and her friend saw us together. They know who you are and where you live. You're not safe here."

I couldn't argue with a thing she said. She had a full-blown case of paranoia, and justifiably so, if there's such a thing as justifiable paranoia. "Where will you go?" I asked mildly.

"I've got a place."

"I don't suppose you'll tell me?"

"You suppose right. I better be going now. Let me know if there's anything interesting on the tape."

"Sure, but how am I gonna do that?"

"Next time I see you."

"I'll see you out," I said. "I've got to lock up the building." I walked her to the corner and hailed a cab, insisting she take one to wherever it was she was going. I gave her ten dollars. It wouldn't surprise me if she gave the driver an address a few blocks away and pocketed most of the ten.

Upstairs again, I braced myself with a stiff bourbon before slipping the tape into the VCR.

The camera clicked on and off again. A man's voice said, "Testing, one, two, three . . . testing." The interior of a bedroom bloomed on the TV screen, and the vidiacon tube adjusted to the low light level. Mumminger was sitting on the bed with Sharon Raynes. He seemed to be demonstrating how to activate the camera. Near the mattress, behind the headboard, was a pressure plate, like a light switch. Judging from the angle of view, the camera must have been hidden behind a two-way mirror, or in a cabinet, opposite the bed. Raynes clicked the camera on and off with delight. Then she and Mumminger began to tussle. "Is it on or off?" she asked. "It's on—no, it's off," he answered. The picture flicked off. "Now it's on," she said, feeling behind the headboard. They continued to wrestle, stripping as the camera clicked on and off and on again each time they changed positions. "Well, what do you think?" Mumminger asked when they were through. "Fantastic," she enthused, and the screen went dark.

It stayed dark for several moments, and then the picture bloomed again. It was Sharon, stylish in a loose-fitting tunic, primping unself-consciously in front of the unblinking lens, like a news anchor waiting for a satellite feed. Finally, she turned and looked directly into the camera.

"My name is Sharon Raynes, and by the time you see this videotape, I will be dead," she intoned dramatically. "The purpose of this tape is to indict my killer. Be warned—some of the scenes you are about to see contain X-rated material, as they say. You won't want to miss them," she added, cracking a lewd grin. "Hold it, just kidding," she laughed, waving a hand in front of the lens and breaking eye contact. She came back sober-faced. "Okay, I know what you are thinking," she said, in character again, voice well modulated, "you're thinking blackmail. And I'll admit that was the original idea of the hidden camera. But after giving the matter some thought, I realize Marc Ransom's not as vulnerable to blackmail as most guys. He isn't married, he's self-employed, and his company's privately held—he's accountable to no one but himself."

Her manner was growing less self-conscious and stilted, her tone more conversational. "There's no reason for him to fear a sex tape. And he'd be a damn fool to pay blackmail. He's many things, but a damn fool ain't one of them. If I were to go public with these tapes, they wouldn't amount to any more than ten minutes' worth of unwelcome notoriety to him. But I'd be leaving myself open to charges of blackmail, plus I'd have nothing to show for my troubles. Well, I'm nobody's fool, either, and that's not the way to go. These hard-core scenes establish my credentials, though, and prove that Marc Ransom and I were more than just friends. However"—she grinned coyly—"that doesn't mean Marc Ransom is off the hook. He is vulnerable to blackmail in business. Yes, indeed, the art of the steal." Her true personality was emerging.

"There's a thing or two I know about Marc Ransom's business dealings that, if they were to be made public, would cause him quite a bit of embarrassment. You're not gonna blow me off that easy, Mr. Ransom. I'm here to stay. Get used to it." She seemed to change moods easily—a family trait, I noticed. "But I'm not a bad person. I can be reasonable. And I want everything to be on the up and up," she said sensibly. "When I get my broker's license, and you've got your brand-new hotel, you can appoint me the agent, and fuck Nellie Rudd. Cut me in for the two percent of the building. I'll even work for it. I think that's fair. A salary, equity, and half a mil annually in revenue. Whatta ya say, Marc? Better say yes, because my next demand's gonna be higher. Isn't that one of your mommy's little tricks? Anyway, that's the deal, take it or leave it. Remember, them that gives, gets. Walk away from this one and I'm gonna blow the whistle on your sweetheart arrangement with Mr. Comptroller. Betcha didn't know I knew about that one, Markie, baby." She stuck her tongue out at the camera. "Look's like I've gotcha by the balls," she gloated, falling back on the bed again, cackling madly to herself. She lay there a moment as though she'd forgotten about the camera. Then she shot back upright and addressed the camera again.

"Well, there you have it, the motive, blackmail," she said solemnly. "I make no apologies, I am what I am. It's a dangerous game I'm playing, but risks are worth it. 'Bye." She grinned, waving a hand in front of the lens, and the camera clicked off.

"Oh, one more thing," she said, clicking back on, "the cast. The stuntwoman in the action shots is Josephine Cyzeski, one of Marc's faithful servants and his occasional playmate. Making a cameo appearance in the prelude is Dean Mumminger. Randell Elliott, the aforementioned Mr. Comptroller, is our second male lead, and our star is, ta-da, the one and only Marc Ransom. And now it's show time!" She flopped back on the bed again. "God, I can't believe I did that," she giggled as the screen went dark.

I stopped the tape. I needed a break. My glass was half empty, I noticed, or maybe I was just being a pessimist. Anyway, I went downstairs for a refill. Sharon Raynes was just as Susan had described her, as nasty as they come, I thought, cracking open a tray of ice cubes. One minute she oozed venom, the next she was inane and supercilious. She was stagy and theatrical, without conviction, like a teenager trying out faces in the mirror. She probably had been in no immediate danger when she made the tape. She hadn't begun to put the screws to Ransom yet. It's one thing to have an intimation of death and another to face it. I had the feeling she didn't really believe things could get so out of hand. But why no mention of Dolly Varden? Sharing in Florine's estate seemed to me like a much bigger proposition than blackmailing Ransom for a piece of the action on the new hotel. I guess the Dolly Varden hustle came later. Sharon Raynes was a greedy girl. She seemed to have had almost as many scams going as Ransom had leases.

I plodded back upstairs with a fresh drink, threw myself on the bed, pressed play on the remote, and became a voyeur again.

Raynes and Randell Elliott were sitting on the bed fully clothed when the picture came back on. There were drinks on the night table, and a hash pipe, too. She was loosening his tie as his hands roamed over her body. She helped him off with his jacket, removed his suspenders, and began tugging at his fly.

"Hmmm . . ." he moaned, "you know, I never could get my wife to do that."

"She doesn't know what she's missing," Raynes lied to his face.

"When the new hotel gets going, I'll see that Marc does the right thing by you, darling," he promised.

"I know you will, baby," she said, going at the task.

"You get your license—"

She stopped work. "You can help me with that, can't you?"

"I can pull a few strings," he said. "I'll see that Marc makes you an agent for the building. How would you like that?"

He seemed to know the kind of pillow talk she wanted to hear, because she went back to work with renewed vigor. It wasn't long before he threw back his head and groaned. She climbed up on the bed and lay next to him while he recovered. His clothing was in disarray; hers was scarcely mussed.

"Randy, honey?" she said after a while, toying with his shirt buttons.

"Hmmm?"

"Well, I was just wondering?" she said, playing the sex kitten. "Do you think I'm a good investment?"

He turned and grinned at her nestled in his arm. "The best, darling. You trying to tell me something? You need a little help with the mortgage?"

"It's easy to see why you're where you are," she said, gazing up at him adoringly. "You're so smart."

"I'll speak to Marc."

"Don't do that."

"Why not?"

"I wouldn't want him to know. I don't want him to know you're seeing me. Don't you see, it will look bad later, when he finds out he's got to appoint me agent for the new hotel. It would be too much."

He frowned. This required some thought. It was plain he was in the habit of having someone else pick up the tab. The comptroller was not a happy camper. While she was waiting for him to come up with a solution, her hand kept inching downward, reminding him of what he couldn't get at home. "Don't worry about it, darling," Elliott said finally, "we'll work something out."

The wandering hand abandoned its search, and she flung her arms around him and kissed him. "I knew I could count on you," she said. "You're so smart."

"I know a good thing when I see one," he said, making a pathetic stab at humor.

"But seriously," she said, "how do you decide where to invest the pension fund money? Why Marc's hotel, for instance?"

"He has a track record, his projects have been winners. That makes Marc bankable."

"But there's plenty of developers as bankable as Marc."

"There are enough of them around."

"And they're all after you to invest in their projects?"

"It seems that way sometimes."

"So why Marc? What's so different about him?"

"Marc understands there is a quid pro quo."

"Like campaign contributions, you mean?"

He pretended to be amazed by this feat of deduction. "Clever girl, aren't you?"

She snuggled closer. "Mmmm . . ." she murmured, and the screen faded to black.

I gargled with a slug of bourbon. The burn had a righteous astringent quality as I swallowed. I don't think Ransom cared who Raynes slept with—he wasn't the jealous type— but he might not like her double dipping on the mortgage. And he certainly wouldn't care to see that exchange on tape. She was a clever girl—too clever.

The tape continued to roll, until suddenly there they were, the main event. Raynes and Josephine scrambled around on the bed squealing like teenagers. This was what Raynes had promised—this or something like this was what I expected to see—and yet it still came as a shock. I stared with a mixture of prurient fascination and repugnance. The women looked good together as they grappled for each other's panties. Josephine depantsed Raynes and waved the trophy overhead. She flung it at an off-camera presence and laughed, "Here, sniff this, creep!" Raynes pinned her and returned the favor. They wrestled awhile, until their grunts and groans gradually turned to sighs and moans. Eventually, Ransom joined them. I hardly recognized him without his glasses and suspenders. The women pounced on him, and he submitted meekly to being hog-tied.

The tape played on, and I ogled it, filled with self-loathing as they took turns using, abusing, and humiliating one other, seemingly without purpose. I'd never met Sharon Raynes, and yet my room seemed permeated with an eerie, musky emanation of her.

Given her taste for pornography, Josephine may not have minded being taped, but she, Ransom, and the comptroller were all unsuspecting performers. They had no idea they were being taped. Mumminger, on the other hand, was aware of the camera, but he must have thought it was for his and Sharon's eyes only, since they were partners in blackmail. That's the problem with this sort of thing, though: you never know who's likely to see it. That's what made watching the tape so creepy. And different from ordinary pornography, which I've heard described as pictures of what prostitutes do for a living. What prostitutes do for a living the rest of us do for love, or recreation. And as dubious as Josephine and Sharon were, I'd give them their amateur standing. I guess that meant the tape wasn't pornographic, only obscene. It wasn't about sex, but death. It stank of death, and death was obscene. Death—that was all I could think of as I watched them moil for gratification. There was no big climax, the tape just trailed off, leaving them in midstroke, the screen turning to snow.

I finished the bourbon and decided I needed a shower. I toweled off humming "I Can't Get No Satisfaction," and went to bed depressed and sworn off sex.

Sleep was slow in coming. I couldn't shut off my mind. What did the tape prove? Nothing, really, except that Sharon Raynes was a blackmailer. It didn't prove Ransom murdered her—only that he had a motive. But so did some others. How would Hannibal see the tape? I wondered. Wouldn't he suspect Mumminger, and Josephine, as much as Ransom? Wouldn't he want to know if they had sufficient motives to murder Sharon Raynes?

And then another thought occurred to me. There must be other tapes, hours of them, just like my surveillance camera . . . and the doctor was the only one other than Raynes who knew about the hidden camera.

31

~~~

It was a restless night of rancid dreams. I woke up at six knowing I wasn't going back to sleep, so I got up, scratched my butt, and rubbed the sleepers out of my eyes, and waited for my brain to climb out of bed. I showered, shaved, brushed, combed, dressed, and brewed a pot of high-octane coffee—all on autopilot. That killed the better part of half an hour. It would be another two and a half hours before the studio began showing signs of life. Today was a lighting day for the first photograph in the carpet ad series, I remembered. The agency people were coming late morning to look the situation over. I hoped we were ready for them. Meanwhile I had a couple of hours to kill. I jogged out for the papers. They ought to be good for an hour, and the crossword puzzle would waste the rest of the time.

Settling down with a cup of coffee, I noticed, from the front page of the *Times*, that Eastern Europe was falling apart, and so were we. Even Japan seemed to be having problems. But planet Earth was still going around. Moving along to the metropolitan news, the crack dealers and the police hadn't shot anyone in the last forty-eight hours, and there were no riots to report, which made it a slow news day in the Moldering Apple. The collapse of the La Fleur was still big news. The pair of unidentified bodies, a black and a Hispanic male found in the ruin, and a new development, a demolition expert's opinion that the hotel had been destroyed deliberately, kept the story front page news. Seems the expert, an explosive's forensics expert hired by the Buildings Department to determine the cause, could tell from the copper residue found in the basement what type and amount of explosives had been used for the job. "Whoever did this knew what they were doing," the *Times* quoted Roy Askling, the expert, as saying. "The charges were placed floor and ceiling on the columns in the basement. These were chevron-shaped RDX charges, which detonate at approximately 277,000 feet per second, and put three million pounds per square inch of pressure on the targeted steel. The penetrating jet from the shaped charges actually creates a plastic flow in the steel, isolating elements in the column and causing the middle section of the column to 'trip out' under the weight of the structure when the top and bottom charges go off. The entire array of charges was ignited by a single electric blasting cap attached to a simple timing device, such as a Baby Ben wind-up alarm clock."

I'd seen how the charges were rigged, of course, and he was right on the money. Askling went on to explain how they had dropped the building on the spot, with minimal damage to the surrounding structures. They had wired the center row of columns with a pound and a half each of RDX, leaving the rear and street columns of the building alone. These columns then were the last to go, causing the building to collapse inward.

It was politically correct to be outraged, and editorial writers for the three major papers were outraged. The Buildings Department chief was outraged. So were the Fire and Police Department chiefs. City Hall was outraged, especially our feisty mayor. He was in high dudgeon; in fact, it was a veritable pissing contest of outrage. But that's how we're governed nowadays. It's the Wizard of Oz, all done with TV sound bites, image, P.R., smoke, and mirrors. It's probably always been that way and I just never noticed it before.

Under Diedre Mahoney's byline there was the story of another sort of collapse that caught my eye. This one had the fingerprints of Strunk and Stein all over it. Mahoney reported that an authoritative source had informed her that "indictments were being handed down in a case involving the looting of a defunct Queens savings and loan association." A convicted swindler, "a world-class con man," it seems, was prepared to testify against the chief loan officer, and former head of the S&L, as well as a syndicate of businessmen whose names, with the exception of one overweight Irishman—Fallon—all ended in vowels. Attempts had been made to get in touch with the usually voluble Mr. Fallon, but he had not returned Mahoney's calls. Ten million skins were missing.

With an indictment and possible conviction hanging over his head, Fallon's usefulness to Ransom was finished, I thought.

The buzzer sounded as I was nearly finished with the crossword puzzle. I found Detective Hannibal beaming at me when I opened the door. I invited him in and fixed him up with a mug of coffee, cream, no sugar. He asked if I had the blowups, and as he studied them impassively, I asked if there was anything new on Sharon Raynes.

"Talked to the doorman."

"Was he cooperative?"

"The building management doesn't pay him enough to lie. He's on the job, and he's got a pension to protect."

"Thought he looked like a cop. What did he say?"

"He said there was a lot of traffic there that day. The Chinese woman—"

"Josephine Cyzeski," I volunteered.

"Her, Ransom, and later, Fallon and the sister, Susan Ferrante."

"He said Ransom and Cyzeski were there?"

"That's what he said."

"When did they leave?"

"He said he didn't know. He didn't see them leave, but there was a blackout that day, and they might have left while the lights were out. Anyhow, he missed them."

"What about the other two, Fallon and Ferrante?"

"Fallon was there before the body was found."

"I found the body. Does that mean he was in the building at the time?"

"Look's that way."

"And what about Susan Ferrante?"

"She came later, after the body was found."

"And they left together. You think maybe Ransom and Cyzeski were still in the building?"

He shrugged. "He said there was another person there that day, a Dr. Mumminger."

"Florine Ransom's doctor."

"Said he came later, after eleven. Had his own key, let himself in. The doorman said he was a regular."

"Did Mumminger know she was dead?"

"Doorman told him. Mumminger told him he'd been calling and got no answer. Did all her boyfriends have keys?"

"I wouldn't know. You'd have to ask Mumminger that. The doorman say how long Mumminger was there?"

"Why?" he asked, eyeing me steadily.

"Just wondering."

"I'm wondering what's your interest in this, Mr. Byrne."

"Me?"

"A woman does a brodie, and a month or so later you come up with some pictures supposedly showing the body was tampered with. How do I know you didn't add the shoe and move the body?" He stared at me, waiting for an answer.

"Why would I do that?"

"Why would you want to get involved in a thing like this in the first place? Unless maybe you've got a score to settle with Fallon, or this guy Mumminger, maybe?"

"Why not include Ransom?"

"Okay, Ransom, too."

"I'm not accusing anyone," I reminded him.

"Maybe you've got pictures you haven't shown me? Seems a little pat, you just happening to find that roll in the camera."

"I didn't take those pictures, my assistant did. He'll be here any minute now if you want to question him."

"I'm just giving you an idea of how it looks from my perspective. You were there, too."

"Yeah, but I wasn't in the Raynes apartment—only Ransom's."

"I know," he said with a disarming smile, "but I gotta wonder what your game is."

"No game, just trying to be helpful."

"Helpful, huh? These pictures are interesting, and it may be more than coincidence that the gang dropped by to see the deceased that day. But our chances of proving murder are slim to none. Raynes was cremated—we don't have a body."

"You've got some bodies now."

He lifted his eyes from the photos and stared at me. "What bodies?"

"The ones they found in the La Fleur."

"What do you know about them?"

"Nothing," I lied, "except that they shouldn't have been there."

"Who are they?"

"I don't know—they haven't been identified yet, have they?" I smiled. "But if they're who I think they are, they're a couple of goons who worked for the landlord evacuating the building."

"You're guessing?"

"Right, just guessing. But the building was intentionally demolished. It's in today's paper. That's manslaughter, at least, isn't it?"

"From what I've read, they don't even know who the landlord is."

"Wait and see—when this has blown over and things calm down, some smart prosecutor'll trace the paper, and guess what they'll find? The owner's a Ransom. Ransom's gonna build a monument to himself on that lot. He wants to show New York that he's got a big one, too."

"What's that got to do with this?" he said, allowing himself a faint smile and gesturing to the photos.

"I don't know, you're the detective. All I know's what I read in the papers, and this morning I read Matty Fallon's about to be indicted."

"So I hear," he said, rocking on his heels.

A key turned in the lock.

"That'll be Tito," I said as he glanced toward the reception area. Tito appeared with his usual brown bag from the Greek's and a copy of the *Daily News*. They'd met before, so introductions were unnecessary. Tito said hello and sat down at the table, spread out the paper, and prepared to eat a fried egg sandwich. I offered Hannibal another cup, and he declined. Slipping the photos back into their envelope, he asked Tito if these were all the pictures he took of Raynes. He said they were.

"Well, what now?" I asked as I walked Hannibal to the elevator.

"I'll speak to Raynes's playmates and see if they've got their stories straight, then we'll see. I'll let you know what happens," he promised before stepping lightly into the elevator.

The dog and pony show with the agency people went an hour longer than it might have because Rodger Pharr horned in on the action. As we reviewed the props and the set, and I went through some lighting alternatives, he took it upon himself to ask and answer his own questions, compelled, as he was, to show what a take-charge kind of guy he was. The only one he succeeded in impressing, though, was himself. The art director was a low-key, middle-aged guy, a seasoned campaigner. He didn't need Pharr's unctuous salesmanship to see that we had it under control. When he'd had enough, he glanced at his watch and announced it was time for lunch. "Where are you taking us, Charles?" said Pharr, delirious at the prospect of cadging a free lunch. "Rossini's?" The A.D. said he already had a lunch date.

"The rest of us, then," said Pharr, appealing to the others. The copywriter, account executive, and brand manager begged off, too. "Another time, perhaps," said Pharr, crestfallen. They began edging toward the door, assuring me how pleased they were with the set and the way the job was shaping up. Before they left, the A.D. rolled his eyes at Pharr, conveying nonverbally he, too, thought Pharr was the last lock on the alimentary canal.

A tall, skinny, sallow, ponytailed freak named Lex, with biker jewelry all over his fingers, wrists, neck, and earlobes, sat staring at the monitor, a Harley cigarette dangling from his lip and a diet Coke in his hand. "Show time," Sharon Raynes said, and fell back on the bed. "Oh, God, I can't believe I did that," she giggled as the screen went dark. "Is she for real?" Lex asked. I said it was a practical joke. He didn't say anything. He was duping the Raynes tape for me. He was the video editor at the same house where we'd had the surveillance tapes duped. "That looks real," he said, watching Raynes and Mumminger at it, "although you can never tell with women." He duped the whole tape, and then transferred the individual sections each to their own cassette. He asked if I'd mind if he made a copy of Josephine and Raynes for his own private collection. I told him I didn't think that was such a good idea. He shrugged and said too bad. But I'll bet he copied it anyway.

When I finished with Lex, I mailed the original tape, with an explanation of how I'd come by it, to Hannibal. Then I called Josephine at work and asked to see her. She said she was busy, I should try again in two weeks. I told her I had something that might turn her on, a tape of her doing the double dildo with Raynes. She asked if I knew a place named Reidy's at Fifty-fourth, between Fifth and Madison. I told her I could find the place. Five-thirty, she said.

It was too early for the dinner trade, and the dining room was nearly empty. I found Josephine at a deuce against the wall, drinking brandy on the rocks. "Hi," she murmured sheepishly as I slid into the opposite seat.

"Hi," I said, putting the cassette on the table and pushing it gently toward her.

She looked at it apprehensively, as though deciding whether it was too explosive to touch. Then she scooped it up and dropped it in the leather handbag resting near her elbow. "Well, I suppose you had fun looking at it?"

The waiter approached and asked if we were having dinner. Just drinks, I told him, and ordered a Perrier and lime. "Not as much fun as Ransom," I said when the waiter'd gone. "Looks like what they say is true—you do sleep with him."

"So what?" she said defiantly. "It's none of your business if I do."

"That's true, you can sleep with Mr. Ed for all I care."

"Anyway, your girlfriend sleeps with him, too."

"He's irresistible." I smiled. She wasn't my girlfriend, but it hurt anyway.

"You want money, I suppose."

"I don't want money."

"Not from me, from Marc. That's what this is all about, isn't it?"

"I don't want any money from Marc."

"What do you want, then?"

"I don't want to see you get hurt."

"Ha, that's a laugh," she said contemptuously. "How do I know there's anything on the tape?"

"Don't take my word for it. You'll find out soon enough. You were burned by Acid Raynes."

"Where did you get it?" she said, nodding at the handbag as though there were a live thing in it.

"I got it from Sharon's mother. Sharon gave it to her for safekeeping. Seems she had a premonition something might happen to her, and she took the precaution of taping your sessions."

Her face went slack with the full implication.

"I know what you're thinking."

"It's on tape?" she gasped. Her face was lovely when calm, beautiful when angry, and ravishing when enthralled, but it was plug-ugly when she was scared.

"The murder?"

She caught herself. "You're fishing. How do I know what's on this tape?"

The waiter intruded to serve the drinks. I asked for the check. "It's not what's on this tape that's important. It's what's on the others."

She considered this. "Do you have the other tapes?" she said finally.

"No."

"Who does, the mother?"

"No."

"You're bluffing," she snapped. "There are no other tapes."

"I'm afraid there are."

"But you don't know who has them. In fact, you don't know anything, isn't that right?"

"I have a pretty good idea who has the other tapes, but one thing I know for certain. You were there when Sharon Raynes was killed."

"You don't know any such thing. You can't prove that," she said hotly. She was almost beautiful.

"I don't have to prove you were there. The doorman's already told the police you were there—you, Ransom, and Fallon."

She suddenly looked very pale. "But her death's been ruled a suicide. Why would the police be asking questions now?"

"Maybe they've come up with some new evidence. Anyway, her death was ruled a probable suicide."

"What new evidence?"

"I don't know."

"They're wasting their time, Sharon jumped."

"Maybe she did, maybe she didn't. You'd know, you were there."

"I'm telling you she jumped."

"A medical examiner would have a difficult time telling whether she slipped, was pushed, or jumped, assuming, that is, she went out the window. A broken neck or a fractured skull would look the same, whether it was sustained in a fall or a brawl. And, if Susan Ferrante told the authorities that her sister was despondent and suicidal, that might have been enough. But if you ask me, I think Sharon Raynes died while the three of you were sporting. Either it was accidental, rough sex, or Ransom went nuts and killed her in cold blood. He was through with her, and she wasn't smart enough to know when to quit. If the tape is any indication of Ransom's sexual tastes, I'd say he was kinky enough to get off on watching her die."

She gazed at me in mute terror.

"Is that how it was?" I asked gently.

She took a swallow of brandy. "I wouldn't go around saying things like that if I were you."

"This is just between you and me. Accidental, or intentional, she died. And the three of you rigged it so it looked as though she took a flying leap. Fallon probably humped the body down the stairs in the dark and planted it in the courtyard."

"Why not dump it out the window?"

"Because, dark as it was, you couldn't take a chance on being seen."

"The stairs seem riskier—you're likely to bump into all kinds of people at a time like that."

"Yes, but you could have run interference, or you might have pretended she was drunk, or sick, propped up between two of you. It was a chance you had to take."

"Why not just leave her in the apartment?"

"Because then there would have to be an investigation."

"This is all speculation—you don't know what you're talking about."

"I'm saying what the cops'll be thinking. When I found the body, it was hastily dressed. The buttons on her blouse didn't line up, the skirt was on backward, she wasn't wearing stockings, or a bra."

"She was home alone, distraught."

"She was dressed in the dark, and quickly. Then, as soon as you got back upstairs, the lights came on. One of you broke the window, and you provided the scream."

"Why are you doing this, Charlie?"

"I'm trying to do you a favor, Josephine. If I can figure it out, so can the cops. Five big units buys a lot of loyalty—I understand that. You're all covering up for the boss. But the way things are going, you're gonna need a good lawyer, and fast. You may have to flip both co-ops to avoid a stretch in Bedford Hills."

"Has anyone else seen the tape?"

"Not yet."

"Have you talked to anyone about this?"

"It's a little too late for the rough stuff, sugar." I smiled warily. "A homicide cop, Detective Sergeant Edward Hannibal, already has a copy of the tape."

She jumped to her feet, snatching up the leather handbag. "You're a real dick, Byrne," she snarled. She turned on her heel and left. A couple of round-bellied suits standing at the bar eyed her as she strode past them.

The waiter had slipped me the check without my noticing. I glanced at it and put a ten and a pair of singles in the tray. I found the pay phone and dialed.

He picked up on the first ring. "The Florine Ransom residence," he said sweetly.

"Charlie Byrne, Bernard."

"Charles, to what do we owe the honor of this call?"

"Is Mumminger there, you silly shit?"

"I'm just trying to be friendly," he said with a pout. "Yes, he's here, why?"

"Put him on."

"Let me find him."

There was a void, but at least it wasn't filled with "Muskrat Love." Finally someone picked up the receiver. "Dean Mumminger here."

"Mumminger, Charlie Byrne."

"Yes, I know. What do you want?"

"Don't move, I'll be right over."

"You can't come here. What's this about, anyway?"

"It's about an instructional video I have in which you and a lady named Sharon Raynes demonstrate reproductive technique."

There was a long silence on his end of the line. "Where did you get it?" he said finally.

"That's not the point."

"You want money, is that it?"

"Jeez, that's all anyone thinks of. Just stay put, I'll be right there."

32

~~~~~

Louise the maid let me in with a sweet smile. I smiled back, and she led me down the hall to Kiernan's office.

"How's the old lady?" I asked.

"A little better," she answered. "She's awake and seems to recognize people, but she's very weak and can't speak."

"It's an improvement, though."

"Definitely."

When we reached Kiernan's office, she asked if I'd like something to drink. I told her no, I'd only be a few minutes, and thanked her. She left.

"Mr. Byrne has arrived, Doctor," Kiernan murmured into an extension phone as he gestured to me to sit. "Well," he said, "this is a sudden and unexpected visit, Charles."

"Louise tells me the old lady's improving."

"It's a miracle. At the rate she's going, she'll be up and doing the fox trot in a day or two," he gushed. His smile faded as Mumminger entered.

"Would you mind, Bernard?" he said, indicating Kiernan should take a hike.

"Well, I see you two want to be left alone," said Kiernan, making an exit.

Mumminger closed the door after him. "You brought the tape?"

I placed the cassette on the corner of the desk. Mumminger walked around the desk, casually retrieving the tape and dropping it in the hip pocket of his double-breasted jacket, where it created an unsightly bulge. To compensate, he unbuttoned the jacket. "That's not the only copy," I said.

His face darkened with the news, and I thought I detected a slight twitch. "What is it you want, Byrne?" he said, sliding into the chair.

"I want to know who killed Sharon Raynes."

"She killed herself."

"Come off it."

"What do you care?"

"Ask a question, get a question," I sighed. "What do you care what I care? Just gimme an answer."

"I'm not in the habit of being interrogated by photographers."

"Well, get used to it. As Paul Newman once said, we all must show our ass sometime, and, buddy, you've been caught with your pants down to your toenails."

"I didn't kill her."

"I know you didn't, or at least I don't think you did."

He was too preoccupied with waiting for the next shoe to drop to say anything.

"Ransom killed her." I waited for a reaction and got none. "Sharon Raynes says so on the tape," I added.

"If you know, what do you want from me?"

"I want you to tell me what you know."

"I know Sharon was not a person with a very high regard for the truth."

"She thought enough of it, though, to ensure it wasn't buried with her," I said. "There are more tapes, aren't there?"

"More tapes—what tapes?"

"Don't get cute. You're a memory if Ransom ever sees a copy of this tape."

He flinched. "You wouldn't do that, would you?"

"I might, unless I get some straight answers."

"Sure you wouldn't care for a drink?"

"I'm sure."

"Mind if I have one?"

He was stalling for time, but it wasn't going to work. "Not as long as you keep talking. I haven't got all night."

He pressed a button, picked up the phone, and requested a vodka martini on the rocks with a twist.

"You and Raynes set up the cameras hoping to blackmail Ransom," I said, prompting him.

"I was only helping her."

"Sure, it's called aiding and abetting."

"It was the comptroller she was really after."

"When it comes to sexcapades, Ransom's more or less blackmail-proof, unless maybe you had a tape of him boinking Lady Di, is that it?"

"Something like that." He cracked a thin smile. "But the comptroller's perfect, he has everything to lose, he's an elected official with a wife and family."

"She was using him to get a piece of Ransom's new hotel."

"That's right. So far, I haven't told you anything you don't already know."

"Don't worry, you will. This stuff's on the tape. Did she really believe Ransom would let her get away with a play like that?"

"I think she did. She was willing to do the job of agent. And I think she thought Marc would respect her if she could show him she was as sharp and ruthless as he is. If she couldn't get a piece of the hotel, well, she always had a piece of the comptroller."

"All Ransom needed was to get one whiff of a blackmail scheme and she'd be doing a sailor's dive into the concrete."

"She was willing to take that risk."

"That's what separates the needy greedy from the just plain greedy—they have to take risks. But something happened, you switched game plans. The two of you cooked up the Dolly Varden scam. Sharing in the old lady's estate was a much bigger score than one or two percent interest in the new hotel."

"Believe me, I wanted no part of it. I never thought it had a prayer. It was all her idea."

"It was you, though, who told her that Dolly Varden was the name of Florine's illegitimate daughter, wasn't it?"

"Sort of."

"What do you mean?"

"Well, Florine can be aphasic. That means she occasionally becomes confused and disoriented."

"I know what it means."

"It's very common in old people, and when she was like that, she'd start to fret about Dolly Varden. Bernard and Louise have heard her, they'll tell you. She'll repeat over and over again to herself, 'What's become of Dolly Varden, what's become of Dolly Varden?' "

"That's funny, she was always alert and sharp whenever I spoke with her. What would cause her to be aphasic?"

"Being overstimulated, or overtired—stress."

"I see, and did you induce the state?"

"No, never."

"Uh-huh, so how'd you get the idea that Dolly Varden was Florine's long-lost daughter? Florine never said that."

"No, in fact I asked her once who Dolly Varden was, and she got quite angry with me, telling me it was none of my business. It was no secret, though, that she'd had a daughter that she'd lost, and gone to considerable expense to try and find, without success."

"She told me the story."

"Well, when I told Sharon about how Florine would go on about Dolly Varden, she jumped to the conclusion it was the long-lost daughter she was referring to."

"And you were willing to go along with that?"

"I told you, I wanted no part of it, but I couldn't stop Sharon. She had it all figured out—her mother was an orphan, she'd pass her off as Dolly Varden."

"Couldn't you do the math? She's not old enough to be the daughter."

"I don't know how old her mother is, and I don't know how old Florine's daughter would be. But the scam never got that far anyway. Sharon approached the old lady once with the idea, that was all, and a few weeks later she was dead."

"Did the old lady tell you she knew that Sharon was an impostor?"

There was a soft knock on the door. "It's Louise, Doctor."

"Come in," said Mumminger.

She served his drink, asked if I wanted anything, and left after I shook my head, quietly closing the door behind her.

Mumminger poked an ice cube with his finger, testing, I suppose, to see if it was chilled enough. Then he took a long swallow and grunted his satisfaction. Finally he raised his eyes to me. "No, Florine never told me she knew Sharon was an impostor. But then, Florine's good at keeping her own counsel." He nodded at the door. "Louise, Bernard, myself —we all report back to Marc. He'll know you were here tonight."

"What happened the day Sharon was killed?" I said, ignoring the last part.

He had another long swallow of vodka. "How would I know, I wasn't there," he said, with more than a trace of the old arrogance. The liquor seemed to have restored some of his courage.

"But you were there later on."

"How do you know that?"

"The doorman's a cop—he told another cop, and that cop told me," I said mildly.

"Christ," he muttered, putting his head in his hand as though he'd just developed a migraine. "I'd been calling all afternoon and evening and got no answer."

"So you dropped by to check up on her. You knew she'd had a date with Ransom that afternoon. You were a familiar figure there. The doorman knew you were one of her boyfriends. You came and went as you pleased. He told you what had happened. If he had any reason to be suspicious, Fallon got to him before the police and paid him to dummy up. You went upstairs, let yourself in with your own key, and picked up the last tape that was playing when the lights went out. You probably came back the next day for the equipment. You couldn't afford to leave it lying around the apartment."

"The police aren't investigating, are they?"

"I'm afraid so."

"But why? Her death was ruled a suicide."

"They must have some new evidence."

"Jesus, Marc's sure to find out. What am I going to do?"

"What's on the tape?"

"The tape?" he said, taking another slug of vodka.

"Yes, the first thing that crossed your mind when you picked it up had to be that this one was different. You knew Sharon wasn't suicidal."

"Because of the power shortage, it isn't clear from the tape what happened."

"It's clear she's alive when the power cut out, though?"

"Yes."

"What's not clear?"

"The picture's not the best, and the angle's bad."

"I know. What else?"

"It appears as though they're struggling."

"For real, or are they playacting?"

"It's hard to say."

"But she's alive?"

"She's alive," he repeated numbly.

"Was he penetrating her when the camera quit?"

"Yes."

"Was Cyzeski in the picture?"

"Yes. It looks as though she's trying to pull him off her."

"Because of what he's doing?"

"Yes. It appears as though he's trying to smother Sharon."

"But it's not clear that's what's happening?"

"No, it's not clear."

"Could he've smothered her?"

"It's possible, but it would have been difficult. They were nearly the same size. Sharon would have put up a fight, and he had Cyzeski to contend with, too."

"So he banged her head against the wall a couple of times, and that ended it. And injuries like that would be consistent with injuries from a fall. The tape sounds damning enough to me. You've still got it, I hope?"

"I've got it," he said, as though he were informing me he had a fatal disease, "and the others."

"You were planning to blackmail him at some point, huh?"

"I hadn't made any plans," he said, evading my gaze.

"If I were you, Mumminger," I said, getting slowly to my feet, "I'd be making plans to get out of town."

Even in the glow of the desk lamp, his face was chalky white. He lowered his head and began massaging his eyes with his thumb and index finger. He gripped the rocks glass in his other hand, perhaps to steady it. He looked like his luck had gotten out of town ahead of him.

"Stay away from open windows," I advised him in parting, "and hang on to those tapes—they may save your ass."

I was trying not to think of the fuse I'd just lit, of the panic I'd touched off in Josephine and Mumminger. I was trying not to think of Susan and Fallon, and that money can't buy happiness, but that it can buy nearly everything else. I was trying not to think about why I should care that Sharon Raynes was murdered. People get away with murder daily. Murder and taxes, the rates of both are out of control—that's what's wrong with this town. And I was trying not to think about the end of it, because it comes soon enough and it's always a disappointment.

Instead, I was thinking about how mild it was for this time of year. The Lord & Taylor windows were dark, their stages lowered to the basement. They were installing the Christmas windows. It was as regular an annual event in New York as opening day at Shea Stadium, or the St. Patrick's Day Parade, and it still came as a shock each year. The windows are wonderful. They make me wish I had the eyes of a child again. But I hated the suddenness of their arrival every year.

I should have been paying attention to where I was going. The first one, the young one, hit me with the speed and force of a blitzing linebacker, slamming me up against the building. The older guy hit me with a punch in the solar plexus that decided the issue then and there. The young guy kicked my legs out from under me and I went down. I curled in the fetal position, trying to protect as much of myself as I could. The older guy squatted and put his face in mine. "Ever see me before, friend?" he asked in a gentle tenor.

"Never," I answered.

"Atta boy." He grinned, rising.

The young guy was winding up to deliver a kick in the head. "Not in the head," said the older guy, checking him, "in the kidneys." He demonstrated with a vicious kick of his own, and they were gone.

A small crowd formed almost immediately. "You all right?" someone asked. I said I thought I was, and was helped to my feet. The attack had been so sudden, it was almost painless—for the moment, anyway. I groped myself to feel if anything was broken. Bruises and contusions mostly, I guessed. Nothing too serious, and nothing that showed. Nice work, guys—you really know how to bust up buildings and people. The kidney worried me, though.

"You should go to a hospital," someone advised.

"I only live a few doors down the block, I'll be all right," I said, my legs beginning to wobble. I'll be all right if I can get there and pull up the drawbridge, I thought.

"Anyone call 911?" someone said.

"I hate to bother them," I said. "Shit happens. Now if you'll excuse me . . . " I lurched forward and the gawkers parted. I dragged myself the last thirty yards home without incident.

Morbid and Curiosity were at the door waiting to be stroked and fed. When all their demands were met, they strolled off with supreme cat indifference to pay a visit to the litter box. It was enough to make me get a dog.

There were no calls on the answering machine. For some reason, it made me feel more alone than I had in a long while. While the tub was filling, I poured myself three fingers of Jack Daniel's, then took another chance on a bourbon and a hot tub. After Michael Beisler and friend's courtesy call, I was in no mood for self-denial.

Later, as I lay on my back dozing through the apocalypse —an Oscar-winning actress was on the tube warning me that I had two weeks to save the rain forest—the phone rang.

33

I fumbled for the receiver and mumbled, "Hullo." The clock on the night table told me I'd been dozing for about an hour.

"Charlie . . ."

"Uh-huh."

"It's Susan. I've got to talk to you."

"I'm listening."

"Not on the phone. I'm downstairs . . . at a pay phone."

"I'll meet you at the kosher restaurant a couple of doors down the block from me. Gimme fifteen minutes."

"Can't I come up?"

"Sure, come up if you want."

"The front door's locked."

"I'll be right down."

"Hurry," she said.

I reached for my shorts and was doubled up with a stabbing pain in my kidneys. I tried it again, more cautiously this time. Easing into my jeans, bending to tie my sneakers, pulling on a sweater—every move was painful, and it would only get worse before it got better.

Mort and Mo were locking up. I held the elevator while they loaded it with watch cartons. We inquired about one another's health as we descended. The old man and I agreed we were in the pink. Mo, as usual, was noncommittal. He was right to be. I don't know what his problem was, but I was a couple of shades off from being in the pink.

She was standing in the doorway, her back to the lobby. She sensed that I was there and turned and faced me with a tentative smile. I tried not to let her see the wince as I knelt to unlock the door. She stepped lightly inside, and I held the door for my friends. While Mort wished me a pleasant evening, Mo gave Susan the once-over, and me an approving grin.

We rode up in the elevator in silence.

"Nice place you've got here, Charlie," she said, looking around the studio.

"Thanks, would you like a drink?"

"Have any scotch?"

"I think so—ice and water?"

"That'll be fine." She wandered around admiring the place while I poured a scotch and a bourbon. "You live upstairs?" she asked as I handed her the drink.

"You didn't drop by to check out my living arrangements, did you?"

"No," she said, lowering her eyes and taking a quick sip of scotch. "I felt I owed you an explanation for the other day."

I gestured for her to sit on the couch, and pulled up a director's chair and waited.

"You're not making this very easy," she said, making herself comfortable. She had another sip of scotch—not that she wanted or needed it, not like Mumminger. It was a bit of business, a prop. She toyed with it, calculating the effect she was having on me. She must have me pegged for a pushover, I thought.

"I'll try and make it easy," I said. "What were you looking for in your mother's storage bin?"

"The tapes," she answered, her gaze steady and solemn, showing she had nothing to hide.

"How did you know about the tapes?"

"That's the wrong question, isn't it?"

"All right, what's the question?"

"You should have said, 'What tapes?'" She smiled.

"Okay, we both know there were tapes. How did you know?"

"Sharon told me. Who told you?" She looked as pleased with herself as though she'd just scored a double word in Scrabble.

"Dolly. What do you want the tapes for?"

She feigned surprise. "Why, to give to Marc, of course."

"Of course, my foot."

"Why not," she said, looking offended, "he'd pay a nice fat finder's fee for them."

"They call it blackmail."

"Not at all. It's gratitude. It's like paying a reward when a cabdriver returns your billfold."

You suddenly see a whole other side to people when there's a little easy money to be made. Maybe that's why I'd missed the resemblance until now. There it was, though, the same cunning glint in the eye Sharon Raynes had had when she talked about "them that gives, gets." Funny I had never noticed it before. Funny how money makes an ordinary liar out of even a package like Susan Ferrante. "What makes you think there's anything on those tapes Marc will be willing to pay for?" I said.

"I don't have to tell you that they're more than home videos," she said. "Sharon feared for her life. Those tapes were her insurance policy."

"For all the good they did her. What makes you think I've seen them?"

"Haven't you?"

"All I know is that they exist," I lied, staring at her.

She blinked first. She made a move toward me. "Charlie," she said, "take me upstairs."

I grabbed her wrists and she went limp. I pushed her back down on the couch. "Does this kind of talk turn you on?" She was looking at me with large, submissive eyes. "Stop it, it's too late for that," I said.

She wasn't listening, though—she was fumbling with her clothes. I still wanted her, and she knew it.

"Did Ransom send you?"

She froze.

"That's it, isn't it?" I said. "This is damage control. Throw the fool a quick one, get the tapes, and get out of here. Anything for the man with the five big units."

"Baby, baby," she murmured, shucking her blouse and coming at me again, "it isn't like that at all."

I flung her back on the couch. "Put your shirt back on," I said, tossing it at her, "it isn't gonna work. I'm not gonna be your chump. You're part of Ransom's string."

"Where'd you hear that?" she said sullenly, clutching the blouse to her chest.

"Josephine," I said, wondering if she liked rough stuff.

"I might have guessed. It's not true."

"What else would you say? Why would she lie? How'm I supposed to know what's true and what's not true?"

"You might listen to me, give me a chance to explain."

"I have. So far all I've heard is you want to sell Ransom some videos."

"Charlie, I know you want me. . . ."

"Maybe I do. So what?"

"I could make you happy. I love you."

"Stop it with that crap."

"It's true."

"It's true, huh—you love me?"

"Yes."

"Okay, so I love you, too. So what?"

She grinned triumphantly.

"What about Fallon? What about Ransom?" I said.

"What about Josephine?" she said.

"She doesn't mean anything to me."

"Neither do they."

"It's true, then—you do sleep with Ransom."

She opened her mouth to say something. "Oh, never mind," she broke off angrily.

"No, no, go on, I wanna hear it."

"It happened," she sighed. "Is that what you want to hear?"

341

"Not particularly."

"You can't just say no to him. . . ."

"I'll bet."

"But it's not what you think. I'm not part of any string."

"What about Fallon?"

"I had a life before I met you. He's just someone I see occasionally."

"If that's the case, how come he was riding shotgun for you the other day?"

"He's just a friend, that's the truth. I swear it."

There was enough to be skeptical about without crowding her on that. "And now I'm supposed to believe you've fallen for me, is that it?"

"Is that so incredible? Is there something wrong with you, Charlie?" She let the blouse drop and casually reached for her drink. There was nothing wrong with her. Her shoulders were smooth and sculpted, her cleavage inviting as she leaned my way.

"Only that I have no money."

"That can be remedied," she said, perched on the edge of the sofa, elbows on knees, the glass cupped in her hands.

"If you're still thinking of selling videos, you can forget about it. It's too late for that. The police have copies of Sharon's tapes."

"That's too bad," she said, turning off the sexy act and becoming thoughtful. "How'd they get them?"

"I gave them to 'em."

"You lied to me?"

"Looks that way."

"You did see them."

"I saw them."

She considered that. "Why'd you give them to the police?" she said finally.

"Because the tapes are evidence in a possible murder case, remember?"

She frowned, then just as quickly brightened and shrugged. "Well, so much for that idea."

"Got any other ideas?"

"Maybe," she said, reaching for her blouse. "You don't happen to know where my mother is, do you?"

"No, I don't."

"Is she safe?" she asked, slipping a slender white arm in the sleeve of the blouse.

"Who would want to harm her?"

"Be serious."

"She's keeping her head down."

"I'm glad to hear that," she said, buttoning the blouse.

"Does this mean the engagement's off?" I nodded at her chest.

"You didn't seem interested." She began tucking in her blouse.

"What happened to 'I love you,' 'You love me'?"

She smirked, and I wanted to smack her.

"Did you get what you came for? Or is it that without the tapes I don't have enough to offer to make it worth your while to drop your pants?"

"I'm sure you've got a lot to offer some lucky girl," she said, getting to her feet.

I grabbed her arm as she brushed by me.

"Take your hands off me," she said.

I released her with a shove, holding up my hands and blocking her path. "Not so fast, sister. Did Ransom send you for those tapes? Or was it Fallon?"

"You mind letting me pass?" She glared from behind a lock of hair, massaging her arm.

"I don't mind letting you pass," I said, poking a finger in her chest, backing her up. "I mind you inviting yourself here thinking all you've got to do is flash your tits at me and I'll turn to Silly Putty and give you anything you want," I said, giving her another jab of the finger. "I mind you thinking I'd go in for blackmail," I said, jabbing her again.

"It's not blackmail. Stop jabbing me with your finger. He wants to buy them."

"I can believe it. I mind you pumping me for information about your mother," I said, giving her another poke of the finger. "And I mind you pretending to give a damn whether she lives or dies," I said. She was ready for me this time and deflected the finger. But I didn't feel like hitting her anymore. The anger had passed, and I was left with a feeling of revulsion. I didn't want to touch her.

"How would you know how I feel about my mother? And what business is it of yours anyway?"

"I know you wouldn't have been terribly upset if she'd been buried under a ton of bricks when the La Fleur collapsed."

"That's a lie."

"You could have fooled me. Could this sudden change of heart have anything to do with the fact Dolly's in line for a share of Florine's estate?"

"I don't know what you're talking about."

"I think you do. The question is, how'd you find out about the change in Florine's will? That's not information you'd be likely to get from Marc, even if he had it."

Her eyes went sullen. Her silence was eloquent.

"Think you're pretty cute, don't you? If you can get ahold of the tapes, you can cut a deal with Marc. If you can't get the tapes . . . well, you've always got Dolly. Provided she can stay alive until Florine dies. The Dolly Varden scam worked after all. Tell me, whose idea was it really? Mumminger's or Fallon's? Or was it yours, maybe?"

"It was Sharon's," she answered, a little too quickly.

"That's what I thought you'd say. But it was your idea to kill Sharon, wasn't it?"

"I don't have to listen to this garbage," she said, exploding, and started for the door.

"I'm not finished with you yet, darling," I said, blocking the way. "That's it, isn't it? Ransom went off on her, but left the job half done. The lights were out. Who knew what was going on in the confusion? When you and Fallon got there, she was still breathing. You hit her in the head, or smothered her, or both, and then you rigged it to look like suicide. You hid in the building—probably in an empty apartment—until the cops arrived, then you appeared and identified the body. You didn't shed any tears over Sharon's death because she'd been nothing but trouble."

"It's not true, none of it," she said in a monotone.

"Maybe not," I said. "Anyway, the guy you wanna see, if you're in the market for some hot tapes, is Mumminger. He's got the tape you're looking for and a whole lot more. You probably know that already, though."

"Are you finished now?"

"I think that about wraps it up," I said, stepping aside.

She paused a moment and eyed me. "You are vile," she said, and brushed past me.

How could it go so fast from, "I love you," to "You are vile," I wondered. "Hey, Susan, wait a minute," I called, remembering I had to let her out.

She stopped and turned. "What is it now?" She glared.

"You're locked in." I grinned, catching up to her.

We rode the elevator downstairs in a stony silence. I glanced at her once out of the corner of my eye. Her eyes flicked off me and focused intently on the floor indicator above the door. I studied my shoes. It was time for a new pair of sneakers. I rushed to get the first set of plate-glass doors. Forgetting about the sidewalk massage I'd received earlier in the evening, which seemed like a lifetime ago, I knelt too quickly and was nearly doubled over with the pain that knifed me in the kidneys.

"Something the matter with you?"

"Just a bad back," I said, hunched over. I held the door and let her pass. Gingerly, I squatted and repeated the procedure with the second set of doors. I straightened up slowly and held the door for her again.

"You're all crippled up." She smiled. "What happened?"

"I said, 'Tastes great,' the other guys said, 'Bleep you.'"

"Hope you have disability insurance," she said, stepping lightly through the open door, "because it wouldn't take much to put you out of commission permanently."

"What's that supposed to mean?"

"What if you were to suddenly go blind? You couldn't very well play photographer then, could you?" She turned and walked away, heels clicking on the pavement, before I could think of something smart to say. A part of me still hated to see her go.

Grimacing, I stooped and began locking up, her parting shot reverberating in my ear. Ransom had probably sent her. He might even have sent her to deliver the threat, although I couldn't be sure of that. Those words could easily have been her own. It was possible Fallon, or Susan, or both of them, had killed Sharon. Maybe they hadn't planned it, but when the opportunity presented itself, they took it. What if Ransom thought he'd done the job, but hadn't? What if Raynes still had been alive when he called Fallon to clean up the mess? How would they explain a fractured skull—if that was what she had—at the hospital? Why risk the scandal trying to save her would surely cause? Why not do Ransom the favor of finishing the job, and let him believe he'd killed her? It was a wicked idea. But Fallon and Susan were both capable of coming up with it. Fallon would have liked it because it would give him something on the boss. And Susan would have liked it, too; her social climbing could continue apace, and she'd be rid of the stigma of her sister. Furthermore, she'd have ingratiated herself with Marc by going along with the suicide cover-up. So far, so good.

Fast forward to the present. There's a bind. Tapes have surfaced of Ransom's romps with Raynes. There may even be a tape of him looking like he's killing Raynes. He's understandably anxious to get his hands on these tapes. Susan, of course, knew about the tapes all along. Sharon told her she'd been taping her playmates. Susan didn't know, however, that Mumminger also knew about the tapes. She must have guessed that Sharon had given tapes to Dolly for safekeeping. But she couldn't have given her the last tape, and the question was, who had it? It must have made them crazy. Susan and Fallon couldn't toss Sharon's apartment in front of Ransom and Josephine. They had to be patient and wait, probably until the next day. By then it was too late, because Mumminger had beaten them to it. They might have suspected Mumminger, but they couldn't say anything without giving themselves away. Now they knew, thanks to me.

I pressed 12 and the elevator doors closed. I gazed idly at the floor indicator as the elevator began its rise. Something about the Mumminger connection was bothering me. And in a chilling flash of intuition, I realized what it was. The next play was his. I glanced at my watch. It was ten-thirty. Two hours since I'd seen Mumminger. Suddenly I felt trapped in the elevator as it seemed to be taking its own sweet time climbing to twelve. Finally it glided to a maddeningly slow halt, and the door opened with robotic deliberateness. I ran to the phone and dialed. Bernard answered.

"Bernard, it's Charlie Byrne."

"Yes, Charles," he said, without a trace of his usual silliness.

"How is the old lady?"

"She passed away about an hour ago," he said solemnly.

"I'm sorry to hear that."

"She died peacefully—she simply stopped breathing."

"Is Marc there?"

"Yes, he is."

"Let me speak to him, will you?"

"I don't know if now's the time—"

"Get him!"

"I'll see if he'll come to the phone."

He put me on hold.

"Hello, Byrne. What do you want?" said Ransom, picking up the receiver after an interminable length of time.

"Sorry to hear about your mother."

"Is that why you called?"

"No, I called to tell you not to let Mumminger sign the death certificate. Get another doctor, get a second opinion, get a medical examiner."

"What are you talking about?"

"Your mother didn't die of natural causes."

34

I called Detective Hannibal next. I had to say I was one of his snitches and it was a matter of life and death before they would give me his home phone. It was too soon for him to have received the tapes, so it took some explaining to get him up to speed. He said he'd get a court order to examine the body, and he'd get someone over there from the M.E.'s office as soon as possible, but that it was going to take time. I told him we didn't have time. He'd do the best he could, he said. "Oh, and Byrne . . . these tapes better be all you say they are."

"You won't be disappointed," I promised. Then I called Stein.

"Aw, no," he said, when I told him the old lady was dead. "It'll take me about forty-five minutes to drive to town. You gonna be there?"

"I'll be there."

"Okay, I'll see you at the Thackeray."

They stopped me at the desk. Ransom must have left

orders. He told me on the phone not to bother coming over, that there was nothing I could do. I took a seat in the lobby and was going to wait there when I was approached by one of the white-gloved palace guards, a fitness freak bulked out on steroids. He informed me I couldn't sit there. Why not? I asked reasonably. No loitering in the lobby, he said. "I'm not loitering, I'm waiting," I replied. He threatened to stick my head up my butt if I didn't move it. That seemed awkward to me, so I moved my butt out to the sidewalk and resumed loitering.

It wasn't long before Hannibal and another plainclothes guy pulled up in an unmarked Plymouth. His pal, Murphy, was a tall, rangy type in his forties, with the face of a basset hound. "Hullo, Byrne," said Hannibal, skipping the introductions. "This better be good, or you're gonna have some explaining to do."

His friend gave me the professional once-over, and we proceeded to the desk and were quickly challenged. Hannibal flashed his potsy and said he'd like to speak to Mr. Ransom. The desk consulted with upstairs in a whisper.

"Is this official business?" the white gloves on the phone wanted to know.

"No, my friends and I just want a room for the night," Hannibal cracked. "Lemme speak to Mr. Ransom."

"Just a moment," said White Gloves, and there was another phone consultation.

"Do you have a warrant?" he asked this time.

"We're not here to search the place," Hannibal explained patiently, "we'd just like a word with Mr. Ransom and the doctor, either here or at the station house, whichever is more convenient."

There was another muffled conversation upstairs.

Murph winked at me. "Probably flushing the evidence down the toilet," he said.

Finally, White Gloves hung up the phone and said, "You may go up now."

I flipped a digit at the bouncer as we filed into the elevator.

Louise greeted us still crisp in her uniform, and led us to the room where I'd had my first interview with the old lady.

"Jeez," Murph murmured, glancing around, "will you look at this place."

"Where is everyone?" I asked Louise.

"They're in Mrs. Ransom's room. Mr. Ransom will be right with you," she said. "Would you like something?"

"Yeah," said Murph, "I'd like this chair, the rug, and the Degas."

"I meant to drink," she said politely.

"No thanks," said Murph, "I'm on the job."

Hannibal asked if he could have some coffee, and that's what we all had.

"Hey, Eddie," said Murph, "have you ever seen a place like this before?"

"Looks like my aunt Margaret's place in Peabody," said Hannibal, "same rugs, same paneling, same everything."

"Aunt Margaret must be loaded," said Murph with a grin, appraising a piece of bric-a-brac.

"She's pretty well fixed, what with her Social Security and Uncle Jack's MTA pension."

"Hmm, Limoges," said Murph, returning the porcelain to its place.

Kiernan opened the doors, and Ransom walked briskly into the room, trailed by Louise with the coffee tray. Hannibal got quickly to his feet and presented his badge. "That wasn't necessary, officer," said Ransom.

"Detective Edward Hannibal," said the cop genially. "This is Sergeant Murphy, and I believe you know Mr. Byrne."

If Ransom thought he was about to be shaken down by the Irish Mafia, he gave no sign of it. "Good evening, gentlemen," he said politely. "As you must know, my mother has just died. I'd appreciate it if we could make this brief."

"My condolences, Mr. Ransom," said Hannibal, taking the cup of coffee Louise offered and declining sugar and cream. "Very sorry to disturb you at a time like this. We'll do our best to make it brief. Is the doctor here?"

"Yes, he is."

"Good, we may want to have a word with him after the medical examiner has had a look at the body."

"Medical examiner?"

"Yes."

"There's no need for a medical examiner, Detective."

"I'm afraid there is. You see, we have reason to believe your mother didn't die of natural causes."

"My mother was a very old lady, detective. She'd had a stroke recently. I can assure you, there's no cause for concern here."

"Nevertheless, if we could have a look at the body," said Hannibal gently.

"Impossible."

"We have a court order—it's on the way with the M.E."

"If I may have a word with you in private, Detective?" said Ransom, drawing the cop toward the door. His thick glasses were like a mask on his face, concealing his eyes and reflecting only the warm light of a table lamp. But the man was less opaque than usual. In fact, for once I felt I could see right through him.

"Marc," Kiernan interrupted, "I've got the senator on the line."

Ransom excused himself and went to the phone.

"The political muscle," Murph commented, sipping coffee with his pinky curled.

Hannibal turned a pair of hard eyes on me. "In about ten minutes there's gonna be a call from One Police Plaza, and it'll be for me. The brass down there'll be climbing all over my ass wanting to know why I'm hassling such a solid citizen."

"Tell them what you told Ransom—that you have reason to believe Florine Ransom didn't die of natural causes—and tell them that her son's not a suspect."

"You think that's good enough? They'll say, if he doesn't think his mother was murdered, then get the hell outta there and leave 'em alone," said Hannibal, his eyes fixed on me. "You better hope for your sake, Byrne, those tapes are all you claim, because if they turn out to be some dopey home videos, I'll personally see to it you get a stretch of five to ten in the slammer on whatever charges I can trump up."

"I appreciate that vote of confidence."

"Look," he said in a milder tone. "I know this thing stinks. Fallon's brother deep-sixing the case tells me as much. I hate to disappoint you, Byrne, but there's no way, on the strength of those photos of Raynes, that a prosecutor's gonna present this case to a grand jury."

"Even with the testimony of the doorman?"

"Even with his testimony. Believe me, this guy's too well heeled to lay a glove on."

"Still, Eddie, you'd think Mr. Ransom might be a bit more friendly, a bit more cooperative," Murph observed.

"He can't cooperate without incriminating himself. He thinks the doctor's got a tape of him killing Sharon Raynes," I said.

"A smart lawyer'd convince a jury they were watching him give her mouth-to-mouth resuscitation," said Hannibal. "It's more than that. Ransom doesn't want any publicity, that's the problem. If this guy Mumminger slipped his mother a hot shot, Ransom'd rather let it slide than see the guy brought to trial and have to face the publicity."

"I see your point," said Murph, and his gaze moved toward the door.

Stein had just appeared, along with a young guy in a raglan-sleeve raincoat and dirty white bucks. He waved a court order in his hand and asked which one of us was Detective Hannibal. Hannibal rose and went to meet him.

"You look like hell, sport," Stein greeted me.

"The La Fleur's demolition team jumped me earlier this evening and worked me over."

"If they were serious, you wouldn't be here," Stein said sympathetically.

"I wish I weren't here. I wish I were home in bed. I've got a big shoot tomorrow."

"We all wish we were home in bed. Where's Marc?" he asked, scanning the room.

"He's on the phone to his senator."

"The Democrat, or the Republican?"

"Whichever one he contributed to."

"He contributes to both of them."

"Figures."

"Detective Hannibal, you're wanted on the phone," Louise announced, before the introductions could be completed.

Hannibal shot me a look and followed her down the hall.

"Getting some heat from downtown, is he?" said Stein.

"Eddie can take the heat," Murph assured us.

Ransom entered the room at that moment, Mumminger slinking in behind him, the two of them looking like a pair of unindicted co-conspirators.

"Henry," said Ransom, with a wary smile, "the news travels fast, I see."

"Only when it's bad," said Stein. "I'm sorry to hear about Florine."

"Thank you," said Ransom stiffly.

"What's all the fuss about?" said Stein, with a nod at the lugubrious cop and the young M.E.

"There's been a misunderstanding," said Ransom. "These gentlemen will be leaving in a moment."

Mumminger fidgeted, and smiled nervously.

"There's something you ought to know, Marc," I said.

He turned toward me with a jerk, light caroming off his glasses. Until now he'd managed to ignore me.

Mumminger sidled closer, nervously chewing on his lower lip. Murph raised a pair of bushy eyebrows and looked on with benign interest. The M.E. flopped on a Chippendale and grumbled, "Hope this doesn't turn out to be a wild-goose chase, 'cause I got 'em stacked up like cordwood at the morgue."

"Follow me," Ransom said finally, and led us to Kiernan's office. He ordered Bernard out and closed the door. "Okay, I'm listening," he said.

Stein and I exchanged glances. "Let me go first," he said. "I feel I owe you this, Marc, on account of my friendship with your mother. You've got a sea of troubles, buddy. The state's got Fallon by the balls and they're squeezing. In a day or so he's gonna wanna cut a deal."

"Matty?"

"Matty," Stein repeated dully. "Two years ago I was part of a sting operation set up by the State Police. We were investigating the defrauding of an S and L in Queens. You may have read about it in the newspapers."

Ransom shook his head—he hadn't.

"Anyway, the long and short of it is, your boy Matty's one of the crooks we caught in the sting. He's looking at some time—five years, at least—and he's gonna sing. You don't own enough politicians to protect yourself from Strunk, the cop running this investigation. He's tough, and honest, and he wants your ass."

Ransom seemed to sag, as though he'd just taken a gut shot.

"This could lead to a RICO indictment," Stein continued, "and you know what that means. If you're convicted, you lose everything you've got."

"Can they do that?" said Ransom, steadying himself with a hand on the desk.

"They can, and will."

"What have they got?"

"They know about Randell Elliott, and they know how you cheat your investors with dummy service companies and overbilling," said Stein. "And that's just for openers. They're gonna know a whole lot more about your business when Fallon get's through singing. Believe me, they can make RICO stick. If I were you, Marc, I'd start hiding my assets now."

"Thanks for the tip, Henry," he said.

"I did it for your mother," said Stein.

Ransom was silent a moment, then he gazed at me, his eyes unnaturally large behind the thick glasses. "What have you got to say?"

"The good news is, Mumminger's bluffing," I said.

"There is no tape?"

"There is a tape, all right, but it's not as bad as it sounds. It doesn't prove anything."

"How do you know this?"

"Mumminger told me, and I can believe it. I've seen some of the other tapes. They're damning enough, especially the one with the comptroller."

"Elliott?" he exclaimed. "Christ . . . the dirty bitch."

Stein eyed him somberly.

"The camera angle's bad," I said, "the lighting is bad, and

the quality is bad, but most important, the lights went out in the middle of it."

He scratched his chin thoughtfully. "Even so," he said after a while, "I can't afford to have a tape like that made public."

"Maybe not, but you didn't kill Sharon Raynes. Mumminger's got nothing on you. You don't have to protect him."

"I can't let them perform an autopsy on my mother."

"Don't you want to know whether he murdered her?" said Stein.

"I know he murdered her. I'll deal with him in due time," he said, with chilling matter-of-factness.

"Why not let the law take care of it?" said Stein.

"I won't have this business dragged through the media, and I don't trust the system to deal with him properly."

Stein shrugged. "Suit yourself."

"I didn't kill her," he mused with a grimace of satisfaction, and in a tone that hovered between a question and an answer. "Who did kill her?" he asked, with genuine interest.

I wasn't going to make it easy for him. "You tell me—you were there."

"Well, yes, but it was dark, there was a lot of confusion, and I wasn't myself at the time," he blustered. "Who knows what actually happened?"

"The killer," said Stein, with a cold stare.

"Fallon must have done it, then," he said. "Yes, it would have had to have been Fallon. I might have guessed."

"Or Susan Ferrante," I suggested.

"Susan? Do you think so?"

"Why not? Or it might even have been both of them."

"Both of them?" He mulled over that possibility. "That would make sense, wouldn't it?" he said finally.

"It's a possibility," I said. "She wanted to be rid of her sister almost as badly as you did. And by going along with the suicide story, she thought she was doing you a favor, getting in tighter with you and your money. As for Fallon, he thought you'd owe him big for cleaning up a manslaughter, which is probably how you would have been charged, if there were charges. Fallon must also have thought he had something he could use on you if push ever came to shove between the two of you."

"So they let me think I'd killed her," he said.

"That's how I see it," I said. "It was a win-win situation for them, or they must have thought so."

"Interesting," he murmured, quietly drumming his fingernails on the desk. "And Susan and Dean must have an understanding."

"Looks that way," I said.

"But the Dolly Varden scheme was a hoax. My mother knew that."

"You should have been patient, Marc," said Stein. "That old hotel meant more to Florine than you knew. She was not about to see it go before she went. You were too clever by half, and she thought she was fixing your wagon buying into the Dolly Varden scam."

"It cost her her life," said Ransom.

"Maybe," said Stein, "but it looks like she's gonna have the last laugh."

"We'll see," said Ransom.

"I suppose you could always have the bag lady killed," Stein suggested.

"Sharon Raynes was as bad as they come," Ransom said, bristling, "but I never suggested for a moment that I wanted her done away with."

"Of course not." Stein grinned.

Ransom seemed uncertain whether or not he was being mocked. "Well," he said, with a curt nod for each of us. "You've been very helpful. I appreciate your coming and telling me this." He threw open the doors with a flourish and waited for us to exit.

Mumminger was pacing in the hall outside the door. He froze when he saw Ransom. But it was a struggle to appear calm. His hands gave him away. They seemed to have lives of their own. One twitched in his pant's pocket, jiggling loose change, the other fooled with the collar of his shirt. Hannibal and Murph were engaged in an amiable conversation, while the young M.E. slumped in the chair, arms across his chest, head down, napping.

"You're still here?" said Ransom, regarding them with some astonishment.

"We'll have a look at the deceased now, Mr. Ransom, if you don't mind," said Hannibal firmly.

Ransom was about to protest when Mumminger blurted out, "I signed the death certificate. There's no reason to question it."

"Please leave this to me, Dean," said Ransom.

"I object, most strenuously, to having my professionalism questioned," said Mumminger, on the verge of hysteria.

"Be quiet," Ransom said sharply. Then, turning to Hannibal and staring at him impassively, he said, "Didn't you get your marching orders from downtown?"

The M.E. was sitting up in the chair, brushing sleepers out of his eyes. Stein beamed and rocked on his heels. Murph grinned broadly, his eyebrows dancing like seismograph needles doing a ten on the Richter scale. I felt a tingle of anticipation myself.

"I'm conducting this investigation, Mr. Ransom"—Hannibal erupted—"not some goddamn hack down at One Police Plaza. Either let us do our job, or I'll arrest you and your boyfriend for interfering with official police business."

"Er, Eddie," Murph said with a grin, "make that 'obstructing governmental administration'?"

"Goddamn bureaucratic jargon," Hannibal complained, "all right, obstructing governmental administration."

Murph nodded approvingly.

"I'd do as he says, Marc," said Stein.

"Excellent advice," Murph said.

The cop and the developer were chest to chest, eyeball to eyeball. Mumminger looked like he was about to fall apart. His knee jiggled inside his trouser leg; his hands flew about, landing fleetingly on cuff, collar, lapel, and tie; his jaw muscle throbbed at the same rate as his pulse. It's Ransom's class the system serves best, and this was uncharted territory, a strange new experience for a man with five big units. He was more used to buying public servants than taking orders from them. But Ransom was also a rational man, and faced with imminent arrest, he blinked. "This way, Detective," he said, turning on his heel.

Hannibal maintained a stony face as he fell into step behind the little megamillionaire. Murph followed, beaming.

"'Bout freakin' time," the M.E. muttered, getting to his feet.

Stein nudged me, and we joined the processional to Florine Ransom's bedroom.

Money was no object when it came to beautiful things, or extreme means, I thought, noticing the intrusion of high-tech modern medical wonders in the otherwise museumlike room. In the end, though, the digital electronic marvels of the Silicon Age had been unable to save the tiny form under the sheet from a killer.

We circled the hospital bed like interns; the cops, the M.E., Stein, and myself. Ransom and Mumminger hung back. The M.E. unceremoniously drew back the sheet and we gazed at the corpse. It was Florine, all right, at least in effigy. She almost looked young again, until I realized it was gravity that pulled the skin smooth over her sharp features. She seemed serene, but when you looked closer, you quickly realized it was just that her face was slack and empty. No face is ever quite that impassive, that composed, except in death. A statue chiseled in stone would be more lifelike than the shell lying in that bed.

"You gonna watch?" the M.E. asked, glancing around.

Stein and I shook our heads mutely and left the room, along with Murph and Ransom.

"It didn't look like her at all," Stein muttered.

"Was there a nurse on duty, Mr. Ransom?" Murph asked, filling in an awful silence.

"There were two," said Ransom, his face nearly as lifeless as his mother's.

"We'll want their names," said Murph gently.

"Of course, Bernard will give them to you."

Murph went in search of Kiernan.

"Would you like a drink?" Ransom asked.

"Thanks, but I don't think so," said Stein.

I shook my head no, remembering wistfully the old lady's good bourbon.

"Why don't we wait in the study?" Ransom suggested.

And we did as suggested, the three of us sitting silently, each lost in his own thoughts. I studied the pattern in the carpet, wondering whether it was Persian, Turkish, Kurdish, or Caucasian, and thinking, if it turned out she had been murdered, as I was sure she had, it was ironic she'd lived as long as she had and then been murdered with so few days left. It was also ironic that she'd inadvertently brought it upon herself. Peripherally I caught a glint of light, and looked up to see Ransom remove his glasses; he was a pathetic figure. He wiped the lenses briskly with a handkerchief and returned the glasses to his face. When Hannibal and the M.E. entered the room, he was composed again. I wondered how well Florine and her son had known each other.

"There's a fresh puncture mark, probably from a needle, on the right buttock, and there are pinpoint hemorrhages in the eyes," said the M.E.

"What's that mean?" said Ransom.

"The pinpoint hemorrhages mean possible asphyxiation," said the M.E.

35

I was too lame to walk home. I said good night to Stein and hailed a cab. The hack license said Rolando Cangialosi. The mug shot showed a scruffy, chubby longhair in his late twenties. I gave him my address and settled back.

"What else do you do," I asked, "when you're not driving a cab?"

"I'm a musician, rock."

I might have guessed. "Tough business," I said, thinking I didn't want to know any more about him.

"I'm good, too good to be driving a hack. I'm thinkin' maybe of trying it in L.A."

He dropped me at Fifth and Thirty-eighth. I paid him and wished him good luck. Tomorrow was a shoot day, I thought, crawling into the building. I didn't bother to stop and scratch the cats, check the answering machine, pour a drink, or brush my teeth. I just stripped and went to bed. The rest of the night was spent tossing and turning. I drug myself out of bed feeling like the Argentine National Soccer Team had kicked me around just for practice. There was no way I was going to cancel the booking, though. I'd shoot from a wheelchair if I had to. And I had one I kept for film and tape jobs.

Things began looking up after a couple of cups of coffee. Surprise, surprise, the sunflower check was in the morning mail. I hardly noticed the pain as I bent to retrieve it from the floor. That was enough to make any day. I had the money in the bank before the clients arrived at ten o'clock.

The A.D. knew exactly what he wanted. I didn't have to scramble around covering the shoot from a hundred different angles. We put the camera on a tripod, framed up, and never moved it. Mom, pop, the kids, and the sheepdog made a cunning, if corny, picture. But that's what they wanted, and that's what we gave them. If it hadn't been for Pharr making a pain in the ass out of himself, the day would have been a piece of cake. Try as he might, he couldn't screw up the shoot, though. In fact, we wrapped early, and the gang from the agency left happy. When the stylist and the makeup artist cleared out, Tito and I unwound with a beer. I thanked him for a job well done. He finished the beer and left to put the film in the lab. That way I could see a test at nine o'clock, run the balance, and deliver first thing in the morning.

Suddenly I was alone—just me, the cats, and an empty set of an idealized suburban living room. When you live in the store, the days begin and end without clear demarcation. I wished I had somewhere to go. That someone was waiting for me. I thought about going for a spin on the Lejeune, but not for long. I was beat, figuratively and physically. I glanced at my watch. It wasn't much past five—four hours to kill before I could see my tests from the shoot. I'd be lucky to stay awake that long.

I wondered what kind of hours journalists kept as I dialed the *Times* and asked to speak to Diedre Mahoney. Charles Byrne, I said, when she picked up. Remember me? Are you the same Charles Byrne about town mentioned in the columns? she laughed. The same, I admitted. What can I do for you? I asked if she was still interested in the bag lady. If you've got something new, sure, she said. I said I had, and asked if we could talk about it over dinner, maybe? She said thanks, but she was married. I said, too bad. She said, no, it was good, she liked being married. She said she hoped being married wouldn't get in the way of a good story, though. Hey, no problem, I said. Good, she laughed. I told her about Florine, and Dolly's inheritance. Interesting, she said. Marc Ransom must be thrilled to death with his new niece. That's what I thought, I said. Think you'll print it? Don't know, but I'll check it out, she promised. Can't ask for more than that, I said, and hung up.

If they did run a follow-up story on Dolly, it might encourage her to resurface, and it couldn't hurt to have on the record who profited the most in the case of her death, should anything happen to her.

When I got back from the lab after seeing the test film, the message light was blinking on the answering machine. I touched playback and the tape rewound.

"Ah . . . sheet, Charlie, id's me, Sonny. . . . Hate tawkin' tuh dese tings . . . damn. . . . Anyhow, called ta tell ya, Aldo's in Bellevue . . . had ah heart ah'tack or sumpting da udder day. . . . Man's nearly ah hunnert . . . don' look too good fo' da ol' fella. . . . We was at OTB when id happen. . . . Ah've had 'bout nuff ah dis place . . . Ah'm hoppin' ah Greyhound fo' Georgia ta night. . . . Ah gotta see mah woman . . . ya know how dat be. . . . Anyway, jus' thought Ah oughta let ya know. . . . Ah'll look ya up sometime if Ah'm ever in da neighborhood. . . . Take care ah yo'self."

That's what I did. I fixed myself a stiff one and watched some tube until I fell asleep. No dreams.

Hannibal dropped by a few days later and reported that the M.E. had found traces of succinylcholine, a pharmacological equivalent of curare, in samples of Florine Ransom's tissue.

"Another M.E. might have missed it completely. You don't tend to find a poison unless you're looking for it. In time, the succinylcholine would have broken down and disappeared without a trace," he explained. "You've got to be able to get close to someone to poison them. The puncture mark was what made him suspicious of Mumminger."

"What about the pinpoint hemorrhages in the eyes?"

"The dose he gave her probably wasn't enough to finish her, just knock her out. The M.E. thinks he smothered her with a pillow. That's what the hemorrhages in the eyes would seem to indicate."

"Jesus," I murmured, imagining the scene. "But can you prove that in court?"

"Murph's getting a search warrant. We'll see if he's still got some of the succinyl. If he does, we'll find out where he got it from, and how much. The case is going to a grand jury whether we find the stuff or not."

"Did you get the tapes I sent you?"

"I got 'em. A regular sperm bank, Sharon Raynes."

"She was with Mumminger on one of those tapes, remember?"

"I remember—they were testing the equipment."

"Then maybe you figured it out already. Mumminger's got the last tape. The one Raynes made the day she died."

"How do you know that?"

"He told me."

"Why would he do that?"

"Because he couldn't deny it. The doorman, the cop?"

"Yeah . . ."

"He put Mumminger at the scene that day, remember?"

He gave me the same hard look I'd seen him give Ransom. "You should have come to me with that information right away."

"I tried to. You weren't around. I sent you the tapes." I shrugged. "Thought you'd like to know what else to look for when you have your search warrant."

"I oughta run your ass in for what you've done."

"Obstructing governmental administration?"

"All right, wiseguy," he said, eyeing me speculatively, "assuming Mumminger did it, why did he kill the old lady?"

"There's only one reason. Money."

"She include him in the will?"

"No."

"What then?"

"It's a long story."

He glanced at his watch. "I've got five minutes."

"Florine Ransom was knocked up and abandoned as a teenager. She had the baby, a girl, and paid a couple she knew to care for it while she went to work as a hooker. When she came back to get her child, the wife had died, and the husband, unable to care for the baby by himself, and not knowing where to get in touch with Florine, had given the child up for adoption."

"Everyone's got a story," he sighed.

"Yeah, but here's where it gets good. When she was a working girl, Florine had used the alias Dolly Varden."

"Wasn't there something in the paper about a Dolly Varden not so long ago . . . a bag lady? They even mentioned your name."

"Diedre Mahoney, in the *Times*."

"I like her stuff. So how'd the bag lady come up with the name Dolly Varden—she read Dickens or something?"

"The bag lady is the mother of Sharon Raynes and her sister, Susan Ferrante," I said, wondering whether Dickens was required reading at the Police Academy.

"And they tried to pass their mother off as the old lady's long-lost daughter?"

"That was the idea, more or less. But the old lady wasn't buying. Back in August, Raynes made the mistake of presenting herself to Florine as her granddaughter, saying that her mother's name was Dolly Varden."

"Florine's old alias. But not her daughter's name."

"Exactly."

"The old lady knew she was a phony."

"From the get-go."

"Why'd Raynes do that? How'd she get the idea Dolly Varden was the daughter's name?"

"She got it from Mumminger most likely, although she might have gotten it from her sister."

"Ferrante?"

"Uh-huh."

"They were all in on it?"

"Including Fallon, that's what I think. Mumminger told

me the old lady was aphasic. Every once in a while she'd wonder out loud whatever became of Dolly Varden. They must have assumed she meant her daughter."

He grinned. "And she was talking about herself."

"Or her alter ego."

"And only the old lady knew who the real Dolly Varden was."

"And she wasn't telling. She had a lot of time on her hands, and was willing to play along with Raynes just for the hell of it."

"Meanwhile Raynes apparently commits suicide."

"That's right, and the old lady forgets about her until Mahoney's story appears in the *Times*. Then I got a call from her, and she asked me to arrange a meeting with Dolly Varden the bag lady, which I did."

"Was the bag lady in on the scam?"

"No way."

"Then why was she using the name?"

"Raynes told her that's what she ought to call herself. She's suggestible, she liked the name, it stuck."

"What happened at this meeting?"

"I don't know for sure, but the two of them must have hit it off in some weird way."

"Is it possible the bag lady could be the long-lost daughter?"

"She's too young."

"This was some scam," said Hannibal.

"Raynes took a chance. If she was caught, she could always say she made a mistake."

"Okay, but why would Mumminger kill the old lady? Who gains?"

"Florine made a fatal error. To spite her son for stealing and destroying the old hotel, which was her first property and held great sentimental value for her, she decided to recognize the bag lady as her granddaughter, and have her share the estate with Marc."

"So the Dolly Varden scam worked after all."

"Unexpectedly, yes, and it nearly cost the bag lady her life. When Ransom learned of the new will, he had Nellie Rudd arrange to have Dolly snatched and planted in the La

Fleur. It was supposed to look like an accident, but I managed to find her and get her out before the building collapsed."

"Where's the bag lady now?"

"I don't know. She's spooked. She's hiding. Mumminger had been waiting for Florine to recognize Dolly as an heir."

"Okay, okay, I've got all that. He snuffed her to ensure the bag lady inherited, but why?"

"Here's what I think. Mumminger and Raynes were partners, the tapes prove that. After Raynes died, her sister stepped in and picked up where Raynes had left off."

"Susan Ferrante?"

"Uh-huh. When it began to look like the Dolly Varden scam might work after all, Ferrante and Mumminger struck a deal. You snuff the old lady, Doctor, and I'll make it worth your while as soon as Dolly comes into her inheritance."

"This is all theory, of course?"

"It works for me."

"Okay, but who killed Raynes, and why?"

"It might have been Ransom, but I doubt it. He wanted to be rid of her, that's true, and she wouldn't go away. According to Mumminger, he definitely went nuts on her, but it's not clear from the tape what really happened. The angle's bad, and you've got to light a scene, even in video."

"The quality of peeper tapes is always lousy."

"Not only that, but there was a power failure that day and the tape cut out at the critical moment."

"Was she alive when the lights went out?"

"Mumminger says she was."

"I gotta see this tape."

"They were all there that day, Josephine Cyzeski—"

"Who's she?"

"The Chinese woman on the tape. And Ransom, Fallon, and Ferrante—"

"And later, Mumminger."

"That's right. Here's what I think happened. Ransom roughed Raynes up pretty good. She was unconscious. He thought he'd killed her, or that she was dying. He called Fallon."

"Mr. Fixit—go on."

"Fallon called Ferrante. When they got to the apartment, Raynes was still breathing. They might have tried saving her, but not without risking a scandal. And that was the last thing any of them wanted. Instead, they decided the thing to do was finish the job themselves and let Ransom go on thinking he'd killed her."

"Her own sister?" Hannibal shook his head in disbelief.

"There was no love lost there. Her sister was as much a pain in the ass for her as she was for Ransom. Both of them wanted to be rid of her. Besides, Ferrante also was one of Ransom's girlfriends. She made the mistake of introducing her sister to Ransom, and he went for her. She was jealous. She didn't like her sister moving in on her action."

"So she saw her chance, she took it. That's cold."

"The woman's got Freon in her veins."

"Now Ransom's rid of his problem, and Ferrante's rid of her problem. Fallon's got a hold on the boss, and Ferrante's solid with Ransom for concocting the suicide cover-up story. Is that it?"

"That's my theory."

"Interesting."

"But you don't like it."

"I didn't say that. It's not a question of what I like or dislike, it's what can be proven in court."

"You've got your work cut out for you, then."

"I might as well start with you. How about giving me a statement?" he said, staring at me as he produced a small tape recorder. "I'll type it up later and ask you to sign it."

"Just the facts, huh?"

"We couldn't ask for anything more, Byrne."

That night, on the eleven o'clock news, there were pictures of a dapper if diffident Mumminger, head bowed and turned from the camera, being hustled by Murph and Hannibal into the station house to be booked. The search warrant had turned up a couple of empty vials of succinylcholine in his office, but not much else. A flashy, high-priced criminal lawyer blustered to the reporter about his client's innocence and how the case would be thrown out of court. A somber Nellie Rudd stood so close to the lawyer, it looked as though he were working him like a hand puppet. A week later, at the corner of Fifty-seventh and Park, in broad daylight, a guy walked up to Mumminger, who was out on bail, put a .22-caliber slug in his head, jumped into a van, and got away. None of the eyewitnesses thought to get the license plate number. They couldn't even agree on the color of the van.

Hannibal never did get to see Raynes's last tape. And without the tape, he had no case. One Police Plaza and the D.A.'s office weren't going to let him reopen a tidy, probably suicide case on the strength of a few photos of the corpse and some home videos of Raynes and her playmates. The man with the five big units had too much clout for that to happen.

In her infinite wisdom, Florine Ransom had left Dolly's share of her estate in trust, appointing Henry Stein the trustee. Diedre Mahoney wrote a glowing piece on Dolly. She closed by telling Dolly she had nothing to fear, and that whenever she was ready to come out of hiding, there were a nice one-bedroom apartment and a German shepherd puppy waiting for her. It didn't take long for Dolly to come knocking on my door, waving Mahoney's article in my face and saying she'd come for her dog. An hour later she was stroking a puppy while Mahoney and I waited for Stein. Somehow, we managed to get her to a doctor, who put her on Clozapine, a drug used to treat schizophrenia. She still dressed zany, but as long as she took her medicine, she would be a reasonable person. Susan made a show of filial concern in the beginning, and then her interest faded when she learned Stein controlled the purse strings. For her part, Dolly was too busy adjusting to a more normal life to notice any strangeness in her only daughter's continued indifference.

The wheels of justice don't necessarily grind exceedingly fine, they just grind. In the World Trade Center, in P.C. Strunk's office, one place where Ransom's money was no good, Matty Fallon was singing a medley of evergreens like he was the fat lady. He sang about bribes and payoffs, about how them that gives, gets, about Ransom writing off millions of dollars a year of taxable income against the Thackeray, about how he defrauds the investors in his syndicates, and about the collapse of the La Fleur Hotel. The grand jury enjoyed the performance so much it handed up a three hundred count indictment, naming Ransom, Rudd, the comptroller Randell Elliott, Lesser, and half a dozen names I didn't recognize.

Speaking of Lesser, it turned out he was the snitch who'd started the ball rolling. Strunk said he ratted on Ransom because Ransom was also banging Jackie Dhiel, and Lesser was jealous. But there might have been more to it than that. Adding to Ransom's misery was the fact that Lesser had taken a powder, and several million dollars were missing.

The State Attorney General, who was running for the Senate against the Republican, said, "Never, in all my years in office, have I seen a case as bad as this one. This indictment lays bare the insidiousness of white-collar crime. I shall prosecute this case with vigor and all the resources at my command." In other words, it was a case he could make his bones on. As if that weren't bad enough, the feds were waiting in the wings for an encore from Fallon. They were preparing to slap Ransom with a RICO indictment. If they could make it stick, Ransom could lose everything he had. Good lawyers don't come cheap, and at the rate he was going, Marc Ransom would soon be scraping by on his last unit. I had a feeling a number of rare antiques would soon be coming on the market. Stein was predicting eighteen months, max. Strunk, the optimist, said thirty months, minimal. Either way, they were certain Ransom was going to serve time before this thing was over.

There were a couple of other things that happened the week Mumminger got popped. The first is really another story, but I got a call from a photographer buddy of mine, Peter Sahula. He wanted to know if I knew a guy named Rodger Pharr. Sure, he's a lowlife creep, I said. What's the problem? The son of a bitch owes me ten grand in fees, and he's taken off with my portfolio. I commiserated with him, telling him about my own experiences with the guy. Yeah, well, I'm gonna kill the bastard if I ever get my hands on him, says Pete. No sooner does he hang up than Jon Riley, another photographer friend, is on the line with a similar story. He says he's hosting a meeting in his studio with a dozen other names in the business who've been burned by Pharr, to try and decide what to do about the situation. He asks if I'd like to come. I tell him I'll be there, and to be sure to invite Peter Sahula. Him, too? he says. Him, too, I say. But as I said, this is really another story.

The other thing that happened was Pharr's press agent planted the third and final item. I found it almost by accident on "The Sauce" page in the *Daily News*. I might have missed it if I hadn't bought a copy from a homeless person to read while waiting in line at the bank. The item went something like this: "Lensman Charles Byrne and main squeeze, couturiere Susan Ferrante, were singing and dancing in the rain last night outside Carnegie Hall after the "Save the Gerbils" concert. Could this couple be contemplating cohabitating?" I winced, and wondered how much of my twenty-five hundred bucks had found its way into the pocket of the press agent.

AN
ARTIE
DEEMER
MYSTERY

LUSH LIFE

"Hilarious....Murphy joins the ranks of authors like Carl Hiaasen and Donald Westlake, writers who can roll suspense and comedy into the same package and leave you wanting more."
—*Albuquerque Journal*

DALLAS
MURPHY

Author of *Apparent Wind*

POCKET BOOKS Available from Pocket Books
mid-September 1993

853